John William Mackail

The Life of William Morris

Vol. 2

John William Mackail

The Life of William Morris
Vol. 2

ISBN/EAN: 9783337415433

Printed in Europe, USA, Canada, Australia, Japan

Cover: Foto ©Raphael Reischuk / pixelio.de

More available books at **www.hansebooks.com**

THE LIFE OF
WILLIAM MORRIS

BY

J. W. MACKAIL

VOLUME II

LONGMANS, GREEN AND CO
LONDON, NEW YORK & BOMBAY
1899

CONTENTS

VOLUME II

CONTENTS

LIST OF ILLUSTRATIONS

VOLUME II

TO FACE
PAGE

THE LIFE OF WILLIAM MORRIS

CHAPTER XII

BUT work among his dye-pots and looms, interesting and fascinating as he found it, could not fill up the whole of his mind. In spite of the variable excitement and the more settled rest of this daily work, voices from an outer world kept calling him more and more imperiously. For a time he tried to think that it was the voice of poetry that was calling, but the fancy brought no real conviction. "As to poetry," he writes in October, 1879, "I don't know, and I don't know. The verse would come easy enough if I had only a subject which would fill my heart and mind : but to write verse for the sake of writing is a crime in a man of my years and experience." He had in fact produced his poetry : the instincts of creation and invention had to find new outlets ; and gradually the fabric of social life itself became the field which, as he had done with specific arts already, he tried to redeem from commercialism and ugliness, and to reinstate on a sounder basis. He recognized the gravity of the enterprise ; yet it did not then seem to him a desperate one. " I have seen a many wonders, and have a good memory for them ; and in spite of all grumblings have a hope that civilized people will grow weary of their worst follies and try to live a less muddled and unreasonable life ; not of course that we shall see much of that change in the remnant that is left of our days."

In this hope, and for work at anything that might lead towards its accomplishment, he was willing to give up ease and leisure, and much of what made life desirable. And one can trace the conviction growing in him very slowly, that towards forwarding the work some renunciation was necessary—it might be, he thought with a sudden pang, the giving up of Kelmscott. "I am sitting now, 10 p.m.," he writes from there in late autumn, "in the tapestry-room, the moon rising red through the east-wind haze, and a cow lowing over the fields. I have been feeling chastened by many thoughts, and the beauty and quietness of the surroundings, which latter, as I hinted, I am, as it were, beginning to take leave of. That leave-taking will, I must confess, though you may think it fantastic, seem a long step towards saying good-night to the world."

His ease, his leisure, in effect we may say his life, he did give up for the sake of this hope : but the giving up of Kelmscott was a pang that was spared to him. Nor would it be right to think of him as habitually occupied by these somewhat sombre broodings. When he did throw off work, his enjoyment remained that of a child. "All right," runs a note of this year to Ellis arranging for a couple of days' fishing, "I think that is best. I am writing to Mrs. Comely to say positively that we will ; so begone dull care: don't forget the worms." Another letter gives a description of his arrival with Webb at Kelmscott through the floods of that wet August. They had been at Salisbury, and he had seen Stonehenge for the first time. "I was much impressed by it," he wrote : "though the earth and sky nearly met, and the rain poured continuously, nothing could spoil the great stretches of

the Plain, and the mysterious monument that nobody
knows anything about—except Fergusson who knows
less than nothing."   From Amesbury they drove north
across the Wiltshire downs.

"We went right up the Avon valley, and very beautiful
it was; then, as the river narrowed, we turned off towards a little scrubby town called Pewsey that lies in
the valley between the Salisbury and the Marlborough
downs: it was all very fine and characteristic country,
especially where we had to climb the Marlborough downs
at a place that I remembered coming on as a boy with
wonder and pleasure: Oare Hill they call it. We got
early in the afternoon to Marlborough and walked out
to see the College, and so strolled away to the Devil's Den,
and back in the dusk. The next morning we set out
early for Avebury, in weather at first much like the day
before; however it cleared before we reached Silbury,
and was quite fine while we were thereabout for two
hours, after which we drove on towards Swindon, intend-
ing Lechlade and Kelmscott that evening. The downs
end at a village called Wroughton, and we could see a
large piece of England from the slope of it, Faringdon
clump not at all in the background. We got another trap
at Swindon, where they warned us that we should have
to go through the waters to get to Lechlade: we went
through Highworth, a queer old village on a hill, and
sure enough we could see waters out from thence, though
they turned out to be only from the little river Cole: at
Highworth we found that they were mending the bridge
into Lechlade town, and that it would be closed; so at
Inglesham we had to turn aside to strike the road that
leads over St. John's Bridge: sure enough in a few yards
we were in deep water enough, right over the axles of
the wheels: the driver lost his presence of mind, not being
used to floods you see, and pretty nearly spilt us in the

ditch, but we just saved the carriage, and after some trouble got into the high road by Buscot Parsonage ; though even there for some time the said road was also a river : so over St. John's Bridge and safe to Kelmscott. But opening the gate there, lo, the water all over the little front garden: in short, I have never seen so high a flood there : there was a smart shower when we got in and then a bright clear evening : the next day was bright and clear between strong showers with a stiff south-west gale : of course we could do nothing but sail and paddle about the floods."

During the following winter the manufacture of the Hammersmith rugs and carpets went busily on at Kelmscott House. By May enough specimens had been successfully produced to allow of a public exhibition of them. The circular written by Morris and issued by the firm on that occasion states the facts very clearly. This new branch of the business was " an attempt to make England independent of the East for carpets which may claim to be considered works of art."

" We believe," the circular goes on, " that the time has come for some one or other to make that attempt, unless the civilized world is prepared to do without the art of Carpet-making at its best : for it is a lamentable fact that, just when we of the West are beginning to understand and admire the art of the East, that art is fading away, nor in any branch has the deterioration been more marked than in Carpet-making.

" All beauty of colour has now (and for long) disappeared from the manufactures of the Levant—the once harmonious and lovely Turkey Carpets. The traditions of excellence of the Indian Carpets are only kept up by a few tasteful and energetic providers in England with infinite trouble and at a great expense, while the mass of the goods are already inferior in many respects to what can be turned out mechanically from the looms of Glasgow or Kidderminster.

"As for Persia, the mother of this beautiful art, nothing could mark the contrast between the past and the present clearer than the Carpets, doubtless picked for excellence of manufacture, given to the South Kensington Museum by His Majesty the Schah, compared with the rough work of the tribes done within the last hundred years, which the Directors of the Museum have judiciously hung near them.

"In short, the art of Carpet-making, in common with the other special arts of the East, is either dead or dying fast; and it is clear to everyone that, whatever future is in store for those countries where it once flourished, they will, in time to come, receive all influence from, rather than give any to, the West.

"It seems to us, therefore, that, for the future, we people of the West must make our own hand-made Carpets, if we are to have any worth the labour and money such things cost; and that these, while they should equal the Eastern ones as nearly as may be in materials and durability, should by no means imitate them in design, but show themselves obviously to be the outcome of modern and Western ideas, guided by those principles that underlie all architectural art in common."

Besides this labour of the loom, the year had been crowded with other more public work. Sweeping restorations were proposed and already in progress at St. Mark's, Venice; and Morris was the soul of the movement of protest, which, though conducted in some quarters with more zeal than discretion in its attitude towards Italy and the Italian Government, at least had a powerful influence in preventing the proposed demolition and rebuilding of the western façade. In support of the movement, which was headed by the Society for Protection of Ancient Buildings, he spoke and wrote untiringly, not only in London, but in Birmingham and Oxford. The Oxford meeting in the Sheldonian Theatre was the first occasion on which he appeared at his own University in any public capacity. In his ardour he even succeeded in prevailing on Burne-Jones to make there, for the first and last time on record, a speech in public.

When he had been at Venice the year before, he had been too ill to take much apparent pleasure in St. Mark's. But his eye had taken it all in, and the impression it made on him rather grew than weakened as time went on. "Always beautiful," he now wrote of it, "but from the first meant to grow more beautiful by the lapse of time, it has now become a work of art, a monument of history, and a piece of nature. Surely I need not enlarge on the pre-eminence of St. Mark's in all these characters; for no one who even pretends to care about art, history, or nature, would call it in question; but I will assert that, strongly as I may have seemed to express myself, my words but feebly represent the feelings of a large body of cultivated men who will feel real grief at the loss that seems imminent—a loss which may be slurred over, but which will not be forgotten, and which will be felt ever deeper as cultivation spreads. That the outward aspect of the world should grow uglier day by day in spite of the aspirations of civilization, nay, partly because of its triumphs, is a grievous puzzle to some of us who are not lacking in sympathy for those aspirations and triumphs, artists and craftsmen as we are. So grievous it is that sometimes we are tempted to say, 'Let them make a clean sweep of it all then; let us forget it all and muddle on as best we may, unencumbered with either history or hope!' But such despair is, we well know, a treason to the cause of civilization and the arts, and we do our best to overcome it, and to strengthen ourselves in the belief that even a small minority will at last be listened to and its reasonable opinions be accepted."

He was also a regular visitor and adviser at the South Kensington Museum and at the Royal School of Art Needlework. And alongside of all the rest, he carried on, until the General Election of 1880, vigorous political work in London. In 1879 he was treasurer of the National Liberal League, an association formed to a large extent from the representatives of that working-class London Radicalism which had organized itself in opposition to the Eastern policy of the Government in 1876. At the meetings of this League he made his first essays in the practice of extempore speech. It was a thing which, partly from constitutional shyness and partly from the pressure of thought behind his language, came to him, so far as it did come at all, with great difficulty. " When he spoke off-hand," a colleague of his at this time notes—and the description is highly characteristic —" he had a knack at times of hammering away at his point until he had said exactly what he wanted to say in exactly the words he wished to use, rocking to and fro the while from one foot to the other."

After the elections of 1880 had replaced a Liberal Government in power, his political partisanship rapidly fell away from him. Like the wave of popular feeling which turned those elections, it had been roused on particular issues, and was kept alive rather by hostility to Lord Beaconsfield's policy than by any great affection for the Cabinet which replaced his. The enthusiasm of 1880 barely lived out the year. The Irish Coercion Bill of 1881 finally destroyed it. In the November following, Morris took an actively joyful part in winding up the affairs of the National Liberal League. The social reforms which he had at heart he saw disappearing amid an ocean of Whiggery, which he no more loved than he did Toryism. "I think some *raison d'être* might be found for us," he wrote in handing over the accounts when he resigned the treasurership, "if we had definite work to do: I do so hate—this in spite of my accounts—everything vague in politics as well as in art." But definite work of the kind he meant was not then in the programme of the Liberal party. Very soon Morris's attitude towards current politics became one of mere irritation and contempt. " Toryism, a system of common robbery, is nevertheless far better than Whiggism—a compound of petty larceny, popular instruction, and receiving of stolen goods": so runs a well-known passage in "The Romany Rye"; and Morris's way of regarding politics had much in common with Borrow's. Gradually but inevitably he became one of a party to whom Canning's famous phrase took a new meaning; and who resolved, if it were possible, to call a new world into existence, not to redress, but to destroy, that balance of the old in which they saw nothing but a door turning back and forward on its hinges.

But this change took time; and it was gradually wrought out through many doubts and even despondencies.

In the summer of 1880 the long-planned voyage of the whole family from Hammersmith to Kelmscott by water actually took place. Price, William De Morgan, and the Hon. Richard Grosvenor were the remainder of the party. All cares were put aside for it, and the light-heartedness of fifteen years before resumed its sway for a happy week.

"Little things please little minds," he writes on the 10th of August; "therefore my mind must be little, so pleased am I this morning. That is not logic, though I suspect the conclusion to be true: but again I doubt if the 'Ark,' which is veritably the name of our ship, can be considered a little thing, except relatively: item, it is scarcely a little thing that the sky is one sheet of pale warm blue, and that the earth is sucking up the sun rejoicing.

" Jenny and I went out before breakfast to see the craft.   She is odd but delightful: imagine a biggish company boat with a small omnibus on board, fitted up luxuriously inside with two shelves and a glass-rack, and a sort of boot behind this: room for two rowers in front, and I must say for not many more except in the cabin or omnibus.   Still what joy (to a little mind) to see the landscape out of a square pane of glass, and to sleep a-nights with the stream rushing two inches past one's ear.   Then after all, there is the romance of the bank, and outside the boat the world is wide : item, we can always hire a skiff for some of the party to row in and stretch their muscles, and in that way I propose to start this afternoon about $2\frac{1}{2}$ after dining here.

" Rathbone can't come, being too hard at work after all; so our males will consist of Crom, Dick, and Meorgan" (this was a child's mispronunciation of De Morgan's name) "besides self. Yesterday morning, also a very beautiful one, I had qualms about leaving the garden here, which really, as De Morgan said on Sunday, is a very tolerable substitute for a garden : item, after doing a good deal of small necessary work at Queen Square I had qualms about leaving my business; but to-day I have none—I think I know now why I fatten so."

("I really think," he says, however, in another letter, written when he was in much trouble and worry over public work, " that Falstaff's view of sighing and grief blowing men up like a bladder was a sound medical opinion.")

" More and more I think people ought to live in one place—pilgrimages excepted. By the way, I give my third lecture to the Trade Guild of Learning in October ; that will be my autumn work, writing it, if I have any quiet time away from home. Also I have promised to lecture next March at the London Institute—subject, the prospects of Architecture in modern civilization. I will be as serious as I can over them, and when I have these two last done, I think of making a book of the lot, as it will be about what I have to say on the subject, which still seems to me the most serious one that a man can think of; for 'tis no less than the chances of a calm, dignified, and therefore happy life for the mass of mankind.

" I shall find my long carpet out of the loom when I come back—but I am not a bit anxious about it now, the river will wash all that away."

The story of the expedition is continued in a long letter from Kelmscott :

" We came to our first lodging (Sunbury, some six miles above Hampton Court) very late, about half-past ten, and queer it was the next morning to note how different the place was to our imaginations of it in the dark : item, the commonplace inn was a blow to the romance of the river, as you may imagine. Crom and I slept on board the Ark that night ; perforce. A cloudy morning when we started, which at first much disappointed me after the splendid evening we had come in by : nevertheless I was in spirits at the idea of getting out of the Cockney waters, and we were scarcely through the lock we had to pass at starting before the sun was out and hot again: the river was nearly new to me really hereabouts and much better than I expected, especially from Chertsey to Staines; it is full of strange character in many places; Laleham, for instance, with its enormous willows and queer suggestions (at any rate) of old houses on the banks: we dined luxuriously on the bank a little below this, and had tea on the grass of Runneymead, which (as I remembered)

is a most lovely place; on such an afternoon as one can
scarcely hope to see again for brightness and clearness.
When we had done tea, it became obvious that we should
never get to Maidenhead (as we had intended) that night,
so after much spilling of wisdom in a discussion of the
kind where no one can see any plan but his own as possible, we agreed to make another day of it; Windsor on
that night (Wednesday) and Marlow on Thursday. Well,
we got to Windsor about eight, and beautiful it was
coming into; and with all drawbacks even when one saw
it next morning seemed a wonderful place : so we only
made 17 miles this day.   We all slept in the inn on the
waterside : that was Wednesday.

" Thursday, Dick took us up to Eton; and again in
spite of drawbacks it is yet a glorious place.   Once more
the morning was grey and even threatening rain (wind N.
N.E.), but very soon cleared up again into the brightest
of days : a very pleasant morning we had, and dined just
above Bray Lock; cook was I, and shut up in the Ark
to do the job, appearing like the high-priest at the critical
moment pot in hand,—but O the wasps about that osier
bed !   We got quite used to them at last and by dint of
care did not swallow any with our food, nor were stung.

" There was a regatta at Maidenhead and both banks
crowded with spectators, so that we had to drop the
tow-rope before our time, and as the Ark forged slowly
along towards the Berkshire side with your servant steering on her roof, and De Morgan labouring at the sculls,
you may think that we were chaffed a little.   After
Maidenhead you go under Cliefden woods, much admired
by the world in general; I confess to thinking them
rather artificial; also eyeing Mr. Dick with reference to
their owner I couldn't help thinking of Mr. Twemlow
and Lord Snigsworthy.   But at Cookham Lock how
beautiful it was: you get out of the Snigsworthy woods

there; the hills fall back from the river, which is very
wide there, and you are in the real country, with cows and
sheep and farm-houses, the work-a-day world again and
not a lacquey's paradise: the country too has plenty of
character there, and may even be called beautiful : it was
beautiful enough that evening at any rate: the sun had
set as we cleared Cookham Lock, and we went facing the
west, which was cloudless and golden, till it got quite dark :
by that same dark we had to get through the Marlow
Lock, with no little trouble, as we had to skirt a huge
weir which roared so that we couldn't hear each other
speak, and so to our night's lodging : Crom and I in the
Ark close to the roaring weir, Dick and De M. in the
inn (a noisy one) and the ladies up town, over the bridge.
We took them there, and as we left the little house, looked
up the street, and saw the streamers of the Northern
Lights flickering all across that part of the sky, just as I
saw them in '71 (and not since) in the harbour of Thors-
haven: it was very mysterious and almost frightening to
see them over the summer leafage so unexpectedly in a
place I at least had not seen by daylight.

"So to bed we went, and again in the morning (Friday)
a grey day that cleared presently into a very hot one: and
once more the river all new to me, and very beautiful: at
Hurley Lock we had to wait for a big steamer that plies
regularly between Kingston and Oxford with passengers:
as I stood up in the lock afterwards I had the surprise of
seeing in a long barn-like building two Gothic arches and
then a Norman church fitting on to it and joined into a
quadrangle by other long roofs: this was Lady Place:
once a monastery, then a Jacobean house, and now there
is but a farm-house, somewhat gammoned, there: we all
went ashore and spent an hour there in great enjoyment,
for 'tis a lovely place: there is a huge dove-cot there with
carefully moulded buttresses of the 15th century: the

church has been miserably gammoned, but kept its old outline.

"I played the cook again a little short of Henley; and we went on again in a burning afternoon through a river fuller and fuller of character as we got higher up: stuck in the mud for 20 minutes at Wargrave: past Shiplake, which is certainly one of the most beautiful parts of the Thames, and so to Sonning for the night: a village prepensely picturesque and somewhat stuffy that hot night, but really pretty, with a nice inn where Crom was at home, having spent some time there when Boyce was painting on the river: but we scattered all over the village and Crom and I slept in the Ark. We started earlier on Saturday, as we had to get to Wallingford, a longer run than heretofore. We had got well used to the Ark by now, and there was Janey lying down and working quite at home: very hot and waspy it was at dinner, on the bank between Pangbourne and Goring, but when we were well past the last place the afternoon got much clouded over for the first time since our start: but now out of the over-rated half picturesque reach of Streatley and Goring here we were on the Thames that is the Thames, amidst the down-like country and all Cockney-dom left far behind, and it *was* jolly.

"We got to stuffy grubby little Wallingford rather early, and got lodging in a riverside pothouse partly and partly in the town. Here it rather tickled me that, an hour or so being to spare before supper, the girls proposed and did a row upon the water as a novel pastime. That was Saturday: well, Sunday morning it had rained in the night, and the look of the dull grey almost drizzling morning made me expect a regular wet day; but it was only dull and cool all day, and we had a very pleasant day of it, and I cooked 'em their dinner just above Culham Lock; we got out at Dorchester to look [at] the

Dykes which Sir J. Lubbock has tried to get into the schedule of his bill and failed; so that the dykes have been partly ploughed over to their hurt: then a bit higher I recognized the place where we stopped for victuals years ago when the Faulkners were with us: and so we got to Oxford a little after nightfall: the banks of the river near the town have been spoilt somewhat since my time; for I have been there but thrice since I was an undergraduate. Well, at Oxford we left the Ark: and Janey the next day (Monday) went on by rail to Kelmscott: while we got up early and by dint of great exertions started from Medley Lock at 9 a.m., with Bossom and another man to tow us as far as New Bridge, where we sent them off, and muddled ourselves home somehow, dining at a lovely place about a mile above New Bridge, where I have stopped twice before for that end.   One thing was very pleasant: they were hay-making on the flat flood-washed spits of ground and islets all about Tadpole; and the hay was gathered on punts and the like; odd stuff to look at, mostly sedge, but they told us it was the best of stuff for milk.

"Night fell on us long before we got to Radcot, and we fastened a lantern to the prow of our boat, after we had with much difficulty got our boats through Radcot Bridge.   Charles was waiting us with a lantern at our bridge by the corner at 10 p.m., and presently the ancient house had me in its arms again: J. had lighted up all brilliantly, and sweet it all looked you may be sure."

A few days later he writes from London to Mrs. Burne-Jones:

"You may imagine that coming back to this beastly congregation of smoke-dried swindlers and their slaves (whom one hopes one day to make their rebels) under the present circumstances does not make me much more in love with London, though I must admit to feeling this morning a touch of the 'all by oneself' independence which you wot of as a thing I like. I found by the way De Morgan a complete sympathizer on the subject of London : however let that pass, since in London I am and must be. The few days we passed at Kelmscott made a fine time of it for me; our mornings were grey and dull, though we had several fine afternoons and two lovely evenings. Thursday we went to Fairford in the afternoon, and I was pleased to see the glass and the handsome church once more. Though the country that way is not remarkable, every turn in the road and every by-way set me a-longing to go afoot through the country, never stopping for a day; after all a fine harvest time is the crown of the year in England; there is so much to look at. On the Friday we went to Inglesham and above the Round House, on what might be called the upperest Thames, for half a mile, to look at Inglesham church, a lovely little building about like Kelmscott in size and style, but handsomer and with more old things left in it. Well, we parted on Sunday morning rather melancholy, but had a beautiful voyage to Medley Lock ; such an evening, and the best of it at Godstow, where the moon began to show red over Wolvercot.

" So here I am again on the lower Thames, finding it grimy; I have just been busy over my carpeteers; all going pretty well. The 'Orchard' being finished is a fair success as manufacture—lies flat on the whole—and as a work of art has points about it, but I can better it next time."

" I can't pretend," he writes again, when on the point of leaving Kelmscott finally that autumn, " not to feel being out of this house and its surroundings as a great loss. I have more than ever at my heart the importance for people of living in beautiful places; I mean the sort of beauty which would be attainable by all, if people could but begin to long for it. I do most earnestly desire that something more startling could be done than mere constant private grumbling and occasional public speaking to lift the standard of revolt against the sordidness which people are so stupid as to think necessary."

The river expedition was repeated in the following year. William De Morgan and Faulkner again joined in it. The party also included De Morgan's sister, and two girls, Miss Bessie Macleod and Miss Lisa Stillman, who came full of the high spirits of youth. "On the whole the hazardous experiment of trying the same expedition twice over has succeeded," was Morris's report after it was over. "Our spirits sank somewhat I think as we neared Kelmscott last night; a thing done and over always does that for people, however well it has gone. For my part I didn't so much feel that as the coming in to Oxford. A kind of terror always falls upon me as I near it; indignation at wanton or rash changes mingles curiously in me with all that I remember that I have lost since I was a lad and dwelling there; not the least of losses the recognition that I didn't know in those days what a gain it was to be there. Perhaps if one dreads repeating a pleasure at my time of life it is because it marks too clearly how the time has gone since the last time, and certainly I feel more than one year older since I came up the water in 1880. At any rate the younger part of us have enjoyed themselves thoroughly ; and indeed so have I. You know my faith, and how I feel I have no sort of right to revenge myself for any of my private troubles on the kind earth : and here I feel her kindness very specially and am bound not to meet it with a long face."

With a long face he did not meet it, whatever his private troubles and perplexities might be. "According to my recollection," Mr. William De Morgan says of these voyages, "we none of us stopped laughing all the way.

The things that come out prominent in my recollection of the two journeys, just as they come, are : 1. Morris sitting cooking the dinner inside the house-boat with the window closed to keep the wind off the spirit lamp, and ourselves outside looking at him through the glass. 2. The party sitting in a circle at dinner on the river-bank, and Morris starting straight off with an Icelandic or other story which kept us all quiet and well-behaved till washing-up time. 3. Detection and conviction by Morris of the Thames Conservancy, which he was always catching at some new misdemeanour. 4. A battle royal at Henley at the hotel where we put up, about whether Mrs. Harris was or was not an abstraction. It began like this: we played Twenty Questions, and Mrs. Harris was the subject to be guessed—I think by me, as I was sent out of the room while the discussion proceeded how my first question, ' abstract or concrete ?' should be answered. I remember being outside the door when the waiter came up from the people in the room underneath to know if anything was the matter. It was a warm discussion ; virtually between Charles Faulkner and Morris. Faulkner maintained that Mrs. Harris was just as much a concrete idea as any other character in fiction. Morris repudiated this indignantly, affirming that she wasn't even a character in fiction, as she doesn't occur in the story except as an invention of Mrs. Gamp, who is herself a character in fiction. It is a delicate question : I recollect discussing it afterwards with Morris in the Merton Abbey days, when I was putting down the foundations of my building there—it was recalled to our minds by the concrete, naturally."

From Kelmscott he wrote on the 4th of September after the second of these voyages: " It has been a great pleasure to see man and maid so hard at work carrying at last. Hobbs began at it on Wednesday morning, and by the next morning the thatchers were putting on the bright straw cap to the new rick : yesterday they were carrying the wheat in the field along our causeway and stacking it in our yard : pretty as one sat in the tapestry-room to see the loads coming on between the stone walls —that was for the other rick though, just beyond the little three-cornered close in front of the house. I am afraid that the last winter has killed us a great many birds here; small ones especially : I don't see the blue tits I look for at this time of the year. I have seen but one moor-hen (yesterday) and was glad to see him, as I feared they were all dead : plenty of rooks however ; they have just left off making the parliament-noise they began about six this morning : starlings also, but they haven't begun to gather in our trees yet.

" The other morning as I was coming up the river by our island I heard a great squealing of the swallows, and looking up saw a hawk hanging in the wind overhead, and the swallows gathered in a knot near him : presently two or three swallows left their knot and began skirting Mr. Hawk, and one swept right down on him and fetched him a crack (or seemed to). He considered for a minute or two, then set his wings slant-wise and went down the wind like lightning, and in an instant was hanging over Eaton Hastings : I remember seeing something like this in the flats about the Arun before."

" We went a most formal expedition on Saturday," says a letter of a fortnight later. " By water to Lechlade: then took a trap there and drove to Cirencester, which turned out a pleasant country town, and to us country folk rather splendid and full of shops. There is a grand church there, mostly late Gothic, of the very biggest type of parish church, romantic to the last extent, with its many aisles and chapels: wall-painting there and stained glass and brasses also: and tacked on to it an elaborate house,

THE MANOR HOUSE, KELMSCOTT, FROM THE KITCHEN GARDEN.

now the town hall, but built doubtless for lodging the priests who served the many altars in the church. I could have spent a long day there ; however, after mooning about the town a bit, we drove off again along the long stretches of the Foss-way (Roman) over a regular down country, the foot-hills of the Cotswolds, pleasant enough, till we came to the valley which the tiny Coln cuts through, where we set ourselves to seeking the Roman villa : said valley very beautiful, the meadows so sweet and wholesome. Two fields were grown all over with the autumn crocus, which I have not seen wild elsewhere in England, though there was plenty of it near Ems. The Roman villa was very interesting, for a show place with a gimcrack *cottage ornée* in front of it, and the place was lovely : we spent our time with the utmost recklessness, so that by then we had had tea at a nice little public by a bridge, and were ready to start down the Coln towards Fairford, it was 6.30, and getting towards twilight. However we saw the first two villages well enough and had some inkling of the others : the scale of everything of the smallest, but so sweet, and unusual even ; it was like the background of an innocent fairy story. We didn't know our way till we had reached the last of the Coln villages, and kept asking and knocking at cottage doors and the like, and it was all very delightful and queer. Our trap put us down at St. John's Bridge, and we trudged thence into Kelmscott, on a night so dark that even Kelmscott lights made a kind of flare in the sky."

It was in the strength of that autumn's stay at Kelmscott, and all the thoughts through which it led him, that he reached a point to which he had not till then attained in width of outlook and depth of insight. An address delivered by him on the 13th of October at the annual meeting of the School of Science and Art connected with the Wedgwood Institute at Burslem, though only published in a locally circulated report, and not at any time very widely known, is both one of the most brilliant and one of the most significant of his published writings.   It contains, in a way which none of his other published lectures of that period seem to approach, the sum of all his earlier and the germ of all his later doctrine.

" I myself," he said in that address, " am just fresh from an out-of-the-way part of the country near the end of the navigable Thames, where within a radius of five miles are some half-dozen tiny village churches, every one of which is a beautiful work of art.   These are the works of the Thames-side country bumpkins, as you would call us—nothing grander than that.   If the same sort of people were to design and build them now, they could not build anything better than the ordinary little plain Nonconformist chapels that one sees scattered about new neighbourhoods.   That is what they correspond with, not an architect-designed new Gothic church.   The more you study architecture the more certain you will become that I am right in this, and that what we have left us of earlier art was made by the unhelped people.   Neither will you fail to see that it was made intelligently and with pleasure.

" That last word brings me to a point so important that, at the risk of getting wearisome, I must add it to my old sentence and repeat the whole.   Time was when everybody that made anything made a work of art besides a useful piece of goods, *and it gave them pleasure to make it.*   Whatever I doubt, I have no doubt of that.

" I know that in those days life was often rough and evil enough, beset by violence, superstition, ignorance, slavery ; yet sorely as poor folks needed a solace, they did not altogether lack one, and that solace was pleasure in their work.   Much as the world has won since then, I do not think it has won for all men such perfect happiness that we can afford to cast aside any solace that nature holds forth to us.   Or must we for ever be casting out one devil by another ?   Shall we never make a push to get rid of the whole pack of them at once ?

"As I sit at my work at home, which is at Hammersmith, close to the river, I often hear some of that ruffianism go past the window of which a good deal has been said in the papers of late, and has been said before at recurring periods.   As I hear the yells and shrieks and all the degradation cast on the glorious tongue of Shakespeare and Milton, as I see the brutal reckless faces and figures go past me, it rouses the recklessness and brutality in me also, and fierce wrath takes possession of me, till I remember, as I hope I mostly do, that it was my good luck only of being born respectable and rich, that has put me on this side of the window among delightful books and lovely works of art, and not on the other side, in the empty street, the drink-steeped liquor-shops, the foul and degraded lodgings.   I know by my own feelings and desires what these men want, what would have saved them from this lowest depth of savagery : employment which would foster their self-respect and win the praise and sympathy of their fellows, and dwellings which they could come to with pleasure, surroundings which would soothe and elevate them ; reasonable labour, reasonable rest.   There is only one thing that can give them this— art."

Two other passages from the same address are memorable.   The first expresses with great lucidity and sympathy the mixture of admiration and impatient despair with which he regarded the work of the Pre-Raphaelite school of painting as it culminated in the art of Burne-Jones.

"The work which is the result of the division of labour, whatever else it can do, cannot produce art : which must,

as long as the present system lasts, be entirely confined
to such works as are the work from beginning to end of
one man—pictures, independent sculpture, and the like.
As to these, on the one hand they cannot fill the gap
which the loss of popular art has made, nor can they,
especially the more imaginative of them, receive the sympathy which should be their due. As things go, it is impossible for any one who is not highly educated to understand the higher kind of pictures. The aspect of this as
regards people in general is to my mind much more important than that which has to do with the unlucky artist:
but he also has some claim upon our consideration ; and
I am sure that this lack of the general sympathy of simple
people weighs very heavily on him, and makes his work
feverish and dreamy, or crabbed and perverse."

The other passage is a piece of straightforward practical advice to designers. In the artist, and therefore in
his · art, a certain moral quality was before all things
essential : the qualities fatal to art were not technical :
they were " vagueness, hypocrisy, and cowardice." And
of these three, vagueness was to Morris as immoral, and
therefore as inartistic, as either of the other vices.

" Be careful to eschew all vagueness. It is better to
be caught out in going wrong when you have had a definite purpose, than to shuffle and slur so that people
can't blame you because they don't know what you are
at. Hold fast to distinct form in art. Don't think too
much of style, but set yourself to get out of you what
you think beautiful, and express it, as cautiously as you
please, but, I repeat, quite distinctly and without vagueness. Always think your design out in your head before
you begin to get it on the paper. Don't begin by slob-
bering and messing about in the hope that something
may come out of it. You must see it before you can
draw it, whether the design be of your own invention or

nature's.   Remember always, form before colour, and outline, silhouette, before modelling, not because these latter are of less importance, but because they can't be right if the first are wrong."

The progress of his mind towards active Socialism during these two years is recorded in the private letters where he set down his thoughts or his beliefs from one day to another with complete transparency.   Through many fluctuations of mood one may trace a gradual advance.   Some people, even among those who knew him well, thought of his Socialism as a sudden and un-accountable aberration; or at all events fancied it a movement into which he flung himself in a sudden fit of enthusiasm, without having thought the matter out, and acting on a rash impulse.   How much this is the reverse of the truth becomes plain when one traces the long struggle, the deep brooding, through which he arrived at his final attitude, and notes the distaste and reluctance which he often felt for the new movement, which at other moments shone out to him as the hope of the world.

"I am in rather a discouraged mood," he writes in a New Year's letter in 1880, "and the whole thing seems almost too tangled to see through and too heavy to move. Happily though, I am not bound either to see through it or move it but a very little way: meantime I do know what I love and what I hate, and believe that neither the love nor the hatred are matters of accident or whim." Beyond all he seems to have been oppressed by a sense of loneliness in his new thoughts.   Any moral support from whatever quarter was hailed by him with touching gratitude.   To misconstruction he had long been ac-customed.   "I have had a life of insults and sucking of my brains," he once said, with no exaggeration of the truth.   A man of means and University education who deliberately kept a shop, a poet who chose to exercise a handicraft, not as a gentleman amateur, but under the ordinary conditions of handicraftsmen, was a figure so unique as to be all but unintelligible. Sometimes, though rarely, he turned upon his persecutors. " It is a real joy to find the game afoot," he breaks out a few months later; "that the thing is stirring in other people's minds besides mine, the poetic upholsterer, as Sir Ed. Beckett calls me, meaning (strange to say) an insult by that harmless statement of fact."

In another letter written on the New Year's Day of 1881 he regards the matter with a greater sense of responsibility and a more practical seriousness.

" I have of late been somewhat melancholy (rather too strong a word, but I don't know another), not so much so as not to enjoy life in a way, but just so much as a man of middle age who has met with rubs (though less than his share of them) may sometimes be allowed to be. When one is just so much subdued one is apt to turn more specially from thinking of one's own affairs to more worthy matters; and my mind is very full of the great change which I hope is slowly coming over the world, and of which surely this new year will be one of the landmarks. Though to me, as I suppose to you, every day begins and ends a year, I was fain to catch hold of ancient custom; nor perhaps will you think it ceremonious or superstitious if I try to join thoughts with you to-day in writing a word of hope for the new year, that it may do a good turn of work toward the abasement of the rich and the raising up of the poor, which is of all things most to be longed for, till people can at last rub out from their dictionaries altogether these dreadful words rich and poor."

Six months later he speaks for the first time clearly of the new day as a thing which (as in the Northern

Mythology) can only arrive through some Night of the Gods, and faces the thought that true civilization may have to be reached through the destruction, and not the transformation, of the existing order.

" I suppose you have seen about the sentence on Herr Most and read Coleridge's most dastardly speech to him : just think of the mixture of tyranny and hypocrisy with which the world is governed! These are the sort of things that make thinking people so sick at heart that they are driven from all interest in politics save revolutionary politics: which I must say seems like to be my case. Indeed I have long known, or felt, say, that society in spite of its modern smoothness was founded on injustice and kept together by cowardice and tyranny : but the hope in me has been that matters would mend gradually, till the last struggle, which must needs be mingled with violence and madness, would be so short as scarcely to count. But I must say matters like this and people's apathy about them shake one's faith in gradual progress.

" As to the Anti-Scrape, I have little comfort there I must say: we have begun too late and our foes are too many; videlicet, almost all people, educated and uneducated. No, as to the buildings themselves, 'tis a lost cause; in fact the destruction is not far from being complete already. What people really say to themselves is this: I don't like the thing being done, but I can bear it maybe—or certainly, when I come to think of it—and to stir in it is such obvious suffering ; so I won't stir. Certainly to take that trouble in any degree it is needful that a man should be touched with a real love of the earth, a worship of it, no less ; and I think that as things go, that is seldom felt except by very simple people, and by them, as would be likely, dimly enough. You know the most refined and cultured people, both those of the old re-

ligions and these of the new vague ones, have a sort of
Manichean hatred of the world (I use the word in its
proper sense, the home of man).   Such people must be
both the enemies of beauty and the slaves of necessity,
and true it is that they lead the world at present, and I
believe will do till all that is old is gone, and history has
become a book from which the pictures have been torn.
Now if you ask me why I kick against the pricks in this
matter, all I can say is, first because I cannot help it, and
secondly because I am encouraged by a sort of faith that
something will come of it, some kind of culture of which
we know nothing at present."

A month later he writes again:

" How people talk as if there were no wrongs of
society against all the poor devils it has driven demented
in one way or other!   Yet I don't wonder at rich men
trembling either: for it does seem as though a rising impatience against the injustice of society was in the air;
and no wonder that the craziest heads, that feel this injustice most, breed schemes for setting it all right with a
stroke of lightning.   There was a curious and thoughtful
letter from America in Tuesday night's Echo, the writer
of which seemed to have been struck by this thought as
to matters over there: quoth he, there is no respect for
people in authority there: every one knows that they are
there by virtue of a bargain struck by selfishness and
selfishness, (I quote his matter only,) and a sort of despair
besets people about it.   All political change seems to me
useful now as making it possible to get the social one: I
don't mean to say that I myself make any wide distinction between political and social; I am only using the
words in the common way."

And once more three weeks later:

" I don't quite agree with you in condemning grumbling against follies and ills that oppress the world at large,

even among friends; for you see it is but now and then that one has a chance of speaking about the thing in public, and meantime one's heart is hot with it, and some expression of it is like to quicken the flame even in those that one loves and respects most, and it is good to feel the air laden with the coming storm even as we go about our daily work or while away time in light matters. To do nothing but grumble and not to act—that is throwing away one's life: but I don't think that words on our cause that we have at heart do nothing but wound the air, even when spoken among friends: 'tis at worst like the music to which men go to battle. Of course if the thing is done egotistically 'tis bad so far; but that again, how to do it well or ill, is a matter of art like other things."

A matter of art like other things! from this position he strayed far, in the opinion of many of his perplexed friends and jeering opponents, in the years when he was an active worker for the Socialist cause: and certainly the storm-laden air that he began to feel round him was partly at least an atmosphere of his own creation : a mirage, a fool's paradise, it was freely called by those who, if they ever strayed into a fool's paradise of their own, would at all events never be lured towards it by any super-flux of sympathy or any ardour of imagination. Yet to look a little deeper, this atmosphere, imagined or created, and created so far as really imagined, is just what art and art alone gives ; and it is well to realize that mankind, if they propose to do without such dreams as this, can buy release from them only by the deliberate destruction of art and renunciation of beauty. Whether the result would be worth the price is a remote and rather abstract question; the price is unpayable.

These last letters are from Kelmscott. The return to London had its natural effect of shaping more or less vague broodings into matters of clear visible right and wrong.

" As to my 'symptoms' on being pitchforked into the dirt and misery of the Centre of Intelligence," he breaks out on his return, " I must hold my peace about them, I suppose : only in sober earnest I must ask you to believe that they are not wholly selfish ; since I could, if I would, more or less escape from this captivity, and would do so if it were not for the cause."

The reference in the use of the word " symptoms " may not be at once obvious.　It is explained by another letter written a few months before.　He knew—or if he did not know it was not for want of telling—that discontent with the existing order of things might be traceable to some merely physical cause, some pressure on the brain, some disorder of the liver, some acrid humour in the blood, that poisoned the springs of energy.　His own temper was naturally passionate, and his gouty habit, with all which that involves when the subject is gathering up for an illness, did not, of course, tend to make him less irritable. That in spite of this his temper sweetened with years was due to an amount of self-control which it is very easy for natures more phlegmatic or of more perfect physical balance to under-estimate.　How sane, how full of ordinary common sense his view of such things was, is illustrated by that other letter, one of his rare excursions into literary criticism.　Even here the criticism passes almost at once, and almost insensibly, into the larger sphere of a criticism of life.

" Last night I took me a book and read Carlyle on Mrs. Carlyle, having read his James Carlyle and Jeffrey before.　I think I never read anything that dispirited me so much ; though read it through one must after having once begun it.　What is one to say of such outrageous blues as this ?　As to what he says about this, that, and the other person now living, I can't see that he gives much offence, I mean to say personally ; he is generally very

unfair and narrow and whimsical about his likes and dis-
likes, but 'tis something in these days of hypocrisy that
he makes distinctions at all—only one wishes his distinctions were something more than whims.   But all that is
nothing to the ferocity of his gloom ; I confess I had no
idea of it till I read the book : and yet I find it difficult
to say that it ought not to have been printed, and I am
sure it ought not to have been garbled, as some folk think
it should.   Only should it not have been called, The history of a great author's liver ?   Not to mention symptoms
too much, I in a small way understand something of that :
to look upon your own natural work, which you have
chosen out of all the work of the world, with a sick disgust, when you are not at it : to be sore and raw with
your friends, distrustful of them, antagonistic to them,
when you are not in their company : to want society and
to hate it when you've got it :—all these things are just
as much a part of the disease as physical squeamishness :
but you see, poor chap, he was so always bad that he
scarcely had a chance of finding that out. But mind you,
I don't believe he didn't enjoy writing his books more or
less, even 'Frederick,' the dullest of them and the one he
groans over most.   After all, my moral from it all is the
excellence of art, its truth, and its power of expression.
Set 'Sartor Resartus' by all this, and what a difference !

"The story of the old father is touching in spite of its
clannishness (which perhaps is not so bad a thing ; holds
the world together somewhat).   He really must have
been a good fellow not to have bullied his queer son.
Only they wouldn't have been the worse for a touch of
definite art up there ; even among those beautiful mountains and moors."

But "the cause," a term perhaps specifically used by
Morris for the first time in the letter quoted above, was
now shaping itself in his mind to something on which the

whole of his life both as an artist and as a human being converged : and it was in London, where he saw the misery of the present most acute, that he also discerned, or thought he discerned, some lifting on the horizon, and some glimmer of future hope. To retreat from the pressure of social problems into "a little Palace of Art of one's own " (in the phrase of five and twenty years back) was now as before possible—was more possible than ever now, when his business as a manufacturer and decorator was firmly established and capable of large expansion. Just at this time he was carrying out decorations on a large scale at St. James's Palace, which included the hanging of the Throne and Reception rooms with specially designed silk damask, the hand-painting of the ceilings and cornices, and the designing of a special paper for hanging the main staircase. This work was, of course, very widely known ; and it had attracted not merely additional attention, but additional respect, to the unique quality of his design and workmanship as a decorator. He had only to accept ordinary commercial conditions and use them for what they were worth, to become a wealthy man, who might live where he chose, and surround himself with a sort of barbed wire fence of beautiful objects. This was just what he would not do: nor would he consent to the less distasteful compromise of giving up the conditions of active production to settle down in quietness at his beloved Kelmscott. The actual problem of civilization, as it was focussed and concentrated in the welter of London, drew him towards it with an invincible attraction ; and upon senses always acutely open, and a brain that never ceased sounding among the bases of things, there fell with ever increasing urgency the cry of a bewildered and unhappy people—*confusæ sonus urbis et illætabile murmur.*

CHAPTER XIII

EVER since the days when Red House was to have been made the centre of a little manufacturing community, the idea of transferring the works of the firm to some place out of London had been in Morris's mind; and now not only was his dislike of London greater than ever, but the increasing scale and complexity of the business made migration more practically urgent. Weaving, dyeing and cotton printing, the three new staples of the firm's work, are all industries that require spacious workshops; for dyeing and its subsidiary processes of bleaching, the necessary air and water could only be had out of London for anything beyond mere experimental work. But in nearly every branch of the business there were difficulties involved by want of proper premises. At every hand something essential to the production of the finished goods had to be procured or executed elsewhere: in some cases the raw material could only be laboriously obtained from Yorkshire manufacturers; in others the designs made at Queen Square had to be sent out to manufacturers for execution. In neither case was it possible to secure the same results as when the whole work was carried out by men trained in Morris's own methods, and working under his own eye. The least that was wanted was a single place in which the business could be so far concentrated that he could dye his own silks and cottons and wools,

weave his own carpets and tapestries and brocades, print
his own chintzes, and put together his own painted
windows. When the separate counting house and show-
rooms in Oxford Street were set up, there was no in-
superable difficulty in the way of transferring the manufacturing part of the business from Queen Square and
Hammersmith to any centre that might be fixed upon.

To transfer the works to the neighbourhood of Kelmscott was an obvious and tempting solution, if the place
had not been so remote and so far from a railway. But
not many miles off lay that Cotswold country which in
the sixteenth and seventeenth centuries had been one
of the principal manufacturing centres of England, and
whose prosperity had only given way towards the end of
last century before northern water-power and the energy
of Yorkshire masters. The slopes and valleys of the
Cotswolds, where the Thames and its tributary rivers
break from the hills, are still thickly set with little towns
that were once thriving seats of commerce, and that still
retain in their decay the traces of older opulence. So
early as the autumn of 1878 the idea of resuscitating the
old local industry in one of these beautiful villages was in
Morris's mind. He had gone over from Kelmscott to
stay for a few days with Price at Broadway Tower. From
Broadway he and Price drove over on the 1st of September to the village of Blockley, near Chipping Campden.
The village stands high up in one of the lateral valleys,
looking down to the plain along which the Roman Foss-
way runs on its straight course northeastward. A stream
runs down the little valley and is gathered in ponds to
work several mills, once busily employed in turning out
silk yarn for the Coventry manufacturers. One after
another they had succumbed to altered conditions and
the fierce competition of more modern machinery: and
now they stood empty. The notices of the last reduction

of wages made, before they had to give up the struggle
for life altogether, were still pasted on the workshop doors.
Morris fell in love with the place.   An ideally beautiful
landscape; clean air and water in abundance; a railway
station within easy distance; skilled workmen still linger-
ing in the half-deserted village, and owners who would
have been glad to make easy terms for what was becoming almost unsaleable property, seemed enough to counter-
balance the disadvantage of being nearly a hundred miles
from London and more remote still from other manufacturing centres.   But to the less enthusiastic mind of his
manager the risks of the scheme seemed much too great;
and at last Morris reluctantly abandoned it.   As time went
on, too, the feeling grew on him that, as a Londoner, he
ought to be loyal to London and do the best by her.

The neighbourhood of London was searched all round.
William De Morgan, who was about to set up pottery
works for the manufacture of his lustred tiles and majolica,
joined in the search, and it was agreed that both factories
should be placed together if possible.   At the beginning
of 1881 the matter became really pressing.   " We shall
have to take the chintzes ourselves before long," Morris
wrote to his wife on the 23rd of February, " and are now
really looking about for premises.   Edgar went to look
at the print-works at Crayford on Monday.   They seemed
promising : how queer it would be if we were to set up
our work there again.   By choice, if 'tis to be had, I had
rather get hold of some place on the Colne, say about
West Drayton : it would take no longer getting down
there, or not so long, as I am to Queen Square now."

On the 3rd of March, " W. De M. is all agog about
premises and has just heard of some at Hemel Hempstead
near St. Albans.   Webb and Wardle are going on Saturday to walk up a stream that runs into Thames at Isle-
worth."

D

"I went with De Morgan to Crayford on Monday," he writes to Mrs. Morris again a week later; "the whole country about seems much spoiled since we were there; but Crayford itself less than most places. However, it wouldn't do: though the buildings were big and solid and very cheap: for one thing the time of getting there is unconscionable, over an hour—on the whole it wasn't to be thought of. I saw Hall Place once more and it made the stomach in me turn round with desire of an old house."

The place finally chosen was nearer London than any of these. "On Monday," he writes on the 17th of March, "De M. and I went to look at premises at Merton in Surrey, whereof more hereafter: they seem as if they would do, and if so, and we can get them, then am I for evermore a bird of this world-without-end-for-everlasting hole of a London." The premises were disused print-works, on the high road from London to Epsom, just seven miles from Charing Cross. They had originally been a silk-weaving factory, started early in last century by some of those Huguenot refugees who had settled in large numbers in the neighbouring districts of Wandsworth and Streatham. The river Wandle, clear and beautiful then, and even now but little spoilt, runs through them, turning a water wheel and supplying water of the special quality required for madder-dyeing. This was one of the prime requisites, and limited the choice of sites materially. "We brought away bottles of water for analysis," Mr. De Morgan says in describing the various searches after the desired factory, "to make sure that it was fit to dye with. I recollect Morris's delight when a certificate was sent from an eminent analyst to the effect that a sample taken from pipes supplying all Lambeth was totally unfit for consumption and could only result in prompt zymotic disease: 'There's your science for you, De Morgan!' said Morris. I explained that if the analyst had known that 250,000

THE MILL POND, WITH THE WEAVING AND PRINTING SHEDS,
MERTON ABBEY.

people drank the water daily he would have analyzed it different. This was in Battersea and never came to anything."

The works stood on about seven acres of ground, including a large meadow as well as an orchard and vegetable garden. They were old-fashioned, though still in good repair. The riverside and the mill pond are thickly set with willows and large poplars; behind the dwelling-house a flower garden, then neglected, but soon restored to beauty when it came into Morris's hands, runs down to the water. The workshops, for the most part long wooden two-storied sheds, red-tiled and weatherboarded, are grouped irregularly round the mill lade. Beyond the meadow are the remains of a mediæval wall, the sole remaining fragment of Merton Abbey. Within a stone's throw Nelson had lived with the Hamiltons for the two years which followed the peace of Amiens, until he went out to the Mediterranean as Commander-in-Chief in 1803. But his house had been pulled down many years before. One drawback to the place was its extreme inaccessibility, considering the smallness of the distance, from Morris's house at Hammersmith, or indeed from almost any part of London. The District Railway was not then extended either to Wimbledon or to Turnham Green. To reach Merton from Kelmscott House Morris had to go by the underground railway from Hammersmith to Farringdon Street, cross the City, and then go down to Merton from Ludgate Hill, a journey that took about two hours. He could, however, stay the night at Merton when there was much to be done. A couple of rooms were fitted up for his private use as at Queen Square: " Papa will have a delightful sort of Quilp establishment there," his daughter wrote when the move was being made.

On the 8th of April he notes that he had "pretty much

come to the conclusion" with the owners. But there were the usual delays and hagglings: it was desired to have power to build kilns for tiles and glass, so that covenants with regard to chimneys had to be drawn up: and the lease was only signed on the 7th of June. The next day he went down with Webb, De Morgan, and George Wardle, and the alterations began to be arranged. Morris would not pull down any of the picturesque and prettily-weathered workshops; but roofs had to be heightened to give free space for looms, and foundations trenched and puddled to keep out damp (for at Merton water lies four feet below the surface of the ground), besides the heavy work of furnishing, the building of carpet-looms, the digging and lining of pits for indigo vats, and the general adaptation of both buildings and grounds to their new uses. One of the first things he did when the season allowed was to plant poplars round the meadow on which the grounds of the calico prints were to be cleared by exposure to the air. Meanwhile he was designing for chintzes with extraordinary rapidity and success; a whole series of these designs, including many of his very best, were turned out during this summer to be ready for the new works to start upon. The move was made at the beginning of winter. His impatience at the inevitable delays was great. "I am in an agony of muddle," he writes early in November; "I now blame myself severely for not having my way and settling at Blockley; I knew I was right; but cowardice prevailed." The agony, Mr. George Wardle tells me, was merely because everything could not move as easily and quickly as he wished. He "could never imagine difficulties," and chose to think that everything would have gone smoothly at Blockley. But before Christmas everything had been cleared out from Queen Square and its annexes, and the new works were fairly set a-going.

A circular issued from Oxford Street when the Merton workshops were in complete order gives a full catalogue of all the kinds of work designed and executed there. The list is as follows :

1. Painted glass windows.
2. Arras tapestry woven in the high-warp loom.
3. Carpets.
4. Embroidery.
5. Tiles.
6. Furniture.
7. General house decorations.
8. Printed cotton goods.
9. Paper hangings.
10. Figured woven stuffs.
11. Furniture velvets and cloths.
12. Upholstery.

Under some of·these headings there are notes of a kind very unlike the usual contents of a manufacturer's catalogue : and the circular may form the text for a brief summary of Morris's methods, and of the personal share he took in the various branches of the work.

In the earlier years of the business Morris had accepted commissions for windows in old as well as new buildings: the most conspicuous instances being the well-known windows in the Latin Chapel at Christ Church, Oxford, and the southern choir-aisle of Salisbury Cathedral. When the Society for Protection of Ancient Buildings was founded, he was forced to reconsider the whole question of dealing with old churches more deeply than before; and the conclusions he drew with regard to the practice of restoration obliged him to take up a very stringent attitude when there was any question of alterations to an ancient building. As regards windows in particular, the casuistry of the matter is exceptionally delicate. " We are prepared as heretofore," Morris wrote in this circular, " to give estimates for windows in churches and other buildings, *except in the case of such as can be considered monuments of Ancient Art*, the glazing of which we cannot conscientiously undertake, as our doing so would seem to sanction the disastrous practice of so-called Restoration." The double ambiguity of the words in which the exception is couched is easily apparent. Even rules laid down with the utmost stringency must in some cases leave room for ambiguities and evasions, and the final decision will fall on the instinct of the artist. But Morris's principles prescribed that in all cases where there was any doubt, an existing building, or any part of an existing building, whether in strict terms a monument of ancient art or not, should be let alone. In most cases there was none. When Dean Stanley asked him to execute a window for Westminster Abbey, and upon his refusal, cited the Vyner window in Christ Church as a precedent, Morris replied that even that window, the excellence of which as a piece of modern work he did not affect to deny, was an intruder where it stood, and alien in character and sentiment from the building in which it was placed.

On the announcement now made and on Morris's own practice under it, Mr. Wardle makes some interesting remarks. " Its object was ill understood," he says, " and moreover so little liked, that we found it necessary to repeat orally and with asseverations our firm intention to abide by it, and at the back of this, to get it believed that we had not given up glass-painting altogether. For a year or two certainly our business suffered from the rumour, not wanting in echoes, that Mr. Morris had given up glass-painting; and we had to make many advertisements to the contrary."

" In the minds of most people," Mr. Wardle goes on,

and here he touches the real truth of the matter, " who took any interest at all in Mr. Morris's work, the *raison d'être* of ' Morris glass ' was its so-called mediævalism, and it was supposed nothing could be more suitable for an ancient building.   The profound misconception which this opinion implied, and the other hopeless mistake which assumed that Mr. Morris's work was purposely ' mediæval,' made it impossible that the circular could be understood.

" The grounds of Mr. Morris's protest were two. The first was the obvious material damage ancient buildings suffer by the process of removing existing glass from the windows and the insertion of new.   We had ourselves several frightful experiences, though we used every precaution in our power : how much damage has been done where no such care was taken, and where it was not even suspected that the original tracery and framing of a window was of any peculiar value ! It was not uncommon, when a painted window was offered to an old church, that as part of the improvement new tracery and mullions were also decided on.   Even when it was intended to preserve the old stonework, it was almost inevitable that some part of it would fall when the support of the ancient glass with its saddle-bars and stanchions was removed : and new stonework would then have to be prepared hastily.   Even if all went well, which would be a large concession—for there was always the cutting of the old stonework for the new saddle-bars, the hammering, and the vibration, most dangerous to old masonry—there was the final blotting out of the entire window by the wire guards.   These guards are almost equivalent to the abolition of the windows as part of the external architecture, since they hide much of the thickness of the masonry and all the refinements of the mouldings and tracery."

The other ground was that laid down with a firm hand by Morris himself in the original statement of the objects of the Society for Protection of Ancient Buildings, and continually impressed and re-impressed by him with tongue and pen whenever he dealt with the subject of ancient art: the essential dishonesty of any process which professed to be "restoration" of the old building; and the essential futility of anything which undertook to replace an original by a copy even when there was not the dishonest purpose of making the copy indistinguishable from the original.

"Never," Mr. Wardle justly adds—and the remark, of course, applies with equal force to the share which Burne-Jones, first as principal and afterwards as sole figure-designer, had in Morris windows—"let people say what they will about the suitability of Mr. Morris's glass to mediæval buildings, do the old and the new rightly harmonize. This last opinion very few were able to adopt, for so few recognized the real originality and modernness of his art. It was supposed to be mediæval. In popular estimation design necessarily takes one of several recognized forms which are called styles, and as his design had many of the characters of mediæval work, he was supposed to be intentionally imitating that style. On the contrary, Mr. Morris was too unaffected, and in the broadest sense natural, in his art to allow himself to imitate, and as he did not intentionally make his work mediæval, he did not pretend that it could be suitable for a mediæval building."

This, then, was Morris's theory, expressed in its rigour. In accordance with it he laid down a self-denying ordinance with regard to supplying painted windows for ancient buildings—self-denying doubly, because not only did this resolution, as has been noted above, injure, and for a time partly cripple, this branch of the business, but because the result in three cases out of four was simply that the owners, or guardians, of the mediæval building went somewhere else ; and the window was filled with glass as much inferior to his in colour and design as it was more alien from the spirit of the Middle Ages, not least so when it was inspired by an insincere and pretentious mediævalism.

By abstaining himself, however, he hoped to set an example that others might gradually follow; and perhaps his action has not been wholly without effect. In a few instances he allowed exceptions: among these may be mentioned the five beautiful windows executed by him for the chancel of St. Margaret's, Rottingdean, at the special request of Burne-Jones. In that case the windows were plain lancets filled with modern glass, some of it unpainted, the rest admittedly and unrelievedly hideous. There was no tracery to injure, and no existing ancient glass to suffer from the juxtaposition of the new.

As regards the personal part which Morris took in this branch of the firm's work, it was the invariable practice in early years, and remained the rule after the Merton Abbey works were started, that the interpretation of the design and the choice of the glass came under his own eye. He seldom at any time, and never in more recent years, made complete designs for windows himself. From the first, the figure-subjects were mainly supplied by those of his colleagues who were professional painters. As time went on, they came almost exclusively from the studio of Burne-Jones, who supplied no cartoons for glass except to the firm. But backgrounds and foliage were, as a rule, of Morris's designing, the animals and certain kinds of ornament being often drawn by Webb.

Morris never made his own glass. He often regretted that he did not; but for organizing this manufacture, time and money alike were required beyond what he could spare.   There is little doubt that in the colouring of glass, as in that of yarns, his personal touch would have produced greater splendours of tone than could be got by other workers.   As it was, his faultless eye for colour had to content itself with doing its best out of the glass supplied by the ordinary manufacturers. If the colour of a Morris window is to the present day unmistakable among all rivals or imitations, this is not from any difference in material, but from the skill in selection and variation which was an instinct in Morris himself, and which to some considerable degree he transmitted to his workmen.

When the cartoons for a window had been drawn, Mr. Wardle notes in speaking of the practice of this period, Morris personally "coloured" the window; that is to say, he dictated in detail to Campfield, the foreman of the painters, what glass was to be used for each part. The various parts were then distributed to the painters, whose work he watched as it went on, though he usually reserved any comments till the painter had done all that he could.   Retouches were then made by his direction, and the glass was burned and leaded up.   When this was done, there came the final review of the window, a work of great difficulty in any case, and to any ordinary eye impossible in the cramped premises in Queen Square, where some of his largest windows were made.   But here his amazing eye and memory for colour enabled him to achieve the impossible: he could pass all the parts of a large window one by one before the light, and never lose sight of the general tone of the colour or of the relation of one part to another.   If any part did not satisfy him, new glass was cut and that piece of the window done again.

The painting of tiles, which had been one of the first occupations of the firm in Red Lion Square, had by this time almost ceased.   It had ceased wholly as regards

THE GLASS-PAINTING SHEDS, MERTON ABBEY, FROM THE DYE-HOUSE.

figure-painted tiles, of which a few sets of great beauty, some of them with verses by Morris also painted on them, had been made for a few years and not in great numbers. Pattern tiles, chiefly meant for use in fireplaces, went on being produced—as they still are—to a limited extent from the early designs. They were all hand-painted, even when the designs were very simple, the touch of the brush being essential towards giving that quality of pattern and surface that made them coherent with the larger decoration of which they formed a part. The manufacture of tiles on a larger scale and with properly constructed kilns had been taken up by De Morgan as a branch of pottery, and it was not necessary that Morris should continue to make his own. Since the premises in Queen Square were abandoned, the firing of both glass and tiles has been executed elsewhere, no kilns having been built at Merton. The premises which De Morgan took in order to establish potteries close to the Merton Abbey works did not prove suitable to their purpose, and the plan of joint, or even contiguous, factories never fully took effect: but he afterwards set up works in Chelsea from which tiles were supplied well suited to take their place among Morris decorations. It may be added that, while the firm never either designed or made pottery of any kind—the tiles used for painting on being got from outside, chiefly from Holland—they did something towards introducing in England the knowledge of some of the best varieties of foreign manufacture, especially the simple and beautiful Grès de Flandre ware, now so common in the shops of London furnishers, which made its first appearance in England, except as a curiosity, in Morris's show-room. Neither did the production of furniture play any important part in the firm's business. There were generally a few pieces, nearly all from Webb's designs, being made; but Morris never designed any himself: it was only when some piece, such as a chest or cupboard, was to be further adorned with gilding or painting, that it came into his hands. Of all the specific minor improvements in common household objects due to Morris, the rush-bottomed Sussex chair perhaps takes the first place. It was not his own invention, but was copied, with trifling improvements, from an old chair of village manufacture picked up in Sussex by Mr. Warrington Taylor. With or without modification it has been taken up by all the modern furniture manufacturers, and is in almost universal use. But the Morris pattern of the later type (there were two) still excels all others in simplicity and elegance of proportion.

The beginnings of the important industry of carpet-weaving have already been recounted. Looms had already been built at Hammersmith for weaving carpets of considerable size, as much as twelve feet across. The great loom at the Merton works is built for making a carpet of no less than twenty-five feet in breadth. The designing of these carpets was wholly, or almost wholly, done by Morris himself. His practice was first to make a drawing on the scale of about one-eighth of the full size, which he coloured very carefully with his own hand. A draughtsman enlarged this coloured drawing on the "point paper"— paper, that is, divided into minute spaces, each representing a single knot of the carpet. The pointing on this paper, a work of immense laboriousness, was done by Morris himself until he gradually trained other workmen to do it with the accurate judgment which makes all the difference between the right and wrong expression of the design. The same laborious work was undertaken by him in the designing of silk damasks, woven tapestries, and all the patterned woven stuffs produced on his looms.

Beyond the preliminary tasks of designing and pointing, the actual work at the loom performed by Morris remained for some years very great: and it became still greater when he set aside the carpet-loom for the tapestry-loom, upon which he revived the splendid and almost extinct art of the fifteenth and sixteenth centuries. In a diary of his daily occupations which he kept in the year of the removal to Merton, the entries of morning work at the tapestry-loom are continual. As early in the year as the 12th of March he puts down " up at 7.30, about four hours tapestry": a week later, "up at $6\frac{1}{2}$, four hours tapestry"; and as the mornings lengthened in April, "up at 6, two hours tapestry," " up at 5.30, three hours tapestry." All through the summer the entries go on: he was seldom up later than six o'clock for several months, and would be at the loom within ten minutes. One day, at the end of May, " wind W.S.W., very fine bright day, cool in evening " (for if Morris kept any diary at all, however scanty, the weather was always the first thing noted in it), the entry is " Up at 5 : $3\frac{1}{2}$ hours tapestry. To Grange. To Queen Square: The green for Peacock " (a woven hanging) " all wrong. Did day books and Friday " (the summing up of the week's business and signing cheques) " besides seeing to this : took away model of G. H. carpet from K. Meeting St. Mark's Committee. Dined A. Ionides." And this was hardly an exceptional day, so crowded was his life with occupation.

The carpet he was making for Mr. George Howard, for the drawing-room at Naworth Castle, which is mentioned in this extract, was by far the largest that he had then executed. It was nearly a year in hand, and the hours he spent in designing and pointing it make up the equivalent of a substantial day's work for a full month. The result of a piece of work of this size and intricacy remained an unknown quantity till the end. " Your carpet has been finished," he wrote to Mr. Howard on the 3rd of November, " for a week or two : I have been keeping it back to try for a fine day to spread it on our lawn, so that I might see it all at once : at present I have only been able to see it piecemeal. So seen, it looks very well, I think, and seems to be satisfactory as to manufacture. What are your orders about it ? as I shall have to send some one down to Naworth to get it into its place : it weighs about a ton I fancy."

The manufacture of Arras tapestry, on which Morris had been experimenting at Hammersmith throughout the year, was only fairly begun after the works were removed to Merton. The first piece made there was a frieze of greenery with birds, which, like the carpet of the previous year, went to Naworth. In reviving this noble art he had nothing in England to guide him, as to the mechanical part of the work, beyond drawings of looms in old books. To see what the mechanism was really like, he had to pay a visit to the Gobelins, where he found the ancient loom still in use, though sunk to the servile task of making copies of oil paintings. The low-warp loom, which had replaced it elsewhere, he at once dismissed as useless for his purpose. In it the task of the weaver is confined to copying the imperfectly seen cartoon stretched under the warp, at which he peers between the threads. The work is almost purely mechanical; the face of the tapestry being below, and the weaving done from the back, the workman has no means of knowing what effect he is producing, and can only trust to a rigid method. The making of tapestry on the high-warp loom approximates in method to the painting of a picture ; the artificer produces his form and colour, stitch by stitch, by the exercise of his own intelligence, and sees, in his little swinging mirror, the actual surface forming itself insensibly under his hand, as if it were a picture on the easel.

When months of daily practice had familiarized Morris

himself with the processes and difficulties of tapestry-
weaving, the next thing was to teach the art to other workmen. The work is of a kind which experience proves to
be best done by boys. It involves little muscular effort,
and is best carried on by small flexible fingers. "He
had another loom built at Queen Square," Mr. Wardle
tells me, "where he taught what he knew to William
Dearle, who was then a boy willing to adapt himself to
anything which gave him a chance of employment. Dearle
got on so well that very soon we took in two other boys,
Sleath and Knight, as his apprentices. When we moved
to Merton therefore we had already three 'hands' fairly
competent in this art. The first piece Dearle accomplished was the Goose-Girl, designed by Walter Crane;
this was begun, and finished, I think, at Queen Square."

"At Merton," Mr. Wardle adds, "the boys, who were
still young, lived in the house. We gave them board and
lodging and a certain weekly stipend. It is worth while
to note that there was no sort of selection of these boys,
or of any others who were brought up by us to one or
other branch of Mr. Morris's business. John Smith,
who is now the dyer at Merton, was taken into the dye-
shop because it was just being set up at the time he was
getting too old to remain errand boy. Dearle was put
to the tapestry because that business then wanted an ap-
prentice; and so of the other two. They were put to
the loom because at the time we were starting this we
were asked to do something for them. We took Sleath
on that ground first of all, and he introduced Knight. The
same rule applied to all others, and its working justified
Mr. Morris's contention that the universal modern
system, which he called that of Devil take the hind-
most, is frightfully wasteful of human intelligence. A
few years later, when we were able to set up a third tapestry-loom, we found a lad with equal facility, without

selection of any kind, the nephew of the housekeeper at Merton.   She happened to tell me, at the time we were getting the new loom ready, that her nephew had left school and was looking for something to do."

This system of setting the nearest person to do whatever kind of work wanted doing was really of the essence of Morris's method as a manufacturer from the beginning; and in his hands it produced surprisingly good results. How it would have worked, whether indeed it would have worked at all, with a man of less genius at the head of the work as a directing and propelling force, is of course a different question.   But, as Morris always insisted, it would have worked just as well, and with much greater certainty, if instead of the solitary man of genius at the head of the work, there had been a living inherited tradition throughout the workshop.   The skilled workman is not as a rule a workman who possesses any remarkable innate skill of hand.   He is one rather whose general intelligence has protected him against that excessive division of labour which cramps and sterilizes the modern artificer.   If a rational latitude were given to manual work of the individual under proper guidance, it might well be that the average skill of hand and eye, stimulated and not repressed by its daily labour, would of its own self rise to a level which at present is only reached in isolated instances.   On this point the evidence given by Morris himself in March, 1882, before the Royal Commission on Technical Instruction, indicates his view with great clearness and precision.   "I often have great difficulty," he said, "in dealing with the workmen I employ in London, because of their *general ignorance.*"   This general ignorance was just what had to be met by general education, not by specific technical instruction.   But drawing, as at the basis of all manual arts whatever, he held to be an essential element in general education which should be worthy of the name. " I think undoubtedly everybody ought to be taught to draw just as much as everybody ought to be taught to read and write."

The principle thus laid down was accepted by the Government eight years later, when by the Code of 1890 drawing was made a compulsory subject in elementary schools for boys. The step thus taken was even then somewhat in advance of public opinion. That children should all be taught to read and write has now so long been the law that it is accepted somewhat as a matter of course, and protests against it are few and faint. But the doctrine that drawing is just as essential a part of any real education is still regarded in many quarters as a foolish, or at best an interesting paradox ; and such instruction in drawing as can be given, in an hour and a half during each week, to children who are allowed to leave school at the age of eleven, is still accepted as the measure of the State's duty.

The divorce between the theory and practice of all the manual arts was a matter against which Morris was always emphatic in his protest. He co-operated loyally in the work done in the teaching of design by the Schools of Art directed from South Kensington. Since 1876, when he first acted as an Examiner to the Art Department, he served year after year until the last year of his life. The work was not interesting to him ; it is arduous while it lasts, and the looking over large masses of thoroughly mediocre work was a severe trial to his patience. But he stuck to it for the sake of the good that might ultimately come of it ; and in the latter years of his life he had the satisfaction of seeing, in London and elsewhere, noticeably at Birmingham, a real school of manual art slowly form itself whose work was directly aimed at practice.

One secret of the excellence of Morris's own designs was that he never designed anything which he did not know how to produce with his own hands. He had mastered the practical arts of dyeing and weaving before he began to produce designs for dyed and woven stuffs to be made in his workshops. "It is a thing to be deprecated," he says in his evidence before the Royal Commission, "that there should be a class of mere artists who furnish designs ready-made to what you may call the technical designers. I think it is desirable that the artist and what is technically called the designer should practically be one." But this is not all. "A designer ought to be able to weave himself. A man employs a designer to draw his patterns. One of two things happens: either the designer has learnt the method of execution in a totally perfunctory manner, and takes no interest in it, but goes only by a certain set of rules, and is therefore cramped and made dull and stupid by going by them: or on the other hand if, as sometimes happens, the manufacturer goes to a more dignified kind of artist, who, knowing nothing of the way in which the thing has to be done, produces a kind of puzzle for the manufacturer, the manufacturer having paid for it takes it away and does what he can with it, chops the design up and adapts it to his purpose as well as he can ; the design is spoilt, and when executed looks not better but worse than the ordinary cut and dried trade design."

"Of late years," he stated in the same evidence, "there has arisen in London a great number of half professional designers, people who would be glad to get work in designing. These people are generally very uneducated in the technique of the arts they design for, which is a great drawback."

Between the workman who had no understanding of design and the designer who had no understanding of execution, the case of the manual arts was hopeless indeed. In both cases alike the root of the evil was sheer ignorance; and this ignorance was directly due to want, in one case as much as the other, of proper education; as that again was due to the false division of labour—the disintegration of labour, as it should more properly be called—which forbade artist and workman alike to know what they were at.

Thus stated the case seems simple enough. But the simplest truths are often the last to be applied to practice. The doctrines laid down by Morris before the Commission were then startling and almost revolutionary; even now but little progress has been made in carrying them out, though their abstract truth is generally admitted. There is a school of designers now, for the most part formed under the influence of Morris's teaching, who design with direct knowledge of the manufacturing processes. But the encouragement given by the State to the art of designing still takes the form of prizes for designs in the air. "Not enough attention is given," Morris said in his evidence, "to the turning out of the actual goods themselves. We cannot give prizes for the things turned out, we can only give prizes for the designs. I think it would be a very good thing to give prizes for the goods themselves." The dislocation between the two sides of the craftsman's education is still so great that this step is thought impossible.

This had been his own experience when he first tried to have carpets made from his own designs by the ordinary manufacturers. He began with the simplest kind, the so-called Kidderminster, a carpet of not more than three colours, in which the pattern is produced by the intersection at fixed points of webs interlaced by the passage of the shuttle through a double or triple-tiered warp. In the trial piece of carpet sent, the design was almost unrecognizable. A suspicion at first crossed his mind that he was being played with: and that the manufacturer, who had frankly said on seeing the design that it was too simple and would not do, had determined to justify his opinion by spoiling it in the manufacture. But this was not the case; he had acted in perfect good faith, and when Morris said to him, "But this is not my pattern," could only answer, "This is how your pattern comes out." Finally an interview was arranged with his "designer," the man who set out the pattern on point paper for the weavers. The root of all the trouble was then found out in five minutes: it was merely this, that the designer could not draw. The pattern was redrawn on point paper in Morris's own workshop, and the carpet (which has become an established pattern and is still the most successful of all the woven carpets produced from Morris's designs) was satisfactorily produced forthwith.

Of Morris's personal share in the firm's work in general decoration and the application of the materials produced by him to their specific purpose, some idea may be formed from fragments of his correspondence about this time with Mr. and Mrs. George Howard. Their house in Palace Green had been recently built by Webb, and was being decorated throughout by Morris. The decoration of the dining-room was unusually careful and elaborate, as it was designed as a setting for a series of paintings on panel by Burne-Jones of the story of Cupid and Psyche.

To Mrs. Howard he writes on the 13th of December, 1879:

"Ned Jones and I went to look at the effect of the gold paper against the picture, and found to our grief that it would not do: yesterday I went there to meet him that we might try something else, but the morning was so bad that he could not come out: this morning I find that you suggest leaving the matter till you come up to town: but meanwhile, I, knowing that it would be impossible to get the work done unless we began at once, have set Leach's men at work to forward the job, so that the drawing-room will be finished next week in the way you wished; and the boudoir has been prepared for final painting and hanging, which would now take less than a week to do at any time: Ned and I are going to look at the room again on Sunday, so that I shall be able to report again on Monday, so that if you agreed to our suggestions there would still be time to finish the room before you get back. I hope I have not done wrong in setting Leach to work: if I have, I must plead the usual excuse of fools, that I have acted for the best.

"Dining-room.—I am bound to ask your pardon for having neglected this job; but I did not quite understand what was to be done except the writing (which by the way is a very difficult business): I am now going to set to work to design ornaments for the mouldings round the pictures, the curved braces of ceiling, and the upper part of the panelling. I fear there is little chance of getting any of this done before your return (I mean executed on the wood-work) but I will do my best to get everything in train to start it on the first opportunity: meantime I have thought it best to tell Leach's man to varnish only the lower part of the panelling, doors, shutters, etc., where the ornament will not come."

And again two days later:

" Ned and I duly went to Palace Green yesterday and our joint conclusion was that the best hanging for the walls of the boudoir would be the inclosed madder-printed cotton: it brings out the greys of the picture better than anything else: also I think it would make a pretty room with the wood-work painted a light blue-green colour like a starling's egg; and if you wanted drapery about it, we have beautiful stuffs of shades of red that would brighten all up without fighting with the wall-hangings : if you could like this and would let me know some day this week, I could get all finished against you come home, but if you still have doubts we would leave the room in a forward state for finishing. To complete the business part of my letter I may as well give you the price of the red stuff: two shillings per yard, yard-wide, which would come to less than the gold sunflower would have done."

The decoration of the house was only completed very gradually. Nearly two years later there is another series of letters to Mrs. Howard :

" Thank you for asking me personally about the patterns: I have been to Oxford Street to-day and told Smith to send off all our patterns that would be of any use to you; I have told him to write ' recommended ' and ' specially recommended ' on certain of them. As to the papers (sunflower and acorn), I will do what I can to soften the colour.

" May I ask what you are going to do about the drawing-room at Palace Green ? Ned tells me that you are going to keep the *Dies Domini* there, and want to hang the room accordingly: we don't like to do anything there till the ceiling is made safe: what do you think of hanging a piece of stuff behind it ? I could get the colour better suited to it so, I believe.   .

" Ned has been doing a great deal to the dining-room pictures and very much improving them : so that the room will be light and pleasant after all, and the pictures very beautiful.

" As to the red dove and rose, for a curtain, it will last as long as need be, since the cloth is really very strong : I can't answer so decidedly as to the colour; but the colours in it when looked at by themselves you will find rather full than not, 'tis the mixture that makes them look delicate : therefore I believe the stuff to be quite safe to use if you fancy it : of course I don't mean to say that any flat-woven stuff can stand sunlight as well as a piled material, and the velvet also is darker, though not so well dyed as the other stuff.

" As to the other version of the dove and rose, if 'tis a smaller sized pattern in green and yellow, you can use it without hesitation ; but if it be of the same size as the red, I should scarcely advise it, if the settees are to have heavy wear : you see we made this stuff for curtains and hangings : I have tried a piece of the purple, turquoise, and yellow as a cushion on a chair of my own on which everybody sits : it has worn better than I expected, but still not like stuff made for it would do.   As to the red silk for curtains, what I am doing (for St. James's) is a very fine colour ; but also you must not forget that I can do pretty well any colour you want, and of sober reds the resources are great.   Item, I can do the most ravishing yellows, rather what people call amber : what would you say to dullish pink shot with amber ; like some of those chrysanthemums we see just now ?   I am going to try that after Christmas.

" The gold and red sunflower is on my board at Queen Square and I will do my best to hit the due colour."

Two letters written about the same time to Mr. Howard, about defects in some painted glass previously executed by Morris for Naworth, are interesting alike as showing the difficulties of working in untested material, and the pride he took in the excellence of his own work.

" 'Tis all too true about the Naworth windows : we (and I believe all other glass-painters) were beguiled by an untrustworthy colour, having borax in it, some years ago ; and the windows painted with this are going all over the country.   Of course we have taken warning, and our work will now be all right.   We have given instructions to our man to take out the faulty glass, which we will—restore !—at once, and pay for that same ourselves—worse luck ! "

" Borax is the name of the culprit : the colour-makers, finding that the glass-painters wanted a colour that would burn well at a lowish temperature, mixed borax with it, to that end ; but unluckily glass of borax is soluble in water, and hence the tears wept by our windows—and our purses.   We use harder colour now, so that if any window of ours goes now it must be from other causes ; bad burning or the like ; I don't think as things go that this is like to happen to us.

" I am very glad indeed that you think the east window a success ; I was very nervous about it, as the cartoons were so good that I should have been quite upset if I had not done them something like justice."

But perhaps the most important new development that the business took after it was moved to Merton Abbey was the production of printed cotton goods, the celebrated " Morris chintzes," which soon became more widely known and more largely used than his woven stuffs or wall-papers.   Their success was so great that deliberate or unconscious imitations of them soon began to be produced by the manufacturers and find a ready market. Their adaptability to many small purposes gave them an advantage over the paper-hangings and tapestries.   To hang a room with good hand-printed paper is a matter of serious expense to many people who would like to do it, but who do not very acutely realize the difference between it and a machine-printed paper that can be produced for one-sixth and bought for one-third of the price. But a mere scrap of these bright and beautifully patterned chintzes can be used to light up a room, as a curtain, or the cover of a chair or a cushion, or in twenty other

THE CHINTZ-PRINTING ROOM, MERTON ABBEY.

ways ; and perhaps the primary use for which these fabrics were meant, that of wall-hangings, is the one to which they have been most seldom applied. Paper-hangings are so much taken for granted as the covering of the walls of rich and poor houses alike, that people rarely pause to consider their many disadvantages. The simpler patterns of his chintzes Morris was able to produce at a price little higher than that of moderately costly wall-papers ; their decorative effect in a room is perhaps ten-fold that of the papers ; and yet his appeal to use them for the purpose for which they were meant fell on the public in vain. People dressed themselves in his wall-hangings, covered books with them, did this or that with them according to their fancy ; but hang walls with them they would not.

Between seventy and eighty designs in wall-papers, and nearly forty in chintzes, were invented by Morris and carried out under his eye in the course of his busi-ness life. These numbers do not take account of the variant designs where a different scheme of colours is applied to the same pattern. If these be counted sepa-rately, the total number of designs from his own hand amounts to four hundred. In all of them the drawing and the choice of colours were alike his own individual work. The cutting of the blocks was done by workmen ; but the cutter's tracing was always submitted to Morris for retouching before it was rubbed off on the wood ; and he kept till late years a vigilant eye both on his own dye-vats and on the colour-pots of the paper-makers. It may give some idea of the prodigious mass of his work as a designer to add that the sum total of his designs for paper-hangings, chintzes, woven stuffs, silk damasks, stamped velvets, carpets, and tapestries (excluding the hand-made carpets and the Arras tapestries, which were each specially designed, and as a rule not duplicated) which were actually carried out, amounts to little short of six hundred, besides countless designs for embroidery.

"Of the work at Merton," Mr. Wardle says, looking back on it perhaps through something of that enchantment that is lent by distance, "there seems nothing to say except that it was altogether delightful." It went on in the ordered tranquillity of spacious and even beautiful surroundings. There were pure water, light, and air in abundance; and the change from the cramped quarters and grimy atmosphere of Bloomsbury reacted on the master's own temper. "It is noticeable," says Mr. Wardle, "in remembering his nervous temperament, that at Merton, though he disliked the journey by rail intensely, he showed no irritation on arriving. There remained a certain impetus in his manner, as if he would still go at twenty miles an hour and rather expected everything to keep pace with him." It was not in his workshops alone that he seemed to expect this, nor was it in his workshops that the expectation was oftenest disappointed.

But indeed even to the present day, as one turns out of the dusty high road and passes through the manager's little house, the world seems left in a moment behind. The old-fashioned garden is gay with irises and daffodils in spring, with hollyhocks and sunflowers in autumn, and full, summer by summer, of the fragrant flowering shrubs that make a London suburb into a brief June Paradise. It rambles away towards the mill pond with its fringe of tall poplars; the cottons lie bleaching on grass thickly set with buttercups; the low long buildings with the clear rushing little stream running between them, and the wooden outside staircases leading to their upper story, have nothing about them to suggest the modern factory; even upon the great sunk dye-vats the sun flickers through leaves, and trout leap outside the

windows of the long cheerful room where the carpet-
looms are built. "To Merton Abbey," runs an entry
in a visitor's diary on a day at the end of April, 1882,
when the new works had settled fairly down to their
routine : "white hawthorn was out in the garden : we
had tea with Mr. Morris in his room in the house, and
left laden with marsh-marigolds, wallflowers, lilac, and
hawthorn." Of these flowers, and of others in their
seasons, Morris often used to bring back bunches to
London with him, and wonder why any one should be
laughed at—as in London one then still was—for carrying flowers.

Nor did it prove to be the case that these humanized
conditions, these pleasant surroundings of the work
carried on at Merton Abbey, were in any way fatal to
the success of the business as a matter of ordinary commerce. It was not from any disastrous experience of
his own that Morris was led to despair of the existing
order of things. In the most striking passage of his
evidence before the Technical Instruction Commission
he speaks of the prospects of art in a spirit of confidence
and even of cheerfulness. "On the whole," he said, in
words which must have been at the time quite sincere—
for irony was a figure which he never used—"one must
suppose that beauty is a marketable quality, and that the
better the work is all round both as a work of art and
in its technique, the more likely it is to find favour with
the public." And the use of technical education was not,
to his mind, to train a select caste of skilled designers and
workers, but one more broadly and indeed quite univers-
ally applicable: "that the public should know something
about it, so that you may get a market for excellence."

This market for excellence he conquered himself,
partly by the mere force of his genius, and partly by
real business ability. He approached matters of busi-

ness in so peculiar a spirit, that the question whether he was really a good business man or not was often debated, and is still debateable. Some of the qualities which go to make up that character he undoubtedly possessed in a high measure : above all perhaps, a certain indefinable driving power—a quality as rare as it is valuable—which was quite distinct from his own energy or industry, and which hardly ever failed to affect those with whom he came into personal contact. In his immediate sub-ordinates—Mr. George Wardle first, and the Messrs. Smith afterwards—he was fortunate in finding men who caught this energy from him and yet retained with it a full measure of shrewdness and caution. But such good fortune, according to the Greek proverb so often quoted by Aristotle, is in itself nearly akin to skill ; and the choice of a good manager is in effect good management.

But for the ordinary processes of competitive com-merce, and this as much before as after he adopted any distinctively Socialistic views, his qualities, whether intel-lectual or emotional, were not such as are calculated to lead to conspicuous success. The truth is that commercial success is an art which must be seriously pursued, and which he, quite apart from any question of morality, was at once too imaginative, too soft-hearted, and too much engrossed by wholly different interests, to pursue seriously. He carried on his business as a manufacturer not because he wished to make money, but because he wished to make the things he manufactured. The art of commerce as it consists in buying material and labour cheaply, and forcing the largest possible sale of the product, was one for which he had little aptitude and less liking. In every manual art which he touched, he was a skilled expert: in the art of money-making he remained to the last an amateur. Throughout he regarded material with the eye of the artist, and labour with the eye of a fellow-labourer. He

never grudged or haggled over the price of anything
which he thought really excellent of its kind and really
desirable for him to have; he would dye with kermes
instead of cochineal if he could gain an almost imper-
ceptible richness of tone by doing so; he would condemn
piece after piece of his manufacture that did not satisfy
his own severe judgment. And in his relations to his
workmen he had adopted the principle of the living wage,
and even of profit-sharing, before he began to study such
questions from a larger point of view. He could hardly
ever be induced to discharge a workman even for habitual
negligence or, in some cases which could be quoted, for
actual dishonesty. Of the feelings of his social inferiors
—or indeed of his social equals—he was sometimes
strangely inconsiderate; but towards their weaknesses
he was habitually indulgent.

So far did he carry this interest in producing the best
work regardless of expense and this careless confidence
in the honesty of his workmen, that without some other
responsible business manager Merton Abbey would have
wrecked the fortunes of the firm. It was encumbered
with old or incompetent workmen paid by time, while
the more skilled hands were put on piece-work; and
similarly in the office the inferior clerks had fixed salaries
for so many hours' work a day and no more, while the
upper clerks were to a certain extent profit-sharers in the
proceeds of the business. This system of profit-sharing
was, even during the later years at Queen Square, in process of extension among the higher grades of the workmen. The result of this mingled generosity and slackness
was that in the staple product of printed cottons the
Staffordshire manufacturers, with their keen eye to profit
and machine-like organization, could supply goods, pur-
porting at least to be the same in quality, forty per cent.
cheaper than they were turned out at Merton: and till

the works were put under more stringent management, the profits of Oxford Street were almost wholly absorbed by the experiments and the leakage of Merton.

In Morris's lectures on Art, and more especially on those lesser arts of life which, though his eye always remained fixed on the greater arts in their culminating glories of architecture and poetry, he had chosen for his own daily province in practice, the outcome of those instincts which had made him a manufacturer, and of that experience which his work as a manufacturer had given him, is visible in many passages of humour or wisdom. In the lecture entitled "Making the Best of it," it is himself whom he describes with complete accuracy in his description of "a handicraftsman who shall put his own individual intelligence and enthusiasm into the goods he fashions. So far from his labour being 'divided,' which is the technical phrase for his always doing one minute piece of work and never being allowed to think of any other, so far from that, he must know all about the ware he is making and its relation to similar wares; he must have a natural aptitude for his work so strong, that no education can force him away from his special bent. He must be allowed to think of what he is doing, and to vary his work as the circumstances of it vary, and his own moods. He must be for ever stirring to make the piece he is at work at better than the last. He must refuse at anybody's bidding to turn out, I won't say a bad, but even an indifferent piece of work, whatever the public want, or think they want. He must have a voice, and a voice worth listening to, in the whole affair."

Such is the ideal handicraftsman whom he thus drew from his own likeness. For what lay at the root of his belief was that this life, the life which he had himself deliberately chosen, should be, and might be, accessible to all. He recognized no essential difference between an

artist and a workman. Until a state of society were
realized in which (according to his version of the Platonic
paradox) artists should be workmen, and workmen artists,
no really sound, and living, and permanent art could exist.
And the hire of the workman in any really civilized community should be precisely, neither more nor less, what he
claimed as his own due, and what he was satisfied with as
his own recompense: " Money enough to keep him from
fear of want or degradation for him and his; leisure
enough from bread-earning work (even though it be pleasant
to him) to give him time to read and think, and connect
his own life with the life of the great world; work enough
of the kind aforesaid, and praise of it, and encouragement
enough to make him feel good friends with his fellows;
and lastly (not least, for 'tis verily part of the bargain)
his own due share of art, the chief part of which will be
a dwelling that does not lack the beauty which Nature
would freely allow it, if our own perversity did not turn
Nature out of doors."

In this last clause of his definition of the ideal life, not
for isolated individuals, nor for a cultured class, but for
universal mankind, he returns to his perpetual insistence
on the value of architecture, in its widest sense, as the beginning and end of all the arts of life. To him, the man
lived in the house almost as the soul lives in the body.
The degradation of architecture and of its subservient arts
of decoration was at once the cause and the effect of the
whole degradation of human life.

But how to begin? His own work as a decorator led
him to see that in the furnishing of the house, such as it
was, a practical beginning, however slight, might be made
by every one. Hence he was led to the formulation of
his celebrated rule—a rule that, as he said without boast-
ing, will fit everybody; " Have nothing in your houses
that you do not know to be useful, or believe to be

beautiful." There is no more brilliant example of a rule that is at once completely universal in its scope, and completely certain in its application.

"To my mind," he says in another lecture, "it is only here and there (out of the kitchen) that you can find in a well-to-do house things that are of any use at all." By this accumulation of useless things not only are beautiful things kept out, but the very sense of beauty is perpetually dulled and ground away. If this pressure were once removed—so at least he thought, and it can hardly be considered an utopian belief—the natural sense of beauty would slowly begin to recover itself, and at last the house that had in it nothing but what was known to be useful would come to have in it nothing but what was really beautiful ; the mistaken or bewildered belief in the beauty of ugly things would disappear, and with the dwindling demand for them they would gradually cease to be produced, and fade away bit by bit out of the world.

Closely connected with this doctrine was his second cardinal axiom : "No work which cannot be done with pleasure in the doing is worth doing." That "natural aptitude for his work so strong that no education can force him away from his special bent" was a quality in him which he could not believe to be unique or even peculiar. "I tried to think what would happen to me," he says in another lecture, that entitled "The Prospects of Architecture in Civilization," "if I were forbidden my ordinary daily work ; and I knew that I should die of despair and weariness. It was clear to me that I worked not in the least in the world for the sake of earning leisure by it, but partly driven by the fear of starvation or disgrace, and partly, and even a very great deal, because I love the work itself." As he accounted labour without pleasure inhuman, so he claimed as the labourer's right an amount of spontaneity in his work that was far

removed from the actual conditions of common labour.
What he could least bear, he used to say, if he were a
workman, was the uninterrupted work required of them
during working hours, and he was sorry for men who had
to do it. While he was working himself it was always
noticeable how he would break off every now and then to
get up and look out of the window, or walk up and down
the room, and yet his actual output would be faster and
more continuous than that of any workman who never
stirred from his bench or took his hand off his machine.
His horror of pleasureless labour made him keenly sympathetic with the working man even in his least lovely
phases. " If I were to work ten hours a day at work I
despised and hated, I should spend my leisure, I hope in
political agitation, but I fear in drinking." Even of the
ideal workman described above, the workman who is an
artist, he confesses that " the capitalist will be apt to call
him a troublesome fellow; and in fact he will be troublesome, mere grit and friction in the wheels of the money-
making machine, yes, will stop the machine perhaps."
And so for the workman who was troublesome without
being an artist, who was grit in the wheels from no high
discontent or haunting ideal, but only from the incompet-
ence and vice he had inherited from a degraded ancestry
and developed in an inhuman environment, he made the
largest allowances and had almost inexhaustible patience.

Thus it was that, before and after the adoption of his
final political creed, Morris carried on his work patiently
from day to day, and thus it was that he exhorted others
by word and example to carry on theirs; " not living
like fools and fine gentlemen, and not beaten by the
muddle, but like good fellows trying by some dim candle-
light to set our workshop ready against to-morrow's daylight." Blessed is that servant, whom his lord when he
cometh shall find so doing.

CHAPTER XIV

OF the year between the establishment of the works at
Merton Abbey and the return of Morris to active political life as a member of the Socialist party at the beginning of 1883, it so happens that there are unusually few
records. Perhaps their scarcity is not altogether accidental. He was working out new theories of life; he was
doing this very much alone; and he had less leisure than
usual, and perhaps less inclination than leisure, for correspondence, or for holiday-making, or for anything beyond
work and thought. "I feel a lonely kind of a chap," he
says of himself, half humorously and half self-pityingly.
Early in the year he had gone down with his elder
daughter to the little house at Rottingdean which Burne-
Jones had bought the year before. From there he wrote
to Mrs. Burne-Jones on the 10th of January:

"Here we are: having just come back from an expedition to Brighton: we spent an hour or more in the
aquarium (where our presence caused astonishment, YE
Old English Fair not having begun till the afternoon, nor
the other damnations which are strung on the much neglected fish). I think I saw more ugly people in Brighton
in the course of an hour than I have seen otherwise for the
last twenty years: as you justly remark, serves me right
for going into Brighton: but you see we went there to
do a little shopping. Yesterday was a lovely day, and

we took a trap and drove to Lewes: you have to go a long way round, as the wheel-roads across the downs are doubtful it seems: it is very beautiful when you get on to the brow of the hill above Falmer: a long way off to the right you can see Lewes lying like a box of toys under a great amphitheatre of chalk hills: the whole ride is very pleasant: Lewes when you get there lies on a ridge in its valley, the street winding down to the river (Ouse) which runs into the sea at Newhaven: on the whole it is set down better than any town I have seen in England: unluckily it is not a very interesting town in itself: there is a horrible workhouse or prison on the outskirts, and close by a hideous row of builders' houses: there are three old Churches in it, dismally restored, but none of them ever over-remarkable: there is the remain of a castle, 14th century: but it is not grand at all.   Never the less it isn't a bad country town, only not up to its position.

" The house is very pleasant and agreeable and suits me to a T; and I am in very good order, and quite satisfied, bating a little unavoidable anxiety, though J. has been hitherto quite well and seemingly very happy. I am hard at work on my Birmingham lecture: I don't feel as if I had much left to say, but must do all I can to say it decently, so as not to discredit the cause."

To write a new lecture was still immense labour and pain to him: " I know what I want to say, but the cursed words go to water between my fingers"; and the discouragement in which he writes to Mrs. Burne-Jones again on his return to London a week later is partly no doubt the effect of this struggle over the lecture on " Some of the Minor Arts of Life," which he was now preparing.   It was delivered at the Midland Institute, Birmingham, on the 23rd of January, and was afterwards printed, under the title of " The Lesser Arts of Life," in the volume of lectures on Art published that year in aid of the funds of the Society for Protection of Ancient Buildings. In both letters it will be noticed that the "cause" still means to him primarily and specifically that of art, though the name of art has taken to him a new and a more profound meaning.

"I am just going to finish my day with a couple of hours' work on my lecture, but will first write you a line, since pen, ink, and paper are at hand, and seeing withal that to-morrow I shall not have any time at all to myself.

"May came to hand safely this morning, thank you kindly for having her. As to Jenny, she has been to my joy very well and in bright spirits all the week, so I have no doubt our sojourn there did her good : it was her birthday on Tuesday: 21 my dear old Jenny was.

"I have perhaps rather more than enough of work to do, and for that reason or what not, am dwelling some-what low down in the valley of humiliation—quite good enough for me doubtless. Yet it sometimes seems to me as if my lot was a strange one : you see, I work pretty hard, and on the whole very cheerfully, not altogether I hope for mere pudding, still less for praise ; and while I work I have the cause always in mind, and yet I know that the cause for which I specially work is doomed to fail, at least in seeming ; I mean that art must go under, where or how ever it may come up again. I don't know if I explain what I'm driving at, but it does sometimes seem to me a strange thing indeed that a man should be driven to work with energy and even with pleasure and enthusiasm at work which he knows will serve no end but amusing himself; am I doing nothing but make-believe then, something like Louis XVI.'s lock-making ? There, I don't pretend to say that the conundrum is a very interesting one, as it certainly has not any practical importance as far as I am concerned, since I shall without doubt go on with my work, useful or useless, till I demit.

" Well, one thing I long for which will certainly come, the sunshine and the spring.   Meantime we are hard at work gardening here: making dry paths, and a sublimely tidy box edging : how I do love tidyness!"

A letter to Mr. George Howard of about the same date shows that he had not yet wholly dissociated himself from the Liberal party, nor given up the hopes which had excited him after the General Election of 1880.   He had then looked eagerly to the formation of an independent Radical wing which might force the Whigs to move forward on penalty of being thrown out of office.   The amalgamation of Whigs and Tories as a powerful constitutional or Unionist party, to prevent such a result, had not yet occurred to him as the natural outlet from this position ; though soon afterwards, and long before the thing actually happened, he foresaw it with much clearness.

" Rottingdean,
" Jan. 10th, 1882.

" My dear George,
      " You see I am away for a few days, which accounts for my not answering your letter at once : we had a letter from the parson's wife of Brampton asking for patterns for that same : I bid them send a big worsted pattern which I thought would be best, as 'tis mostly blue, which I fancy the Church wants: only you must think that under that very bright window all woven stuffs will look grey.   If the blue looks too grey, I fear there is nothing for it but the brightest red : we have a woollen stuff very bright and telling (3-ply pomegranate), or would red damask silk be too costly?

"I suppose your election is the North Riding: I haven't seen a paper for four days, so don't know how it's going; so can only wish you good speed: I make, with all apologies for my impudence, the unpolitical remark, that I hope you have got a good candidate: 'tis better to be beaten with a good one than be successful with a bad one. I guess there will be a fine procession of rats before this parliament is over: that will teach us, I hope, not to run the worst man possible on all occasions. Excuse the spleen of a kind of Radical cobbler.
"With best wishes from
"Yours affectionately,
"WILLIAM MORRIS."

Two months later he writes again to Mr. Howard in a much less philosophic vein. A sudden risk had arisen that the works at Merton Abbey might be ruined by the cutting off of the water-supply of the Wandle.

"Merton Abbey,
"March 16th, 1882.

"My dear George,
"I am in a fix—for look here; I took this place muchly for the sake of its water-power, and for the water of the Wandle; and now the Wandle is going to be dried up—no less—there is a bill before a committee on Monday, as I hear suddenly, to enable the London and South Western Water Company to tap the head springs of the river at Carshalton: the river is almost wholly fed from these springs, and tapping them thus would reduce it to a muddy ditch. As to myself I don't much care, as I always said we ought to have gone into the country, but on public grounds I could burst when I think of it: the Wandle from here upwards is a most beautiful stream

as perhaps you know.　I shall try to see you on Saturday morning; but meantime can you do anything in the House to help to stop such a damned iniquity?

　　　　　　　" Yours affectionately,
　　　　　　　　　" WILLIAM MORRIS."

He unburdens himself on the same subject in the letter to Ellis which follows.　The first part of it relates to alterations in the channel of the upper Thames recently made by the Conservancy, which had the effect of draining off the Kelmscott backwater and making the boat-house there useless.　Ellis had just brought up some perch from Kelmscott to stock the water at Merton Abbey.

　　　　　　　" Kelmscott House,
　　　　　　　　　" March 22nd, 1882.

" My dear Ellis,

　　" Thank you for your note : I imagine I understand what they are going to do, although your explanation would have been helped by a plan : I had heard something of this before, but hoped it would not take place in our time.　However something they will leave behind them so long as the old house stands; only strange it is that we are tumbled just into the time when these things go quickest : after us in a while I think things will mend; before us change was slower.　Meanwhile I ought to have thanked you for your perch before, especially as I know what a trouble it is to bring such wet goods up to town : only, news for news, nay, water news for water news, I have suddenly discovered that it may not be long that they will have water to swim in; whereas a society, calling itself the London and South Western Spring Water Company, has a bill in Parliament to enable them to sink a well at Carshalton which will drain the Carshalton Wandle, and give us a muddy ditch instead of my water

and water-power: jolly isn't it? there are 7 miles of
Wandle and 40 mills on that 7 miles, and here we are to
be landed without compensation just to put some money
into promoters' pockets, unless we can manage to get
the bill thrown out in Committee. You see that 'tis
jobbery (not mastery) that mows the meadow: what
compensation we should have got, if this had been public
money that was in question! However there is a strong
opposition to the thieves, so perhaps my perch may die
a natural death (by hook to wit) after all. I was up
the water to-day to see about this matter, and at Carshalton for the first time; a pretty place still in spite of
the building.

> "Yours ever truly,
> "WILLIAM MORRIS."

The opposition to the Bill, in which Morris had, of
course, the hearty support of the other thirty-nine mill-
owners immediately concerned in the Wandle as a source
of water-power, was successful. "The water company,"
he writes at the end of March, "terrified by our bold
front, has climbed down and has agreed not to meddle
with the Wandle: so this time I am quit for the fright,
and whatsoever part of £50 the lawyers' conscience will
let them grab of me. Cheap at the price both for me
and the public I think, since I have seen more of the
river. On Wednesday Wardle and I went up the river
and saw as much as we could get at: a wild day of
storm and bitter wind it turned out, yet I think we enjoyed it. As we got to Wallington I thought I would
go and call on Arthur Hughes, and did so to my pleasure:
we were very glad to see each other, though perhaps
when we got to talking were somewhat gravelled: he
lives in a beautiful place, and the Croydon branch of the
Wandle sweeps round his bit of close.

" I went up the water again on Friday with G. Howard and R. Grosvenor and had a pleasant half rainy day, seeing a great deal of the water, much of it quite quiet and unspoiled; it is really very beautiful, crystal clear in spite of all the mills.   When you come on the ponds at Carshalton, where it rises or seems to rise, the surprise is most delightful and strange : a village green, only the green is the pond, quite bright and clear, the road across the fall of it from one level to another, and springs bubbling up amidst it all over.   The whole river swarms with trout."

This peril over, work at Merton went on pleasantly and successfully.   " I have just twice as much to do since we began at Merton," he writes in June.   "At the same time I think it likely enough that my carpet business may fail commercially.   I shan't like that ; but as to giving up the whole affair because of it, if I say so it is mere ill-temper on my part, always supposing we can struggle on somehow."   But his daughter's severe and repeated illnesses during the summer and autumn upset the whole year for him.   It is not putting the case too strongly to say that for the time they thoroughly shattered his nerve, though the private correspondence in which this appears is neither meant nor suited for a wider public.

This household anxiety coloured all the world to him : and even Kelmscott that year could not charm away his melancholy.   The sense of change seemed brooding everywhere, and a dim shadow of unhappiness clung about the " sweet-looking clean waterside."   He felt it even at Godstow, " less changed than any beautiful place I know, the very fields that stretch up to Wytham much the same as they always were with their wealth of poplar and willow trees, the most beautiful meadows to be seen anywhere."   " So it will be," he goes on, "till civilized life is quite changed, every alteration in the material world will be for the worse."

The same desperate concentration of mind, the feeling of one thing, and one thing alone, being needful, reappears in another letter which is one of the extremely rare instances of his criticism of a contemporary writer. It was written soon after the publication of Mr. Swinburne's " Tristram of Lyonnesse."

" As to the poem, I have made two or three attempts to read it, but have failed, not being in the mood I suppose : nothing would lay hold of me at all. This is doubtless my own fault, since it certainly did seem very fine. But, to confess and be hanged, you know I never could really sympathize with Swinburne's work; it always seemed to me to be founded on literature, not on nature. In saying this I really cannot accuse myself of any jealousy on the subject, as I think also you will not. Now I believe that Swinburne's sympathy with literature is most genuine and complete ; and it is a pleasure to hear him talk about it, which he does in the best vein possible ; he is most steadily enthusiastic about it. Now time was when the poetry resulting merely from this intense study and love of literature might have been, if not the best, yet at any rate very worthy and enduring : but in these days when all the arts, even poetry, are like to be overwhelmed under the mass of material riches which civilization has made and is making more and more hastily every day ; riches which the world has made indeed, but cannot use to any good purpose : in these days the issue between art, that is, the godlike part of man, and mere bestiality, is so momentous, and the surroundings of life are so stern and unplayful, that nothing can take serious hold of people, or should do so, but that which is rooted deepest in reality and is quite at first hand : there is no room for anything which is not forced out of a man of deep feeling, because of its innate strength and vision.

"In all this I may be quite wrong and the lack may be in myself : I only state my opinion, I don't defend it ; still less do I my own poetry."

He was thinking in these last words, no doubt, of his own unwritten poem on the same subject, the story of Tristram and Iseult: the one which his " soul yearned to do " twelve years before, when he had just completed " The Earthly Paradise," and which was the episode of the whole Arthurian cycle that held his imagination most strongly.

On the 23rd of August he writes more cheerfully to Mrs. Burne-Jones :

" We went on Saturday to call on the De Morgans at Witley and found them lodging in a newish red brick house, the surroundings of which rather reminded one of Mrs. Bodichon's Scalands : afterwards we drove down with them and the Allinghams through woodland lanes up on to the great commons and Hind Head Hill on the Portsmouth Road : covered it was, much of it, with heather and ling, all in blossom at this season, and seeming to me not the best chosen of colours though so very bright ; but the place is very beautiful, and amazingly free from anything Cockney-base, considering how near it is to London : the best part of it the beauty of the oaks, now in their new foliage hanging about the rare corn-fields ; for the tilth is scanty in this sandy woodland country. Allingham's dwelling is in a very pleasant and beautiful spot, but the house highly uninteresting though not specially hideous, nor the get up inside of it very pleasant (though not very bad), as you might imagine : the garden too that discomforting sort of place that a new garden with no special natural gifts is apt to be : I should like to have made them better it. As to that country in general, in spite of all its beauty, it didn't quite touch me (except as pleasant hills and meadows and lanes). For one thing it is very thinly inhabited, and looks more than most countrysides as if it were kept for the pleasure of the rich, as indeed it is : but I don't know anything of it but this one visit. I must take a turn of walking through it one day: for this thing interests me in it, that if ever I am to live out of London (as I don't suppose I ever shall), and Merton goes on, somewhere thereabouts I should have to pitch my tent.

"I am much encouraged by your interest in our Merton Crafts, and shall do my best to make it pay so that we may keep it going, though, as I have told you, I can't hide from myself that there is a chance of failure (commercial I mean) in the matter : in which case I must draw in my horns, and try to shuffle out of the whole affair decently, and live thereafter small and certain if possible : little would be my grief at that same. This is looking at the worst side, which I think one ought to do; but I *think* we shall on the whole succeed ; though a rich man (so-called) I never either can or will become: nay, I am trying in a feeble way to be more thrifty— whereof no more, lest I boast now and be disgraced at Christmas.

"I have been reading more of Carlyle's life, and find it deeply interesting in spite of Froude; usually I find biographies dull to extremity, I suppose because they are generally a mass of insincerities and platitudes : but in this book is a man speaking who can say what he thinks even in a letter (I wish I could). I like him much the better for having read this book, after that other mass of moodiness, and I fare to feel as if he were on the right side in spite of all faults.

"I have to go now to Oxford Street and then to the Mansion House to the Icelandic Relief Committee, which

I am afraid owing to the time of the year is like to be a dead failure."

A week later he writes again :

"I have not been well, and there have been other troubles also of which I won't speak, and the sum of all has rather made me break down.

"I hope I am not quite unhumble, or want to be the only person in the world untroubled; but I have been ever loth to think that there were no people going through life, not without pain indeed, but with simplicity and free from blinding entanglements. Such an one I want to be, and my faith is that it is possible for most men to be no worse. Yet indeed I am older, and the year is evil; the summerless season, and famine and war, and the folly of peoples come back again, as it were, and the more and more obvious death of art before it rises again, are heavy matters to a small creature like me, who cannot choose but think about them, and can mend them scarce a whit.

"However, to stand up for oneself and tip them Long Melford, as Miss Berners says (and also in his way old Carlyle), is the only cure; and indeed I try it at whiles."

With the exception of two lectures given on behalf of the Society for Protection of Ancient Buildings, the Iceland Famine Relief Fund was the only public matter in which Morris took any part during the year. In the depths of his own household anxiety this work came as a kind of relief; and during August and September he was busy over it, writing letters to the newspapers and making personal appeals to all his acquaintance. "For those," he wrote to the Times on the 5th of August, "who have never been in Iceland nor read its ancient literature there still remains the undoubted fact that they are a kindly, honest, and intelligent people, bearing their lot, at the best a hard one, with singular courage and cheerfulness, and keeping up through all difficulties in their remote desert (for such indeed is the land in spite of its beauty and romance) an elevation of mind and a high degree of culture, which would be honourable to countries much more favoured by nature." But the work could not distract him long from his own thoughts. "I have had a bad time of it lately and feel ten years older than I did in June," he writes again six weeks later. "I saw to-day about a book written by an Italian peasant (near Verona) complaining of their misery. How shocking it seemed to me that all the riches of rich lands should be wasted till they are no better than the poorest for most men. Think what the constitution of civilized society must be when the Italian peasant is not better off, but worse off (taking one year with another), than his brother of Iceland!"

In connexion with this Icelandic famine and the work of the Mansion House Committee there is a most characteristic note to Ellis written from Kelmscott on the 29th of September. It should perhaps be explained that there had been correspondence in the London papers making little of the distress in Iceland, and questioning whether there were in fact any famine at all there. Mr. Magnússon had just started for Reykjavik with the money and provisions already collected, in order to investigate matters on the spot.

"I am so vexed that you should have had all this trouble; except for the circumstances which you know of, I would have made a point of staying in London and seeing the matter through. I cannot find that beastly letter. When I saw you Monday week I put what letters I thought would be wanted into an envelope which I intended to give you, but I was so muddled by my own troubles that I daresay I did not; nor can I be sure that

the letter was in it. Meantime I have written a letter
to the bloody Times which I also inclose; if you think it
worth while please send it on : after which I really don't
see what any of us can do till Magnússon comes back.
I repeat I am so vexed that you should have been let in
for such worrits—I am reminded of Swinburne's view of
providence when he said that he never saw an old gentleman give a sixpence to a beggar, but he was straightway
run over by a 'bus."

But apart from all private anxieties, the pressure on
Morris's mind during these autumn and winter months
seems from several indications to have been greater than
it was either before or since. It is a curious sign of his
loneliness and self-absorption at this time, that no two of
his friends (so far as I am able to ascertain) agree in
their view of the steps by which he became a convinced
Socialist and the main influences—whether men or events
or books—that served to shape his course at this time
precisely in the way it took. His own letters of the time,
so far as they exist, give little clue to any changes which
were going on in his mind. The account which he himself gave some ten years later is no doubt abstractly accurate. " A brief period of political Radicalism," he
then wrote, " during which I saw my ideal clear enough,
but had no hope of any realization of it, came to an end
some months before I joined the Democratic Federation,
and the meaning of my joining that body was, that I had
conceived a hope of the realization of that ideal." But
for the growth of this hope no one cause can be assigned.
He once said to Mr. G. B. Shaw that he had been converted to Socialism by Mill, in his posthumously published papers analyzing the system of Fourier, in which
he " clearly gave the verdict against the evidence." In
the article already quoted, Morris alludes to these papers,
and says that they put the finishing touch to his conver-

sion. It may be doubted whether even this modified statement is not an unconscious over-statement, and whether Morris does not here mix up the causes of his conversion with the reasons by which that conversion could be justified. For some considerable time after he became a professed Socialist, he worked hard at the task of proving his belief. " I put some conscience into trying to learn the economical side of Socialism, and even tackled Marx, though I suffered agonies of confusion of the brain over reading the economics of that work." But the belief, while it was not unreasoned, was not the outcome (if any belief be) of abstract economic reasoning.

While it is true to say that during these months Morris was moving towards Socialism, it would also be true to say that Socialism was moving towards him. It was " the consciousness of revolution stirring," he says himself, which " prevented me, luckier than many others of artistic perceptions, from crystallizing into a mere railer against progress on the one hand, and on the other from wasting time and energy in any of the numerous schemes by which the quasi-artistic of the middle classes hope to make art grow when it has no longer any root." His own beliefs and sympathies changed little, while the tendency of public thought was changing fast, and he might reasonably claim that, both before and after this so-called parting of the ways, he had, since he first began to think for himself, been consistent throughout his life. The history of the Socialist movement in England during the years which succeeded the war of 1870 has yet to be written; and a biographer would be straying far beyond the limits of his appointed task if he became an analyst of social conditions or a historian of institutions. But it must be noted that just at this time, that spirit of profound discontent, which is also a spirit of hope—which, unable to rest in the present, looks forward and not backward—

was widely in the air. "All countries and all individuals hang to the past, but seem hardly to think of the future. I suppose we should, like the Jewish prophets, get the habit of looking onwards to the future and not backwards to the past." Such, a generation earlier, had been the words of one of the great formative intelligences of the age, as he observed, not without a large degree of sympathy, the Chartist movement and the Christian Socialism of Kingsley and Maurice. It seemed now as if this spirit were once more in the ascendant. "The era of administration has come" was a phrase much in the mouths of economic writers. The Irish legislation of successive Governments had already, in the judgment of dispassionate observers, committed one, if not both, of the two great political parties to what might be properly called a Socialist programme. The International, though as an organized force it had been broken up in 1872, had even in its dispersion scattered widely the seeds of a cosmopolitan revolt against the domination of capital and of the middle classes. Its doctrines had to some extent permeated the leading English Trades Unions. Intelligent London artisans had in large numbers familiarized themselves with the doctrines of Karl Marx and the more recent theories of Henry George. At meetings of working men there were shouts for Revolution. The repressive measures taken in France and Austria after the Commune, and in Germany by Bismarck some years later, had incidentally filled London with foreign refugees, whose influence spread silently in many directions. The position may be summed up in Morris's own words by saying that there was no longer, among the mass of the working class in London, any decided hostility to Socialism, and that the working man who took an interest in politics was generally in favour of Socialist tendencies so far as he understood them.

In 1881 an effort had been set on foot to organize the various Radical clubs of working men in different parts of London, and to give the organization a definite bias in favour of what were becoming known as Socialistic principles.   The result was the formation of a body known as the Democratic Federation.   Its programme was, broadly speaking, that of the political Radicalism of the time, and directed towards alterations in the mere machinery of government—annual Parliaments, payment of Members, abolition of the House of Lords, and the like.   The only distinctively "Socialist" article in its creed was a claim, not further defined, for the nationalization of land.

But as time went on the Federation became, partly by the secession of members who belonged to the older school of Radicalism, partly by a new enthusiasm among the younger men, more and more Socialist in general tendency and sympathy: and the practical changes which it advocated all went in the direction of setting up a State Socialism of a somewhat drastic kind.   The "Democrat without ulterior views" of the previous generation was becoming a Social Democrat ; was asking what was the use of democratic institutions, and whether they were an end or only a means.   Once this question was fairly raised, the whole existing system of society began to rock and waver. To the new analysis, the status of a middle class was as artificial, and therefore as capable of removal, as all the privileges and anomalies which had been swept away by that middle class itself, when once it took the pains to organize itself and set hand to the work.   People were even beginning to ask themselves, with a sudden shock of disenchantment, what reason there was for the existence of a middle class at all.

" Numbers of young men," such was the account given some seven years later by one of the most thoughtful leaders of the movement, which had then parted with some of its unreasoning enthusiasm and lost the dazzle of its earlier hope, " pupils of Mill, Spencer, Comte, and Darwin, roused by Mr. Henry George's 'Progress and Poverty,' left aside evolution and free thought; took to insurrectionary economics; studied Karl Marx; and were so convinced that Socialism had only to be put clearly before the working classes to concentrate the power of their immense numbers in one irresistible organization, that the Revolution was fixed for 1889 (the anniversary of the French Revolution) at latest. The opposition we got was uninstructive: it was mainly founded on the assumption that our projects were theoretically unsound but immediately possible, whereas our weak point lay in the case being exactly the reverse."

By one of those large and gradual changes of opinion which are seldom traceable to any distinct cause, the middle class had just then become deeply discredited. Matthew Arnold, after a lifetime spent in persistent efforts to arouse it to a sense of its own shortcomings, had abandoned the task in despair and given utterance to a new creed, that of hope in the working class; the creed which he formulated in an address delivered to the Ipswich Working Men's College under the title *Ecce convertimur ad Gentes*. The change—so far as it was a change —that had passed over Morris was somewhat parallel, but led him towards utterance more violent in proportion to his imaginative ardour and the impatience of his temperament.

" I have no very ardent interest," Arnold said in that address, " in politics in their present state in this country. What interests me is English civilization; and our politics in their present state do not seem to me to have much bearing upon that. Both the natural reason of the thing and also the proof from practical experience seem to me to show the same thing; that for modern civilization some approach to equality is necessary, and that an enormous inequality like ours is a hindrance to our civilization. Our middle classes know neither man nor the world; they have no light, and can give none." So far the two men are in complete agreement; and though Morris might have expressed himself in phrases less lucidly temperate, there is even a curious and quite unpremeditated likeness in the language which they use. "Can the middle class regenerate themselves?" Morris asks, and answers the question essentially as Arnold answered it. "At first sight," are his words, "one would say that a body of people so powerful, who have built up the gigantic edifice of modern commerce, whose science, invention, and energy have subdued the forces of nature to serve their everyday purposes, and who guide the organization that keeps these natural powers in subjection in a way almost miraculous; at first sight one would say, surely such a mighty mass of wealthy men could do anything they please. And yet I doubt it. Why do not you—and I—set about doing this to-morrow? Because we cannot."

"For twenty years," Arnold went on in the Ipswich address, "I have been vainly urging this upon the middle classes themselves. Now I urge it upon you. Carry it forward yourselves, and insist on taking the middle class with you." But Morris could not stand aloof to give counsel; he must needs be in the thick of the conflict. A passage in a lecture delivered at the beginning of 1884 seems to express his attitude precisely in the way that he felt and meant it. "The cause of art," he there says, "is the cause of the people. We well-to-do people, those of us who love art, not as a toy, but as a thing necessary to the life of man, have for our best work the raising of the standard of life among the people. How can we of

the middle classes, we the capitalists and our hangers-on,
help? By renouncing our class, and on all occasions
when antagonism rises up between the classes, casting in
our lot with the victims; those who are condemned at
the best to lack of education, refinement, leisure, pleasure,
and renown; and at the worst, to a life lower than that
of the most brutal of savages. There is no other way."

There can be little doubt that this passage, though
not written till after he had joined a Socialist organization, expresses with great accuracy the frame of mind
which made him take the step of joining it. In addressing
middle-class audiences this was the offer which he distinctly made them: " To these I offer a means," were his
words, repeated again and again on public platforms,
" of renouncing their class by joining the only body in
this country which puts forward constructive Socialism
as its programme."

That, if the privileged classes became merged in a
Third Estate, national equality and national unity would
be the result, is a thesis which may be variously argued
either in abstract logic or from the lessons of history.
But it is perhaps more to the point to ask how far it is
possible in the nature of things that a man should renounce his class. Into that class he was born: in it he
has grown and lived: it environs him with the constant
pressure of an atmosphere : he clings to it and draws his
daily life out of it by a thousand filaments of inherited
tradition and acquired habit. To many it may seem that
Arnold, and not Morris, in this instance pointed out the
true path. Morris's own language with regard to the
matter, while not always strictly consistent, often indicates
that he saw as clearly as any man the hopelessness of any
attempt to elevate the working class from without. He
never deceived himself into thinking that, by taking his
stand thus on the side of those whom he called the

workers, he had ceased himself to be a professional man, a hanger-on (for so he defined the term "professional man") of the capitalist class. His hope was that at the touch of an external impulse leaders among the workers themselves might arise, with whom or under whom he might himself be permitted to work. It was only after years of disappointment that he realized that the time for this had not yet come. But his whole life bore witness to the sincerity and self-sacrificing devotion with which he followed the path he conceived to be that of his highest duty.

This renunciation of his own class at all events, so far as such a thing could be actually done, presented itself to him as a step which now more than ever would have, so far as he himself was concerned, real value and significance. His position in the eyes of the world was more than respectable; it might even be described, within limits, as famous. He had a recognized place in the first rank of living poets. He had no less recognized an authority on all matters relating to the theory and practice of the decorative arts. He was a well-known and (in spite of the temporary embarrassments which attended the first year of the work at Merton Abbey) a prosperous manufacturer, whose goods travelled far, and carried their own guarantee of excellence in design and workmanship. He might speak of renunciation as one who had something not inconsiderable to renounce. Just at the moment when he was making up his mind to take some decisive step, he was unanimously elected an Honorary Fellow of his College at Oxford ; a distinction which, always rare, is generally reserved for old members who have attained the highest official rank in their profession, and implies a tribute to very special distinction in one who is not a Bishop or a Privy Councillor. This honour was conferred on him on the 13th of January, 1883.

PART OF THE DRAWING-ROOM, KELMSCOTT HOUSE, HAMMERSMITH.

He had gone down to Bournemouth that day to see his daughter. "Such a pile of letters I found waiting me," he wrote to her on the 17th, after coming back to London, "some of them like those of David Copperfield after he had become an author." That same day he enrolled himself as a member of the Democratic Federation.

On his card of membership, which is signed by H. H. Champion, he is described as "William Morris, designer." It was on his status as a workman that he based his claim to admission into the fighting rank of a working-class movement. The step, which in a sense cut him definitely away from respectability, was in no way a merely formal one. He took it with a full sense of its import. "I am truly glad," were his words, with something of the grave joy of a convert, "that I have joined the only society I could find which is definitely Socialistic." His support of the new movement, even before he formally joined it, had not been confined to theoretical sympathy. In the previous October he had sold the greater part of his valuable library, in order to devote the proceeds to the furtherance of Socialism. Though he was not exactly a bibliophile, many of these treasures cost him a pang to part with, from the "De Claris Mulieribus," which had been his first purchase among the masterpieces of the early printers, down to oddly printed collections of Sagas from the Skálaholt Press, which he had acquired in Iceland. "If the modern books are unsaleable," he wrote to Ellis, "perhaps you would let me take them out after your valuation, as I have no idea what they are worth to sell (though beastly dear to buy), and though I hate them and should be glad to be rid of them as far as pleasure is concerned, they are of some use to me professionally—though by the way I am not a professional man, but a tradesman."

A few letters to Bournemouth during the winter indicate how his daily work went on, notwithstanding the excitement of the new departure. "Yesterday," he writes on the 6th of December, "I spent the day at the South Kensington Museum. My opinion was wanted as to the value of a set of textiles which old Canon Bock has offered them: there were some very interesting pieces among them: a noble piece of Sicilian woven stuff of a pattern I haven't seen before; a fine piece of 13th century Syrian silk with (real) Arab writing in it: some fragments of the very early cloths also, and a great quantity of good 17th century patterns; also a good collection of printed goods from the 14th century till the beginnings on the Wandle. I had also to decide as to whether the Museum should buy three large pieces of tapestry (of about 1530), but I refused them, as they were not really good, and had been gammoned badly: also they were too dear, £1,200 for the three and not worth more than £400 at the most. I have made three new patterns for embroidery, two small table-cloths, and one cushion."

And on the 19th from Merton:

"It is a lovely day here, though it was dark and thick in town; but I cannot get about the works, for the gout has made another grab at me: it feels so queer to be here and a kind of prisoner to the house: however I have ordered the cab to be here at 6 to take me back to Hammersmith, and I have plenty of small designing work to do meantime. As to our printing, we are really not quite straight yet: I am quite ashamed of it: however they are doing Brother Rabbit successfully, and the Anemone will go on now, and when we are once out of this difficulty, I really think we shall have seen the worst of it. Item, we are going to get our wheel set straight during the Christmas holidays, so as not to stop work; the poor critter wants it very badly, for every now and then when there is not much water on, it really seems as if he stopped to think, like a lazy boy turning a grind-stone. Well, here is an end of my paper, and Mr. Barret the wood-cutter come to see about cutting the design I made down there—I shall call it Christchurch, not Bournemouth."

On New Year's Day he writes again:

"I duly went to Merton on Thursday, and found the wheel by no means finished as they had promised : indeed it all looked like a boy who has pulled his watch to pieces and can't put it together again; however I expect to find all going to-day. I am going to sleep at Merton to-night I fancy : because on Wednesday I have to go to an Icelandic meeting at 12 (noon). There will be no contested election here : I could have wished a real Radical could have been found to stand against Dilke, but then the Tories would have run a man, and probably got him in. Do you see the Pope is going to canonize Sir Thomas More? the Socialists ought to look up, if that is to be their (late) reward."

More's "Utopia" had been one of the books he had read aloud at Kelmscott during his melancholy autumn holiday, and it had no inconsiderable influence over him ; much more, it seems, than the professedly Socialistic treatises—Marx's "Capital," Wallace's "Land Nationalization," and the like—which he had been rather dispiritedly ploughing through. Socialists more versed in abstract economic theories than himself were inclined to accuse him of sentimentalism ; and in this, as in other spheres of activity, the demands of the romantic imagination were as imperious in him as ever. A fairly complete list happens to be extant in a private diary of what he read aloud at the Grange, where he still regularly spent Sunday morning and one other evening every week, during the year just ended. The only new book in the list is " Erewhon," one of the first and ablest of those modern Utopias which were coming into fashion, and a book that Morris greatly admired.   The rest are all old and tried friends ; Monte Cristo, The Three Musketeers, Redgauntlet, David Copperfield, Great Expectations, Tales of Old Japan, and on the last evening of the year his earliest love of all, the Arabian Nights.

CHAPTER XV

FOR the two years during which Morris was a member
of the Democratic Federation, there is little in his life to
chronicle which is not directly connected with that organization, and with his own development under its influence
into a more logical and uncompromising type of Socialist.
For reasons which are easy to appreciate, and of which
his own statement will be given later, he did not, either
when he joined it as an active member or afterwards,
abandon his own profession as a manufacturer, or his
own status as a man of letters. But it took up a principal, and, as time went on, an absorbing share of his
time, thought, and energy. His production in pure
literature, whether prose or verse, fell for these years
wholly into abeyance : his production as a designer was
greatly curtailed ; and his management of his business
became more and more perfunctory. Fears were often
expressed by his friends that the effect on the business
might be grave, if not disastrous. But it had been solidly
founded, and was kept up by the skill and energy of his
managers, Mr. George Wardle and Messrs. F. and R.
Smith, who were now practically partners as well. Morris
himself was nearly always ready to respond to the call for
new designs that were really needed, and to apply his
strong common sense to questions that were submitted
for his decision.

There are several indications that when he now plunged into politics, he was on the brink of a new departure in the field of romance.   One may even conjecture the path it would have taken.   The heroic cycle of Iran had long held in his mind a place next to those of Greece and Scandinavia.   "He loved everything Persian," Sir Edward Burne-Jones says, "including the wild confusion of their chronology."   His profound study of Oriental design in its application to pottery and textiles had recently reinforced his interest in the Persian epic.   At the beginning of 1883 he was deep in Mohl's French translation of the Shah Nameh, and had begun a version of his own from the French into English, of which a considerable fragment was executed.   But now, under a constraining sense of social duty, this and all other literary plans were given up by him for the service of the Federation.   It was nearly three years later before he once more returned to imaginative work—though still with a political aim and inspiration—in "The Dream of John Ball."   In those three years he had indeed produced a large volume of writing. But it was not of a kind which possessed literary value, or was meant for permanence.   With the exception of some dozen fragments of poetry, and as many lectures on the relation of art to social conditions, and to the life of mankind, it was professedly and even ostentatiously journalism.

An interesting light is thrown on his attitude of mind at this time by a letter written in January to Mr. Manson, his old colleague on the executive of the National Liberal League.   It was in answer to some question which Mr. Manson had put to him in connexion with the exhibition of Rossetti's pictures and drawings which was then being held at the Burlington Fine Arts Club. Rossetti himself had died in the previous April.

" I can't say," he writes, " how it was that Rossetti

took no interest in politics; but so it was: of course he was quite Italian in his general turn of thought; though I think he took less interest in Italian politics than in English, in spite of his knowing several of the leading patriots personally, Saffi for instance. The truth is he cared for nothing but individual and personal matters; chiefly of course in relation to art and literature, but he would take abundant trouble to help any one person who was in distress of mind or body; but the evils of any mass of people he couldn't bring his mind to bear upon. I suppose in short it needs a person of hopeful mind to take disinterested notice of politics, and Rossetti was certainly not hopeful."

The difference here touched, whether or not the explanation offered of it be right, was real and deep. Morris had himself always been one of the people to whom personal matters bear far less than their normal share in life. He was interested in things much more than in people. He had the capacity for loyal friendships and for deep affections; but even of these one might almost say that they did not penetrate to the central part of him. The thing done, the story, or the building, or the picture, or whatever it might be, was what he cared about in the work of his contemporaries and friends no less than in that of other ages or countries: and in his mind these things seem to have been quite independent of the story-teller, or the architect, or the painter, and not merely substantive things, but one might almost say substantive personalities. So too in the ordinary concerns of life he was strangely incurious of individuals. On one side this quality of mind took the form of an absolute indifference to gossip and scandal, and a capacity of working with the most unsympathetic or disagreeable colleagues, so long as they were helping on the particular work in hand. On another side it resulted in an almost equally marked inconsiderateness. He sometimes seemed to have the aloofness of some great natural force. For sympathy in distress, for soothing in trouble, it was not to him that one would have gone. The lot of the poor, as a class, when he thought of it, had always lain heavily on his spirit. "Indeed, the poor man is always much at the mercy of the rich"—those noble and melancholy words, used just a century before by Johnson to Boswell, express a feeling which was at the root of all Morris's social doctrine. But the sufferings of individuals often only moved him to a certain impatience. Many years before, Rossetti, in one of those flashes of hard insight that made him so terrible a friend, had said of him, "Did you ever notice that Top never gives a penny to a beggar?" Inconsiderate and even unscrupulous as Rossetti was himself in some of the larger affairs of life, this particular instinct of generosity was one which never failed him. For the individual in distress—were it a friend in difficulties, or some unknown poor woman on the street—he was always ready to empty his own pockets, and plunge deeply into those of his friends. Morris's virtues were of a completely different type. Scrupulously just in his dealings, incapable of driving a hard bargain, liberal up to and even beyond his means in the support of an object which had gained his sympathy, he had not in his nature that touch of lavishness that gives a human warmth to generosity, and may elevate even inconsiderate profusion into a moral excellence. That habit of magnificence, which to the Greek mind was the crown of virtues, was Rossetti's most remarkable quality. In the nature of Morris it had no place. "I am bourgeois, you know, and therefore without the point of honour," he had written many years before to Madox Brown in a moment of real self-appreciation; and his virtues were those of the bourgeois class—industrious, honest, fair-minded up to their lights, but unexpansive and unsympathetic—so far as the touch of genius did not transform him into something quite unique and incalculable.

There is a pleasant sketch of one of his frequent visits to Paris, in company with Mr. Armstrong, on the affairs of the South Kensington Museum, in a letter to his daughter at the end of that January. They crossed together on a stormy moonlit night, "so that we could see the waves at any rate, and they were very fine indeed. We slept on the road to Paris after a fashion, but it was so cold that it was a sort of dog-sleep, and the inn-room and wood-fire and coffee and rolls were sweet to us when we got there. Armstrong took me to dine at a simple place he knew, where we were welcome and paid but moderately: by the way, seeing *goujons* on the bill, I insisted on having them, and very good they were. The trees in the Tuileries gardens have suffered very much even since we were there: it is sad to see, for I remember when I first came to Paris and was high up aloft with Aunt Henrietta at Meurice's they were so thick they looked as if you could walk on their tops. We were very busy over our proper business both days, but managed to see the Cluny, being close by; also a new Museum of casts of Gothic sculpture at the Trocadéro, very interesting. As to the sale we were beat, a sort of French S.K.M. bought the things over our heads, but Armstrong thinks he can borrow the best book of the pattern books, which was very good, had a lot of old Indian and Persian printed cloths in it."

Of Morris's first appearance at a meeting of the Democratic Federation the following account is given by Mr. Scheu:

"In the early winter months of 1883 the Democratic Federation had arranged some meetings at the Westminster Palace Chambers. I attended the first of those meetings (I forget the exact date), Mr. Hyndman in the chair. The order of the day was the passing of some resolutions on the question of education, normal working-day, and the housing of the working classes. The business had scarcely been started when Banner, who sat behind me, passed me a slip of paper, 'The third man to your right is William Morris.' I had read of but never seen Morris before, and I looked at once in the direction given. I was struck by Morris's fine face, his earnestness, the half searching, half dreamy look of his eyes, and his plain and comely dress.

" When the resolution *re* artisans' dwellings was proposed, I rose and took exception to the notion that only artisans needed rational dwellings, and proposed to alter the wording into ' people's dwellings.' The amendment was frowned upon by the chair, but when Morris got up and seconded it with a few sympathetic words, it was carried almost unanimously."

That random shot—for such perhaps it was—struck home : for it was characteristic of Morris to welcome with almost exaggerated gratitude any remark from a stranger that pointed towards the same conclusions to which his own lonely thoughts had led him. The amendment was meant to protest against limiting the movement in favour of better dwellings to the class of skilled workmen. But to Morris the necessity of rational dwellings for the rich no less than the poor was a primary article of belief. " I have at least respect for the dwellers in the tub of Diogenes ; indeed I don't look upon it as so bad a house after all. I have seen worse houses to let for £700 a year." So he said afterwards with perfect sincerity, and the housing of the rich was to him one of the most distressing features of modern civilization.

At the same meeting " Rowland, for whom we voted for our School Board," Morris writes, " was there, and spoke hugely to my liking; advocated street-preaching of our doctrines as the real practical method: wisely to my mind, since those who suffer (more than we, or they, can tell) from society as it is, are so many, and those who have conceived any hope that it may be changed are so few." This belief, to which he clung against hope for several years, had momentous consequences in his life; for in the task of street-preaching outdoors, and work equivalent to street-preaching indoors, he broke down his health, and to some extent wore away the keen edge of his mind. But for the moment the new task seemed to lend him additional vigour. A month later there is a glimpse of him in the first flush of his enterprise in an entry from a private diary:

" Feb. 22. At Ned's. Top came in to breakfast as usual on Sundays: was extremely brilliant as soon as he had shaken off a little drooping of spirits owing to bad news about Jenny: was very angry against Seddon for replacing old Hammersmith Church ('a harmless silly old thing') by such an excrescence. He was bubbling over with Karl Marx, whom he had just begun to read in French. He praised Robert Owen immensely. He had been giving an address to a Clerkenwell Radical Club—found the members 'eager to learn but dreadfully ignorant.' ' All Socialists are agreed as to education.' Finely explosive against railways. Some imitation-Morris wall-paper was 'a mangy gherkin on a horse-dung ground.' Spent the evening at Top's—a long talk on birds: T.'s knowledge of them very extensive: can go on for hours about their habits: but especially about their form."

About the same time Morris wrote to Mr. T. C. Horsfall, who had made his acquaintance four years earlier in connexion with the formation of the Manchester Art Museum:

"I think on reflection that I have not much to add to what I have written in my little book" ("Hopes and Fears for Art"). "I have, as you will note, guarded myself against the imputation of wishing to get rid of all rough work. I would only get rid as much as possible of all nasty and stupid work, and what is left I would divide as equitably as might be among all classes.

"You see it was not necessary in my lectures to tell people that I am in principle a Socialist, and would be so in practice if there should ever in my lifetime turn up an occasion for action: add to this fact that I have a religious hatred to all war and violence, and you have the reason for my speaking and writing on subjects of art. I mean that I have done it as seed for the goodwill and justice that *may* make it possible for the next great revolution, which will be a social one, to work itself out without violence being an essential part of it."

But economy of truth was never a thing possible for Morris, and any advance in his own views was reflected immediately in his public as much as in his private utterances. On the 6th of March he gave an address on "Art, Wealth, and Riches" at the Manchester Royal Institution, in which the Socialist doctrine was so pronounced as to meet with much hostile criticism. On the theory of art people were willing to hear him gladly, much as they would hear a preacher from the pulpit on the theory of religion. They would even to some degree consent to translate his doctrine into practice in the decoration of their houses. But when he attacked the structure and basis of the life they led in these houses, there were murmurs of alarm and resentment. "Does not that raise another question than one of mere art?" they asked in perplexity or indignation. To a letter in the Manchester Examiner which put the question in these specific words Morris took the opportunity to reply thus :

"It was the purpose of my lecture to raise another question than one of mere art. I specially wished to point out that the question of popular art was a social question, involving the happiness or misery of the greater part of the community. The absence of popular art from modern times is more disquieting and grievous to bear for this reason than for any other, that it betokens that fatal division of men into the cultivated and the degraded classes which competitive commerce has bred and fosters ; popular art has no chance of a healthy life, or, indeed, of a life at all, till we are on the way to fill up this terrible gulf between riches and poverty. Doubtless many things will go to filling it up, and if art must be one of those things, let it go. What business have we with art at all unless all can share it ? I am not afraid but that art will rise from the dead, whatever else lies there. For, after all, what is the true end and aim of all politics and all commerce ? Is it not to bring about a state of things in which all men may live at peace and free from over-burdensome anxiety, provided with work which is pleasant to them and produces results useful to their neighbours ?

"It may well be a burden to the conscience of an honest man who lives a more manlike life to think of the innumerable lives which are spent in toil unrelieved by hope and uncheered by praise; men who might as well, for all the good they are doing to their neighbours by their work, be turning a crank with nothing at the end of it ; but this is the fate of those who are working at the bidding of blind competitive commerce, which still persists in looking at itself as an end, and not as a means.

"It has been this burden on my conscience, I do in

all sincerity believe, which has urged me on to speak of popular art in Manchester and elsewhere. 1 could never forget that in spite of all drawbacks my work is little else than pleasure to me; that under no conceivable circumstances would I give it up even if I could. Over and over again have I asked myself why should not my lot be the common lot. My work is simple work enough; much of it, nor that the least pleasant, any man of decent intelligence could do, if he could but get to care about the work and its results. Indeed I have been ashamed when I have thought of the contrast between my happy working hours and the unpraised, unrewarded, monotonous drudgery which most men are condemned to. Nothing shall convince me that such labour as this is good or necessary to civilization."

Of Merton Abbey and his work going on there he writes to his daughter on the 28th of February. The tapestry of the Goose-Girl, from a design by Mr. Walter Crane, was the first figure-subject executed at Merton on the high-warp loom. It was succeeded by the Flora and Pomona pieces, in which the figures were designed by Burne-Jones.

"At Merton there are some daffodils out already. The almond tree is blossoming there beautifully: some of these fine days the place *has* looked pretty, the water sparkling among the twigs. We are getting tidy now, but haven't quite cleared up about the big filtering bed, which still wants something doing to it, as the tail was red with madder the other day. We are not getting on quite as fast as we should with the printing; it is very tough work getting everything in due order, the cloths seem to want so much doing to them before they can be printed, and then so much doing to them after they are printed. We have had a grand cleaning of the blue Persian carpet at Merton. My word, wasn't it dirty: caked with dirt: it looks very much better, the pattern being quite plain to see except just at the end for about a foot. I was frightened though at first: for after we first put it into the river it cockled up like a sheet of crumpled paper, the cotton warp shrinking with the wet. I thought my £80 had gone down the Wandle: but all came right when it was dry. In about a fortnight we shall have finished the Goose-Girl tapestry: Uncle Ned has done me two lovely figures for tapestry, but I have got to design a background for them; I shall probably bring that down next time I come for my holiday task. Tell dear May that I have devoted about twenty minutes to the lace—it is a drawback to have to be always washing one's hands for a fidgety person like me. Neither have I done much to the Shah Nameh: you see the lecture has swallowed up my literary time."

Under the pressure of opposition which, at Manchester and elsewhere, he was now beginning to feel, a hardening of his tone about this time begins to be perceptible. " I am tired of being mealy-mouthed," he breaks out in a letter. In April he was lecturing regularly, " preaching my sermon " as he calls it, in different parts of London, and becoming more plain-spoken in each fresh draft of his message. In May he was put, rather against his will, on the executive of the Democratic Federation ; " so I am in for more work. However I don't like belonging to a body without knowing what they are doing. Without feeling very sanguine about their doings, they seem certainly to mean something ; money is chiefly lacking, as usual."

To meet this lack of money among a small and struggling group of enthusiasts, the drain on his own resources was already heavy, and became heavier as time went on. " *You* have no revolution on hand on which to spend your money," he wrote to Ellis in the same week. " By the way," he adds, suddenly turning to another and an earlier interest, " the May-fly does not visit Wandle: they are eating the alder and the cocktail now. Wardle got a fish (not in our water) on Monday evening, a 2 lb., I heard." Himself now he found no time for fishing or for any relaxation. The absorption of his time by his new work amounted to two full working-days, besides odd evenings, out of every week. " I haven't had two consecutive hours to call my own since I saw you three weeks ago," he writes to Mrs. Burne-Jones later in the summer; "my time has been a mere heap of chopped straw."

So far as concerns his attitude at this point towards politics and the ideas of that middle class which he had not yet renounced, two long and clearly reasoned letters written this summer to Mr. C. E. Maurice give his thought fully and frankly.

" Kelmscott House,
" June 22, 1883.

" Dear Mr. Maurice,

"I think you might be able to help a friend of mine with advice in the following case: A poor woman comes to her asking for a ticket for her son for the Consumptive Hospital: son obviously ill, but *not* with consumption: woman herself ill, sore throat and out-of-sorts: husband ill also: very bad smell in the house; the rent-collector or landlord, when asked to mend matters by the tenant, won't do anything; won't even give his address; inspector when written to by tenant don't answer: Can you tell me who is the proper inspector or board to apply to ? and forgive my troubling you on such a simple question.

" I should have been glad to have continued our conversation last Friday night; as I so much desire to convert all disinterested people of good will to what I should call active and general Socialism, and to have their help: I think that you, like myself, have really been a Socialist for a long time, and I know you have done your best, as you would be sure to do, to carry out your views. For my part I used to think that one might further real Socialistic progress by doing what one could on the lines of ordinary middle-class Radicalism: I have been driven of late into the conclusion that I was mistaken; that Radicalism is on the wrong line, so to say, and will never develope into anything more than Radicalism: in fact that it is made for and by the middle classes and will always be under the control of rich capitalists: they will have no objection to its *political* development, if they think they can stop it there: but as to real social changes, they will not allow them if they can help it: you may see almost any day such phrases as "this is the proper way to stop the spread of Socialism" in the Liberal papers, the writer of the phrase never having taken the trouble to find out what Socialism meant, and also choosing to ignore the discontent, dumb indeed for the most part, which is widely spread even in England. Meantime I can see no use in people having political freedom unless they use it as an instrument for leading reasonable and manlike lives; no good even in education if, when they are educated, people have only slavish work to do, and have to live lives too much beset with sordid anxiety for them to be able to think and feel with the more fortunate people who produced art and poetry and great thought. This release from slavery it is clear cannot come to people so long as they are subjected to the bare subsistence wages which are a necessity of competitive commerce; and I cannot help thinking that the workmen will be soon finding out that for themselves: it is certain that Henry

George's book has been received in this country and in America as a new Gospel: I believe that Socialism is advancing, and will advance more and more as education spreads, and so believing, find my duty clear to do my best to further its advance, and in the same time, in what poor way I can, to soften the ruggedness, and refine the coarseness which centuries of oppression have hammered into it, so to say.

" A word about the Democratic Federation : as far as I know it is the only active Socialist organization in England : under the above mentioned circumstances therefore I found myself bound to join it, although I had heard beforehand (to speak plainly) that it was a sort of Tory drag to take the scent off the fox.   From all I can hear I believe that to be a calumny : or, to speak English, one of those curious lies for which no one seems responsible, but which stick very tight to the object they are thrown at.   However that may be, I cannot see how a Society which has declared openly for Socialism, including Land Nationalization, can serve the Tory cause, whatever the Tory intention may be : for the rest, from what I can see of their proceedings the Executive seem to me to mean work ; and if their opinions hurt the Liberal party (where is it by the way ?) it is the fault of the Liberal party for allowing itself to stiffen into Whiggery or practical Toryism, as it seems to me it is fast doing.

" I won't make any excuses for this long letter, as I know you are deeply interested in the matter, and I believe your uprightness of thought will see through my clumsy sentences into what I have in my mind.

" I am, dear Mr. Maurice,
" Yours faithfully,
" WILLIAM MORRIS."

　　　　　　　　　　　　　　　" Kelmscott House,
　　　　　　　　　　　　　　　　" July 1st, 1883.

" Dear Mr. Maurice,

　　　"I am sitting down to write my promised letter to you, but to begin with find it somewhat difficult to do more than define my own position a little more than I did in my last. You see I think we differ to start with in this, that you think that the present system of Society has certain hitches in it; certain wrongs resulting from blunders persisted in, till they have become very difficult to deal with, but which hitches and blunders are removable, and when removed will leave us a society which can be kept straight by careful attention to the general duties of good citizenship. I confess I go much further than that: true it is that I cannot help trying to remove obvious anomalies or helping what I can to palliate the effects of the obstinate blunders which we both see, but I do so with little hope, because I believe that the whole basis of Society, with its contrasts of rich and poor, is incurably vicious: I might be content that the change which I think must come about before this can be righted should be a gradual one—or say I *must* be content; but I do not see that those who are at the head of the political advance have any intention of making a real change in the social basis : for them it seems a part of the necessary and eternal order of things that the present supply and demand Capitalist system should last for ever; though the system of citizen and chattel slave under which the ancient civilizations lived, which no doubt once seemed also necessary and eternal, had to give place, after a long period of violence and anarchy, to the feudal system of seigneur and serf; which in its turn, though once thought necessary and eternal, has been swept away in favour of our present contract system between rich and poor. Of course I don't do you the injustice to suppose that you defend the finality of any system, but I am quite clear that the ordinary Radical of to-day does do so, and there I join issue with him.

" Also of course, I do not believe in the world being saved by any system,—I only assert the necessity of attacking systems grown corrupt, and no longer leading anywhither : that to my mind is the case with the present system of capital and labour : as all my lectures assert, I have personally been gradually driven to the conclusion that art has been handcuffed by it, and will die out of civilization if the system lasts.   That of itself does to me carry with it the condemnation of the whole system, and I admit has been the thing which has drawn my attention to the subject in general : but furthermore in looking into matters social and political I have but one rule, that in thinking of the condition of any body of men I should ask myself, ' How could you bear it yourself? what would you feel if you were poor against the system under which you live ? '   I have always been uneasy when I had to ask myself that question, and of late years I have had to ask it so often, that I have seldom had it out of my mind : and the answer to it has more and more made me ashamed of my own position, and more and more made me feel that if I had not been born rich or well-to-do I should have found my position *un*endurable, and should have been a mere rebel against what would have seemed to me a system of robbery and injustice.   Nothing can argue me out of this feeling, which I say plainly is a matter of religion to me : the contrasts of rich and poor are unendurable and ought not to be endured by either rich or poor.   Now it seems to me that, feeling this, I am bound to act for the destruction of the system which seems to me mere oppression and obstruction ; such a system can only be destroyed, it seems to me, by the united discontent of numbers ; isolated acts of a few persons of the middle and upper classes seeming to me (as I have said before) quite powerless against it: in other words the antagonism of classes, which the system has bred, is the natural and necessary instrument of its destruction.   My aim therefore being to spread discontent among all classes, I feel myself bound to join any organization whose object seemed to me really to further this aim : nor in doing so should I be much troubled by consideration of who the leaders of such an organization might be,always supposing that one believes them genuine in their support of certain *principles*.   It has always seemed to me that the worship of leaders has been a sign of the lifelessness of ordinaryRadicalism of late, and that opinion has received fresh confirmation in my mind by last year's events in Ireland and Egypt (especially the latter, where the Liberal ' leaders ' ' led ' the party into mere Jingoism).

" But further I earnestly wish that the middle classes, to whom hitherto I have personally addressed myself, should look to all these matters, and become discontented also, as they certainly should be, since they themselves suffer from the same system which oppresses the poor; their lives made barren and dull by it; their hopes for a higher standard of life repressed: besides I am quite sure that the change which will overthrow our present system will come sooner or later : on the middle classes to a great extent it depends whether it will come peaceably or violently. If they can only learn the uselessness of mere overplus money, the poisonousness of luxury to all civilization, they will not be so likely to cry out ' confiscation and robbery and injustice ' at a system which, while it proposes to give to every man what he really *needs,* will have no call to take from any man what he can really *use :* in short, what we of the middle classes have to do, if we can, is to show by our lives what is the proper type of a useful citizen, the type into which all classes should melt at last. I remember a little time ago meeting a clever man in a train who enlarged (without letting me get a word in edgewise) on the woes of the middle class, and how they suffered in comparison with the pampered working classes. I am sorry to say that I was not ready enough to say to him what I afterwards thought: 'my friend, if you would only allow yourself to become a member of this pampered working class, then would all your woes be at an end, by your own showing.' His line of argument is common enough, and is founded on the assumption that one class must be masters of the other: but to my mind no man is good enough to be any one's master without injuring himself at least, whatever he does for the servant. Well, I don't know if I have explained myself at all ; I daresay I haven't, but I have told you of certain things which were on my mind ; and you will at least see that I am your ally in trying to deal with the lives of our own class.

"I much agree with what you say about the shop-keeping class, and think with you that they have been very unjustly scolded at for a position which they cannot help, and which is I know very often hard enough for them: whatever political grievances they lack, I think they have a social grievance heavy enough : for instance, the more refined classes do usually assume in their dealings with them that they will as a matter of course cheat the buyer, though all the while the buyer is eager for what he calls a 'bargain,' *i.e.*, that he should cheat the seller. Doesn't this bring home to us all the waste and disgrace which is the essence of our present system of Commercial War ?

" Well, I have spun you a very long yarn, and have not attempted to answer your objections directly; because

I saw from your letter that you could not be expected to join in such a Society as ours at present, though I cannot help thinking that you one day will take some such step.

"Meantime I have begun a little essay on the subject you were good enough to suggest to me : when it is finished I will send it you, and if you approve of it I would read it somewhere and be prepared to answer further questions on the subject—which however I cannot help feeling will eventually lead us back to Socialism by another road.

"By the way a friend sent me Hampstead paper cuttings, containing 1st, an irate letter from some one who was 'touched up' by my lecture; and 2nd, a very handsome answer to him by yourself, for which I thank you heartily, especially as it made clear to me that you quite understood what I had been saying on that occasion.   You must remember by the way again that I was sent by the Democratic Federation to lecture there; so I thought I was acting within my rights in distributing their circular, and speaking for them.

"I am, dear Mr. Maurice,
"Yours faithfully,
"WILLIAM MORRIS."

In more touching and intimate words he wrote on the 21st of August to Mrs. Burne-Jones, who had made a renewed effort to urge him back to writing poetry :

"I am touched by your kind anxiety about my poetry; but you see, my dear, there is first of all my anxiety, which I am bound to confess has made a sad coward of me; and then, though I admit that I am a conceited man, yet I really don't think anything I have done (when I consider it as I should another man's work) of any value except to myself: except as showing my sympathy with history and the like. Poetry goes with the hand-arts I think, and like them has now become unreal: the arts have got to die, what is left of them, before they can be born again. You know my views on the matter; I apply them to myself as well as to others. This would not, I admit, prevent my writing poetry any more than it prevents my doing my pattern work, because the mere personal pleasure of it urges one to the work; but it prevents my looking at it as a sacred duty, and the grief aforesaid is too strong and disquieting to be overcome by a mere inclination to do what I *know* is unimportant work. Meantime the propaganda gives me work to do, which, unimportant as it seems, is part of a great whole which cannot be lost, and that ought to be enough for me."

Within the ranks of the Democratic Federation meanwhile, which had set out so gaily to conquer working-class opinion and use it as a lever against the established order of things, disruptive tendencies were already showing themselves, and its middle-class leaders were already beginning to mistrust one another. "I am like enough to have some trouble over my propagandist work," Morris writes at the end of August, "let alone that I am in for a many lectures: for small as our body is, we are not without dissensions in it. Some of the more ardent disciples look upon Hyndman as too opportunist, and there is truth in that; he is sanguine of speedy change happening somehow, and is inclined to intrigue and the making of a party; towards which end compromise is needed, and the carrying people who don't really agree with us as far as they will go. As you know, I am not sanguine, and think the aim of Socialists should be the founding of a religion, towards which end compromise is no use, and we only want to have those with us who will be with us to the end. But then again, if the

zealots don't take care they will blow the whole thing
to the winds; all the more as the religious or theological
difficulty is on us, or threatening to be so. In the midst
of all this I find myself drifting into the disgraceful
position of a moderator and patcher up, which is much
against my inclination.

" Meantime it is obvious that the support to be looked
for for constructive Socialism from the working classes
at present is nought. Who can wonder, as things now
are, when the lower classes are really lower? Of vague
discontent and a spirit of revenge for the degradation in
which they are kept there is plenty I think, but that
seems all. What we want is real leaders themselves
working men, and content to be so till classes are
abolished. But you see when a man has gifts for that
kind of thing he finds himself tending to rise out of his
class before he has begun to think of class politics as a
matter of principle, and too often he is just simply ' got
at ' by the governing classes, not formally, but by circumstances I mean. Education is the word doubtless ;
but then in comes the commercial system and defends
itself against that in a terrible unconscious way with the
struggle for bread, and lack of leisure, and squalid
housing—and there we go, round and round the circle
still."

It was not only the business of moderating and patching up that was now beginning, but the equally endless
task of explaining to a quite light-hearted and careless
world distinctions which perpetually became more crucial
as their scope was narrowed, but which those beyond
the circle could never be induced to see as distinctions
at all. "The manifesto spoken of in to-day's Daily
News," he wearily writes, "is not ours ; nor is it Social
Democratic, which is what we are, but Anarchist. We
consider them dangerous ; for you see they have no pro-

gramme but destruction, whereas we are reconstructive. People in general are quite ignorant of the whole matter."

At the beginning of September he wrote the first of those hymns of the new movement which were issued under the title of " Chants for Socialists." The fine and stirring verses, entitled "The Day is Coming," are included in the volume of " Poems by the Way." In sending a copy of the newly-written poem to Mrs. Burne-Jones he once more recurs to the objection, urged by her and by many of those whose sympathy he sought to enlist, that education was the primary necessity, and that it was hopeless to attempt to reconstruct society with the existing materials.

" As to the D. F., you need not be anxious about me. I went into the affair quite with my eyes open, and suspecting worse things of it than are likely to happen : for you understand I by no means suppose Hyndman or any of the leaders not to be in earnest, though I may not always agree with them. I naturally find it harder work to understand the subject of Socialism in detail now I am alongside it, and often get beaten in argument when I know all the same I am really in the right : but of course this only means more study. Every one who has thought over the matter must feel your dilemma about education ; but think of many not uneducated people that you know, and you will I am sure see that education will not cure people of the grossest social selfishness and tyranny unless Socialistic principles form part of it. Meantime I am sure it is right, whatever the apparent consequences may be, to stir up the lower classes (damn the word) to demand a higher standard of life for themselves, not merely for themselves or for the sake of the material comfort it will bring, but for the good of the whole world and the re-generation of the conscience of man: and this stirring up is part of the necessary education which must in good truth go before the reconstruction of society : but I repeat that without laying before people this reconstruction, our education will but breed tyrants and cowards, big, little and least, down to the smallest who can screw out money from standing by to see another man working for him.

"The one thing I want you to be clear about is that I *cannot help* acting in the matter, and associating myself with any body which has the root of the matter ; and you know, and it may ease your kind heart respecting me, that those who are in the thick of it, and trying to do something, are not likely to feel so much of the hope deferred which hangs about the cause as onlookers do."

In the same spirit, though from a somewhat different position, and in a rather more militant tone, he wrote about the same time to Mr. Horsfall:

"I have long felt sure that commercialism must be attacked at the root before we can be on the road for those improvements in life which you and I so much desire. A society which is founded on the system of *compelling* all well-to-do people to live on making the greatest possible profit out of the labour of others, must be wrong. For it means the perpetuating the division of society into civilized and uncivilized classes : I am far from being an anarchist, but even anarchy is better than this, which is in fact anarchy and despotism mixed : if there is no hope of conquering this—let us eat and drink, for to-morrow we die.

"Of course I do not discuss these matters with you or any person of good will in any bitterness of spirit : but there are people with whom it is hard to keep one's temper ; such as the philistine middle-class Radical ; who think, or pretend to, that now at last all is for the best in this best of all possible worlds."

"I am working at lectures and chintz-patterns hard," he writes a fortnight later; "perhaps poems will come too." But this was hardly meant seriously, or if it was, represented a momentary lapse from the tension up to which he had worked himself, and which his new colleagues naturally took no pains to relieve. At the end of October Mr. Charles Rowley, who was then still personally unknown to him, though it only needed a first meeting to make them friends, had written to ask him to come to Manchester and give a Sunday lecture to the Ancoats Brotherhood. Morris's reply was prompt and straight:

> "Kelmscott House,
>   "Oct. 25th, 1883.
>
> "My dear Sir,
>   "I have only one subject to lecture on, the relation of Art to Labour: also I am an open and declared Socialist, or to be more specific, Collectivist, and whatever I say would be coloured by my opinions on these matters: if you think under these circumstances a lecture from me would come within the scope of your scheme, and be acceptable as an expression of opinions for which of course you would not be responsible, I should be very happy to be one of those who lecture to you.
>   "I am, dear Sir,
>   "Yours faithfully,
>   "WILLIAM MORRIS."

Mr. Rowley was not frightened by this reply: and the lecture which Morris gave was the first of many that he delivered in the New Islington Hall at Ancoats, and the beginning of an intimate cordiality and affection between the two men.

The manifesto of the Democratic Federation, issued in June and signed by Morris together with the rest of the

Executive Committee, had gone far in advance of anything that was in his mind, or in the minds of most of his colleagues, when he had joined it at the beginning of the year.   For the rapid development of doctrine there were several causes, any of them sufficient.   In an association which is itself formed by the detachment of the Extreme Left (to use the convenient French term) of a great party, the inevitable tendency is to become more and more extremist.   Waverers relapse on to the main body, and the control of the movement passes more and more into the hands of enthusiasts.   Such a situation gives a terrible power to logic.   Friends and enemies alike are quick to detect and eager to pounce upon inconsistencies; and in human affairs, inconsistency can only be avoided by falling back from compromise after compromise to the extreme limit of abstract theory.   Nor does the evil stop here.   As an abstract logic becomes more and more the dominant guiding force, the refined distinctions to which logic lends itself become articles of faith over which divisions are multiplied.   The more a party holding extreme doctrines defines the consequences of its principles; the more it purges itself of the ambiguities of an unformulated creed and the inconsistencies of moderate opinion: the more violent does the conflict become among the remnant left, on points that have only arisen in the course of argument.   The path between right-hand heats and extremes and left-hand defections is always narrowing.   In the seventeenth chapter of " The Heart of Midlothian " the master-hand of Scott has drawn an imperishable picture of the disintegration that ensues, and the loss, first of moving power on the world without, and then of vital energy within, that has overtaken so many kingdoms of the Saints.   The world takes its own way, regardless of logic, impatient of theory, merciless to failure: nor is it until the years have heaped

their dust over the asperities of the conflict that understanding comes with pity. Yet in the simple faith of such
a despised remnant, and not in the facile contempt of the
majority, may have lain that seed of spiritual ardour which
has kept the soul of man alive.

On the same day that Morris declared himself an open
Socialist with only one subject on which he could give
public utterance, he wrote to Mr. Horsfall in reply to a
letter of anxious and amazed questioning:

" In few words what I have to say about the manifesto
is, that, though I may not like the taste of some of the
wording, I do agree with the substance of it (or I should
not have signed it). This does not however prevent me
from agreeing with you that the rich do not act as they
do in the matter from malice. Nevertheless their position (as a class) forces them to 'strive' (unconsciously
most often I know) to keep the working men in ignorance of their rights and their power.

" Where I think I differ from you of the means where-
by revolution may be attained is this: if I do not mis-
represent your views, you think that *individuals* of good
will belonging to all classes can, if they be numerous and
strenuous enough, bring about the change: I on the contrary think that the basis of all change must be, as it has
always been, the antagonism of classes: I mean that
though here and there a few men of the upper and middle
classes, moved by their conscience and insight, may and
doubtless will throw in their lot with the working classes,
the upper and middle classes as a body will by the very
nature of their existence, and like a plant grows, resist
the abolition of classes: neither do I think that any
amelioration of the condition of the poor on the only
lines which the rich *can* go upon will advance us on the
road; save that it will put more power into the hands of
the lower class and so strengthen both their discontent

and their means of showing it : for I do not believe that starvelings can bring about a revolution. I do not say that there is not a terrible side to this : but how can it be otherwise ? Commercialism, competition, has sown the wind recklessly, and must reap the whirlwind : it has created the proletariat for its own interest, and its creation will and must destroy it : there is no other force which can do so. For my part I have never under-rated the power of the middle classes, whom, in spite of their individual good nature and banality, I look upon as a most terrible and implacable force : so terrible that I think it not unlikely that their resistance to inevitable change may, if the beginnings of change are too long delayed, ruin all civilization for a time. Meantime I must tell you that among the discontented, discontent unlighted by hope is in many places taking the form of a passionate desire for mere anarchy, so that it becomes a pressing duty for those who, not believing in the stability of the present system, have any hopes for the future, to lay before the world those hopes founded on *constructive* revolution."

An opportunity soon occurred for him to announce his attitude more dramatically to a larger audience. In November he had been invited to Oxford to give an address to the Russell Club, a society of Liberal undergraduates with a tendency towards the newer developments of Radicalism. Social questions, under the stimulating influence of Arnold Toynbee and his disciples, had at that time risen to the first place among the intellectual interests of younger Oxford. Toynbee's recent death had only given a fresh impulse to the movement. The so-called University Settlements were in the air. Social reform was the current subject of discussion in College debating societies and filled the pages of the Oxford magazines. Mr. Henry George had lectured at Oxford in support of his scheme of land nationalization, and had been received with a studied incivility which aroused a strong reaction in his favour.

The authorities, always willing to follow the lead of any strong undergraduate feeling, and not averse from allowing the new movement to spend its force in vague discussion, threw no obstacles in the way of the meeting. When Morris accepted the invitation of the Russell Club, the hall of University College was lent to them for the evening. The title announced for the address was "Democracy and Art"; two subjects not obviously explosive when brought into contact. The College hall was crowded, and all went smoothly till at the end of his address Morris boldly passed from theoretic ground, announced that he spoke as the agent of a Socialist body, and appealed to his audience to join it. The platform sat aghast; and the Master of University at once rose to explain that the College when they lent their hall had not known that Mr. Morris was the agent of any Socialist propaganda, and that all they had meant was to give to an eminent man the opportunity of expressing his opinions on art under a democracy : "a subject with which" (so the report of the meeting gives Dr. Bright's words) "he was unusually well acquainted, and a knowledge of which, in the existing condition of social questions in England, was a most desirable part of the education of every young man."

For the misunderstanding, if misunderstanding there were, Morris at all events was in no way to blame. He had taken the utmost pains to explain his position clearly before he came. To Faulkner, through whom as one of the Fellows the request for the use of the College hall had been made, he had written as follows on the 23rd of October. The original proposal had been that he and Mr. Hyndman should both speak; but Mr. Hyndman's doctrines were known to be revolutionary, and the methods he advocated were believed to be violent.

"As to Hyndman lecturing in your hall I would ask you to lay before the Master the fact that I am quite as much a Socialist as he is; that I am an officer of the same Association, and am distinctly going to lecture as a delegate from it: also that if the subject is to be stirred at all, it is surely worth while to listen to a man who is capable of giving a definite exposition of the whole doctrine. I am rather anxious about this matter, as if Hyndman is shut up I shall feel rather like a fool, and as if I were there on false pretences. For the rest, Hyndman is an educated man if Trin: Coll: Camb: is capable of educating (which is doubtful), and though he is perhaps not as polite as the Devil is usually said to be, is at least politer than I am : neither has he horns and hoofs, as I am prepared to swear: neither (as a Secretary of the S. P. A. B.) will I allow him to blow up any *old* building in Oxford. Would it be any good my writing to the Master stating these facts in conventional language; and also stating what seems to me to be true, that people do seem just at this moment to want to know something about Socialism? though to tell you the truth I misdoubt me that that may be but a passing wind of fashion."

"We must leave the matter in the hands of the Russell Club," he wrote to Faulkner again on the 25th; "I have undertaken to give my lecture and will not back out of it, but will deliver it where they think advisable. Please to thank the Master on my behalf when you see him; I don't doubt he has done his best for us."

Notwithstanding these repeated explanations, the College authorities appear to have been possessed by the fixed idea that Morris, as a man of means and a man of letters, could not be a Socialist in the same sense as his colleagues; and they persisted, with a sort of obstinate innocence, in believing that his address would be confined to generalities which could do no harm. When they found that he had really meant what he said, their feeling was one which approached consternation. The meeting had, at all events, a success of scandal, and henceforth Morris was widely known as a declared Socialist.

In spite of all his labours as a peacemaker the year ended gloomily for him. The party had got rid of its moderate members. It had modified its name to that of the Social Democratic Federation in order to make its position as a Socialist body quite clear. It was about to start a weekly newspaper for the purpose of spreading its doctrines among the working classes. But internally it was already a distracted chaos. "I went to Merton for a little time on Thursday," says Morris's last letter of the year, "and found all well there. Now I'm off to see Fitzgerald (that's our editor) about ' Justice,' the prospects of which I am not sanguine over. The fact is, we really want a good steady business man over the D. F. affairs: a man who could give up most of his time and who wouldn't be excitable. For lack of it I fear we shall fall to pieces. I am much worried by the whole business just now : but in any case I shall try to save something out of the fire and keep a few together."

Throughout 1884 this desperate work of mingled proselytizing and patching up went on unceasingly. In January " he can talk about little else, and will brook no opposition." For a time there was almost a breach between him and several of his older friends. " I was rather disconcerted," one of them has recorded, "when I found that an honest objection to Bulgarian atrocities had been held to be one and the same thing as sympathy with Karl Marx, and that Morris took it for granted that I should be ready for enrolment." Just at present Morris had quite lost his capacity for good-humoured argument.

"I have a dim recollection," says Mr. William De Morgan, "of a discussion on Socialism which ended in a scheme for the complete reconstruction of society exactly as it is now, so as to meet the views of both revolutionaries and Conservatives: however, this was in the earlier days of Socialism—as he got more engrossed in the subject, this sort of chat became less and less possible."

The first number of the weekly paper of the Democratic Federation, "Justice: the Organ of the Social Democracy," appeared on the 9th of January. Besides practically paying out of his own pocket for the weekly deficit in its balance sheet, Morris contributed articles to one-half of the numbers which appeared up to the end of December. These contributions included three more of the "Chants for Socialists," and one brief article on that year's exhibition of the Royal Academy, expanded by him in a longer paper which was published in the July number of the secularist magazine "To-day." Like the single piece of literary criticism he had printed twenty-eight years earlier, this single piece of art criticism is more interesting as a fragment of unstudied autobiography than from its remarks on the special works singled out for praise or blame. A few sentences from it are worth quoting as summing up in brief and incisive words the view he held, and had held all his life, of the function and excellence of the painter's art.

"In considering such an exhibition it is necessary to have a clear idea of what the aims of a painter should be. Something like this, I think, will embrace them all: 1st. The embodiment in art of some vision which has forced itself on the artist's brain. 2nd. The creation of some lovely combination of colour and form. 3rd. The setting forth a faithful portraiture of some beautiful, characteristic, or historical place, or of some living person worthy to be so portrayed ; in either case so as to be easily recognizable by a careless observer, and yet to have a reserve of more intimate facts for a careful one. 4th. Mastery over material; the production of a finished and workmanlike piece, as perfect in all ways as the kind of work admits of.

"Success in any of the three first of these aims, *together with the last*, will give a picture existence as a work of art. Most pictures that impress us seriously have achieved success in more than one of the three joined to the fourth, while great works of art have all the four qualities united, yet in due subordination to the master one of them, whichever it may be, which produces the greatest impression on us; this subordination is what is meant by the word ' style.'

"Skill of execution is the first thing we must seek for, since without it a picture is incapable of expressing anything, is a failure and not a picture. Well, there are signs here and there on the walls of the Academy of skill of a certain kind, but what does it amount to? does it give us any reasonable hope of establishing by our present method of artistic life a workmanlike traditional skill, continuous and progressive, so that while there may be hope for a man of genius for pushing forward the standard of excellence, no one, be he of genius or not, need waste half the energies of his life in half-fruitless individual experiments, the results of which he cannot pass on to others? What signs are there of collective skill, the skill of the school, which nurses moderate talent and sets genius free? Scanty signs indeed: at best a plausible appearance of workmanlike execution, a low kind of skill which manages to get through the job, but in so dull and joyless a way that one's eye almost refuses to rest upon the canvas, or one's brain to take in any idea it may strive to express. That is all, I fear, that can claim to represent anything like traditional workmanlike skill. What other skill of execution is visible is chiefly, almost entirely, an amateur-like cleverness, experimental, uncertain, never successful in accomplishing a real work, in expressing a fact or an imagination simply and straightforwardly, but often enough succeeding in thrusting itself forward and attracting attention to itself as something dashing, clever, and—useless; the end, not the means. Of this kind of skill there is a good deal; and to speak plainly it is on this quality, such as it is, that most of the pictures must rest their claim to attention."

Lecturing, in and out of London, had now become his most serious occupation. At Manchester he mournfully notes that "the workmen seem on the whole to identify themselves with the middle classes." Elsewhere "there was a funny old ex-Chartist present, an old man of seventy; he said it made him feel twenty years younger." At Edinburgh "a very good audience, and we fished two additional members, not much you will say, but things go slowly." Bradford, Leeds, Blackburn, Leicester, Glasgow, were among the other provincial centres where he gave these addresses. " I am in a hurry, as I always am now," is one unusual, and coming from him, even pathetic sentence in a letter. In March, writing to Faulkner about the formation of a branch of the Federation at Oxford, he expresses in a few strong words the uncompromising attitude he had taken up towards those who sympathized and hesitated, or whose tenets did not wholly coincide with his own. A number of liberal Churchmen—most of them belonging to the advanced High Church party in matters of ritual and doctrine— had once more taken up the Christian Socialism of Maurice and Kingsley. " Meantime," he comments, " the Christian *Church* has always declared against Socialism; its mainstays must always be property and authority. A worthy Irish Catholic member of the S. D. F. resigned on those grounds when we declared for Socialism. Of course as long as people are ignorant, compromise *plus* sentiment always looks better to them than the real article."

In April the weekly evening at Burne-Jones's house, which had been the habit of so many years, finally ceased, crowded out by the multiplicity of new engagements. The one gleam of real pleasure that the year brought him was a reconciliation, of which one of his visits to Manchester was the immediate occasion, with Madox Brown. "You are aware," he wrote of it to Mr. Rowley, "that there has been a cloud between him and me, and I am more than rejoiced it should be cleared off in such a pleasant way by my old friend himself, for whom I have always had the greatest respect and affection."

A Hammersmith Branch of the Democratic Federation had been formed in June in order to organize work among the labouring population of the district. The manifesto which it issued was written by Morris. It is a striking instance of the belief which he then undoubtedly held, and from which it took long time and hard teaching to remove him completely, that the re-organization of society which he advocated was immediately practicable, and that it had only to be effected to make all the misery of the world cease. "There is now a constant war," runs this leaflet, "between Capital, or the rich men who make profits out of work without working themselves, and Labour, or the poor men who produce everything and have no more share in what they produce than is necessary to keep them alive. While the rich enslave the poor, they themselves are not happy, and are always trying to ruin each other. Socialism will end this war by abolishing classes: this change will get rid of bad housing, under-feeding, over-work, and ignorance."

Such were the sweeping promises then held out by the Federation to a working class whom experience had made deeply incredulous of all promises, or of any great and sudden change in the existing order of the world.

At the great Franchise meeting in Hyde Park on the 21st of July Morris was one of the small knot of Socialists who tried to convert the enthusiasm of the occasion to their own uses, with little obvious success. In the main they were unnoticed and swallowed up in the vast crowd. They had provided themselves with a little cart with a red flag, from which they distributed their manifesto and tried to sell their newspaper. "We found it easy work getting rid of the gratis literature," he wrote next day, "but hard to sell anything." The attempts at speaking from the mound of the reservoir in the Park were little more successful. A contemptuous reference by one of the speakers to John Bright raised a storm of hooting in the audience; the crowd began to push and sway, and the ring of friends round the banner was broken up and dispersed. There was no actual violence; a suggestion that the unpopular speaker should be put in the Serpentine was not taken up: but the day was over as far as any attempt to influence the crowd was concerned.

By this time the internal jealousies and divergent aims of the Federation were leading up to a crisis that could not be much longer delayed. Its leaders profoundly mistrusted one another, and personalities and accusations of intrigue and duplicity were flying thick. The peace-maker's task was plainly hopeless.

"The time which I have foreseen from the first," Morris writes in August, "seems to be upon us, and I don't see how I can avoid taking my share in the internal conflict which seems likely to rend the D. F. into two or more. More than two or three of us distrust

Hyndman thoroughly: I have done my best to trust him, but cannot any longer. Practically it comes to a contest between him and me. If I don't come up to the scratch I shall disappoint those who I believe have their hearts in the cause and are quite disinterested, many of them simple and worthy people. I don't think intrigue or ambition are amongst my many faults; but here I am driven to thrusting myself forward and making a party within a party. However I say I foresaw it, and 'tis part of the day's work, but I begin to wish the day were over."

The affair dragged on for several months more. The mere idea of breaking up the party did not distress Morris deeply: "half-a-dozen people," he says, "who agree and are friends, that is, can trust each other, are worth a hundred jealous squabblers." But he was heartily annoyed and, to say the truth, frightened, at the prominence into which he found himself being pushed by his faction.

" My habits are quiet and studious," he wrote, with an almost pathetic self-depreciation, to a colleague who was urging on him the duty of leadership, " and if I am too much worried with ' politics,' *i.e.*, intrigue, I shall be no use to the cause as a writer. All this shows, you will say, a weak man : that is true, but I must be taken as I am, not as I am not." With a great effort of self-effacement he had placed himself at their orders, in the indistinct hope that he might elude responsibility by simply doing loyally what he was told : now to his dismay he found himself called upon to become a leader, and responsible not only for his own action, but for the continued existence of his party.

What brought the quarrel to a point was a jealousy so trivial that it can hardly now move anything beyond a faint smile. A small knot of Socialists in Edinburgh (the same to which two further recruits were added by Morris's visit and address that autumn) had been organized into a society by Mr. Scheu, whose business had taken him there during the summer. To give it a more imposing air, and also to conciliate the national susceptibility, it was not made a branch of the English Democratic Federation, but was started as a separate organization under the name of the Scottish Land and Labour League. The fat was in the fire at once. Mr. Hyndman called for the instant dissolution of the newly-founded league in the name of the Federation One and Indivisible. " Discord has arisen in this Council," ran the reply of his opponents, " owing to the attempt to substitute arbitrary rule therein for fraternal Co-operation, contrary to the principles of Socialism." The scenes of the Convention of the Year Two were repeated on a microscopic scale. Hyndman was denounced as a tyrant; Scheu was denounced in turn as certainly a foreigner, and probably a traitor in the pay of the police. Accusations were flung back and forward of underhand intrigue, of deliberately wrecking the work of colleagues, of being bribed by capitalist gold. The extreme men on both sides gave the impression that, if it had been possible, they would cheerfully have sent their opponents to the guillotine. Things were finally fought out at a full meeting of the Council of the Federation held in London at Christmas. The details and the result may be given in Morris's own words.

" My merry Christmas "—this is written on Christmas Eve—" is like to be enlivened by a scene or two at all events. Last night came off to the full as damned as I expected, which seldom happens: and the worst of it is that the debate is adjourned till Saturday, as we couldn't sit any later than midnight yesterday. It was a piece of degradation, only illumined by Scheu's really noble and

skilful defence of his character against Hyndman: all
the rest was a mere exposition of backbiting, mixed
with some melancholy and to me touching examples of
faith. However, Saturday I *will* be out of it. Our lot
agreed beforehand, being I must say moved by me, that
it is not worth fighting for the name of the S. D. F. and
the sad remains of ' Justice ' at the expense of a month
or two of wrangling: so as Hyndman considers the S.
D. F. his property, let him take it and make what he
can of it, and try if he can really make up a bogie of it
to frighten the Government, which I really think is about
all his scheme; and we will begin again quite clean-
handed to try the more humdrum method of quiet propaganda, and start a new paper of our own. The worst
of the new body, as far as I am concerned, is that for the
present at least I have to be editor of the paper, which
I by no means bargained for, but it seems nobody else
will do.

" I went to Chesterfield and saw Carpenter on Monday, and found him very sympathetic and sensible at the
same time. I listened with longing heart to his account
of his patch of ground, seven acres: he says that he and
his fellow can almost live on it: they grow their own
wheat, and send flowers and fruit to Chesterfield and
Sheffield markets: all that sounds very agreeable to me.
It seems to me that the real way to enjoy life is to accept
all its necessary ordinary details and turn them into
pleasures by taking interest in them : whereas modern
civilization huddles them out of the way, has them done
in a venal and slovenly manner till they become real
drudgery which people can't help trying to avoid.
Whiles I think, as in a vision, of a decent community as
a refuge from our mean squabbles and corrupt society;
but I am too old now, even if it were not dastardly to
desert."

On the 28th he resumes, writing from Merton Abbey: "Saturday evening did see the end. We began at 6 and ended at 10.30. I don't think it would interest you to go through the affair in detail, and to say the truth I am so sick of it that I don't think I could write it all down. There was a good deal of speaking, mostly on their side, for Hyndman had brought up supporters, who spouted away without in the least understanding what the quarrel was about. It finished by H. making a long and clever and lawyer-like speech: all of which, as in the House of Commons, might just as well have been left out, as either side had made up their minds how to vote from the first. Accordingly we voted, and the result was as expected, ten to eight, majority of two on our side. Whereon I got up and after a word or two of defence of my honour, honesty, and all that, which had been somewhat torn ragged in the debate, I read our resignation from the paper prepared thereto, and we solemnly walked out. This seemed to produce what penny-a-liners call 'a revulsion of feeling,' and most of the other side came round me and assured me that they had the best opinion of me and didn't mean all those hard things: poor little Williams cried heartily and took a most affectionate farewell of us. Of course we did right to resign; the alternative would have been a general meeting, and after a month's squabble for the amusement of the rest of the world that cared to notice us, would have landed us first in deadlock and ultimately where we are now, two separate bodies. This morning I hired very humble quarters for the Socialist League, and authorized the purchase of the due amount of Windsor chairs and a kitchen table: so there I am really once more like a young bear with all my troubles before me. We meet to inaugurate the League tomorrow evening. There now, I really don't think I have strength to say anything more about the matter just now. I find my room here and a view of the winter garden, with the men spreading some pieces of chintz on the bleaching ground, somewhat of a consolation. But I promise myself to work as hard as I can in the new body, which I think will be but a small one for some time to come."

CHAPTER XVI

"I CANNOT yet forgo the hope," Morris had written in July, 1884, when the disruption of the Democratic Federation was already looming ahead, " of our forming a Socialist *party* which shall begin to act in our own time, instead of a mere theoretical association in a private room with no hope but that of gradually permeating cultivated people with our aspirations." After the first spasm of disheartened disgust at the break-up of December was over, he was not disinclined to set to work again to form such a party out of what he believed was a thoroughly loyal remnant. To this task he now set himself in fresh courage and with even higher hope. The conflict had made him examine his own ground more carefully: he was more satisfied than ever of the truth of his principles, and of the reasonableness of his position. But the prominence now forced upon him as a leader at once exposed him to a redoubled storm of misrepresentation and obloquy. Socialism had once been regarded by ordinary middle-class opinion as a thing that went on abroad. When there was no longer any doubt that it had reached England, it was still looked on for a time as a silly or perhaps even an interesting craze. But now it had roused a genuine fear among a large body of people. The attitude of Gallio was passing away, and a strong feeling arising in its place which regarded the new Gospel, in the words applied by the Rome of Nero to the not wholly dissimilar doctrine of the early Christian Church, as a destructive superstition which drew upon itself the natural hatred of the human race.

But this was not all. In the curious imbroglio into which politics were then drifting, the name, and some at least of the doctrines, of Socialism had been seized by various parties as weapons of attack and defence. The famous speech in which Mr. Chamberlain laid down the doctrine of "ransom" was delivered a few days after the foundation of the Socialist League. On the part of both the Radical and the Tory-Democratic wings of the two great political parties there was a tendency to believe that Socialism in some sense or another was a real force, and a desire to attach that force and use it for all it was worth. Overtures were made from both sides by persons who might fairly be regarded as responsible politicians. Attacked by some and courted by others, the Socialist party became an object of widespread and increasing interest. It was enough to upset many Socialists who were not old hands in politics, and make them believe that a great movement of public opinion was about to take place towards Socialism.

On Morris personally the attack was a double one. It consisted on the one hand in renewing, with additional zest and less attention to ordinary manners, the familiar sneers at the strange figure of a poet-upholsterer; and on the other, of denouncing him for inconsistency or hypocrisy in being a Socialist who was also a capitalist manufacturer. In his first public utterance after the formation of the Socialist League, he had expressed his hope and his aim in words of studied moderation. He spoke of the social re-organization which he advocated as something not only desirable in itself, but involving a high conception of duty, and containing in it the elements of solid permanence. " When the change comes, it will embrace the whole of society, and there will be no discontented class left to form the elements of a fresh revolution. It is necessary that the movement should not be ignorant, but intelligent. What I should like to have now far more than anything else, would be a body of able, high-minded, competent men who should act as instructors. I should look to those men to preach what Socialism really is—not a change for the sake of change, but a change involving the very noblest ideal of human life and duty: a life in which every human being should find unrestricted scope for his best powers and faculties." The Saturday Review, with characteristic suavity, seized this occasion to point its finger at " this spectacle of the intellectual disaster of the intelligence of a man who could once write ' The Earthly Paradise ' and can now formulate these two propositions about the disappearance of all discontented classes and the change involving a life in which every human being finds unrestricted scope for his best powers and faculties." This last phrase, indeed, to judge by the number of times it recurs in the article, was found humorous to an uncommon degree. That such a life should be conceived of as possible, that any attempt should be made to realize it, seemed quite preposterous to the critic and to the large body of opinion which he represented. The laws of nature were invoked to sustain the conclusion that a state of things in which the larger number of the human race were permanently poor, ignorant, and brutal was certainly necessary and in all probability desirable.

The inconsistency of Morris's own position as a capitalist employer of labour was a matter on which he might more reasonably be challenged by a criticism which was not either purposely unfair or obviously unintelligent. It had formed the ground of the earliest attacks made on

him when the Oxford address of November, 1883, had
excited general attention to the case. To an attack
made by an anonymous correspondent in the Standard,
Morris had then replied in simple and dignified words,
which come near the truth of the matter, though, as
Morris himself felt, they require further definition.

"I think I may assume," he then wrote, "that your
correspondent had no wish to cast any personal imputation on my motives, but wished to call attention to the
position of those who, like myself, are well-to-do employers of labour (as I am) and hold Socialist views.

"I freely admit that this position is a false one, but it
seems to me that its falseness is first felt by an honest
man, not when he begins to express his opinions openly,
and to further openly the spread of Socialism, but when
his conscience is first pricked by a sense of the injustice
and stupidity of the present state of society. Your correspondent implies that, to be consistent, we should at
once cast aside our position of capitalists, and take rank
with the proletariat ; but he must excuse my saying that
he knows very well that we are not able to do so ; that
the most we can do is to palliate, as far as we can, the
evils of the unjust system which we are forced to sustain; that we are but minute links in the immense chain
of the terrible organization of competitive commerce,
and that only the complete unriveting of that chain
will really free us. It is this very sense of the helplessness of our individual efforts which arms us against our
own class, which compels us to take an active part in an
agitation which, if it be successful, will deprive us of our
capitalist position."

"I have been living," he writes a few days afterwards
from Merton Abbey, "in a sort of storm of newspaper
brickbats, to some of which I had to reply : of course I
don't mind a bit, nor even think the attack unfair. My

own men here are very sympathetic, which pleases me hugely; and I find we shall get on much better for my having spoken my mind about things: seven of them would insist on joining the Democratic Federation, though I preached to them the necessity of really understanding it all."

What is quite certain is that the reproach of inconsistency was never made against Morris by any of his own workmen. The attacks on this score which he had to meet came in the main from educated people, who attached their own meaning to the term Socialism, and were confident in their condemnation of doctrines the purport of which they had never taken pains to ascertain. The fixed idea which most of them had was that Socialism meant the redistribution of individual property in equal shares. From this point, however, they pursued divergent lines of argument. Some contented themselves with remarking that if individual property were divided equally to-day, inequality would have begun to reinstate itself before to-morrow. Others argued that any employer who believed in the principles of Socialism could carry them out in practice by sharing the profits of his business equally among himself and each of his workmen. But among the latter class of objectors were some for whose good opinion Morris had a respect; and it was implicitly in answer to them that he drew up, in June, 1884, a memorandum going into the matter, not only on the principle, but in detailed figures.

The business was then organized as follows. Morris himself, George Wardle his chief manager, and four other sub-managers or heads of departments, shared directly in the profits of the business. Two others, the colour-mixer and the foreman dyer, shared in them also, but indirectly, in the form of a bonus on the goods turned out. The rest of the staff were paid fixed wages; the greater number (including all the most efficient workmen) by the piece ; a smaller residuum, partly consisting of men who were getting past work on the one hand, or on the other as yet imperfectly trained, by the hour. Both piece-workers and time-workers were paid on a scale somewhat over the ordinary market price of their labour. " Two or three people about the place," he adds, " are of no use to the business, and are kept on on the live-and-let-live principle, not a bad one I think as things go, in spite of the Charity Organization Society."

On an analysis of the figures, Morris found that if he gave up his own share of the profits, which, of course, included not merely the remuneration for his own labour as manager, designer, and artificer, but interest on the whole capitalized value of the business, by that time representing some £15,000, and took in lieu of it a foreman's or a highly-skilled workman's wages of £4 a week or £200 a year, there would be a sum divisible which would represent £16 a year, or about six shillings a week, for each of the workmen. " That would, I admit," he adds, " be a very nice thing for them ; but it would not alter the position of any one of them ; it would leave them still members of the working class, with all the disadvantages of that position. Further, if I were to die or be otherwise disabled, the business could not get any one to do my work for £200 a year, and would in short at once take back the extra £16 a year from the workman."

" I have left out," he goes on with admirable sincerity, "a matter which complicates the position, my family. We ought to be able to live on £4 a week, and if they were quite well and capable I think they ought not to grumble at living on the said £4, nor do I think they would." There are perhaps few families of the richer middle class to whom so splendid a compliment could be paid.

But what, the memorandum goes on, would be gained

by taking such action? A small knot of working people would be somewhat better off amidst the great ocean of economic slavery, but with what probable or necessary result? Like himself, the workmen were imprisoned in an existing social system. " If the manufacturer were to give up his gains to them, they would set to work to save, and would become, or try to become, small capitalists, and then large ones. In effect this is what mostly happens in those few factories where division of profits has been tried. Now, much as I want to see workmen escape from their slavish position, I don't at all want to see a few individuals more creep up out of their class into the middle class; this will only make the poor poorer still. And this effect of multiplying the capitalist class (every member of which is engaged in fierce private commercial war with his fellows) is the utmost that could result from even a large number of employers giving up their profits to their workmen. The men would not know how to spend their newly gained wealth. Even now there are at times artisans who receive very high wages, but their exceptional good luck has no influence over the general army of wage-earners, and they themselves have in consequence only two choices: the first, to rise out of their class as above; the second, to squander their high earnings and remain in the long run at the ordinary low standard of life of their brethren. The really desirable thing, that, being still workmen, they should rise in culture and refinement, they can only attain by their whole class rising."

But this, as things go, he continues, is impossible; because the competition for subsistence keeps the standard of life, taking labour all round, from rising seriously for any long period. Trades Unions have in England raised it, for a time, for skilled labour. But their effect can in the nature of things be only partial and temporary: for on the one hand the movement, not being an international one, allows other nations to undersell us; and on the other, it does not include the unskilled labourer, whose wage of subsistence finally determines the rate of the wages of labour all round, and who is scarcely in a better position than he was fifty years ago.

The choice, then, which lies before a capitalist, or before the hanger-on of the capitalist class known by the name of a professional man, whom reflection has turned into a convinced Socialist, is this.   Shall he ease his conscience by dropping a certain portion of the surplus value which reaches him, in order to bestow it in charity on a handful of workers (for it is but charity after all, since their claim is not on him personally, but on the class and system of which he is a mere unit)? or shall he, continuing his life under existing conditions, do his best, by expenditure of his money and his whole powers, to further a revolution of the basis of society?   If he can do both, let him do so, and make his conscience surer.   But if, as must generally be the case, he must choose between suffering some pangs of conscience and divesting himself of his power to further a great principle, "then, I think," Morris concludes, "he is right to choose the first."

It is true that there is a third alternative, that of complete individual renunciation, which, illogical as it may be, has often, as with the earliest Christians, with the mendicant friars of the great religious revival of the thirteenth century, and since then in many splendid isolated instances, affected mankind more powerfully through the imagination than they have ever been affected by arguments or enactments.   *If thou wilt be perfect, go, sell what thou hast, and give to the poor, and come, follow me.*   Such a course would have accorded with Morris's own early dreams at Oxford of a monastic life, lived by friends in common in the single pursuit of poverty and art.   But now it seemed to him to mean practically, though not formally, abandoning the principles for which Socialists contended, and giving up the struggle in a spirit not far removed from cowardice. "If these were ordinary times of peace, I might be contented amidst my discontent to settle down into an ascetic, such a man as I should respect even now. But I don't see the peace or feel it: on the contrary, fate or what not has forced me to feel war, and lays hands on me as a recruit: therefore do I find it not only lawful to my conscience, but even compulsory on it, to do what in times of peace would not perhaps be lawful, and certainly would not be compulsory. If I am wrong I am wrong, and there is an end of it. Whatever hope or life there is in me is staked on the success of the cause. Of course I don't mean to say that I necessarily expect to see much of it before I die, and yet something I hope to see."

This, then, was the conclusion to which Morris came as to what was right for him to do with his income as a capitalist. To distribute it among his own workmen would be to waste it; he could as little satisfy his conscience by wasting as by hoarding: his duty was to spend it; to devote it, as he devoted all else that belonged to him, to the furtherance of one great purpose.

How it could be so spent was sufficiently plain. The newly-founded Socialist League was practically without funds except so far as he supplied them. That it should spread its doctrines by means of a newspaper was taken for granted from the first, and preparations for bringing out the "Commonweal," the first number of which appeared at the beginning of February, were begun the first moment that the League was constituted. "I intend," he wrote on the 4th of January, "to turn it into a weekly if possible: but paying for 'Justice' has somewhat crippled me, and I shall have to find money for the other expenses of the League first."

The Manifesto of the Socialist League, which was printed at full length in the first number of the Commonweal, declares in uncompromising terms for a complete revolution in the basis of society. Co-operation, Nationalization of Land, State-Socialism which left the existing system of capital and wages still in operation, are reviewed and dismissed as equally useless with merely political movements such as constitutionalism or republicanism. The League is stated to have been founded on the 30th of December, 1884, and to have taken temporary offices at 27, Farringdon Street. Morris is named as having been appointed Treasurer of the League and Editor of its journal, the control of the journal, however, being in the hands of the Council. The twenty-three persons whose signatures, as members of the Provisional Council, are appended to the manifesto, were mainly members of the little group of Socialists, English and foreign, settled in London: but they included also an old veteran of the Chartist movement, a few members from the great manufacturing centres of Leeds and Glasgow, and among them all, the one friend who had followed Morris unfalteringly through all his life from the Oxford days till now, as member first of the Brotherhood, then of the Firm, and now finally of the League, Charles Faulkner.

The beginnings of the venture were not discouraging. "They have sold 5,000 and are in a second edition," Morris writes on the 10th of February: "I have written a poem for the next number, not bad I think." This poem, "The Message of the March Wind," which appeared in the March number, has touches in it of the natural magic which had filled his early poetry. It opened a series of poems, forming a more or less continuous narrative, which, under the title of "The Pilgrims of Hope," appeared at irregular intervals in the Commonweal for upwards of a year. With all its faults, this series of poems is perhaps the only contribution to the first year's issue of the Commonweal which appeals to a wide circle or has any permanent value as literature. It contains passages of extreme beauty : the two sections reprinted in "Poems by the Way" under the names of "Mother and Son" and "The Half of Life Gone" stand high among his finest work. But the narrative of which they form parts has much of the same weakness and unreality as his prose novel of fifteen years earlier : and like it, dwindles away and finally stops with the unfulfilled promise "To be Concluded" in July, 1886. Of his prose contributions, signed and unsigned, and ranging from carefully written leading articles down to brief notes hastily set down to fill up a column, there is little to say except that he no more than other men escaped the vices of journalism when he took to being a journalist.

Another visit to Oxford in February was more eventful than the one of fifteen months before, so far at least as the behaviour of the meeting went. The Clarendon Rooms had been refused for this meeting on account of the fear of disturbance, and it was held in the Music Room in Holywell. Opinion on both sides had stiffened ; and Faulkner had, two or three weeks before, for a speech he had made to a little Socialist meeting in Cowley, been stigmatized in the sedate columns of the Oxford Magazine as an alehouse anarchist. The social enthusiasm which had been so strong in 1883 was beginning to cool down among a fresh generation of undergraduates. But for the healthy young Tory Morris had always a lurking sympathy, and he writes the account of his experiences in the highest spirits.

" Wednesday I went to Oxford with the Avelings : we went by the early train, and all turned out well, and even amusing : we walked about Oxford a good deal,

and even with all the horrors done to it, it looks very
well and beautiful on such a bright afternoon as we had.
There were terrible threats about what the lads were going to do, which I didn't suppose would come to much :
we met, some of us, in University Common Room to
settle the meeting, and it seems the enemy sent in a spy,
which however we survived. Charley had asked a great
many very young persons to dinner, and their ingenuous
visages made me feel rather old. So to the meeting we
went, in a room in Holywell, which I daresay you have
forgotten : it used to be the room of the Architectural
Society when I was a boy, and is now a music room : it
is just opposite where Janey used to live—Lord, how old
I am ! Well, we had a fine lot of supporters, town and
gown both, who put on red ribbons and acted as stewards,
but the 'enemy' got in in some numbers, and prepared
for some enjoyment. Charley was in the chair and led
off well, and they heard him with only an average amount
of howling: you must understand that there were but
some 20 or 30 of those enemies, and perhaps 100
declared friends, with some 250 indifferents who really
came to listen to us ; the hall was quite full. I had to get
up when Charley sat down ; I was rather nervous before
I began, as it was my first long speech without book, but
the noise and life braced me up, and after all I knew my
subject, so I fired off my speech fairly well I think: if I
hadn't, our friends the enemy would have found it out
and chaffed me with all the mercilessness of boys. Of
course they howled and stamped at certain catchwords, and
our people cheered, so that it was very good fun. Aveling
came next : they had really listened to me, even the noisy
ones ; but it seems they had agreed that A. at any rate
should not be allowed to speak ; but he began very
cleverly and won their ingenuous hearts so that they
listened to him better than they did to me. Then came

question-time, and that was more than they could bear;
after two or three questions asked and answered, the joke
of the evening came off by one young gentleman letting
off a bottle of chemical which made a horrible stink, and
the respectables began to leave and both the fighting
[bodies] to draw nearer to the platform. Then by
Aveling's advice Charley, who was by the way getting
a bit nervous, broke off the meeting, and we 'got';
which I suppose was the best thing to do, as more horse-
play might have made what was serious enough ridiculous.
After all the best joke was what we heard next day, viz.,
that the disturbers were so angry with their ringleader
for not making a better job of it that they broke all his
windows that same night. I hope this piece of frankness
touches your hard heart as it did mine. We had some
serious talk at our inn after the meeting with the best
of the lads; and then some of them took us into New
College cloisters to see their loveliness under the moon."

From Mr. Edward Carpenter's house at Millthorpe
he writes on the 28th of April, on his way home from
giving Socialist addresses in Edinburgh and Glasgow:

" I have been getting on pretty well in Scotland, but
whether pock-pudding prejudice or not, I can't bring
myself to love that country, 'tis so raw-boned. But I
had my reward by the journey (the first time in daylight)
from Carlisle to Settle : 'tis true that the day was most
splendid, but at any rate 'tis the pick of all England for
beauty. I fared to feel as if I must live there, say somewhere near Kirkby Stephen, for a year or two before I
die : even the building there is not bad; necessitous and
rude, but looking like shelter and quiet. There is a
good deal of this lovely country; the railway goes right
up into the mountains among the sheepwalks : there was
a little snow lying in bights of the highest crags. I
needn't enlarge on an entry into the Yorkshire manfactur-

ing country after this; but I was so elated by the beauty we had passed through that I did not feel it as much as usual. I read a queer book called 'After London' coming down: I rather liked it: absurd hopes curled round my heart as I read it. I rather wish I were thirty years younger: I want to see the game played out."

"After London," the unfinished masterpiece of Richard Jefferies, was a book that Morris afterwards was never weary of praising. It put into definite shape, with a mingling of elusive romance and minute detail that was entirely after his heart, much that he had himself imagined; and he thought that it represented very closely what might really happen in a dispeopled England. The effect of the book is perhaps visible in another letter of the 13th of May:

"I am in low spirits about the prospects of our 'party,' if I can dignify a little knot of men by such a word. Scheu is, I fear, leaving London again, which is a great disappointment to me, but he must get work where he can. You see we are such a few, and hard as we work we don't seem to pick up people to take our places when we demit. All this you understand is only said about the petty skirmish of outposts, the fight of a corporal's guard, in which I am immediately concerned; I have more faith than a grain of mustard seed in the future history of 'civilization,' which I *know* now is doomed to destruction, and probably before very long: what a joy it is to think of! and how often it consoles me to think of barbarism once more flooding the world, and real feelings and passions, however rudimentary, taking the place of our wretched hypocrisies. With this thought in my mind all the history of the past is lighted up and lives again to me. I used really to despair once because I thought what the idiots of our day call progress would go on perfecting itself: happily I know now that all that will

have a sudden check—sudden in appearance I mean—
'as it was in the days of Noë.'"

On the 27th of May he writes again, giving in a few
touches a vivid picture of what the little meetings, over
which he was spending so much time and energy, were
really like.

"On Sunday I went a-preaching Stepney way. My
visit intensely depressed me, as these Eastward visits always do: the mere stretch of houses, the vast mass of
utter shabbiness and uneventfulness, sits upon one like
a nightmare: of course what slums there are one doesn't
see. You would perhaps have smiled at my congregation; some twenty people in a little room, as dirty as
convenient and stinking a good deal. It took the fire
out of my fine periods, I can tell you: it is a great drawback that I can't *talk* to them roughly and unaffectedly.
Also I would like to know what amount of real feeling
underlies their bombastic revolutionary talk when they
get to that. I don't seem to have got at them yet—
you see this great class gulf lies between us."

The numbers of the League grew only very slowly.
In July, when stock was taken of the progress made,
they only amounted to a little over two hundred all told,
over all the branches in both England and Scotland. But
they were working on hard in the hope of an ampler
harvest from some sudden movement of popular feeling.
In June they had taken new premises in Farringdon
Road, which included a printing office and a large lecture
room. The output of leaflets and pamphlets, as well as
their monthly journal, was carried on to the utmost limit
of their means; and it had been determined to turn the
Commonweal into a weekly paper as soon as sufficient
guarantee could be procured against the further loss of
money on it that was then certainly to be expected.
Morris himself, beyond his other work for the League,

had set on foot a branch at Hammersmith, to whose use
he gave up the large room where he had begun his carpet-
weaving. Sunday evening addresses were regularly given
there by himself or others of his colleagues; and as regularly on Saturday afternoons and Sunday mornings he
spoke at outdoor meetings in different parts of London.
At these, as a rule, knots of working men and casual
passers-by listened with a languid interest. But in September the action taken by the heads of the Metropolitan
Police with regard to an open air meeting in Limehouse
raised the Socialistic movement into increased notoriety,
and gave it the greatest access of popular support that it
had yet found.

A space in that part of London, at the corner of Dod
Street and Burdett Road, had long been in common use
for public gatherings and open-air speaking on all kinds
of subjects, especially on Sundays, when there was practically no traffic. The Social Democratic Federation and
the Socialist League had both held meetings there repeatedly. Of late there had been some friction with the
police, and notice had been given that the meetings must
be stopped. The joyful expectation of a disturbance drew
a crowd estimated at about a thousand people to the place
that Sunday. Against this crowd, which was quite determined not to be dispersed so long as there was the chance
of seeing any fun, the dozen or so of police who had been
drafted to the spot found themselves almost helpless.
Several ineffective attempts had been made to get at the
group of speakers who were on a drag in the middle of the
concourse, and the police, jeered at and hustled by an unsympathetic crowd, began to lose their tempers. Meanwhile one o'clock struck; and the signal of the opening of
the public houses caused the greater part of the crowd to
disperse. Hot, weary, and angry, and not wishing to
think that all their unpleasant morning's work had ef-

fected nothing, the policemen charged among the remnant, knocked down two banners, and marched eight men off to the nearest police station, where they were charged with obstructing a public thoroughfare and resisting the police in the execution of their duty.

When the prisoners were brought up at the Thames Police Court next morning, there was the usual amount of confused and contradictory evidence given as to the amount of obstruction that had really happened, and the degree of violence used by or against the police. Finally, after some rather irrelevant remarks about the nationality of the prisoners and the contents of the bills announcing the meeting, Mr. Saunders, the sitting magistrate, sentenced one of them to two months' hard labour and imposed fines all round on the rest. What is known as a scene in court followed; there were loud hisses and cries of " Shame !" In these Morris, who was in court with other members of the League, joined : there was some hustling before order was restored, and he was arrested and charged on the spot with disorderly conduct and striking a policeman. To this charge he gave a direct negative. No evidence was called on either side, but the following curious dialogue ensued.

Mr. Saunders : What are you ?

Prisoner : I am an artist and a literary man, pretty well known, I think, throughout Europe.

Mr. Saunders : I suppose you did not intend to do this ?

Prisoner : I never struck him at all.

Mr. Saunders : Well, I will let you go.

Prisoner : But I have not done anything.

Mr. Saunders : Well, you can stay if you like.

Prisoner : I don't want to stay.

He was accordingly discharged, and left the court. It was the one instance in which he was stung into asserting his own reputation in public, and the incautious words were long remembered against him.   But the whole proceedings were a substantial victory for him and his party.   The right of free speech is of all the privileges of citizenship the one which the ordinary Englishman guards most jealously : and interference with that right, when it seems to encroach on customary limits, is fiercely resented by the most orderly classes.   More especially is this so in London, where the police are under the direct control of the Imperial Executive, and where any suspicion that they have been used by the party in power to suppress hostile criticism is enough to shake the strongest Government.   The London Radicals rallied to the defence of a threatened privilege, and letters of protest poured into the newspapers from opponents as well as friends of Socialism.   Many people who took no interest in politics at all were indignant: "already," one of them wrote to the Daily News, " police interference has caused more obstruction and disturbance than twelve months of Socialistic lecturing."   A weak Conservative Government was then in office : a General Election was imminent : and angry charges were made that this attack on a Socialist meeting was an insidious attempt to prepare the way for interference with open-air Parliamentary meetings.   The Socialist League rose with a bound to something like popularity.   The following Sunday a procession of many thousands of people, organized by the East London United Radical Club, held a meeting on the forbidden spot (the few policemen present, under fresh instructions, not attempting to interfere), and then dispersed in a quiet orderly way, good-tempered with victory.   "All goes well," Morris wrote : "we Socialists have suddenly become popular, and your humble servant could hardly have received more sympathy if he had been racked by Mr. Saunders.   All this has its absurd, and even humiliating side, but it is encouraging to see that people are shocked at unfairness and persecution of mere opinion, as I really think they are."

Unfortunately for the prospects of the League, the ground thus gained was soon lost by the old trouble of ill-assorted colleagues and internal jealousies. Morris himself, who had been working and travelling much beyond his strength, was laid up immediately afterwards for a month or six weeks with the severest attack of gout he had yet had, and in his absence the others fell to quarrelling with one another. On the 31st of October, while still completely crippled by his illness, he wrote to Mrs. Burne-Jones:

" Here I am still more or less on my back, though I am getting better; I have not had any very bad pain, but have been so dead lame that till yesterday it has been a month of wheeling me in on a sofa from my room to the dining-room. I think I was much like this at Venice, only not so lame. There, enough of symptoms. It has been beautiful weather here till to-day, and I am glad of that for your holidays' sake: also I have enjoyed it myself: it was quite a luxury to lie here in the morning and let the sun creep over me and watch the clouds. I am afraid that when I get about again I shall find myself very lazy; I have picked up terrible habits of novel-reading and doing nothing this spell. I don't think it comes from my knocking about to meetings and the like, but rather from incaution as to diet, which I really must look after. You see, having joined a movement, I must do what I can while I last, that is a matter of duty. Besides, in spite of all the self-denying ordinances of us semi-anarchists, I grieve to have to say that some sort of leadership is required, and that in our section I unfortunately supply that want; it seems I was missed last Monday, and stupid quarrels about nothing took place,

which it was thought I could have stopped. All this
work I have pulled upon my own head, and though in
detail much of it is repulsive to the last degree, I still
hold that I did not do so without due consideration.
Anyhow, it seems to me that I can be of use, therefore
I am impelled to make myself useful.

"It is true, as I think I have said before, that I have
no great confidence in the stability of our party : but in
the stability of the movement I have every confidence;
and this I have always said to myself, that on the morrow
of the League breaking up I and some half-dozen must
directly begin a new organization ; and I believe we
should do so.

" You see, my dear, I can't help it. The ideas which
have taken hold of me will not let me rest : nor can I
see anything else worth thinking of. How can it be
otherwise, when to me society, which to many seems an
orderly arrangement for allowing decent people to get
through their lives creditably and with some pleasure,
seems mere cannibalism ; nay worse, (for there might be
hope in that,) is grown so corrupt, so steeped in hypocrisy and lies, that one turns from one stratum of it to
another with hopeless loathing. One must turn to hope,
and only in one direction do I see it—on the road to
Revolution : everything else is gone now. And now at
last when the corruption of society seems complete, there
is arising a definite conception of the new order, with its
demands in some sort formulated. In the details of that
I do not myself feel any great confidence, but that they
have taken so much form is hopeful, because unless the
new is near to the birth, however rotten the old may be,
rebellion against it is mere hopeless grumbling and rail-
ing, such as you used to reproach me with.

" Meantime what a little ruffles me is this, that if I
do a little fail in my duty some of my friends will praise

me for failing instead of blaming me. I have a pile of worry about the party ahead of me when I am about again, which must excuse me for dwelling on these things so much."

" They made it up last night," he writes a few days later of the particular quarrel which was then agitating the party. " Even such things as this—the army setting off to conquer all the world turning back to burn Jack's pigstye, and tumbling drunk into the fire—even this don't shake me : means one must use the best one can get; but one thing I won't do, wait for ever till perfect means are made for very imperfect me to work with. As to my not looking round, why it seems to me that no hour of the day passes that the whole world does not show itself to me."

Such was the courage with which Morris met apparent failure. He was soon to be more seriously alarmed by a sudden though elusive prospect of premature success. It was being borne in on him by bitter daily experience how unripe the Socialist party was ; how discordant in its aims, how unfixed in its principles, how incapable of forming or guiding any large popular movement. On the 8th of February, 1886, a meeting of the London unemployed in Trafalgar Square had been followed by a riot which caused an immense sensation, and to the imaginations of many persons seemed the beginning of a really revolutionary movement. When the meeting was over, a mob made its way through several of the main streets of the West End of London, hurling stones at the windows of the club-houses, stopping carriages and demanding money from the occupants, and break-ing into and plundering several shops, less it would seem from any distinct plan of robbery than as a rough practical joke. Morris's own shop, or at the least its windows, only escaped destruction by a few minutes ; the shutters were put up and the door locked just as the crowd began to pour into Oxford Street out of North Audley Street. But by that time they had become a mere rabble, and were easily dispersed by the police. "Contemptible as the riot was, as a riot," Morris wrote of it, "it no doubt has had a great effect, both here and on the Continent." Nothing of the sort had happened in London for many years. Parliament had just met and a change of Ministry was in progress. The rumours of Mr. Gladstone's proposed Irish legislation had raised politics to a high tension, and there was all abroad a general uneasiness and excitement which needed little to inflame it. To the Socialists, at least to the more thoughtful among them, excitement was mingled with a sort of terror. They had been working for a revolution, hitherto with little belief that anything could be effected for a long time to come. Was the revolution, beyond their expectation and almost beyond their hope, already at the door? In the next number of the Commonweal, Morris took the opportunity to issue a weighty statement of policy.

The article opens in a tone that gives little promise of applying either light or wisdom to the situation. It was the time when the vices of that debased journalism with which he had deliberately associated himself infected Morris most deeply. The description of the riot itself, and the forecast of what might ensue from it, are not free from qualities most deeply alien from his own nature, tumid metaphor and tawdry declamation. So far the writing is characteristic not of himself, but of his party, or of any party of undisciplined and half-educated men, whether reactionaries or revolutionaries. But once he has paid this sacrifice to the taste of his colleagues, he speaks in his own voice with grave good-sense and temperate foresight.

" I should like to say a few words with the utmost seriousness to our comrades and supporters, on the policy of the Socialist League. I have said that we have been overtaken unprepared, by a revolutionary incident, but that incident was practically aimless. This kind of thing is what many of us have dreaded from the first, and we may be sure that it will happen again and again while the industrial outlook is what it is ; but every time it happens it will happen with ever-increasing tragedy. It is above all things our business to guard against the possible consequences of these surprises. At the risk of being misunderstood by hot-heads, I say that our business is more than ever *Education.*

" The Gospel of Discontent is in a fair way towards forcing itself on the whole of the workers; how can that discontent be used so as to bring about the New Birth of Society ? That is the question we must always have before us. It is too much to hope that the *whole* working class can be educated in the aims of Socialism in due time, before other surprises take place. But we must hope that a strong party can be so educated, educated in economics, in organization, and in administration. To such a body of men all the aspirations and vague opinion of the oppressed multitudes would drift, and little by little they would be educated by them, if the march of events should give us time; or if not, even half-educated they would follow them in any action which it was necessary to take.

" Let me ask our comrades to picture to themselves the consequences of an aimless revolt unexpectedly successful for the time ; we will even suppose that it carries with it a small number of men capable of government and administration, though that is supposing a great deal. What would be the result unless the people had some definite aim, however limited ?

" The men thus floated to the surface would be powerless, their attempts at legislation would be misunderstood, disappointment and fresh discontent would follow, and the counter-revolution would sweep them away at once. But, indeed, it would not even come to that.   History teaches us that no revolts that are without aim are successful even for a time; even the failures (some of them glorious indeed) had a guiding aim in them, which only lacked completeness.

" The educational process, therefore, the forming a rallying point for definite aims, is necessary to our success; but I must guard against misunderstanding.   We must be no mere debating club, or philosophical society; we must take part in all really popular movements when we can make our own views on them unmistakably clear; that is a most important part of the education in organization.

" Education towards Revolution seems to me to express in three words what our policy should be; towards that New Birth of Society which we know must come, and which, therefore, we must strive to help forward so that it may come with as little confusion and suffering as may be."

In issuing this manifesto Morris, while not taking any step that brought him nearer the other wing of the Socialist party, the Parliamentarians and opportunists with whom he had broken a year before, also cut himself definitely away from the more violent section of his own supporters, who were already beginning to class themselves as Anarchists.   It became a question whether the midway course he had chosen would attract towards it the best men of both extremes, or whether, on the other hand, he and his following would find themselves a mere thinning remnant between two divergent and increasing camps.

To Burne-Jones, who had written to him after the riot of the 8th of February asking him not to do anything rash, he answered :

"Many thanks, my dear Ned, for your anxiety, but lay it aside for the present. I shall not shove myself into assemblies that are likely to turn into riots ; and for the rest I don't think that the Government will be such doited fools as to attack mere *opinion*. If they do, all liberal-minded persons will be on our side and they will be ig-nominiously beaten. At the worst as far as I am con-cerned it cannot come to much more than a mere joke of a Police-Court case ; and that not till the summer. I think the present excitement (it is little more) will die out ; or rather be flattened out into a sort of dull discon-tent favourable to our propaganda, but not likely to lead people into mere aimless rioting. So I am not a bit anxious about myself. My mind is quite made up as to my position ; I daresay you would not agree with me as to my views on that matter, but you would have to ad-mit that I was right, judging the thing from my starting point, namely that I am impelled to take action of some sort.

"I will talk of this matter when we meet : meantime, old chap, I send my best love to you for troubling about me.

"I wish I were not so damned old. If I were but twenty years younger ! But then you know there would be the Female complication somewhere. Best as it is after all."

"I have often thought," he says in another letter of the same date, "that we should be overtaken by the course of events—overtaken unprepared I mean. It will happen again and again : and some of us will cut sorry figures in the confusion. I myself shall be glad when this ferment sinks down again. Things industrial are bad—I wish they would better: their doing so would not interfere with our propaganda, and would give us some chance of getting at working men with intelligence and some share of leisure. Yet if that will not come about, and the dominating classes *will* push revolution on us, let it be ! the upshot must be good in the end. If you had only suffered as I have from the apathy of the English lower classes (woe's me how low !) you would rejoice at their awakening, however ugly the forms it took. As to my capacity for leadership in this turmoil, believe me, I feel as humble as could be wished: yet after all it is my life, and the work of it, and I must do my best."

The ferment sank down; and though his forecast of trouble with the police in summer was to be literally verified, he had soon resumed the regular routine of his work. "We had a very crowded meeting here on Sunday," he writes to Mrs. Morris on the 3rd of April: " I am going to Croydon to-morrow. Murray is in town, come back to Graham's sale : I saw him at Charing Cross the other day. I go to Dublin on Thursday evening. I see people are making a great fuss about Walker's pictures : I don't *much* sympathize, but the one that they have bought for the National Gallery is the best he did. Ned's and Gabriel's are to be sold to-day. Millais's Vale of Rest fetched a long price : but at any rate 'tis worth a cartload of the wretched daubs he turns out now."

" I came back from the Irishry all safe last night," he resumes on the 15th ; " but I am off to Leeds and Bradford on Saturday and shall not be back thence till Tuesday: after that, peace as far as travelling is concerned till the end of June. I had a good passage back, and did 50 lines of Homer on the boat. Dublin on the whole I rather like : there is a sort of cosy shabbiness about it

which, joined to the clear air, is pleasant. The last meeting
on the Tuesday evening was peaceful and even enthusiastic.
The day I had spent up among the Wicklow mountains,
and found it very beautiful. On whatever other points
the Irishry are wild, they are quite cool, sensible, and
determined on the Home Rule question. I met some
very agreeable middle-classers there and had much talk—
far too much in fact; I doubt if there is an iron pot in
Dublin with a leg on it by this time.

"I was very glad to get home and am very loth to leave
it I can tell you. However, the wine is drawn and must
be drunk."

The translation of the Odyssey to which this last letter
alludes had been just begun; and its inception marks the
point at which the extreme tension of the last three years
began to relax. For as long a period to come he continued equally active and conscientious in the work of
spreading Socialist doctrine, but creative work in art and
letters began now to resume its normal place in his mind.
The effect on his spirits and temper was soon obvious.
In May, when the fortunes of the first Home Rule Bill
were still swaying heavily in the balance, he could take
note of the wild words that were flying in the air with a
humorous side glance at the hardly wilder words of the
extremists among his own colleagues. "Rebellion is
getting quite fashionable now; I shall have to join the
Quakers. I wonder if the Queen will order herself to
be arrested after having hoisted the flag of rebellion on
Buckingham Palace. I don't think, mind you, that there
is *much* else than brag about the Orangemen; I suppose
it would end in a riot or two. But you really should
read the St. James's now and then; Hyndman at his
wildest is nothing to it."

Indeed he seems now and then to have found it necessary to brace himself up against a moderation that was

stealing over him almost against his will.   " I do not love
contention; I even shrink from it with indifferent persons.   Indeed I know that all my faults lie on the other
side: love of ease, dreaminess, sloth, sloppy good-nature,
are what I chiefly accuse myself of.   All these would not
have been hurt by my being a 'moderate Socialist'; nor
need I have forgone a good share of the satisfaction of
vainglory: for in such a party I could easily have been a
leader, nay, perhaps *the* leader, whereas amidst our rough
work I can scarcely be a leader at all and certainly do not
care to be.   I say this because I feel that a very little self-
deception would have landed me among the moderates.
But self-deception it would have been."

That recovered sweetness of temper (which no one
but himself would ever have thought of describing as
sloppy good-nature, or good-nature of any kind but the
simplest and soundest) is apparent in a series of his
letters to his daughter during June.

June 2. "Such a knockabout day as I had on Monday!
I saw in the Daily News that our men had been 'run
in' at Stratford, and expected what followed; namely
that as soon as I got home I had to go off to West Ham
Police Court (which is the Lord knows where) and see
about cash for paying their fines: for we foolishly let too
many men be run in, so that though the fines were small,
it came to £5 17s. in all.   I am very busy lecturing all
this week, and have plenty of regrets for the rest of
Kelmscott and your dear company; but what will you?
it is part of the day's work."

June 5. " Stories I have none to tell you: 'tis all meeting and lecture, lecture and meeting, with a little writing
interspersed.   It was Margaret's birthday on Thursday
when I went to the Grange I found.   She is ever so old,
20 actually, just think, and she the baby of the lot!
Both the Hammersmith and the Merton gardens are look-

ing very nice now, though even the latter is commonplace compared with Kelmscott. A lady who came on Thursday sent us yesterday a lot of peonies, single ones of various kinds, very handsome: they are Chinese flowers and look just like the flowers on their embroideries.

" Your old Prooshian Blue (only 'tis indigo)."

June 15. " There is a good deal to tell you about since I wrote last. Though I forget if I told you how I went to speak on the disputed place at Stratford on Saturday week. Well, I went there rather expecting the police to ' run me in.' In which case I should have been fined the following Monday after a wearisome morning. However the meeting was so orderly that they didn't venture, perhaps all the more as two of the Radicals spoke also ; the meeting also was somewhat short. Last Saturday however they did ' run in ' Mowbray and fined him 20s. and costs yesterday, which seemed to me absurd ; I mean to say that they let us alone and got him. We are not going to give it up however yet, but shall try to get the Radicals to go into it heartily, as really an ordinary meeting makes no obstruction at all. In any case I shall not go there on Saturday, because on the Monday after I am to go on the Scotch journey of which I told you, and shall be away for a week. As to my coming to see you, my darling, if I possibly can this week I will ; though it will have to be but a short visit.

"As to other events, we had our Conference on Sunday ; all day long it lasted ; May and I getting home about 11.30 p.m. It was rather a weary job that Conference, and as I was not a delegate, I had not got to speak ; though that was after all rather a blessing, as the main subject in dispute was the alteration of the Constitution —not of the British Empire, but of the League. However all went well ; the alterers were defeated and bore

their defeat with good temper; but I am very glad that
there is a respite of a year before we can have another.
Yesterday (Monday) we had our outing and I rather enjoyed it, though we did not distinguish ourselves by much
organization in it, wandering about rather aimlessly: also
the day was not brilliant, as in the afternoon there was a
sort of cloudy drizzle on the hills: yet we escaped a good
ducking.   The place, Box Hill, is really beautiful, with
a famous box-wood at the top: you and I must go there
when you are back in London.   We finished off in
Dorking, not however at the Markis of Granby, but the
Wheatsheaf, where we had tea, beer, singing and recita-
tion.   I regret to state that in the town generally we
were taken for a detachment of the Salvation Army.   In
fact Dorking is a very quiet place, and I don't suppose
they have yet heard the word Socialist.   I forgot to say
by the way, that though I didn't speak at Stratford on
Saturday I did so at Hyde Park near the Marble Arch.
I was quite nervous about it, I don't know why: because when I was speaking at Stratford I was not nervous
at all, though I expected the Police to attack us.   At
Hyde Park we had a very quiet and rather good audience,
and sold four quires of Commonweal: and I spoke twice,
the second time not at all nervously.

"As to the Bill, my dear, we expected it to be defeated, though not by so large a majority.   The question
now is what the country will say about it.   Again I expect Gladstone will be beaten, though this time he ought
not to be, as he is in the right.   I thought his last manifesto (of yesterday) was good and straightforward: there
will be all sorts of trouble if the Home Rule matter is
not soon settled.   I am rather enjoying myself to-day
after the last two days' excitement, in being quietly at
home on a nice fine fresh day, though I am obliged to
work very hard."

June 23: Arbroath. "I am here all safe and well: not a bad sort of a town for Scotland: all stone built, and all the older houses roofed with stone slates, right on the sea: it is in fact Fairport of 'The Antiquary.' The remains of a very fine Abbey Church and buildings stand for St. Ruth, the Musselcraig is identified, and so forth. I slept a good deal on the road: woke as the train went out of Stirling and showed a very raw-boned town but a lovely country,: plain and mountains with Forth amidst it very lovely. Perth also blue-boned, but a most beautiful situation, especially down the water of Tay. I have been walking on the sea-shore *not* trying to remember Miss Isabella Wardour; and now want my dinner."

Even the long-looked-for collision with the police over the matter of open-air meetings, when it came, came in the mildest and most good-humoured form. On Sunday morning the 18th of July, in accordance with advertised arrangement, Morris was addressing an outdoor meeting in a street off the Edgware Road. An Inspector of police appeared on the scene; the crowd groaned, but made way for him. He came up "mighty civil" and told Morris to stop speaking: Morris refused; his name and address were taken, and the Inspector went away again. Morris was summoned two days afterwards at the Marylebone Police Court: the technical offence of obstructing the highway was, of course, indisputable, and he was fined a shilling and costs. This was his last encounter with authority in the cause of freedom of speech. Public interest in the matter had for the time died away. Since their experience in Limehouse the year before, the police had been acting more sensibly, and avoided purposeless friction. The public were getting a little tired of the meetings on waste grounds or at street corners, which they vaguely classed with those of the Salvation Army as probably well-meant but certainly foolish, and best treated with neglect. The Radical clubs, which had rallied to the cry of free speech the year before, now hung back, and very reasonably suggested that if there were to be any common action, the Socialists had better first make up their own differences, which had for long been no secret. Always eager for peace, Morris took on himself once more the task of approaching the Social Democratic Federation to try to patch up the quarrel.

The attempt at peacemaking proved quite futile. Morris found the leader of the other faction " stiff and stately, playing the big man, and complaining of being ill-treated by us, which was a Wolf and Lamb business." Indeed most of the grievances, on whichever side the cause of offence first arose, seem now as they seemed to Morris then, " preposterously petty." At Dod Street— so the leaders of the Social Democratic Federation in- sisted, and made this the front of the offence—there had been a distinct breach of faith as regards the order of speeches on the 27th of September the year before. Angry words had passed at the time about this, and the Council of the Socialist League had passed a resolution expressing its " pity for Mr. Hyndman's tools." The insult was never forgotten. Since then each party had roundly accused the other of trying to break up its local branches by open abuse and underground insinuations. " How *can* we make common cause," they asked, " with people who are perpetually calling us all liars, rogues, intriguers ? " For Morris personally indeed his opponents expressed unaltered regard. To accuse him of intrigue would have been plainly preposterous in the most heated adversary : and little as they took a lesson by it, the simple goodness of his nature impressed itself on even the most jealous, the vainest, the most vindictive of the men whom he longed to call his comrades, and for whose faults and vices, so long as he believed they had the root of the matter somewhere in them, he had a patience that was all but inexhaustible.

" Well, I think I have done with that lot," he writes when this last negotiation had broken down. " Why will people quarrel when they have a serious end in view ? I went to Merton yesterday and worked very hard at my patterns and found it amusing. I have finished the 8th book of Homer and got into the 9th, Lotus Eaters, Cyclops, and so on. How jolly it would be to be in a little cottage in the deep country going on with that, and long walks interspersed—in the autumn country, which after all I love as much as the spring."

CHAPTER XVII

THE return to literature, which began early in 1886 with
the translation of the Odyssey into English verse, was to
some degree both the cause and the effect of a gradual
change in Morris's attitude towards active Socialism. For
between three and four years he had forced himself, under
the impulse of a great hope and the continuous sense
of a primary duty, into a more contracted and perhaps a
less effective life than was consonant with his real nature.
His principles had changed little when he became a declared Socialist: they changed even less now: but the
movement of things was lifting him slowly away from
the path that had coincided with or deflected his own,
and insensibly he began to swing back into his own
orbit. He held as strongly as ever that Education
towards Revolution was the end to be steadily pursued.
But the terms Education and Revolution both began
to shift and enlarge their meaning. As the strain of
an excessive concentration on a single task relaxed, the
joy of work returned in a fuller measure. " It is right
and necessary "—such was the claim he had made con-
sistently from the first on behalf of human life—" that
all men should have work of itself pleasant to do; nay
more, work done without pleasure is, however one may
turn it, not real work at all, but useless and degrading
toil." The educational, no less than the creative, work

which he did in the latter years of life resumed this pleasurable quality, which for a time, under the compulsion of what seemed an overpowering duty, had been almost beaten out of it. In the strenuous self-devotion to the labours exacted of him by his party—sometimes distasteful to him in the highest degree, sometimes of a kind for which he had little native aptitude—there had been an element of what he himself felt to be unnatural. His energy had become forced and feverish. In his own beautiful words, it was the " power of the strong man yearning to accomplish something before his death, not the simple hope of the child who has long years of life and growth before him." That simple hope is a thing which, once broken, can never be wholly restored. But in his work for the cause henceforth there was, in spite of all discouragements, the hope and the joy that come of work which looks to no immediate results, and is checked by no apparent failure, but sows the seed and leaves it to quicken: as if a man should cast seed into the ground, and should sleep and rise night and day, and the seed should spring and grow up, he knoweth not how.

The translation of the Odyssey had been begun in February, but made little progress till summer, when he took to it with keen interest and advanced with it rapidly. " The Odyssey is to my mind much the most interesting of the two," he had written to Ellis when he first took up the translation, " but I may do the Iliad afterwards. It is hard work, much more so than the Virgil, owing to the great simplicity of the original, which never has a redundant word in it, or a word without a meaning : however it is very pleasant work." As it went on, its soothing effect over his nerves became more and more marked. At the beginning of September he alludes to its progress in a letter promising a visit to W. Bell Scott in his northern home at Penkill :

" I am of course much more from pillar to post since I have taken to the pernicious practice of what may be called professional agitation, professional though unpaid, except by general loss of reputation, which however is of no importance, and by no means balances on the wrong side the pleasure on the right side of being engaged in an important movement.   Things seem to us more and more tending to a great change, though no doubt it will take time, and also there is a great expenditure of patience necessary to meet all the petty worries that encumber the progress of even great movements.   I am also at work, as perhaps you have heard, at translating the Odyssey: this is very amusing: and a great rest from the other work: I am in the middle of the 9th book now."

On the 7th of September he writes to Kelmscott:

" Dearest Jenny,

" I am just writing a line to say that I am well and busy, though somewhat sulky at being dragged away from Kelmscott.   The garden here is going the way of all London autumn gardens; but there is still a sort of pale prettiness about it, and there are a good many flowers in it, chiefly Japanese anemones and ' Chaynee oysters.'   The gardener is busy to-day tidying up.   Yesterday M. Guerrault called wanting work; Mr. York Powell (who is working with Gúdbrandr Vigfússon at Oxford) was with him: the conversation I regret to say was chiefly between Powell and me, as Guerrault talks little English and I—well.   Powell is a very nice fellow, a good deal of a Socialist and very genial: he was born and bred in Walthamstow, though a Welsh one of blood: he used as a boy to come to Leyton House, he told me. I go to Merton Abbey to-day, and in the evening to a Fabian meeting, where it seems our people expect me to speak against the party of compromise.   Young Tom Wardle was summoned for speaking at the Harrow Road Station, some weeks ago, and appeared at the police-court yesterday: he was committed for trial: he says he will not pay a fine—item his father says *he* won't.   The Temperance people sent a deputation to us on the beautiful Monday that we others went to the White Horse on; they are quite prepared to work with us, and in fact we have made an alliance offensive and defensive with them: I think we shall beat the police in the long run after all.   Even at the place where T. Wardle was summoned they have not interfered with us for three weeks.

"Dear me! my Jenny, what a nice four days I did have down there with you; I doubt if I ever enjoyed myself so much in my life: it was delightful and dear.

"I have a long letter from Mr. Birchall this morning about semi-Socialism: he is really a very sensible man: and Mr. Turner says he has very good knowledge of archæology.   Well, my dear, I must now go to Merton. Best love, dear: also to all the party.

"Your loving father,

"W. M."

Later in the month he went to Edinburgh to give an address.   On the journey, "I amused myself partly with Homer (110 lines) and partly with reading a new book which is very interesting, Russian Epic Songs to wit. The smoke hung low on Edinburgh, so that the mountains looked like strong outlines against the sky, and the ugly detail of the houses was a good deal hidden: so that there was something very fine about the whole view from the Castle Hill, to which I wandered before getting into the church where our window is.   Our window is fine, and looks a queer contrast with its glittering jewel-like colour to the daubs about it.   There is no station hotel at Edinburgh, so I had to make a shot at one, and it was a bad one too; dull and not over clean. It was quite respectable however, although its dulness was relieved by a sudden fight between the head waiter and a quarrelsome gentleman more or less in liquor. The waiter got the best of it and quite deserved to do so, as far as I could see. It was a curious piece of drama to note the attempts of the quarrelsome gentleman to get away with some kind of dignity, while his old antagonist, become the polite waiter again, brushed past him taking other people's orders."

Already literature both in prose and verse was filling up his mind. At the end of October he was full of new projects: " it really would be rather convenient to me to have a little gout in order to do some literary work." One of these projects, never carried out, was to rewrite and complete the fragments of the poem which had appeared in the Commonweal under the title of "The Pilgrims of Hope." The first half of the Odyssey was nearly completed. And he had begun to write the flower of his prose romances, the work into which he put his most exquisite descriptions and his deepest thoughts on human life, "The Dream of John Ball." It also was first published in the Commonweal, beginning in the number for the 13th of November, 1886, and concluding in that for the 22nd of January, 1887.

Even in his direct work for the party—for he still took his full share of duty as a Socialist speaker and on the executive of the League—the reviving literary instinct was beginning to show itself unmistakably. No sooner was "John Ball" completed than he began to write an elaborate diary of his work and of the movement of things generally in the world about him, with the view of compiling an exact contemporary chronicle. Like the Iceland diary of 1871, it was written with some more or less defined view of publication ; " I am writing a diary," he says in a letter to his daughter, " which may one day be published as a kind of view of the Socialist movement seen from the inside, Jonah's view of the whale, you know, my dear."   But it was carried on for only three months : and three months' experience may have sufficed to convince him that this sort of literature—if literature it was strictly to be called—was not on his own strongest side and was hampering him in more important work.   The fragment has a double interest, both from passages which seem to show that he still treasured the hope of some sudden and surprising revolution in civilized life, and from other passages in which he criticises his party from the outside with a curiously dispassionate clearness.   In both alike, and indeed all through, it has the unique transparency of a record of his actual thoughts at each moment, without any attempt at consistency, or at altering his forecasts in the light of actual events.   The fragment has no heading.   It opens with the words, " I begin what may be called my diary from this point, January 25th, 1887 "; and then goes on without any further preface, " I went down to lecture at Merton Abbey last Sunday."   One of its most noticeable features is the keen and even excited interest he takes in the course of current politics, both domestic and international.   This is not indeed surprising in itself, for the time was one of uncertainty and excitement, but it contrasts curiously with the tone of lordly indifference adopted in the official journal of the Socialist League towards things that lay outside their own movement.   The extracts which follow show what immense labour he continued to spend in the service of the League, and how clearly nevertheless he saw the weakness of their machinery and the futility of the greater part of their efforts, and of his own.

" I went down to lecture at Merton Abbey last Sunday : the little room was pretty full of men, mostly of the labourer class : anything attacking the upper classes directly moved their enthusiasm ; of their discontent there could be no doubt, or the sincerity of their class hatred : they have been very badly off there this winter, and there is little to wonder at in their discontent ; but with a few exceptions they have not yet learned what Socialism means ; they and Frank Kitz were much excited about the Norwich affair, and he made a very hot speech : he was much exercised about the police being all about the place, detectives inside and so on : I fancy their game is to try to catch the club serving non-members with beer or in some way breaking the law. But there is no doubt that there is a good deal of stir amongst the labourers about there ; the place is wretchedly poor.

" I slept at Merton, and in the morning got the Norwich paper with a full account of the trial of Mowbray and Henderson ; the Judge's summing up of the case was amusing and instructive, as showing a sort of survival of the old sort of bullying of the Castlereagh times mixed with a grotesque attempt at modernization on philanthropical lines : it put me in a great rage.

" The Daily News printed my letter ; it had also a brief paragraph asserting that Germany would presently ask France the meaning of her war preparations, and an alarmist article therewith. I did not know but what the other papers had the same news, and was much excited at the idea : because whatever one may say, one cannot help hoping that such a huge turmoil as a European war could not fail to turn to some advantage for us. Coming to town however I found that the evening papers poh-poh it as a mere hurrying up of the belated Daily News. Yet there may be something in it.

" At the Council of the Socialist League in the evening : the Avelings there mighty civil, but took no part in the proceedings. A dullish meeting, both sides rather shy of the Norwich matter, which but for the heaviness of the sentences would be but a pitiful affair : a committee was appointed to see after Mowbray's wife and children while he is *in :* a letter came from Norwich with the news of their having held a great meeting of 6,000 in the market-place on Sunday, at which they passed resolutions condemning the sentence, and in favour of the Social Revolution : though I fear few indeed out of the 6,000 knew what that meant. They were getting up a petition to the Home Secretary.

"Our attempt to get up an Irish meeting of the Radicals led by the Socialists will fail: we are not big enough for the job : the Radical clubs are civil to us but afraid of us, and not yet prepared to break with the Liberals. . . .

"Jan. 26th. Went to South Kensington Museum yesterday with Jenny to look at the Troy tapestry again since they have bought it for £1,250 : I chuckled to think that properly speaking it was bought for me, since scarcely anybody will care a damn for it. A. Cole showed us a lot of scraps of woven stuff from the tombs of Upper Egypt ; very curious as showing in an unusual material the transition to the pure Byzantine style from the Classical: some pieces being nothing but debased Classical style, others purely Byzantine, yet I think not much different in date : the contrast between the bald ugliness of the Classical pieces and the great beauty of the Byzantine was a pleasing thing to me, who loathe so all Classical art and literature. I spoke in the evening at the Hammersmith Radical Club at a meeting to condemn the Glenbeigh evictions, the room crowded, and of course our Socialist friends there ; my speech was well received, but I thought the applause rather hollow, as the really Radical part of the audience had clearly no ideas beyond the ordinary party shibboleths, and were quite untouched by Socialism: they seemed to me a very discouraging set of men; but perhaps can be got at somehow—the frightful ignorance and want of impressibility of the average English workman floors me at times.

" 27th. I went to Merton yesterday on a lovely day. Wardle told me the whole story of what they are doing and are going to do at St. Mark's at Venice. I was incoherent with rage: they will soon finish up the whole thing there—and indeed everywhere else. . . .

" Parliament is to meet to-day: that is not of much importance to ' we-uns ': it is a matter of course that if the Government venture to bring forward a gagging-bill they will not venture to make it anything but an Irish one. For my part I should rather like the Liberals to get in again: for if they do, they must either push on the revolution by furthering Irish matters, which will be a direct gain to us ; or they must sneak out of the Irish question, which would be an indirect gain to us, but a far greater one, as it would turn all that is democratic sick of them. It seems that they by no means want to get in, and I don't wonder, considering that dilemma.

" News this morning that Goschen has lost Liverpool. . . . It is curious to see how equally the parties are balanced in the electorate, by the way: and this again is hopeful for us, because it will force the Liberals to be less and less democratic, and so consolidate the Party of Reaction.

" Feb. 3rd. Went down to Rottingdean on Friday 28th and spent three or four days there: was very glad to leave the Newspapers alone while there : did Homer and an article for Commonweal. . . . I was very loth to come back ; though as for holidays 'tis a mistake to call them rests: one is excited and eager always; at any rate during a short holiday, and I don't know what a long one means. The ordinary drifting about of a 'busy' man is much less exciting than these sort of holidays. . . .

" Feb. 7th (Monday). On Friday I went up to the Chiswick club, where Mordhurst (one of our Hammersmith Branch) was to have opened a debate on the Class-war, but as he didn't turn up, I was called on to take his place: the room was not large; about twenty people there at first, swelling to forty perhaps before the end: the kind of men composing the audience is a matter worth noting, since the chief purpose of this diary is to record my impressions on the Socialist movement. I should say then that the speakers were all either of the better-to-do workmen or small tradesmen class, except Gordon Hogg, who is a doctor. . . . My Socialism was gravely listened to by the audience, but taken with no enthusiasm, and in fact however simply one puts the case for Socialism one always rather puzzles an audience : the speakers, except Hogg and a young timid member of our branch, were muddled to the last degree; but clearly the most intelligent men did not speak : the debate was adjourned till next Friday, but I was allowed a short reply in which I warmed them up somehow. This description of an audience may be taken for almost any other at a Radical club, *mutatis mutandis.* The sum of it all is that the men at present listen respectfully to Socialism, but are perfectly supine and not in the least inclined to move except along the lines of Radicalism and Trades' Unionism. . . .

" Yesterday (Sunday) we began our open-air meetings at Beadon Road, near the Broadway there. I spoke alone for about an hour, and a very fair audience (for the place, which is out of the way) gathered curiously quickly; a comrade counted a hundred at most. This audience characteristic of small open-air meetings, also quite mixed, from labourers on their Sunday lounge to ' respectable ' people coming from church: the latter inclined to grin: the working men listening attentively trying to understand, but mostly failing to do so: a fair cheer when I ended, of course led by the three or four Branch members present. . . .

" Feb. 12th. I have been on League business every night this week till to-night " (Saturday). " Monday the Council meeting peaceable enough, and dull. . . . Tuesday I took the chair at the meeting to protest against the (possible) coming war at Cleveland Hall, Cleveland St., a wretched place once flash and now sordid, in a miserable street. It is the head-quarters of what I should call the orthodox Anarchists : Victor Dave the leading spirit there. Of course there were many ' foreigners ' there, and also a good sprinkling of our people and I suppose of the Federation also. It was rather hard work getting through all the speeches in the unknown tongues of French and German, and the natives showed their almost superstitious reverence for internationalism by sitting through it all patiently: the foreign speakers were mostly of the ' orthodox Anarchists '; but a Collectivist also spoke, and one at least of the Autonomy section, who have some quarrel which I can't understand with the Cleveland Hall people : a Federation man spoke though he was not a delegate ; also Macdonald of the Socialist Union : the Fabians declined to send on the grounds of the war-scare being premature : but probably in reality because they did not want to be mixed up too much with the Anarchists : the Krapotkine-Wilson people also refused on the grounds that bourgeois peace *is* a war, which no doubt was a genuine reason on their part and is true enough. . . . On Wednesday I went to lecture at a schoolroom in Peckham High Street. . . . Thursday

I went to the Ways and Means Committee at the League: found them cheerful there on the prospects of Commonweal. I didn't quite feel as cheerful as the others, but hope it may go on. Friday I went in the evening to finish the debate begun last week : the room full. Sparling made a good speech ; I didn't.

"Feb. 16th. Sunday I spoke on a very cold windy (N.E.) morning at the Walham Green Station: the people listened well though the audience was not large, about 60 at the most. . . . I lectured on 'Mediæval England' to a good audience here in the evening: lecture rather 'young.'

"Monday, Council meeting very quiet and short. . . . In the afternoon Bax called with Champion, who thinks of starting a new weekly, a private paper not so much a party journal as Commonweal, and bigger, as he is to be backed by money. He wanted my goodwill, which he is welcome to ; but I distrust the long endurance of a paper at all commercial, unless there is *plenty* of money at its back. Champion spoke in a friendly way and was quite open and reasonable ; but seems out of spirits about the movement: he has been extremely over-sanguine about getting people to 'show their strength,' which of course they won't do at present, as soon as it looks dangerous, and so he is correspondingly depressed at the poor performance of the Social Democratic Federation in agitation lately.

" Next Sunday they are going to have a ' Church-parade, at St. Paul's : but unless they can get an enormous crowd, it will be a silly business, and if they do there will be a row ; which got up in this way I think a mistake ; take this for my word about the sort of thing : if a riot is quite spontaneous it does frighten the bourgeois even if it [is] but isolated ; but planned riots or shows of force are no good unless in a time of action, when they are backed by the opinion of the people and are in point of fact indications of the rising tide. . . .

"Feb. 23rd. I had a sort of threat of gout the last days of last week, so kept myself quiet at home.

"Sunday for same reason I did not speak out of doors. I went to Mitcham (the branch) on Sunday evening and spoke extemporary to them at their club-room, a tumble-down shed opposite the grand new workhouse built by the Holborn Union: amongst the woeful hovels that make up the worse (and newer) part of Mitcham, which was once a pretty place with its old street and greens and lavender fields. Except a German from Wimbledon (who was in the chair) and two others who looked like artisans of the painter or small builder type, the audience was all made up of labourers and their wives: they were very quiet and attentive except one man who was courageous from liquor, and interrupted sympathetically: but I doubt if most of them understood anything I said; though some few of them showed that they did by applauding the points. I wonder sometimes if people will remember in times to come to what a depth of degradation the ordinary English workman has been reduced; I felt very downcast amongst these poor people in their poor hutch whose opening I attended some three months back (and they were rather proud of it). There were but about 25 present: yet I felt as if I might be doing some good there. . . .

"Monday was Council-night again, and I attended. Poor Allman had been before the magistrate that day and fined 40s., and was sent to jail in default of payment: his offence was open-air preaching close to the meeting-place of the Hackney Branch: so we are beginning our troubles early this year; which is a great nuisance; but I don't see what is to be done: we can't give up street-preaching in spite of what Bax and one or two others say about its uselessness: yet the police if they persist can put us down ; and unless we can get up a very good case of causeless interference on their part, and consequent presumption of unfairness against us, we shall not be able to enlist the Radical clubs on our side, which is our only chance.   At the Council we agreed not to pay Allman's fine, as he cried out loudly against it ; and I believe meant it, as he is a courageous little man. . . . I may note here for the benefit of well-to-do West-enders that the police are incredibly rough and brutal to the poor people in the East end ; and that they treated Allman very ill. . . . I may as well say here that my intention is if possible to prevent the quarrel coming to a head between the two sections, parliamentary and anti-parliamentary, which are pretty much commensurate with the Collectivists and Anarchists : and this because I believe there would be a good many who would join the Anarchist side who are not really Anarchists, and who would be useful to us : indeed I doubt if, except one or two Germans, etc., we have any real Anarchists amongst us : and I don't want to see a lot of enthusiastic men who are not very deep in Socialist doctrines driven off for a fad of the more pedantic part of the Collectivist section. . . .

" Yesterday all day long with Bax trying to get our second article on Marx together : a very difficult job : I hope it may be worth the trouble.

"News of the German elections to-day: the Socialists seem to be going to lose seats (and no wonder considering Bismarck's iron fist), but they are gaining numbers according to the voting.

" Sparling went down on Monday night to Reading to try to found a branch, after the good reception which he and Carruthers had there last week : but it was a dead failure : a good many had given their names to attend, but when it came to the scratch 'with one consent they all began to make excuse': I note this because it is characteristic of the present stage of the movement; for as above said there was plenty of agreement at the meetings we have held there. This hanging-back is partly fear of being boycotted by the masters; but chiefly from dislike to organization, for a question which the 'respectable' political parties ignore; and also fear of anything like revolt or revolution. . . .

"March 3rd. Sunday I spoke at Beadon Road; fair attendance of the usual kind; I met a *posse* of horse police going to St. Paul's *apropos* of the S. D. F.'s Church-parade there; and there were also a crowd of police at the Metropolitan station. . . .

"The S. D. F. Church-parade went off well: they ought not to spoil it by having inferior ones at small churches now; but should change the entertainment. Which remark points to the weak side of their tactics: they must always be getting up some fresh excitement, or else making the thing stale and at last ridiculous; so that they are rather in the position of a hard-pressed manager of a theatre—what are they to do next? . . .

"March 9th. It is clear that the Government is in a shaky condition. The Union Liberals are beginning to see that the cat is going to jump the other way: Trevelyan made a speech at Devonshire House this week as good as renouncing the Tory alliance: so it seems the Liberal party is to be re-united on the basis of a Compromise Home Rule Bill; which will last as long as the Irish find convenient. Meantime the Government are threatening a very harsh Coercion Bill: indeed I shouldn't wonder if they were to make it as stiff as possible in order to insure their own defeat, and then were to appeal to the country on the ground of law and order. All this is blessed bread to us, even the re-union of the

Liberal party; because after all, that means the Whigs still retaining their hold of it, the stripping it more and more of anything which could enable it to pose as a popular party; while on the other hand it cripples the Radicals, and takes away all chance of their forming a popular party underneath the more advanced Liberals: so that in politics the break-up of the old parties and the formation of a strong reactionary party goes on apace. . . .

"Sunday I went to the new premises of the Hoxton Branch (the Labour Emancipation League) to lecture: I rather liked it: a queer little no-shaped slip cut off from some workshop or other, neatly whitewashed, with some innocent decoration obviously by the decorator member of the branch: all very poor but showing signs of sticking to it: the room full of a new audience of the usual type of attenders at such places: all working men except a parson in the front row, and perhaps a clerk or two, the opposition represented by a fool of the debating club type; but our men glad of any opposition at all. I heard that our branch lecture was a wretched failure. The fact is our branch, which was very vigorous a little time ago, is sick now; the men want some little new thing to be doing or they get slack in attendance. I must try to push them together a bit. I attended the Council meeting on Monday. It was in the end quarrelsome. . . . We passed a resolution practically bidding our speakers not to draw on quarrels with the police: though I doubt if they will heed it often: as some of them are ambitious of figuring as heroes in this 'free-speech' business. This is a pity; as if the police stick to it, they can of course beat us in the long run: and we have more out-a-door stations already than we can man properly. . . .

"March 20th. The annual meeting of our Hammersmith Branch came off: a dead failure, as all our meetings except the open-air ones have been lately.   However I really think the savage second winter has had something to do with it; we have had a hard frost for nearly a fortnight now, and often a bitter blast of the N.E. with it; and our stable-meeting-room is not very warmable under such conditions.

"I lectured in the Chiswick Club Hall and had a scanty audience *and* a dull.   It was a new lecture, and good, though I say it, and I really did my best; but they hung on my hands as heavy as lead.   The open-air meeting at Walham Green in the morning was very creditable considering the cold weather and the underfoot misery.

"March 24th. 53 years old to-day—no use grumbling at that."

The diary is continued for a month longer, but becomes more fragmentary as it goes on, and is filled in at longer intervals.   On the 27th of April it ends, with the note, "I have been busy about many things, and so unable to fill up this book."

Among these many things was his Odyssey.   "I have just finished the 16th book," he writes to his daughter on the 18th of February, " and am getting the first volume through the press."   This first volume was published early in April, and the second volume followed in November.   It was received with the respect due to its merits.   The first edition was sold out in six weeks: but it never became really popular, nor has it taken a place as the standard English version of Homer.   It is perhaps one of the cases in which the disparity between the nature of the original and the method of rendering is no less vital because it lies below the surface.   When Morris published the translation of the Æneid, the first criticism that occurred to many of his readers was that Homer rather than Virgil, and of the Homeric poems the Odyssey rather than the Iliad, was what he would render with the greatest sympathy and success. This may now be doubted. Notwithstanding his deep love and admiration for the Icelandic epics, notwithstanding the essentially Homeric tone of his own great Volsung epic, the romantic element in Virgil was perhaps more nearly akin to his own most intimate poetical instincts than the broader and more impersonal treatment which puts the Iliad and Odyssey in a class of poetry by themselves. It may further be questioned whether the metre chosen, admirably as it represents the Greek hexameter as regards length of line and rapidity of movement, is not one which lays traps for a translator by the very ease and variation of which its rhythm admits.

Morris prided himself upon the fidelity of his version to the original: " My translation is a real one so far," he wrote of it to Ellis while it was in progress, " not a mere periphrase of the original as *all* the others are." But a translation, whether of Homer or of any other great poet, which sets out to be literal, must of necessity incur the risk of a certain flatness and commonness in passages where the original is only poetical by virtue of some un-transferable quality. More especially is this the case in rendering from the Greek. That wonderful language almost makes poetry of itself; it is at once the model and the despair of all other languages. A translation which aims at a high standard of literal accuracy doubles the difficulty, in any case immensely great, of reproducing the continuous dignity and elevation of Homer. And a metre of loose structure invites the evasion of difficulties which are perhaps insoluble, and at all events are not solved in the least by being evaded. The epic hexameter, with all its elasticity, is accurately uniform in its metrical structure: it carries the poem forward unswervingly and unfalteringly. But the Sigurd-metre of Morris's Odyssey, with an elasticity equal to that of the Greek hexameter itself, and a power (due to the great variation of which it admits) of attaining certain astonishing effects, suffers from this very quality in a tendency to relapse into formlessness. It is apt to revert into the mere inchoate metre from which it and the hexameter are both historical evolutions.

This tendency acts in two ways: in one way by stripping the metre, as one might say, to the bone. The couplet,

They sat and fell to feasting, and men of worth rose up
And poured the wine unto them in many a golden cup,

goes back to the metre of the Niebelungenlied, of Nævius's " Punic War," and in all probability of the lost Greek epics, out of which was gradually evolved what we know by the name of Homer. But on the other hand it is apt to become overloaded. In lines like

Whether he should pray to the fair-faced, laying hand
     upon her knee,

or,

Bides she still with my child, and steadfast yet guardeth
     all my good?

the laxity of the metre allows it to pass into something that is barely metrical. In original writing the ear and taste of a good craftsman will keep him safe from both extremes. But in a translation, as all translators know, there is a temptation almost irresistible to take advantage of any licence the metre allows, a little here and a little there, till at last the accumulated result goes far beyond what the translator had meant or what the reader can readily approve. This is the reason why a successful verse translation, be it of Homer or Virgil or any other great poet, must be executed in a metre of accurate structure.

Morris was too conscientious an artist, and too deeply in sympathy with the spirit of the Saga, whether Greek or Northern, to make things easier for his readers by modernizations of language or sentiment, or by slurring whatever in the original is weak, or verbose, or in any way repellent to modern feeling. There is a measure of truth in what he said of the translation himself before it appeared: " I don't think the public will take to it; it is too like Homer." In fact, when due allowance is made for this defect in the medium chosen, one may well wonder that in a language which is so different from Greek, and which, with all its own merits, has so little of the specific Greek beauty, Morris succeeded in producing such radiant effects as he does. And if his translation has not become the standard English version, it is only because that place still remains empty.

Of another kind of calls on his time there is a ludicrous instance in a letter to his daughter written this spring. "Comes me here on Tuesday one of our Oxford Street chaps and says will I go call on a lady near Hans Place about some decoration. So yesterday I go—grumbling, but thinking like John Gilpin about the loss of pence: and coming to Hans Place find it a very architectoora-looral region: knock at the door: am shown into the drawing-room, when enter to me a lady who, after a very short preamble, requests me to look at some decoration that *she* was doing in the poker-style you know, burning the pattern in: and with a view of my helping her to a sale of these articles; her husband by the way being a swell in the War Office. My dear, the impudence of women is great; ask your Mama if she don't think so. Moreover I was too much amused, and also flabbergasted, to walk out of the house without a word, so I had to finish my morning call with great gravity; a morning call also for which I can't see my way for charging. How May did laugh at me when I came home!"

"I must tell you, my dear," he says in another letter a little later, "that I am getting famous, or at least notorious, in Hammersmith town. The other day opposite the Nazareth a covered greengrocer's cart hailed me as 'Socialist!' and then as 'Morris!' I don't think this was meant to be complimentary. Also a week ago as I was going down Rivercourt Road, lo a small boy, chubby, about seven years old, sitting swinging on one of the iron gates, very uncomfortably I should think, as they have sort of cabbage ornaments, sings out to me: 'Have a ride, Morris!' At these two places I was known: but last Sunday it befel me to go to Victoria Park (beyond Bethnal Green) to a meeting. Now I have mounted a cape or cloak, grey in colour, so that people doubt whether I be a brigand or a parson: this seemed too picturesque for some 'Arrys who were passing by, and sung out after me, 'Shakespeare, yah!'"

All through that hot summer of the Queen's Jubilee he stayed in London, busily trying to keep the Socialist League together, and working hard at Merton against the continued depression of trade, but not too anxious to enjoy life in a way that he could hardly have done the year before. A few extracts from letters written during these summer months may be added here.

"I am trying to get the League to make peace with each other and hold together for another year. It is a tough job; something like the worst kind of pig-driving I should think, and sometimes I lose my temper over it. It is so bewilderingly irritating to see perfectly honest men, very enthusiastic, and not at all self-seeking, and less stupid than most people, squabble so: and withal for the most part they are personally good friends together."

"It was almost too good to be true to hear the rain tinkling on the leaves when I woke about half-past four, and O how pleasant it did feel! I have looked at Lewis Morris's Ode; and looked away from it in wonder why people write odes: as Huck Finn would say, if I had a yaller dog that took to writing odes I would shoot him."

"On Tuesday our water-party did actually come off, Aglaia, Opie and Mr. Leaf being the other ones besides Janey, Jenny and self. It turned out quite a success; we went by train to Richmond and then took a boat and went up to Hampton Court by slow degrees, rowing, sailing, and towing. We got to the Palace just half an hour before closing-time of the building, but didn't mind about that. Our other male-man got out coming back at Surbiton, so that we were rather late; didn't get to Teddington Lock till after 8; so that it was full night when we came out of it. So I had to set poor Aglaia to steer in the dark, or the dusk rather, as Jenny is short-sighted and Janey was too tired, and the two girls had been rowing a good bit already, so that I had to row till we were close to Richmond again. Aglaia was (naturally) nervous and kept on mistaking 'nature's boskage,' or its shadow rather, for barges: but she did very well after all and we mightily enjoyed ourselves; Jenny especially, who was delighted with the night rowing and the glitter of the lights of Richmond Hill in the water, and the rather terrifying mysteries of a river by night.

"An improvement is to be noted at Hampton Court by the way. They have cleaned the tapestries; and taken the piece that used to be under the gallery and hung it in the Drawing Room so that it is quite visible, and have added another piece to it which I have never seen before and which is very fine. The Triumph of Time, also at the end of the Drawing Room, now it is cleaned shows a most splendid work: also they have opened a small room next to the Drawing Room, and that also is hung with tapestries, inferior to these, but still very beautiful."

" This morning, as it is fresh and fair after the rain, I am going to throw dull care away and have a holiday, to wit I am going to Hampton Court *by myself* to look at the tapestries and loaf about the gardens."

" I don't know if you saw an article about the Working Men's Clubs in the Daily News t'other day. I who know a good deal about these institutions grinned sardonically at its conventional rose-water. There is only a very small nucleus of really political working men: at Chiswick with a membership of 300 there are about 14 who interest themselves in politics: the Hackney Club 1,600 members, and about 100 political ones. Sunday beer, and weekday cards and billiards, are the real attraction. Moreover quite in contradiction to what the D. N. states, the only political working men's clubs at all that are even worth mentioning are much infused with Socialism."

" I have had one holiday this week: I went to see the Flowers (human) at Tangley Manor. It is a very beautiful old house: the old 14th century hall, at least its chief beam, being built up into a house of 1582. I grudged the vanishing of the older house in spite of the beauty of the other. A moat it has and a stone wall with holes in it, and many things desired by the righteous; and the country around is pleasant. But Lord! if I lived there, what a state of terror I should be in lest they should begin to build up round about. There is a beautiful pile of old barns fronting it which does not belong to Flower, but to a man who thinks that he looks upon them as an eyesore and wants to buy them to pull them down ; and therefore he keeps them up, in order to stimulate Flower to bid a higher price for the land than it is worth."

"I have now" (August 25th) "committed the irremediable error of finishing the Odyssey, all but a little bit of fair-copying.   I am rather sad thereat."

"It is a beautiful bright autumn morning here, as fresh as daisies: and I am not over-inclined for my morning preachment at Walham Green, but go I must, as also to Victoria Park in the afternoon.   I had a sort of dastardly hope that it might rain.   Mind you, I don't pretend to say that I don't like it in some way or other, when I am on my legs.   I fear I am an inveterate word-spinner and not good for much else."

"I had three very good days at Kelmscott" (in September) : "once or twice I had that delightful quickening of perception by which everything gets emphasized and brightened, and the commonest landscape looks lovely ; anxieties and worrits, though remembered, yet no weight on one's spirits—Heaven in short.   It comes not very commonly even in one's younger and brighter days, and doesn't quite leave one even in the times of combat."

Late in that autumn was produced the most singular of all Morris's literary adventures, the little play entitled "The Tables Turned, or Nupkins Awakened."   "I have been writing," he says on the 24th of September, "a—what?—an 'interlude' let's call it, to be acted at Farringdon Road for the benefit of Commonweal."   It was performed there on the 15th of October, Morris himself acting in it, and was so successful that it was repeated three times.   The dramatic form was one which he had essayed long before in a very different material. "Sir Peter Harpdon's End," "The Fall of Troy," and "Love is Enough," are a trilogy which is strangely concluded by this satyric piece.

In the contemporary theatre and in the modern actor's art Morris had not, and never affected to have, the slightest interest. From a very different point of view, he had for many years come to the same conclusion as Matthew Arnold in pronouncing the modern English theatre the most debased in Europe. Since the days of his early enthusiasm for Robson and Kean he hardly ever had gone to a play, unless on some rare occasion when he took his children or was dragged off by a friend. Nor has "The Tables Turned" anything that can be called a plot, any dramatic artifice, or any characterization beyond that of a mediæval mystery play. "If he had started a Kelmscott Theatre," says one of the most enthusiastic and most paradoxical of his followers, "instead of the Kelmscott Press, I am quite confident that in a few months, without going half a mile afield for his company, he would have produced work that would within ten years have affected every theatre in Europe." As a personal impression this assertion is interesting, but unverifiable. As a matter of fact nothing came of the experiment in which the method of the Townley Mysteries was applied to a modern farce. "Morris was so interested," the critic just quoted adds, "by his experiment in this sort of composition that he for some time talked of trying his hand at a serious drama, and would no doubt have done it had there been any practical occasion for it, or any means of consummating it by stage representation under proper conditions, without spending more time on the job than it was worth. It was impossible for such a born teller and devourer of stories as he was to be indifferent to an art which is nothing

more than the most vivid and real of all ways of story-
telling."   It is certainly true that he was just then casting about for some new method of expressing the thought
working inside him, and getting rid of his superabundant
creative energy.   So it had always been in all his practice of the arts: no sooner had he mastered one art—
were it illuminating, or carpet-weaving, or narrative
poetry—than he passed eagerly on to master another :
and just now, " rather lost," as he says, " with the conclusion of my Odyssey job, and on the look-out for
another," he may have thought now and then of the
dramatic form as one in which he might begin a new
and interesting series of researches and experiments in
order to recover, as in the other arts, the dropped thread
of the mediæval tradition.   But if so, it was not seriously,
nor for long : and in the series of prose romances which
he began soon afterwards, and which were continued
through the remaining years of his life, he found a
vehicle of new expression more satisfying to his imagination and better suited to his familiar methods.

The part which Morris himself took in the play was
that of the Archbishop of Canterbury, who was supposed
to have been called as a witness for the defence in a
police prosecution of a member of the Socialist League.
The charge was one of obstruction and incitement to
riot by speaking from a stool (as Morris so often did)
on a Sunday forenoon at Beadon Road, Hammersmith.
" Under the pretext of paying a visit to my brother of
London," the Archbishop had got into a cab and gone off
to see what these Socialist meetings were like. " To the
best of my remembrance," he states in evidence, " there
were present at the commencement of your discourse but
three persons exclusive of yourself"—namely, a colleague
of the lecturer, the Archbishop himself, and a small boy.
The discourse " was a mass of the most frightful incen-

diarism. He even made an attack on my position, stating (wrongly) the amount of my moderate stipend." The audience, he further states, had increased to ten by the time the orator concluded. The scene, which was received by the audience, most of them familiar with those Sunday street meetings, with uncontrolled amusement, gave the ludicrous side of a bitter truth. Often Morris had himself spoken, both in doors and out of doors, to as small an audience. A few months earlier, a lecture on Feudal England, into which no other man alive could have put an equal combination of historical knowledge, imaginative insight, and romantic sympathy, had been delivered to an audience of nine people, not one of whom probably understood what it was about. That such entire public apathy regarding the Socialist ideal should co-exist with the presence of revolution actually at the door (the trial in this play is broken off by its triumphal outbreak) is a situation well enough suited for a farce which is intentionally and wildly extravagant. But it seems that even then the combination was one in which the more ardent members of the League had not in the least abandoned belief.

For that strange belief, in which Morris no doubt had once to a certain degree shared ("as his way was about everything, to make it something different from what it was," the habit of boyhood surviving undiminished into mature life), the events of the next month in London gave some sort of colour. A long-continued depression of trade had made the question of the unemployed, in London and elsewhere, more than usually serious; and the restlessness among the working classes culminated in the famous scenes of the 13th of November, "Bloody Sunday," in and round Trafalgar Square. A meeting in the Square had been announced to protest against the Irish policy of the Government: it had been proclaimed by the police, and became converted into a demonstration on a huge scale. No one who saw it will ever forget the strange and indeed terrible sight of that grey winter day, the vast sombre-coloured crowd, the brief but fierce struggle at the corner of the Strand, and the river of steel and scarlet that moved slowly through the dusky swaying masses when two squadrons of the Life Guards were summoned up from Whitehall. Morris himself did not see it till all was nearly over. He had marched with one of the columns which were to converge on Trafalgar Square from all quarters. It started in good order to the number of five or six thousand from Clerkenwell Green, but at the crossing of Shaftesbury Avenue was attacked in front and on both flanks by a strong force of police. They charged into it with great violence, striking right and left indiscriminately. In a few minutes it was helplessly broken up. Only disorganized fragments straggled into the Square, to find that the other columns had also been headed off or crushed, and that the day was practically over. Preparations had been made to repel something little short of a popular insurrection. An immense police force had been concentrated, and in the afternoon the Square was lined by a battalion of Foot Guards, with fixed bayonets and twenty rounds of ball cartridge. For an hour or two the danger was imminent of street-fighting such as had not been known in London for more than a century. But the organized force at the disposal of the civil authorities proved sufficient to check the insurgent columns and finally clear the streets without a shot being fired. For some weeks afterwards the Square was garrisoned by special drafts of police. Otherwise London next day had resumed its usual aspect.

Once more the London Socialists had drawn into line with the great mass of the London Radicals, and a formidable popular movement had resulted, which on that Sunday was within a very little of culminating in a frightful loss of life and the practical establishment of a state of siege in London. But the English spirit of comprom se soon made itself felt. While on the one hand the impotence of a London crowd against armed and drilled forces had been crushingly demonstrated, on the other hand the public were startled into seriousness. Measures were taken for the relief of the unemployed. Political Radicalism resumed its normal occupations; and by the end of the year the Socialist League had dropped back to its old place, a small body of enthusiasts among whom an Anarchist group were now beginning to assume a distinct prominence. The only other important public occasion in which Morris took part during the rest of the year was on the 18th of December. A young man named Alfred Linnell had died in hospital from injuries received from the police in the struggle of Bloody Sunday. A public funeral was organized. In pouring rain a great but orderly crowd marched through the mid-winter dusk from Soho to Bow Cemetery, where the burial service was read by the light of a lantern. The stately verses which Morris wrote for the occasion are well known. Less known, but perhaps not less worthy of remembrance, is the brief speech which he delivered over the grave. The other speakers—Mr. Tims of Battersea, Mr. Dowling of the Irish National League, Mr. Quelch of the Social Democratic Federation—had improved the occasion with obvious sincerity, but in phrases that were rapidly becoming mere commonplaces of journalism and losing any definite meaning: protesting against what they described as the autocracy of the police, speaking of hired murderers in uniform, and a ruling class trembling in its shoes. Morris's words, spoken to a crowd fast melting away in the darkness and rain, tried to recall the larger and nobler issue. "Our friend who lies here has had a hard life, and met with a hard death; and if society had been differently constituted, his life might have been a delightful, a beautiful, and a happy one. It is our business to begin to organize for the purpose of seeing that such things shall not happen; to try and make this earth a beautiful and happy place."

"The scene at the grave," he writes a few days afterwards, "was the strangest sight I have ever seen, I think. It was most impressive to witness; there was to me something aweful (I can use no other word) in such a tremendous mass of people, unorganized, unhelped, and so harmless and good-tempered."

This feeling of pity for the helplessness of the masses had throughout stood alongside of his indignation at the practical barbarism of the commercial system as the dominant force in his mind. When he saw the multitudes—if we may recall in so different a context the august words of the Evangelist—he was moved with compassion on them, because they fainted, and were scattered abroad as sheep having no shepherd. The direct result of all his efforts to bring them together and lead them on was indeed little enough. The smallness of the numbers of really convinced supporters, however much the opportunist section of English Socialists might try to swell them out by various bodies of men in buckram, was a fact to which he never blinded himself, nor was he less keenly alive to the prodigious difficulty of accustoming men's minds in England to conceive the possibility of any changes being effected by other than the familiar Parliamentary methods. "I have always known," he writes on the 26th of February, 1887, to Ellis, "that if ever there were a Socialist *party* in England they would have to send men to Parliament, though

I certainly wouldn't be one of them. But 'tis no more use a *sect* blustering about getting itself 'represented' than it is about its conquering the world by dynamite and battle. 'Tis barely possible to get a Radical returned as a Radical, let alone a Socialist. Still things have moved much within the last four years, and they will no more stop for the capitalists than they will hurry for me." But it was not all waste labour. "Men fight and lose the battle," says John Ball, "and the thing that they fought for comes about in spite of their defeat, and when it comes turns out not to be what they meant." The silent permeation of a new spirit was making itself felt. The doctrines on which Socialism is founded were slowly beginning to modify common thought. Education towards revolution, Morris's own watchword as a Socialist, was in one sense or another rapidly becoming the order of the day. In the larger sphere of politics a change of tone was beginning to be manifest. Significant utterances began to be heard from supporters of the existing organization. The celebrated words, "We are all Socialists now," had already been uttered by an ex-Minister in the House of Commons. Professed Socialists had been invited to read papers at the Church Congress, and a Bishop had startled his colleagues by publicly declaring the contrast between the rich and poor to be so appalling that serious consideration was due to any scheme, no matter how revolutionary, that promised relief. And about Morris himself a group of artists and craftsmen were gathering, who, without following his principles to their logical issues or joining any Socialist organization, were profoundly permeated with his ideas on their most fruitful side, that of the regeneration, by continued and combined individual effort, of the decaying arts of life. Among these men, a small body, but growing in numbers, strong in youth, ardent

in assured conviction, Morris's final words on the
Beauty of Life were at last working with their full
force.   " To us who have a cause at heart, our highest
ambition and our simplest duty are one and the same
thing.   For the most part we shall be too busy doing
the work that lies ready to our hands to let impatience
for visibly great progress vex us much.   And surely,
since we are servants of a cause, hope must be ever
with us."

*Cela est bien dit, répondit Candide, mais il faut cultiver
notre jardin.*   Such too had been the last word of the
despised eighteenth century.

CHAPTER XVIII

THIS group of craftsmen were drawn together from many
different quarters and worked in very various methods;
but each in his own sphere, all alike consciously aimed at
a Renaissance of the decorative arts which should act at
once through and towards more humanized conditions of
life both for the workman and for those for whom he
worked.   There were few if any among them who would
not readily have acknowledged Morris as their master.
The seed sown twenty-seven years before in the little
workshop in Red Lion Square had long been silently and
unostentatiously bearing fruit. Of those whose practice
had long been moulded by Morris's influence, there
were not a few for whom the ideas which underlay the
whole of his work had, when they took definite shape
as a body of doctrine, added a quickened impulse and a
higher enthusiasm.   Socialism, less as a definite creed or
a dogmatic system than as a way of looking at human
life and the meaning of the arts, was widely diffused among
a younger generation of artists. Among these Mr. Walter
Crane, by his versatility and energy, as well as the acknowledged excellence of his artistic work, held a leading
place. Mr. T. J. Cobden-Sanderson brought to the movement an energy as great, united with the gift of a copious
and persuasive eloquence. Among the younger men

Mr. Heywood Sumner, Mr. W. R. Lethaby, and Mr. W. A. S. Benson may be singled out as prominent members of the group. Only a few out of the whole body were, either then or subsequently, professed Socialists. Some of them were Conservative or even ultra-Conservative in politics. But they all in their special lines of work carried out ideas of which Morris was the original source. To them, and to many others, he has been, both while he lived and afterwards, an inspiring and guiding influence of the first importance.

Alongside of this movement, or rather essentially included in it, was another movement towards a re-integration of labour, a practical socialism of handicraft as applied to the arts. This movement expressed itself in two ways. On the one hand it aimed at a new organization of work within the single workshop, so that the manager, the designer, and the artificer should cease to be three distinct persons belonging to different social grades, differently educated and differently employed, working without mutual sympathy, or even each in active hostility to the others. On the other hand it expressed itself in the co-ordination of these workshops, hitherto isolated units of productive energy, whether by means of formal guilds and associations, or through more intangible links of common ideas and kindred enthusiasms, into the beginnings of a trained organism of handicraftsmen, with a mutual intercommunication, and a cumulative force of trained intelligence. What Morris himself had, in earlier days, done by the mere unassisted force of his own genius, was now being attempted on all sides with a conscious purpose. His own work in the early sixties had been based on two principles: the first, that nothing should be done in his workshops which he did not know how to do himself; and the second, that every form of decorative art could be subsumed under the single head of architecture, and had only a real life and intelligible meaning in its relation to the mistress-art, and through the mistress-art to all the other subordinate arts. Following out these principles, his pupils were now occupied, first, in learning what it was they had to deal with by actual work at the lathe, or the dye-vat, or the mason's yard, and then in forming, by the co-ordination and communication of this practical knowledge, the basis for a really popular art such as had not existed within the memory of men now living.

The sense of corporate life among this group of artists and workmen had by this time reached a point where it demanded some visible expression. There was already a sort of freemasonry among them. The Art Workers' Guild, established in March, 1884, had become a great influence towards solidarity. But now an increased motive power might, it was thought, be given to the movement by arranging for periodical public exhibitions of work done. These exhibitions were to be combined with some amount of instruction by acknowledged masters in both the theory and the practice of the various handicrafts. The beginning of this project has been dated from a correspondence which had been carried on some three years before in the Times on the subject of reform of the Royal Academy. It had long been a surprise or scandal to many that the Academy of Arts should confine itself rigidly to painting and sculpture and what may be called abstract architecture, and should ignore all the other decorative and applied arts. But public opinion could not be roused to press for the reform of this bad tradition. The attempt to do so, not for the first or last time, came to nothing: and it was then that the suggestion arose of a separate exhibition of products of applied art. So early as 1858 the question had been raised by Madox Brown in connexion with the exhibitions held by the newly-founded Hogarth Club. The committee of the club had then refused to hang his designs for furniture, as not being examples of " fine art proper." Their decision was quite in consonance with the traditions of that day. But the Pre-Raphaelites themselves were strongly represented on the committee, and even among them the proposal found little or no favour. Probably this was due to a certain excessive purism which had its legitimate and intelligible source in the desire to withdraw art from all taint or suspicion of commercialism. In any case the decision then taken had practically put the matter off for a whole generation. Perhaps the delay was not without its uses.

The first step towards carrying the scheme now once more suggested into actual working was taken by Mr. Benson, who, since he left Oxford in 1876, had been engaged first (like Morris himself) in an architect's office, and then in founding and carrying on a business as a decorative metal-worker and cabinet-maker, and had been throughout that time intimate with Morris on the side of theory and of practice alike. In concert with two or three others, he succeeded, early in 1886, in effecting the formation of a provisional committee of some five and twenty members. Nearly all of them were also members of the Art Workers' Guild ; and it was the existence of the Art Workers' Guild, Mr. Benson thinks, which made the Arts and Crafts Exhibition Society possible. Of less import, but not without a large result both for good and harm on the new movement, were the various associations which had sprung up in recent years under the names of Home Arts, or Cottage Arts Societies, or Village Industries. These associations had been formed chiefly by the energy or caprice of individuals. Some of them were direct attempts at following the teaching of Ruskin. Others represented a mixture of charity and patronage, and their only effect was to multiply the productions of amateur incompetency. In a few cases, according to the view taken by skilled judges, good work had been produced by them, and in a few more, a slow but steady progress towards good work was visible; but on the whole they were of little value either as productive or as educational agencies.

The newly-formed association was at first known by the name of the Combined Arts. The name of the Arts and Crafts was the invention, at a somewhat later stage, of Mr. Cobden-Sanderson. He was also in the main responsible for another of the new departures made in the first Arts and Crafts Exhibition, that of publishing the names of the designer and executant as the joint-authors of any given piece of work which was exhibited.

That such a thing should be thought of at all marked a great advance from the ideas of a generation earlier. The large firms of decorators and furnishers looked on the notion with suspicion or contempt ; and several of them refused point blank to have anything to do with a scheme under which the work of art should have any name attached to it except that of the proprietor and vendor. It was contrary to their practice, and injurious, as they conceived, to their interests, that even their own "designer," the artist whom they paid to produce patterns for their workmen to execute, should be known by name, or have any substantive existence, or separate recognition, outside their workshops. As a body of designers—for such in the main they were—the members of the Arts and Crafts Exhibition Society were fighting for their own hand in insisting that he should be so recognized. The further doctrine that the name of the executant workman should, where possible, be given, as well as that of the designer, was no doubt in a measure due to the working of Socialistic, or at all events semi-Socialistic ideas. To Morris, who had thought the whole matter out for years, and was never the victim of phrases, the point seemed a trivial one ; it was not by printing lists of names in a catalogue that the status of the workman could be raised, or the system of capitalistic commerce altered in the slightest degree. As a matter of fact, this was essentially a designers' movement: and it was as such that Morris approached it. Any elements of militant Socialism which appeared in it came from other sources ; and some of those who had been his own disciples, up to the measure of their capacity, in Socialist doctrine, were surprised, and a little indignant, at the cool view which Morris took of the " responsible executants " of his own designs, and the civil contempt with which he treated the rules and regulations framed by his colleagues or pupils. Here, as always whenever it came to be a question of practical production, he understood exactly how to make the best of things as they are, and was no more the slave of new theories than of old conventions.

Towards the movement which thus took shape, the way here, as in so many other instances, had been pointed out by the far-ranging genius of Ruskin long before any steps were, or could be, taken towards its realization. The prophet had, as usual, been long before his age. The whole of the Socialism with which Morris identified himself so prominently in the eighties had been implicitly contained, and the greater part of it explicitly stated, in the pages of " Unto This Last " in 1862, when Morris had just begun the work of his life as a manufacturer. And so now, the new movement in art, which has had so powerful an effect in the succeeding decade, took a direction which had been suggested by Ruskin ten years earlier. Writing to Morris on the 3rd of December, 1878, Ruskin, after thanking him for being the only person who went " straight to the accurate point of the craftsman's question," added these striking words : "How much good might be done by the establishment of an exhibition, anywhere, in which the Right doing, instead of the Clever doing, of all that men know how to do, should be the test of acceptance!" The times were not then ripe. But now this was one main object with which the Arts and Crafts Society was founded, and this was the test which, to the best of its power and will, it attempted to apply.

The project had taken form in the latter months of 1887. Morris, though for it, as for the whole movement out of which it sprang, he was so largely the ultimate source, had no share in its origination, and was at first, with his strong common sense, inclined to lay stress on the difficulties that stood in the way. "One thing will have to be made clear," he wrote on the last day of that year, "*i.e.*, who is to find the money. I can't help thinking on reflection that some money will have to be dropped upon it: for I don't think (again on reflection) that you will find commercial exhibitors willing to pay rent for space, and the shillings at the door will not, I fear, come to much after the first week or two : the general public don't care one damn about the arts and crafts ; and our customers can come to our shops to look at our kind of goods ; and the other kind of exhibits would be some of Walter Crane's works and one or two of Burne-Jones : those would be the things worth looking at: the rest would tend to be of an amateurish nature, I fear. In short, at the risk of being considered a wet blanket, a Job, or Job's comforter, and all that sort of thing, I must say I rather dread the said exhibition : this is of course my private view of the matter, and also of course I wish it success if it comes off."

A month later he writes again : " I am convinced that the only time of the year available for the exhibition is from the middle of March to the middle of August. Any other time it would only be visited by the few who are really interested in the subject. Isn't it now too late to get the thing afoot during this period this year?"

But the scheme was already fairly afoot: and Morris seems to have under-estimated, not indeed the actual progress that had been made in the production of good work rightly done, but the amount of feeling towards such production which was stirring, and the amount of public interest which had been at last, though languidly and tardily, aroused in the difference between good and bad decorative art. When once the decision was taken, he gave the scheme his hearty support : and in this, as in the succeeding exhibitions held, his work attracted a wider and more intelligent interest than could have been counted upon. The lectures and papers which he contributed had also a real stimulative and educative value. Limited as was the number of people interested in the subject, they were to be counted by hundreds where those interested in theoretic Socialism could be reckoned on the fingers of one hand. When he resumed educational work in connexion with what was, after all, his own proper subject, on which he spoke with the ease and authority of an absolute master, he may indeed have felt that he was not striking at the root, but must also have recognized that he was not spending his blows on the air.

The echoes of the Trafalgar Square disturbances died slowly away. Popular attention in England was soon transferred to the action of the Government in Ireland under the Crimes Act of 1887 : but Morris refused to be so turned off the point. "As to Blunt and his imprisonment," he wrote on the 14th of January (Mr. Wilfrid Blunt was a personal friend of his own, for whom he had a great liking), " from what I hear, the

Irish prisons are better than the English. I don't see that we take it quietly specially because it is in Ireland: there are dozens of poor fellows in prison in England over the Trafalgar Square business, some of them for four or six months, for the same offence as Blunt's, and I fear little enough is said about them. However it is a bad business enough, nor do I deny that an English prison is torture, and is meant to be so. Doubtless it is bad that political prisoners like Blunt and the so-called rioters should be treated as criminals; but then the criminals are not treated as if they were human beings. The whole prison system in its folly, stupidity, and cruelty, is a disgrace to mankind; and the treatment of political prisoners is only one instance."

But though there were crowded meetings to welcome the Trafalgar Square prisoners on their release, the excitement, so far as not artificially kept up by the temporary alliance between Socialists and Irish Home-Rulers in vindication of the right of free speech in both countries, had already dwindled away. "On the whole," Morris writes again in March, "I think things will be pretty quiet till next October or November, when it will begin simmering again. I have been reading Tolstoi's 'War and Peace,' which I find I can get through with much approbation but little enjoyment, and yet (to take the horse round to the other side of the cart) with a good deal of satisfaction. There seems to be a consensus of opinion in these Russian novels as to the curious undecided turn of the intellectual persons there: Hamlet (Shakespeare's I mean, not the genuine Amloði) should have been a Russian, not a Dane. This throws some light on the determination and straightforwardness of the revolutionary heroes and heroines there; as if they said, 'Russians must be always shilly-shally, letting I dare not wait upon I would, must they? Look here then, we will throw all that aside and walk straight to death.'

"I don't think I shall tackle 'Anna Karenina'; I want something more of the nature of a stimulant when I read. I am not in a good temper with myself: I cannot shake off the feeling that I might have done much more in these recent matters than I have; though I really don't know what I could have done : but I feel beaten and humbled. Yet one ought not to be down in the mouth about matters; for I certainly never thought that things would have gone on so fast as they have in the last three years; only, again, as opinion spreads, organization does not spread with it."

"The Dream of John Ball" was published as a book that month, and was followed two months later by the volume of lectures and addresses entitled "Signs of Change." This volume once cleared out of the way, his mind reverted with full force to the romance and simplicity of a remoter past. An epoch of swift change, even were it in the nature of progress, was distasteful to his temperament. He was continually seeking refuge from it in dreams of some settled and seeming-change-less order, whether seen as a vision of the future or re-created from a tradition of the past. The old world which he had summoned up in "John Ball" was one that had none of this stability. Its period was that of the breaking up of the mediæval system, and the be-ginnings of times of change, destruction and unsettle-ment. In the new romance which he now began to write, he went back from the close of the Middle Ages to their earliest beginnings, and from a complex artificial society to the simplest of all known to history. This story, "The House of the Wolfings," was the first of a series of prose romances which he went on writing almost continuously down to the end of his life.

"I am a little dispirited over our movement in all directions," he writes to Mrs. Burne-Jones on the 29th of July. "Perhaps we Leaguers have been somewhat too stiff in our refusal of compromise. I have always felt that it was rather a matter of temperament than of principle; that some transition period was of course inevitable, I mean a transition involving State Socialism and pretty stiff at that; and also, that whatever might be said about the reception of ideal Socialism or Communism, towards this State Socialism things are certainly tending, and swiftly too. But then in all the wearisome shilly-shally of parliamentary politics I should be absolutely useless : and the immediate end to be gained, the pushing things just a trifle nearer to State Socialism, which when realized seems to me but a dull goal—all this quite sickens me. Also I know that there are a good many other idealists (if I may use that word of myself) who are in the same position, and I don't see why they should not hold together and keep out of the vestry-business, necessary as that may be. Preaching the ideal is surely always necessary. Yet on the other hand I sometimes vex myself by thinking that perhaps I am not doing the most I can merely for the sake of a piece of 'preciousness.'

"I have done another chapter to the tale, rather good I think, and shall get on with it as I can; and when finished shall set about revising before I get it into type."

The work of editing the Commonweal, which even in its first hopeful days had been unpleasant, had now in this altered frame of mind grown inexpressibly irksome. "I have been writing hard all the morning," he says on the 11th of August, "but not at what I like; have been simply pitching into Balfour and Salisbury, who will never see my scathing periods and wouldn't care if they did." The scathing periods, as they may still be found in the file of the Commonweal, make very dull reading now, as they made dull writing then. The only chances of writing what he liked that the scope of the Commonweal gave him he seized with avidity: just at this time he was in the middle of a vivid and detailed account of the Revolt of Ghent in the fourteenth century, including long passages of admirable translation from Froissart, which runs through the issues of seven weeks.

"I am prepared," he writes again a few weeks later, "to see all organized Socialism run into the sand for a while. But we shall have done something even then, as we shall have forced intelligent people to consider the matter; and then there will come some favourable conjunction of circumstances in due time which will call for our active work again. If I am alive then I shall chip in again, and one advantage I shall have, that I shall know much better what to do and what to forbear than this first time."

In this settled low content he spent not an unhappy autumn, as a series of letters in August and September sufficiently show. But before quoting from these I may be pardoned for inserting a letter of the same autumn, addressed to "the baby of the lot" who had been children together through the past twenty years, Miss Margaret Burne-Jones. She was married this year on the 4th of September.

" Kelmscott House,
" August 21st, 1888.

" Dearest Margery,

"I have bidden our Mr. Smith to send you an 'article' called a Hammersmith Rug (made at Merton Abbey) which Janey and I ask you to take as a small and unimportant addition to your 'hards.'   If it should at any time get dirty (as is likely, since London will not be pulled down for a few months, I judge) if you send it to Merton we can wash it as good as new.

" Also with this little gift take my hearty good wishes for your happiness, which you will easily believe are not at all conventional, since you will remember how prettily and dearly you have always behaved to me since you were a dear little child, in the days when I was really a young man, but thought myself rather old. Also as the wish is not conventional, as really meaning what it says, so it is not conventional as saying something which I do not think will happen: as indeed I think you have every chance of being happy, both because of your fortunate surroundings, and your good choice, and especially because I think you have it in you to be happy, and to be all along the dear little child of those times I was reminding you of.

"I went away in a hurry last Sunday, which I was sorry for, as I should have liked to have said good-bye. But I shall hope to see you very soon after September.

" Meantime good-bye, and good luck in all senses of the word.

" Your affectionate friend,
" WILLIAM MORRIS."

The following are extracts from letters to his daughter Jenny at Malvern.

August 18th. " Well, my dear, as to Worcester I have only been there once, since the days when I sucked at a bottle, of which your Granny will tell you. That once was when I went to see my Aunts thirty years ago, and I was not so well informed on archæology as I am now. But I do remember Prince Arthur's Chantry and the tombs and also the general look of the Church. The town I don't remember except as a mass of red brick broken by a few half-timber houses.

"Yesterday I went to Birmingham all by myself to see the new window: my work was over there in five minutes, for it was quite satisfactory; it was rather a long journey for so short a piece of work. Well, I must tell you about the Norwich journey, my dear. We went down rather a jolly company though the day was dull. The comrades work one pretty hard when they get hold of one in Norwich, and I left most of my voice behind me there. I spoke three times on the Sunday, twice in the market-place, once indoors, and twice in the market-place on the Monday, besides taking the chair for Mrs. Besant in the evening indoors; and being photographed (in groups) twice, and going a row (in five boats, cost 15d.) in the afternoon. However I enjoyed it all and was pleased that it was so successful : there were between seven and eight thousand people present at the meeting in the market-place on Sunday afternoon; and all the meetings were good. After the Sunday afternoon meeting Mrs. Besant proposed a walk, and we went down towards the Close; but Lord ! such a tail as we took with us, including a lot of boys who were fascinated by us, expected I think to see us hanged presently; the others except the boys mostly tailed off when we got into the Close, but not the boys; the only resource we had was to cross the ferry at the other side of the Close, which charges $\frac{1}{2}d$. for the transit ; this threw out our younger brethren and we got away quietly.

"The river I went on was a branch of the Wensum ; it was very beautiful ; the water awash with the green banks, willows nearly meeting over the water ; no rushes or reeds, no weeds except some kind of long grass growing up from the bottom, no stream scarcely, and the water deep and clear as glass. All quite different from the rivers I am used to: in fact I always feel in a foreign land when I go to Norwich."

August 21st.   "I suppose your mother told you we are going down to Kelmscott to-day: you see your mother doesn't like it to eat its head off, and for my part I have been rather driven lately and want to be quiet. I am taking down a piece of Oxford Street work which I must do, and I shall hope to get on with my story, perhaps nearly finish it."

August 28th.   "We had a beautiful day on Sunday: we all went up the water along with Mr. Radford, who suddenly turned up on Saturday evening on a bicycle, asking for lodging, having come over from Didcot through Wantage. The morning opened most lovely; we started at eleven, and by twelve were sheltering our-selves from a driving rain under Mr. Birchall's yew tree ; then it cleared a little, and we got to dinner close to where we dined so merrily, my dear, with Ellis, and lo by two the sun was hot and bright, and the day straight on most lovely. We got out at the Round House, and walked nearly a mile up the canal, which is really very pretty, the water without stream and clear and bright: it made me long for an expedition. Your mother and Crom and I went up to the Church after-wards over perilous ditch-bridges, leaving Radford and May lazing by the boat. It went to my heart on that beautiful afternoon to see the neglect and stupidity that had so marred the lovely little building : yet it still looked lovely. As we passed by Buscot, there were the Birchalls in their goat-mead, and we exchanged a few words with them, as we rather expected Walker to meet us : we had left the house quite empty of Frank and everybody, the key under the doormat and a letter pinned to the door for Walker, who duly came and walked on to meet us and fell in with us just as we were opening Buscot Lock. So we had a merry evening together, and I so wished you had been with us, my darling."

September 6th. " Yesterday the weather, which had been drizzly in the morning, clearing up somewhat in the afternoon, we set off about 2.30 to go to Rushey, thinking we might get to Bampton, which your mother has never seen, and we got down there comfortably enough: we intended coming straight back by boat, as we seemed too late to get up to Bampton and back, (it is two miles from the lock there,) but strolling up towards the town over the fields we thought we would go there and get a trap for the ladies, and that Walker and I would go back and pull the boat home: so we did this; but Mrs. Walker could only go so slow that it was quite late before we got to Bampton. However we managed to see the church, which is a very fine one, but has been shockingly restored. There is Norman work in it, and transition ; and a fine decorated nave with a most beautiful western doorway. The tower and spire is very pretty; much the same date as Broadwell but handsomer. Near the church is a very pretty little house used as a grammar school, and another house called the Deanery. The town is the queerest left-behind sort of a place : when Walker and I first came into the street there were two other persons visible, a small boy and a small girl. Well, it was nearly dark when W. and I set off to walk to Rushey, and quite dark before we were well under way. I had to steer all the way, as Walker didn't like the job. It was a very dark night with drizzle now and then, and often one could barely see the bank. However we scarcely touched the bank at all, and got in about 10 o'clock. Frank had been sent out with a lantern to meet us, and we perceived the same as we came to Welly-Hole Reach, looking like a

' bright particular star.'   It seems he had been nearly down to the Old Weir to look for us."

The autumn holiday lingered late.   On the 8th of October he wrote to Ellis, who had been staying with him at Kelmscott:

" I am really surprised at your not liking ' Tom Sawyer,' especially as it so *very* like Shakespeare, not to say Shelley.

" I went out in the afternoon of Saturday, and a most grim and stormy afternoon it was : I caught nothing except that just as I was going away a $\frac{1}{2}$ lb. chub took my gudgeon and insisted on being caught.   Saturday night was as cold as need be ; but yesterday was better, and to-day is a mild beautiful morning : unhappily there is no river for me to-day, as we are all going to Fairford.

" I wish you had been here instead of the new comer, whose shortcomings I am not used to like I am to yours and mine ; so that we have no standing cause of quarrel ; which I think is a necessity to a really good understanding."

At the end of October, when " the river has grown small and bright and the fish won't bite," he regretfully left Kelmscott.   On the 1st of November he lectured on Tapestry-weaving at the first Exhibition of the Arts and Crafts Society, to the catalogue of which he had already contributed a short paper on Textiles.   Three Arras tapestries from the Merton Abbey looms were among the objects exhibited.   The great series of tapestries from the Morte d'Arthur now hung at Stanmore Hall were then being put in hand.   " The House of the Wolfings," too, had been finished during the autumn, and was through the press early in December.

Apart from other reasons this book has a special interest as marking the beginning of Morris's practical dealings

with the art of typography.   Hitherto he had been content to let his books be printed in the common way, without any special attention to matters of type or arrangement
of page.   His attention had been lately turned to the
matter through an increasing intimacy with his neighbour
at Hammersmith, Mr. Emery Walker, whose enthusiasm
for fine printing was accompanied by a thorough practical
acquaintance with it as a modern handicraft.   The early
printed books, which Morris had hitherto collected and
prized mainly for their woodcuts, now took a fresh
interest and value to him as specimens of beauty in type.
In consultation with Mr. Walker he fixed on a fount of
type belonging to Messrs. Whittingham for the new book.
It had been cast as an experiment about half a century
before, and was modelled on an old Basel fount ; and it
had already been used in some of the trial pages of the
illustrated " Earthly Paradise " which had been set up
in 1868. " It will be a pretty piece of typography for
modern times," Morris said of the book before it appeared ; and so pleased was he with it, that he could not
bear for a while to hear any adverse criticism even on the
demerits of the type, especially on an over-conspicuous
e of the lower case which he silently altered in his next
book, " The Roots of the Mountains."

The story itself well deserved the words "your delightful and wonderful book," with which it was hailed
by Mr. Swinburne. For the first time since " The Earthly
Paradise " had been completed, Morris was writing with
complete enjoyment and perfect ease.   The life of the
Germanic tribes of Central Europe in the second or third
century was one which was at once sufficiently known to
allow of copious and detailed description and sufficiently
undetermined to give full scope to a romantic imagination.
The use, as the vehicle of the story, of a mixed mode of
prose and verse, was a device not perhaps suited for fre-

quent repetition, but excellently adapted for this particular purpose. It was suggested by the Icelandic Sagas, but used in a fresh and quite delightful way. By the use of prose for the main narrative, he avoided the languor which is almost inseparable from verse as a medium of continuous narration ; and in speeches and ornate passages, where prose in its turn would flag, the rolling verse— that of " Sigurd the Volsung " revived in much of its first freshness—seems the natural medium of the heightened emotion.

Like " The Roots of the Mountains," it belongs to what may be called the epic or Icelandic side of the author's imagination. In the later prose tales he reverted to a softer and sweeter world, that of a vaguely mediæval life, with churches in it and houses of monks, and a faint air of the thirteenth century, the world of his own earlier masterpiece in the story of " The Man Born to be King." This primitive Gothic world of older gods and more heroic men was less fully his own. In " The Roots of the Mountains," though the supposed date of the story can hardly be later than the seventh century, he tends to slip back now and then into the later romantic world, full of beautifully forged armour and grey carved stone, and gardens standing thick with pinks and lavender. But here all the sensuous ornament of mediæval romance is as strictly excluded as it is from the stories of Sigurd and of the dwellers in Laxdale. Even when the hero makes pictures for himself of some golden life that is to be when fighting is over, it is no such world of cloistered green places, " faint with the scent of the overworn roses and the honey-sweetness of the lilies," to which his dreams turn, but the hard open life of the earlier world. " There he was between the plough-stilts in the acres of the kindred when the west wind was blowing over the promise of early spring ; or smiting down the ripe wheat in the hot afternoon amidst the laughter and merry talk of man and maid; or far away over Mirkwood-water watching the edges of the wood against the prowling wolf and lynx, the stars just beginning to shine over his head; or wending the windless woods in the first frosts before the snow came, the hunter's bow or javelin in hand; or coming back from the wood with the quarry on the sledge across the snow, when winter was deep, through the biting icy wind and the whirl of the drifting snow, to the lights and music of the Great Roof, and the merry talk therein and the smiling of the faces glad to see the hunting-carles come back; and the full draughts of mead, and the sweet rest a night-tide when the north wind was moaning round the ancient home."

His first satisfaction in the appearance of the book was soon replaced by a keener desire to improve upon it. "I am very glad that you like the new book," he writes to Ellis a few days after it was published. "I quite agree with you about the type; they have managed to knock the guts out of it somehow. Also I am beginning to learn something about the art of type-setting; and I now see what a lot of difference there is between the work of the conceited numskulls of to-day and that of the 15th and 16th century printers merely in the arrangement of the words, I mean the spacing out: it makes all the difference in the beauty of a page of print. If ever I print another book I shall enter into the conflict on this side also. However this is all grief that comes of fresh knowledge and I am pretty well pleased with the book as to its personal appearance."

On the 10th of January he writes to his daughter:

"Dearest own Jenny,

"I came back yesterday from Hadham; Auntie was pretty well, and the Granny in very good spirits but very deaf. She went a walk with me to the Church in the morning : they are ' restoring ' the nave ; a wanton piece of stupidity, as there was really nothing to do with it.   However there was no excuse for touching the roof, which is quite sound ; so they left that alone: in short the only harm is the new plaister, and the new modern glass, but that is considerable. They have found one or two bits of painting, which they have left : one a good patch of that imitation of patterned stuff such as we know at Fairford and Burford, but not so elaborate ; a rough bold good pattern. I went to see the Berrys with them ; and thought the house very nice ; it is really a 16th century building much faked up : but the rooms with that pleasantness of an old house : some of them with that regular old panelling in them where the mouldings are not ' mitred,' but the horizontal ones die off before they meet the vertical. I was there two nights and played backgammon both with Auntie and Granny : the latter beat me one night (to her great delight), but they, and especially Auntie, played with the utmost recklessness.

" This is a bad business of the burning of Clouds, isn't it ? When I saw it (the year before last I think) it looked so solid that one could not think of its being destroyed. I was at the Grange this morning and Aunt Georgie read me a letter to Margaret from one of the daughters which gave a really good account of the scene. It was touch and go for some of them. I saw Webb yesterday, and he made light of it, as he would be likely to do. It seems it will be rebuilt, which is a good thing ; but there is a certain feeling of weariness in the proceeding, isn't there, dear ? Webb says that some of the walls may be all right, especially as they are mostly built of sandstone, not limestone : the lower rooms, or some of them, were not burnt. The walls were 3 feet thick.   One of Uncle Ned's cartoons that he did for the church in Rome was there and was burnt; but that is the only important unreplaceable thing I have heard of. Our long carpet was, I imagine, saved.

" The weather changed on Tuesday and yesterday, which was a bright beautiful day: but to-day is cold; rainy, sleety, but not frosty.   I think I should care mighty little about it (in January) if I were at Kelmscott, but bad weather, especially fog, does make London wretched : indeed I feel very like not going out in it this evening; but I think I must, as it is a Ways and Means evening at the League.

" Well, darling Jenny, good-bye with this not very brilliant letter.   By the way you will be glad to hear that Faulkner shows signs of mending.   Good-bye, my dearest child.

" Your loving father,
" William Morris."

Charles Faulkner, the constant friend of so many years, had been struck down by paralysis in the previous October.   He lingered in a state of living death for upwards of three years, with just so much intelligence left as allowed of his being amused a little by the company of his friends.   Through all that period, his sister, Miss Kate Faulkner, was his devoted and unweariable nurse; and next to her, his old companions, Webb and Morris, were the most constant in their attention.   Between Morris and Faulkner the intimacy and affection was perhaps the stronger that it was founded on a deeper and subtler bond than community of tastes or even association in work.   A fine mathematician and a man of high proficiency in the mixed mathematics of engineering, Faulkner had no native bent towards art, and no apparent creative power.   He had, however, qualities at least as attaching : unconquerable courage, transparent honesty, and deep-rooted affection ; and his devotion to Morris knew no limit. He had followed him into the Socialist League as he had followed him into the firm of Red Lion Square, and lectured on Socialism for him as he had painted tiles and cut wood-blocks five and twenty years earlier, with perfect simplicity and sincerity. The work and all the load of toil and obloquy it involved had almost been too much even for Morris's immense energy and abounding vitality : on the weaker constitution of Faulkner it would seem to have acted with dangerous and finally fatal result.

"The Roots of the Mountains" had been begun as soon as "The House of the Wolfings" was through the press. "Did I tell you in my last," he writes to his daughter on the 29th of January, "that I had begun a new tale ? I don't know whether it will come to anything, but I have written about twenty pages in the rough. This time I don't think I shall 'drop into poetry,' at least not systematically. For one thing the condition of the people I am telling of is later (whatever their date may be) than that of the Wolfings. They are people living in a place near the Great Mountains. I don't think it is worth while telling you anything more of it till you hear some of it done, as the telling the plot of a story in cold blood falls very flat."

Though he still lectured regularly for the Socialist League, addresses on Art, principally given to the students of Art Schools, were taking a more and more prominent place in his activity. The way in which the two kinds of work were at present combined is well illustrated by a letter of this February. "I go to-morrow, Saturday," he writes from Hammersmith, "by night train to Glasgow, and lecture for the branch on Sunday evening. On the Monday I lecture to certain art students

on Gothic Architecture, which I daresay will be rather a
new subject to them, and will a good deal surprise them.
On the Tuesday I give an address at the School of Art
on Arts and Crafts. On Wednesday I go to Edinburgh
and lecture for the branch there : on Thursday I go to
Macclesfield and lecture (Arts and Crafts) to the School
of Art there: Friday I come home, with pretty well
enough of it."

On this visit to Glasgow, " I went," he says, " to Pro-
fessor Nichol to guest: he is a ' literary man,' not with
a wooden leg; but there is something crippled about his
mind all the same; a very clever and able man, but soured
and disappointed ; mainly I think because his capacity is
second- and his ambition first-rate. He is talkative and
amusing, and was very cordial with me. That day I
lectured on Gothic Architecture to an Institute of students.
I am afraid that they did not know much about the subject, so that my matter was rather over their heads. Lecture over, I underwent a bore—to wit dining at a solemn
dinner at the Arts Club : Lord Provost (*i.e.*, Mayor)
present, also professors and big-wigs. The business of
the evening to make speeches; toasts and thanks for
them. *I* had to return thanks for Music and Literature,
curious conjuncture ! which I turned the flank of by alluding to the Scotch Ballads and their old tunes. Tuesday
I had to address the art-school after a sort of private
public dinner; the place was full, although J. Chamberlain was speaking to a big meeting elsewhere, and the
folk seemed pleased."

Through all the wear and tear of this work " The Roots
of the Mountains" was making steady progress. At
Kelmscott in March, " the rooks and the lambs both
singing around me," he writes that " I have been writing
out my rough copy of my story and have done a good
deal of it. I am half inclined not to kill my Bride, but

to make her marry the brother: it would be a very good alliance for the Burgdalers and the Silverdalers both, and I don't think sentiment ought to stand in the way."

On Easter Monday he writes again from Kelmscott to Mrs. Burne-Jones:

"As I have been away some time I will hereby bestow some of my tediousness on you. I only got here on Thursday and feel as if I had been staying here a long time; not that I have been bored with it, as I have enough to do what with my story, what with other work which I ought to do and don't. The country is about six weeks backward; more backward by a good deal than it was last year, though that was late: neither the big trees (except the chestnuts) nor the apple trees show any sign of life yet. The garden is very pretty, though there are scarce any flowers in blossom except the primroses; but there are such beautiful promises of buds and things just out of the ground that it makes amends for all. The buds of the wild tulip, which is one of the beautifullest flowers there is, just at point to open. Jenny and I went up into Buscot wood this morning: it is such a change from our river plain that it is like going into another country; yet I don't much care about a wood unless it is a very big one; and Buscot is scarcely more than a coppice; but the blue distance between the trunks was very delightful. As to the weather, bearing in mind that things are so much behindhand, it is not bad. To-day has been March all over; rain-showers, hail, wind, dead calm, thunder, finishing with a calm frosty evening sky. The birds are amusing, especially the starlings, whereof there are many: but some damned fool has been bullying our rooks so much that they have only got six nests, so that we haven't got the proper volume of sound from them.

"One grief, the sort of thing that is always happening

in the spring : there were some beautiful willows at Eaton Hastings which to my certain knowledge had not been polled during the whole 17 years that we have been here ; and now the idiot Parson has polled them into wretched stumps.   I should like to cut off the beggar's legs and have wooden ones made for him out of the willow timber, the value of which is about 7s. 6d.

" I am so very sorry to hear of poor Kate's misfortune, and am not a little uneasy about it.   I didn't see her last Wednesday, though I called.   She was poorly then, having had some bad nights with poor dear Charley.   It is such a grievous business altogether that, rightly or wrongly, I try not to think of it too much lest I should give way altogether, and make an end of what small use there may be in my life."

The following beautiful description of a visit to western Wiltshire on business of the Society for Protection of Ancient Buildings is also from a letter to Mrs. Burne-Jones written on the 13th of May :

" Thursday afternoon was grey and stormy : the lightning twinkled over the White Horse as we passed by, and just at Swindon down came the rain in floods.   However I had rather a pleasant journey to Westbury, as the rain didn't last long, and every field corner was lovely. Some way off I saw the downs rise mountainous above the town, and remembered them by token of a modern White Horse which somewhat spoils the lovely headland they push into the plain.   The town is little and, as I expected, dull, dull, dull : no old houses, a great big church much spoiled by restoration, and my dull, but not ugly inn close to it.   I got in about seven, so had a longish time before bed, which I partly got rid of by going a little way up the down after my dinner : so you see gout was not rampant.   The resources of the Lopes Arms were not great ; but they (with all civility) provided me

for breakfast with what to me has been of late a rarity;
to wit, a genuine addled egg. However their hearts were
in the right places if their eggs were not.   Next morning
I drove to Edington along the feet of the Downs, which
are very fine: also the villages push up right into their
buttresses with cottages and trees, so that it is lovely;
the building being tolerable: so came I to Edington,
which was like one of my dream-churches, so big and
splendid: the whole population of Edington and its two
neighbours could easily go to church in one of its transepts.   Beside it a beautiful little fifteenth-century house
with pretty garden, and beyond, the Abbey gardens and
fish-ponds and a village green on the other side : except
that the parson is a lubber-fiend and that the people are
as poor as may be, nothing need be better. So back to
Westbury, and in early afternoon to Bradford. Quite a
pretty town and as gay as gay ; away from the downs
in a steep little valley built all up the southern-looking
slope; all up and down with steps and queer nooks : of
stone every house, most of them old, a good many mediæval.   The bridge fifteenth century, with a queer little
toll-house on it.   The church a very big and fine one,
but scraped to death by G. Scott, the (happily) dead dog.
Close by, the Saxon chapel, a very beautiful little building, but shamefully vulgarized by restoration, cast iron
railings, and sixpence a head.   Out in the meadow,
awkwardly near the Railway Station, Barton Farm with
old house and farm buildings, the big fourteenth-century
barn one of them.   It is very fine, but I think Great
Coxwell is bigger, and I like it better."

At Kelmscott again on Midsummer day " haymaking
is going on like a house afire; I should think such a hay-
time has seldom been; heavy crop and wonderful weather
to get it in.   For the rest the country is one big nose-
gay, the scents wonderful, really that is the word; the

THE MANOR HOUSE, KELMSCOTT, FROM THE GARDEN.

life to us holiday-makers luxurious to the extent of
making one feel wicked, at least in the old sense of be-
witched.

" We went to Great Coxwell yesterday, and also to
Little Coxwell, where there is a funny little church with
a 14th-century wooden roof over the nave, the church
much smaller than Kelmscott. We were delighted with
the barn again. The farmer turned up and seemed a
nice sort of chap; he said his family had been there for
hundreds of years. William Morris was, it seems, lord
of the manor there: we saw his brass again, it is really
a very pretty one. The harvest being now out of the
barn, we saw the corbels that support the wall pieces:
they are certainly not later than 1250, so the barn is
much earlier than I thought. The building of the walls
and buttresses is remarkably good and solid.

" The roses are not at their best, yet I shall bring
you a good bunch. The pink martagon lilies have been
very fine. Raspberries any amount, but none to eat for
a fortnight at least: no strawberries yet."

In July Morris was one of the English delegates to
an international Congress of Socialists held in Paris to
celebrate the hundredth anniversary of the fall of the
Bastille. The proceedings there did not re-inspire him
with confidence in the prospects of the cause or the
wisdom of its leaders. He left Paris before the sittings
of the Congress were concluded, and so escaped the final
scenes of confused recrimination among the various sects
which ended in the violent expulsion of the dissentient
minority. The great London dock strike of the following August and September was hailed by him with a
greater hope: for here at least there was an instance of
labour organizing itself for a definite end, and being
supported in the struggle by a powerful minority, if not
an actual preponderance, of educated opinion. The end

in question was indeed a particular one, yet it involved issues of immense width. Almost for the first time in the social history of England the organized trades took their part definitely on the side of unskilled and unorganized labour, and the principle of a minimum payment for human work began to emerge. The "docker's tanner" of 1889 was the germ more fully developed in the famous "living wage" of 1893.

Morris was at Kelmscott when the strike began; but on returning to London he at once realized its importance. "I went straight to the League," he writes on the 31st of August, "and found our people there in a great state of excitement about the strike, the importance of which I had not at all understood in the country: only you see we are two days late for news at Kelmscott. However I thought that perhaps our folk a little exaggerated the importance of it, as to some of them it seemed that now at last the revolution was beginning. Whereas indeed it began before the Mammoth ended, and is now only going on. Yet I don't want to belittle the strike, which *is* of much importance, chiefly as showing such a good spirit on the part of the men. They will, I fear, be beaten; and perhaps their yesterday's manifesto will not do them good as mere strikers. On the other hand it was a step which they were sure to take, if the masters held out; as in spite of the assertions of the daily press the tendency has been Socialistic; and I am very glad that they have taken it, since as aforesaid the real point of the strike is the sense of combination which it is giving to the men, and their winning or losing matters little, especially as what they ask for is so small. That the capitalistic press should turn against them for the said manifesto, is a matter of course, so after this hint at a general strike (it can be no more than a hint) it is clear that there is a feeling abroad wider than a mere attack on these muddling dock directors. I am told, and believe it, that the attack is on sweating in general. Our people have been very active; the Hammersmith branch alone having collected (mostly on Sunday and Monday last) nearly £20; a large sum for Socialists to handle."

" I went on Wednesday to Yarmouth," says a letter of the same date, " and had many thoughts of Peggotty. It really is a jolly old ramshackle place: the country about curious and fascinating : sand banks very low, all covered with heather and ling and bracken, so that if you were lying there you would expect to see highland crags above you; instead of which, two feet below spread out miles upon miles of alluvial meadows with slow rivers running through them, as you judge by the great sails moving over the pastures. The great church has been woefully restored, indeed almost ruined outside; I believe by John Seddon: but inside there is a good deal to see: a huge spacious church without any clerestory anywhere; exhilarating to behold after the modern shabbiness."

The Arts and Crafts Exhibition Society held a second exhibition at the New Gallery in autumn, of which a selection of Morris's woven stuffs and printed cottons was a prominent feature. To the catalogue he contributed a charming and luminous essay on the art of dyeing; and he opened the series of lectures given in the rooms of the exhibition by an introductory address on Gothic Architecture, which expressed within brief compass and in simple words the whole knowledge and enthusiasm of a lifetime.

He was also one of the leading speakers at an Art Congress held in Edinburgh in November, which was only conspicuous for a curious attempt, made by a section of its promoters, to capture it for Socialism after having sacrificed to decorum by meeting under the presidency of the Marquis of Lorne. Before he went, Morris frankly called his journey a fool's errand. When it was finished he wrote home: " It was rather a dull job, and imagine one in the chair hour after hour listening to men teaching their grandmother to suck eggs, and I on my good behaviour too ! I am very tired of it ; but since the Tory evening paper here declares that Crane and I have spoiled the Congress, you may imagine we have not let all go by default. In point of fact, with the exception of Richmond, who gave a good address yesterday, there was nothing of any interest said except by Crane and me; and my lecture on dyeing to the workmen was really a success." This lecture was one of a series given to working men by experts on the principles and practice of their crafts. The others were given by Mr. Crane, Mr. Emery Walker, and Mr. Cobden-Sanderson, all of them either declared Socialists or in full sympathy with Socialism. " On the whole the working men were good and attentive," Morris says, " and stood our Socialism well, in fact seemed to relish it."

" I have finished my book (last night)," he writes to Kelmscott on the 10th of October, " and there will not be many more proofs I think. I have a mind to begin a short story again soon; but shall say no more about it till it is under way. I have been to Oxford Street and Merton, and find business good: the girls were hard at work on the yellow carpet, but had not done very much to it yet. I was busy at pointing all the day. The tapestry is going on well, though not very fast. We have sold the 'Peace' exhibited at the Arts and Crafts for £160, which I am glad of. As for the Exhibition, I think it will be a success : the rooms look very pretty ; and there are a good many interesting works there. The visitors come pretty well : these first three days they have taken more than double than they did in the same time last year ; so this looks good."

" The Roots of the Mountains " was published in the middle of November. The study of typography as a fine art, which had been begun in " The House of the Wolf-ings," was here carried out much more fully, and the result was a page of great beauty. " I am so pleased with my book," Morris said soon after it was published, "—typo-graphy, binding, and must I say it, literary matter—that I am any day to be seen huggling it up, and am become a spectacle to Gods and men because of it." As to the " literary matter," he said afterwards that this of all his books was the one which had given him the greatest pleasure in writing. For combination and balance of his qualities it may perhaps be ranked first among his prose romances. It has not the strength of its predecessor, " The House of the Wolfings," nor the fairy charm of its successor, " The Wood beyond the World." But in its union of the gravity of the Saga with the delicate and profuse ornament of the romance it may perhaps take the first place among the three as a work of art.

The binding which pleased him so much was one of his own chintzes, used for a small number of copies of the book printed on hand-made paper. His own cooler judgment recognized that it had defects for this use both in pattern and texture, and the experiment was not re-peated. But his interest in the production of printed books was now fully aroused on all its sides ; and he was already beginning to plan out the printing and pro-duction of such books himself.

" I think before my next book comes out," he wrote to Ellis on the 21st of November,. " I shall design a chintz for bookbinding, and if I do I shall get it cal-endered so as to keep the dirt off—what do you think ? As to the printing, the difficulty of getting it really well done shows us the old story again. It seems it is no easy matter to get good hand-press men, so little work is done by the hand-press : that accounts for some defects in the book, caused by want of care in distributing the ink. I really am thinking of turning printer myself in a small way ; the first step to that would be getting a new fount cut. Walker and I both think Jenson's the best model, taking all things into consideration. What do you think again ? Did you ever have his Pliny ? I have a vivid recollection of the vellum copy at the Bodleian."

Such was the first inception of the Kelmscott Press. In December Mr. Emery Walker was asked by Morris to go into partnership with him as a printer. He was unable to accept the offer ; but the starting of a printing press was nevertheless definitely resolved on, and the latest great interest of Morris's life begins from this point.

The last letter of the year is as follows :

"Kelmscott House,
"Dec. 24th, 1889.

"Dearest Mother,

"Thank you very much for your kind letter, and for sending me the paper knife. We are all well; and as for me I rather like the weather for winter-weather. Yesterday morning was indeed beautiful, and Jenny went with a friend to the Chiswick Horticultural Gardens, which are still in existence though sadly built up. I remember as clearly as if it were yesterday going with father there when I was quite a little boy, and have never been inside the place since. How the neighbourhood must have altered since then ! Indeed it has altered very much, and that for the worse, since we first came to Turnham Green.

"I have been so very busy lately with the work at Oxford Street and Merton, that I have had no time to turn round, or I should have come down and seen you. I will do so shortly after Christmas. Janey and I remembered that you liked that champagne which I sent you last year, and I'm sure it will do you good to drink a glass now and then ; so we are sending you a little more, which ought to reach you before the New Year. I hope you will like it, dearest Mother.

" I shall be writing to Henrietta as well as you, but give her my best love, which I send her, and to you, my dearest mother, my best of love and good wishes.

" The paper knife has not come yet or I would tell you what I think of it.

" Good-bye, dearest Mother.

" Your most affectionate son,
"WILLIAM MORRIS."

CHAPTER XIX

WHILE Morris's attention was becoming absorbed in
other fields, the affairs of the Socialist League had been
going on from bad to worse. Such part of their doctrines
as was of essential truth or immediate practical value had
been absorbed by, and was bearing fruit among, the larger
body of persons who were interested in social theories, but
more concerned about what was immediately possible than
in dreams, however high or however bloodthirsty. The
real battle-ground had been transferred to the Independent
Labour Party, and, in the metropolis, the recently created
London County Council. To these bodies a number of
the best members of the League now transferred their
energies. The remnant became more and more a group
of impracticable visionaries whom the movement of things
had left behind. In 1889 the control of the executive
was captured by a group of professed Anarchists. One
of their first acts was to depose Morris from the control
of the Commonweal, replacing him by an extremist named
Frank Kitz. "The League," says one of its members,
" became a romping ground of more than dubious characters "—he gives names which I forbear to quote—
" who, being suspected of relations with the police, drove
the better elements away in disgust, and finally broke up
what was left of Morris's organization." With infinite

patience, Morris continued for some time yet to bear the demands made on his purse to meet the expenses of the Commonweal; and it was after his removal from the editorship that he contributed to it, from the 11th of January to the 4th of October, 1890, the successive chapters of his romance, "News from Nowhere." In the issues of July and August there was also printed in numbers a lecture by him on the Development of Modern Society. On the 12th of May he reappeared on the stage in support of the fast sinking funds of the journal, taking a part in a one-act play, "The Duchess of Bayswater and Co.," which was performed by members of the League in a hall in Tottenham Court Road. This was one of the last desperate efforts made to restore the League to solvency. Though the Commonweal never followed the example of a sister journal conducted by Communists and Anarchists at Buenos Ayres, for which any payment was purely voluntary, the number of copies sold was dwindling away almost to nothing, and the appeals repeated in nearly every number for renewal of lapsed subscriptions had little effect. As the task of keeping the League together became more impracticable, the interest taken in it by Morris, as a thoroughly practical man of business notwithstanding all his high idealism, also fell away. In July he writes, " I have been somewhat worrited by matters connected with the League, and am like to be more worrited ; but somehow or other I don't seem to care much." Vague efforts were made from time to time to promote union with other Socialist bodies, but they were futile. The disintegrating forces were too strong to be stopped. The doctrine of freedom from dictation was worked out in the quaintest ways. At a Revolutionary Conference held in August "it was unanimously agreed"—so the official record runs—" to dispense with any such quasi-constitutional official as a chairman, and all red-tapeism and quasi-authoritarianism were banished." At the same time articles began to appear in the Commonweal gravely discussing the methods of putting up barricades in London streets.

Morris had learned his lesson. "Such finish to what of education in practical Socialism I am capable of," he wrote a few years later with a touch of acid humour, " I received from some of my Anarchist friends, from whom I learned, quite against their intention, that Anarchism was impossible, much as I had learned from Mill, against *his* intention, that Socialism was necessary." But before severing his connexion with the League, Morris made a final statement and appeal. It appeared in the Commonweal for the 15th of November, 1890, and summed up his attitude towards the cause which he had, in spite of all disillusionments, as deeply as ever at heart. He reviews the strange history of the movement with calmness and not without a certain pride.

"It is now some seven years," he writes, "since Socialism came to life again in this country. To some the time will seem long, so many hopes and disappointments as have been crowded into them. Yet in the history of a serious movement seven years is a short time enough ; and few movements surely have made so much progress during this short time in one way or another as Socialism has done.

"For what was it which we set out to accomplish? To change the system of society on which the tremendous fabric of civilization is founded, and which has been built up by centuries of conflict with older and dying systems, and crowned by the victory of modern civilization over the material surroundings of life. Could seven years make any visible impression on such a tremendous undertaking as this?

"Consider, too, the quality of those who began and

carried on this business of reversing the basis of modern society ! A few working men, less successful even in the wretched life of labour than their fellows ; a sprinkling of the intellectual proletariat, whose keen pushing of Socialism must have seemed pretty certain to extinguish their limited chances of prosperity; one or two outsiders in the game political ; a few refugees from the bureaucratic tyranny of foreign Governments; and here and there an unpractical, half-cracked artist or author.

"Yet such as they were, they were enough to do something. Through them, though not by them, the seven years of the new movement toward freedom have, contrary to all that might have been expected, impressed the idea of Socialism deeply on the epoch.

"It cannot be said that great unexpected talent for administration and conduct of affairs has been developed amongst us, nor any vast amount of foresight either. We have been what we seemed to be (to our friends I hope)—and that was no great things. We have between us made about as many mistakes as any other party in a similar space of time. Quarrels more than enough we have had; and sometimes also weak assent for fear of quarrels to what we did not agree with. There has been self-seeking amongst us, and vainglory, and sloth, and rashness ; though there has been at least courage and devotion also. When I first joined the movement I hoped that some working-man leader, or rather leaders, would turn up, who would push aside all middle-class help, and become great historical figures. I might still hope for that, if it seemed likely to happen, for indeed I long for it enough ; but to speak plainly it does not seem so at present. Yet, I repeat, in spite of all drawbacks the impression has been made, and why ? The reason has been given in words said before, but which I must needs say again: because that seemingly inexpugnable fabric of modern society is verging towards its fall; it has done its work, and is going to change into something else.

"So much at least we have to encourage us. But are not some of us disappointed in spite of the change of the way in which Socialism is looked on generally? It is but natural that we should be. When we first began to work together, there was little said about anything save the great ideals of Socialism; and so far off did we seem from the realization of these, that we could hardly think of any means for their realization, save great dramatic events which would make our lives tragic indeed, but would take us out of the sordidness of the so-called 'peace' of civilization. With the great extension of Socialism, this also is changed. Our very success has dimmed the great ideals that first led us on; for the hope of the partial and, so to say, vulgarized realization of Socialism is now pressing on us. I think that we are all confident that Socialism will be realized: it is not wonderful, then, that we should long to see—to feel—its realization in our own lifetime. Methods of realization, therefore, are now more before our eyes than ideals: but it is of no use talking about methods which are not, in part at least, immediately feasible, and it is of the nature of such partial methods to be sordid and discouraging, though they *may* be necessary.

"There are two tendencies in this matter of methods: on the one hand is our old acquaintance palliation, elevated now into vastly greater importance than it used to have, because of the growing discontent, and the obvious advance of Socialism; on the other is the method of partial, necessarily futile, inconsequent revolt, or riot rather, against the authorities, who are our absolute masters, and can easily put it down.

"With both of these methods I disagree; and that

the more because the palliatives have to be clamoured for, and the riots carried out, by men who do not know what Socialism is, and have no idea what their next step is to be, if contrary to all calculation they should happen to be successful.   Therefore, at the best our masters would be our masters still, because there would be nothing to take their place.   *We are not ready for such a change as that!*

"I have mentioned the two lines on which what I should call the methods of impatience profess to work. Before I write a very few words on the only line of method on which some of us *can* work, I will give my views about the present state of the movement as briefly as I can.

"The whole set opinion amongst those more or less touched by Socialism, who are not definite Socialists, is towards the New Trades' Unionism and palliation.   Men believe that they can wrest from the capitalists some portion of their privileged profits, and the masters, to judge by the recent threats of combination on their side, believe also that this can be done.   That it could only very partially be done, and that the men could not rest there if it were done, we Socialists know very well; but others do not.

"I neither believe in State Socialism as desirable in itself, nor, indeed, as a complete scheme do I think it possible.   Nevertheless, some approach to it is sure to be tried, and to my mind this will precede any complete enlightenment on the new order of things.   The success of Mr. Bellamy's utopian book, deadly dull as it is, is a straw to show which way the wind blows.   The general attention paid to our clever friends, the Fabian lecturers and pamphleteers, is not altogether due to their literary ability; people have really got their heads turned more or less in their direction.

"Now it seems to me that at such a time, when people

are not only discontented, but have really conceived a hope of bettering the condition of labour, while at the same time the means towards their end are doubtful; or, rather, when they take the very beginning of the means as an end in itself,—that this time when people are excited about Socialism, and when many who know nothing about it think themselves Socialists, is the time of all others to put forward the simple principles of Socialism regardless of the policy of the passing hour.

" My readers will understand that in saying this I am speaking for those who are complete Socialists—or let us call them Communists. I say for us *to make Socialists* is *the* business at present, and at present I do not think we can have any other useful business. Those who are not really Socialists—who are Trades' Unionists, disturbance-breeders, or what not—will do what they are impelled to do, and we cannot help it. At the worst there will be some good in what they do; but we need not and cannot heartily work with them, when we know that their methods are beside the right way.

" Our business, I repeat, is the making of Socialists, *i.e.*, convincing people that Socialism is good for them and is possible. When we have enough people of that way of thinking, *they* will find out what action is necessary for putting their principles in practice. Therefore, I say, make Socialists. We Socialists can do nothing else that is useful."

This grave and reasoned statement drew forth a volley of shrill protest and abuse from the Anarchists of the League. " Our comrade lectures us!" one of them writes indignantly in the next number of the journal; and another replies by a frantic appeal to use dynamite and make open war upon society. But Morris had already left the League. The moment he did so it began to crumble away like sand. The offices of the League in

Farringdon Road had been already given up for a year, and the Commonweal had been issued from small premises in Great Queen Street. Now the rent was not forthcoming for these; they were in their turn vacated, and for the remainder of its brief and restless life the Commonweal was issued from a temporary address in Lamb's Conduit Street, where some of the members of the League kept a small grocery store under the sounding name of the Socialist Co-operative Federation. The weekly issue of the Commonweal at once ceased. It continued a struggling life as a monthly for upwards of a year. Its preaching became more and more violent. At last the slow-moving arm of authority came down upon it. In April, 1892, certain men describing themselves as Anarchists had been arrested and tried at Walsall on the charge of manufacturing high-explosive bombs; and four of them were sentenced to long terms of penal servitude. A violent article appeared in the next issue of the Commonweal, declaiming against the Home Secretary, the Judge, and the Inspector of Police who had conducted the case, and asking if such men were fit to live. The authorities were weary of this perpetual recurrence of what was on the face of it incitement to murder, and determined to make an end of it once for all. C. W. Mowbray and D. J. Nicoll, the former registered as printer and publisher, the latter as proprietor, of the Commonweal, were arrested a few days later. When tried on the criminal charge, Mowbray, who asserted that he had disapproved of the particular article in question, and was able to prove that he had taken no active part in the publication of the Commonweal for two or three months back, was acquitted; Nicoll was convicted and sentenced to eighteen months' imprisonment. This was the end of the Commonweal, and with it of the last remnants of the Socialist League.

By that time Morris was too busy with other things to be deeply concerned; nor had the treatment he had received from his unfortunate colleagues been such as a patience not absolutely inexhaustible could survive. One allusion to the matter is preserved in his correspondence. Writing to his daughter on the 21st of April, 1892, " You will be sorry to see," he says, " that Nicoll and Mowbray, two of our old comrades, have got into trouble with the Commonweal. It was very stupid of Nicoll, for it seems that he stuck in his idiotic article while Mowbray was away, so that the latter knew nothing of it. I think Mowbray will get off. I am sorry for him, and even for the Commonweal."

While therefore Morris's withdrawal in November, 1890, from the membership of the Socialist League by no means meant that he had ceased to be a convinced Socialist or had in any important way modified his doctrine, it did imply an important change in the conduct of his own life. The weary work of militant Socialism was now over for him. To make Socialists, mainly by the quiet influence of ideas; to keep the flame alive till the slow advance of time and thought had prepared the fuel for it, remained still what he conceived of as his duty: but this was rather a way of living and thinking than an active struggle, an expenditure of time and money, or that expense of spirit which was even a heavier and a more wasteful drain. A small body of his own immediate circle, those connected with him by friendship or neighbourhood, had hitherto been organized as the Hammersmith Branch of the Socialist League. They now seceded along with him, and formed themselves into an independent body named the Hammersmith Socialist Society. The secession was resolved upon on the 21st of November. Two days afterwards they met, to the number of about a dozen, and organized themselves

under a very simple body of rules.   The circular, drafted
by Morris, which they sent out to the other branches of
the Socialist League in England and Scotland—by this
time their number had dwindled to ten, four in London
and six in the provinces—is studiously quiet in its wording.

" We think it proper," he wrote, " to write you a
brief explanation of the action which the Hammersmith
Branch of the Socialist League has thought it necessary
to take in separating itself from the League.

" It has been impossible for us to be blind to the fact
that there have been once more growing up two parties
in the League, one of which has been tending more and
more to Anarchism, and the other has been opposed to
that tendency; the paper of the League, the Commonweal, has, by a vote of the last Conference, been put into
the hands of those who represent the Anarchist views:
and the majority of the Council are of that way of thinking.   Several articles have appeared in the Commonweal
with the approbation of the majority of the Council,
which we have felt did not represent our opinions.   Under
these circumstances there were two courses for us to
pursue; first to remain in the League, and oppose whatever seriously thwarted our views, and secondly to withdraw from it and carry on our propaganda independently.
We have chosen the second course; because we believe
in the sincerity of our comrades with whom we disagree;
and we think that however much they might be disposed
to yield to us and to keep articles which we should not
approve of out of the paper, they could not do so without looking upon us as a drag upon their freedom of
speech and action.   And moreover a great part of our
time which should be spent in attacking capitalism would
have to be wasted in bickering with our own comrades.
Therefore we think it much better to retire in a friendly
way, keeping our own freedom and not interfering with

that of others, and thus have formally withdrawn ourselves from the League.

"We have reconstituted ourselves under the name of
the Hammersmith Socialist Society, and hope and believe
that our efforts in pushing forward Socialism will be
rather stimulated than retarded by the new position that
we have been forced into, and that we shall take every
opportunity, whenever we feel ourselves able to do so, of
acting cordially with all bodies of Socialists both in and
out of the Socialist League."

The conditions of membership in the Society were
limited to a general agreement with the principles of
Socialism, as explained in the manifesto to be issued by
it, and a payment of a shilling as annual subscription.
Its object was defined, or was left undefined, as the
spreading of the principles of Socialism. Its place of
meeting was named as being at Kelmscott House, and a
few simple regulations as to officers and candidates made
up the remainder of its constitution. Mr. E. Walker
was, and still is, the secretary of the Society. Morris
himself was treasurer. The old room in Kelmscott
House continued to be at the service of the members
for meetings, which were held twice a week for several
years. As time went on they became more intermittent;
and at last the Society continued to exist only in the
sense that it never was formally dissolved.

"I have got to rewrite the manifesto for the new
Hammersmith Society," Morris writes on the 9th of
December, 1890, "and that I must do this very night:
it is a troublesome and difficult job, and I had so much
rather go on with my Saga work."

The manifesto does not throw any fresh light on his
principles or methods. It is in the main a re-statement
of the case against a capitalist system of society; to
which a further definition of the aims of the newly-

founded body is added, disclaiming State Socialism as a final ideal, but repudiating with much greater energy any doctrine which tends towards Anarchism. "It is not the dissolution of society for which we strive, but its re-integration. The idea put forward by some who attack present society, of the complete independence of every individual, that is, of freedom without society, is not merely impossible of realization, but when looked into, turns out to be inconceivable." Passive resistance is proclaimed as the limit of opposition to the existing order, however tyrannical; and the hope of the future is indicated as a general combination of labour which will slowly drive capitalists from position after position, until at last they find themselves in possession of responsibility without privilege, and voluntarily abdicate an untenable position.

Throughout the year the project of his new printing press and the work to be done in connexion with it had swallowed up all other interests. Even his own work in romance-writing and translating Sagas from the Icelandic took a second place to it. But at these employments, and at his Merton Abbey work, he was also fairly busy, and well contented with them all. In February the magnificent Arras tapestry of the Adoration of the Kings which now hangs in Exeter College Chapel was finished to his complete satisfaction; nothing better of the kind, he said, had ever been done, old or new. The admission to partnership in the firm of Morris & Co. of Messrs. F. and R. Smith, the two principal sub-managers after Mr. George Wardle's retirement, had relieved Morris from a great deal of the purely mechanical or commercial details of management. The romance entitled " The Story of the Glittering Plain " was written this spring, and was published in the English Illustrated Magazine, in the four numbers for the months of June to

September.   It is perhaps best known as the first book printed at the Kelmscott Press. But it is likewise notable as marking the full and unreserved return of the author to romance. In "The House of the Wolfings," and even to some degree in "The Roots of the Mountains" also, there had been a semi-historical setting, and an adherence to the conditions of a world from which the supernatural element was not indeed excluded, but in which it bore such a subordinate place as involved no violent strain on probability. Here the imagined world is of no place or time, and is one in which nothing is impossible. The dreamer of dreams has returned to that strange Land East of the Sun, mingled of Northern Saga and Arabian tale, through which the Star-Gazer had passed two and twenty years before in the days of "The Earthly Paradise": a land in which, like Odysseus and his comrades in the isle of Circe, " we do not know where is the dusk nor where the dawn." The book which the King's daughter shows to Hallblithe in his dream on the Acre of the Undying is a sort of figure of that glittering world, rich with all imagined and unimaginable wonders, into which Morris had entered long ago, and the door of which always remained open to him.

"She had in her hand a book covered outside with gold and gems, even as he saw it in the orchard-close aforetime : and he beheld her face that it was no longer the face of one sick with sorrow; but glad, and clear, and most beauteous. Now she opened the book and held it before Hallblithe and turned the leaves so that he might see them clearly ; and therein were woods and castles painted, and burning mountains, and the wall of the world, and kings upon their thrones, and fair women and warriors, all most lovely to behold, even as he had seen it aforetime in the orchard when he lay lurking amidst the leaves of the bay tree.

"So at last she came to the place in the book where-in was painted Hallblithe's own image over against the image of the Hostage; and he looked thereon and longed. But she turned the leaf, and lo ! on one side the Hostage again, standing in a fair garden of the spring with the lilies all about her feet, and behind her the walls of a house, grey, ancient, and lovely : and on the other leaf over against her was painted a sea rippled by a little wind and a boat thereon sailing swiftly, and one man alone in the boat sitting and steering with a cheerful countenance; and he, who but Hallblithe himself.　Hallblithe looked thereon for a while and then the King's daughter shut the book, and the dream flowed into other imaginings of no import."

"News from Nowhere" had been revised about the same time and was published as a cheap volume in paper covers, which had a large circulation.　It is a curious fact that this slightly constructed and essentially insular romance has, as a Socialist pamphlet, been translated into French, German, and Italian, and has probably been more read in foreign countries than any of his more important works in prose or verse.　The romance itself—if it would not be more correct to speak of it as a pastoral—is of such beauty as may readily win indulgence for its arti-ficiality.　A pastoral, whether it places its golden age in the past or the future, is by the nature of the case arti-ficial, and perhaps as much so, though not so obviously, as when it boldly plants itself in the present.　The im-mediate occasion which led Morris to put into a connected form those dreams of an idyllic future in which his mind was constantly hovering was no doubt the prodigious vogue which had been obtained the year before, by an American Utopia, Mr. Bellamy's once celebrated "Look-ing Backward."　The refined rusticity of "News from Nowhere" is in studied contrast to the apotheosis of machinery and the glorification of the life of large towns in the American book ; and is perhaps somewhat exaggerated in its reaction from that picture of a world in which the *phalanstère* of Fourier seems to have swollen to delirious proportions, and State Socialism has resulted in a monstrous and almost incredible centralization.

Indeed a merely materialist Earthly Paradise was always a thing Morris regarded with a feeling little removed from disgust. That ideal organization of life in which the names of rich and poor should disappear, together with the things themselves, in a common social well-being, was in itself to him a mere body, of which art, as the single high source of pleasure, was the informing soul. "Mr. Bellamy worries himself unnecessarily," he had said in an article in the Commonweal on this very book and its ideas in June, 1889, "in seeking, with obvious failure, some incentive to labour to replace the fear of starvation, which is at present our only one ; whereas it cannot be too often repeated that the true incentive to useful and happy labour is, and must be, pleasure in the work itself." That single sentence contains the sum of his belief in politics, in economics, in art.

The thought is thus expanded in the same article. "It is necessary to point out," he writes, "that there are some Socialists who do not think that the problem of the organization of life and necessary labour can be dealt with by a huge national centralization, working by a kind of magic for which no one feels himself responsible : that on the contrary it will be necessary for the unit of administration to be small enough for every citizen to feel himself responsible for its details and be interested in them ; that individual men cannot shuffle off the business of life on to the shoulders of an abstraction called the State, but must deal with it in conscious association with each other : that variety of life is as much an aim of true

Communism as equality of condition, and that nothing but an union of these two will bring about real freedom : that modern nationalities are mere artificial devices for the commercial war that we seek to put an end to, and will disappear with it: and finally, that art, using that word in its widest and due signification, is not a mere adjunct of life which free and happy men can do without, but the necessary expression and indispensable instrument of human happiness."

On the 10th of June Morris writes from Kelmscott House to Mrs. Burne-Jones :

" I have had three outings,—no, four—two of them business though. Item, to Chislehurst after a job : villas (some desperately ugly, others according to the new light) in the beautiful woods with lots of oak growing in them which to me is a treat, as I see so little oak about Kelmscott. Yes, villas and nothing but villas save a chemist's shop and a dry public house near the station : no sign of any common people, or anything but gentlemen and servants—a beastly place to live in, don't you think ?

" Next place was better—in a way—a house of a very rich—and such a wretched uncomfortable place ! a sham Gothic house of fifty years ago now being added to by a young architect of the commercial type—men who are very bad. Fancy, in one of the rooms there was not a pane of glass that opened ! Well, let that flea stick on the wall. Stanmore is the name of the place : it is really quite pretty about, though only about ten miles from London (near Harrow), great big properties all about, the wall of one park next to the wall of another, which has at any rate preserved the trees. Smith and I walked thence to Edgware over most beautiful meadows with scarce a house to be seen till you come to Edgware, which is a little melancholy town or large village ; old, not ugly, but too visibly the home of most abundant poverty.

"The next outing was an Anti-Scrape one to Lincoln. That was exceedingly delightful to me. The town has a terrible blot on it, a great factory for machines down by the river, which seems to take a pleasure in smoking; indeed I suppose its masters are practically the masters of the whole town. However that is the worst of it : there is a longish oldish street on the flat, and at the end of it a beautiful gate across, now the Guildhall, and it rises steeper and steeper till before you come to the close you almost have to crawl, and most of the way the long leaden roof of the minster is the horizon; the houses mostly oldish red brick and pantiles. There is another most beautiful gate into the close, over which show the different planes of the minster most wonderfully. The whole place is chock full of history : there is work of the first Norman bishop, Remigius, who strangely enough moved his see there from Dorchester on the Thames, so well known to me. The rest (and almost all) is in gradated periods of Early Pointed ; outside one may perhaps find fault with parts, especially the East Front (only I had a pleasing feeling that I was not responsible for them). But when we got inside all criticism fell, and one felt—well, quite happy—and as if one never wanted to go away again. I had seen it all more than twenty years ago, but somehow was much more impressed this time : the church is not high inside, though it is long and broad, but its great quality is a kind of careful delicacy of beauty, that no other English minster that I have seen comes up to: in short a miracle of art, that nowhere misses its intention. There is a little stained glass (early thirteenth century) as good as the best, and some of the sculpture at least belongs to the best work of the time. Outside the church and close to it is a huge Norman Castle, the *enceinte* quite complete, a piece of the keep left : a horrible modern prison and court house inside the old walls. Five minutes from the close gate towards the open country you come on the gate of the Roman town, quite unornamented, but sound and well-built. Down the slope of the hill are still left two twelfth-century houses. One of them, in honour surely of little Sir Hugh, is called the Jew's House ; I cheapened an old chest there of a lady somewhat of Mrs. Wilfer's type, who received us with the dignity of a fallen Queen."

The fourth outing was a brief visit to Kelmscott. " I am steadily at work," he writes ten days later, " reading my own poems, because we are really going to bring out a one-volume ' Earthly Paradise ' this autumn. Some people would say the work was hard. ' The Glittering Plain ' I have finished some time, and begun another."

On the 8th of July he writes again : " I have undertaken to get out some of the Sagas I have lying about. Quaritch is exceedingly anxious to get hold of me, and received with enthusiasm a proposal to publish a Saga Library : item he will give me money (or perhaps I ought to say old books). We have got six letters of our new type done and have even had a scrap printed."

This type, the first produced for the Kelmscott Press, cost Morris almost infinite pains. " What I wanted," he writes of it himself in the Note on his aims in founding the Kelmscott Press, " was letter pure in form ; severe, without needless excrescences; solid, without the thickening and thinning of the line which is the essential fault of the ordinary modern type, and which makes it difficult to read ; and not compressed laterally, as all later type has grown to be owing to commercial exigencies. There was only one source from which to take examples of this perfected Roman type, to wit, the works of the great

Venetian printers of the fifteenth century, of whom Nicholas Jenson produced the completest and most Roman characters from 1470 to 1476. This type I studied with much care, getting it photographed to a big scale, and drawing it over many times before I began designing my own letter; so that though I think I mastered the essence of it, I did not copy it servilely; in fact, my Roman type, especially in the lower case, tends rather more to the Gothic than does Jenson's."

By the middle of August eleven punches had been cut for the new fount, and Morris had determined that Caxton's "Golden Legend" should be the first large work produced by his press. He himself had recently acquired a copy of the edition of 1527 printed by Wynkyn de Worde. The Kelmscott "Golden Legend" was, however, set up, not from this, but from Caxton's own first edition of 1483. The almost priceless original was borrowed, under a heavy bond in case of loss or injury, from the Cambridge University Library for this purpose. It was transcribed for the press—a work of such laborious magnitude, and one executed so patiently and carefully as to deserve commemoration—by Miss Phillis M. Ellis, the daughter of his old friend and collaborator. Ellis himself took the chief part in superintending the accuracy of the text, a work of no small difficulty.

On the 29th of August, 1890, Morris writes to him from Kelmscott:

" Please pardon me for not answering your letter sooner; you know my little ways. Also I did want to weigh between the Golden Legend and the Troy book for reprinting: now I have borrowed a Recueil of the Histories of Troy (the Wynkyn de Worde of course) from Quaritch, and have no doubt that the G. L. is by far the most important book of the two: so I accept your kind offer with many thanks indeed, and will begin printing as soon as the type is free from the Glittering Plain, which I take it will be the first book printed in the regenerate type or Jenson-Morris.

"I inclose a specimen (over-inked) of as far as we have gone at present. I hope you admire its literature—due of course to the compositor. Kind regards to the young she-scribe that is to be."

The idea of becoming a publisher as well as a printer was one which had not yet occurred to him. An experiment was talked of later, but never carried out, of dispensing with a publisher by printing off a book and then selling the whole edition by auction. For "The Golden Legend" an agreement for publication was entered into with Mr. Bernard Quaritch. "I don't mind having a publisher," Morris said, "so long as he has nothing whatever to do with any question except purely business ones. As to the 'prophet' I want none of him: I only want not to have to drop much, say not above £100." On this footing it was arranged. The agreement, signed on the 11th of September, 1890, provides that the publisher shall pay for the expenses of paper, printing, and binding, and that Morris is to have sole and absolute control over choice of paper and type, size of the reprint, and selection of the printer. The last-named provision indicates that Morris was then still uncertain whether to start a press of his own or to have his new type printed from by some existing firm of printers. The following two letters to Ellis continue the details of the enterprise.

"Kelmscott House,
"Sept. 7th, 1890.

"My dear Ellis,

"I gave Quaritch your letter in person, and we had a talk about the matter: by this time you will have had a letter from him. It seemed to me a matter of

course to agree, as far as I am concerned, with his pro-
position to take the whole expense on himself and do
what he can with the 250 copies, since it will then cost
us nothing but our work: only it seems to me that your
share of the work will be so much the heaviest that I
feel rather uncomfortable about it, and think it somehow
ought to be made up to you.   What I have now chiefly
to do is to push on the type-founding side of matters : I
will do all I possibly can on this side, so that we may
begin as soon as possible. I should think that we might
get some type about Christmas time ; but of course I
cannot be sure. Wishing you good luck (I had little
with the gudgeons),

" I am yours ever,
" WILLIAM MORRIS."

" Kelmscott,
" Sept. 14th, 1890.

" My dear Ellis,
     " I have sent on Q.'s copy and now send back
yours.   Of course I should like the reprint to be of the
same *form* as the original if the Roman type can do it,
which I doubt, as black letter takes up less room: in
any case some kind of folio it will have to be. As to
paper I have heard of two people who may help us, one
whom Walker knows and whose mill I propose to visit
with Walker almost at once ; and one employed by
Allen, Ruskin's publisher. We can do nothing with
Whatman but take what he has on the shelves. In one
thing I think I differ from you a little, *i.e.*, about the
joined letters or queer signs : since our book is to be a
reprint, not a fac-simile, I do not think that we need reproduce these : indeed I should extend the abbreviations
in order to make the book more readable. However I
am open to correction on this point. Don't rest too

much on my date of Christmas for the type: we seem to be getting on very slowly with it at present, and I have only eleven letters cut yet. I can only hope for the best.

" Yours ever,
"WILLIAM MORRIS."

By the middle of October " the type is getting on: I have all the lower case letters (26), also I have been designing ornamental letters, rather good I think." His excitement over the work was so great that for once he left Kelmscott, when autumn ended, with little regret. " We are coming to London to-day," he writes from there on the 16th of October. " The weather has been very good; our best day was Monday, when I hear you had a fog; it was a miracle of a day here: the sort of day when you really can do nothing but stand and stare at it. I am not sorry to come to town. I want to cease from being bumbled up and down. I want to work hard at my easy work."

The breaking up of the Socialist League and the constitution of the Hammersmith Socialist Society, though it took up a measure of his time for the next six weeks in London, hardly disturbed him materially, and did not check the progress of his other work. By the end of the year all but two of the punches for the type, both upper and lower case, were completed, and a compositor and pressman, Mr. William Bowden, had been engaged. The paper was made from linen rag by Messrs. Batchelor & Son of Little Chart, near Ashford, after an Italian pattern of the fifteenth century, which Morris supplied. Such care was taken in its manufacture, that the wire moulds were woven by hand to reproduce the slight irregularity in the texture of those used by the earliest printers. Morris went down to Little Chart himself with

Mr. E. Walker to see about this paper. With unabated interest in any form of manual art, he must take off his coat and try to make a sheet of paper with his own hands. At the second attempt he succeeded in doing very creditably what it is supposed takes a man several months to master.

In the course of the year Morris had made one more experiment in the use of type other than his own. This was a small edition of his own translation of the Gunnlaug Saga, which he had printed at the Chiswick Press in a Gothic type copied from a fount used by Caxton. The initials in this little book were left blank in order to be rubricated by hand; and Morris put them in himself on two or three copies: but the whole project went no further, and the little book was never published.

On the last day of the year he writes to Ellis:

" I am very glad that you are getting on so well and like the work. As for me I expect to have my type in a month, and shall take a room and see about comps. at once. The paper also will not be later, though this matters less as to our date of beginning. One thing may disappoint you—to wit, that we cannot make a double-column page of it, the page will not be wide enough. For my part, I don't regret it: double column seems to me chiefly fit for black letter, which prints up so close. Jenson did not print even his Pliny in double column. But it is a case of *a fortiori* in modern printing : because we have no contractions, few tied letters, and we cannot break a word with the same frankness as they could : I mean we can't put whi on one side and ch on the other. This makes the spacing difficult, and a wide page desirable.

" Would you kindly give me the Initial letters of the first few sheets of our copy ; I mean state whether they are A's B's and what not ; I want this for our 'blooming-letters,' so that I may get ready those which are most wanted."

With the beginning of 1891 the Kelmscott Press actually started working. Its first premises, a cottage on the Upper Mall of Hammersmith a few yards from Kelmscott House, were taken possession of on the 12th of January. A proof-press and a printing-press were got and set up there. The first sample of the paper arrived on the 27th, and the first full trial page was set up and printed on the 31st. During February a sufficient working stock of both type and paper was delivered, and the regular working of the Press began. Mr. Bowden's son, who continued to work at the Press until it was closed, was engaged as compositor, and a third workman as pressman.

Meanwhile his research after fine specimens of fifteenth-century printing went on with unabated zeal. The following letter to J. H. Middleton refers to some of his most recent purchases, made from a dealer named Olschki, whose prices Morris thought rather exorbitant. Middleton was also in dealings with Mr. Olschki on behalf of the Fitzwilliam Museum at Cambridge, of which he was then Director.

"Kelmscott House,
"Jan. 20th, 1891.

"My dear Middleton,

"One of those books of Olschki's is a fine book otherwise (John Zeiner, Ulm, 1474) and rare doubtless, and has moreover a *very* fine woodcut border to first page and some curious initials: I am not buying it because there is, oddly enough, the same border in another of his books (by the same printer, 1475) which is much cheaper. This border is however so fine and so very well printed that I thought you might like it for the Fitzwilliam, since though I think it Jew-dear, I should have kept it if I had not got the other. The price is £15, but I daresay O. would take less. Shall I send it you to look at? I have just bought a very fine and interesting book: Speculum Humanæ Salvationis (in Dutch), Culembourg, Veldener, 1483. That says little; but the point of it is that it has in it *all* the cuts from the block-book Speculum (116) and 12 more seemingly of the same date. These are not recut, but are printed from the original blocks sawn in two down the columns of the canopies: some of these cuts are to my mind far away the best woodcuts ever done, and generally the designs are admirable: at once decorative, and serious with the devotional fervour of the best side of the Middle Ages. The date of the cutting you know is probably about 1430.

"Do you know if they have a copy at the University Library? If they have not I should like to show Mr. Jenkinson the book when I come your way. My copy belonged to the Enschede people, who you may know were a very old firm of type-founders.

"By the way I expect my press will be at work in about a month.

"Yours affectionately,
"WILLIAM MORRIS."

On the 11th of February he writes to Ellis:
"This is the state of things. The punches all cut, and matrices all struck: I had a little lot of type cast to see if any alterations were required, and set up a page of the 4to as there was not enough for the folio; I had the g recut because it seemed to me too black. I then ordered five cwt. of the type, which I am told is enough, and am expecting to have it towards the end of this week or beginning of next. As soon as I get it I will set up a trial page of the G. L.

" Then paper—the trial lot turned out not quite right, not sized quite hard enough, though I think better than any modern paper I have come across.   He is going to size it harder.   But it is only a little lot (9 reams), therefore I intend printing a little edition of the Glittering Plain on it.   Moreover we had better not be too cocksure about the paper, we *might* find it desirable to make a bigger sheet.   In any case however we might set up a section or so of the G. L. and let the type be till we had got the paper right.   I was not going to send you a specimen of the type till we could set up a page of the G. L.   But I can sympathize with my pardner's anxiety ; and accordingly send him a page of the G. P., of course full of defects, but on the paper and with the types.   I don't know what you will think of it ; but I think it precious good.   Crane when he saw it beside Jenson thought it more Gothic-looking : this is a fact, and a cheerful one to me."

The first sheet of " The Story of the Glittering Plain," which owing to this accidental collocation of circumstances was the first book printed at and issued from the Kelmscott Press, was printed off on the 2nd of March, and the last on the 4th of April.   Only two hundred copies on paper, besides six on vellum, were printed.   It was issued in May by Messrs. Reeves and Turner, Morris's ordinary publishers.   The printing had been carried through under great difficulties.   Towards the end of February Morris was laid up for several weeks with a severe attack of gout, attended by other symptoms of an alarming kind.   On consultation the kidneys were found to be gravely affected ; and he was told that henceforth he must consider himself an invalid to the extent of husbanding his strength and living under a very careful regimen.

In the height of the attack, and before he was able to

hold a pen,—" my hand seems lead and my wrist string"
—he writes to Ellis with unconquerable spirit:

"And now as to the joint enterprise: I have got my
type and am hard at work on the Glittering Plain, which
I hope to get out in about six weeks time; about the
same time I expect the first instalment of my due stock
of paper; and I don't see why we then should not be
ready to go ahead with G. L., only I certainly must see
you before we settle matters. Meantime, as soon as I
can stand up, or before, I will get a mere trial page or
two of the G. L. set up, and then you can get some idea
of the number of pages.

"Yes, 'tis a fine thing to have some interesting work
to do, and more than ever when one is in trouble—I
found that out the other day."

From Folkestone, where he had gone to pick up his
strength after this illness, he writes a month later, "I
think I shall make some scratch of a border to each life
or section. I want to make it grand. I have a specimen
of the new paper this morning, it is *admirable*—couldn't
be better." While there, he designed the ornamental
border for the first page of "The Golden Legend," and
several of the large floriated initials, or "bloomers," as
they are called in the traditional slang of the press. As
soon as he came back to London, a regular pressman
was permanently engaged (the one got in to help in the
printing of "The Story of the Glittering Plain" had only
been taken for the job) and the printing of "The Golden
Legend" began to go steadily on. The first sheet was
printed off by the middle of May: and before the end of
that month the Press had been removed into larger
premises in Sussex House, next door to the cottage first
occupied by it.

"The new printed sheets of the G. L. look very well
indeed," says a letter of the 20th of May. "Pleased as I

am with my printing, when I saw my two men at work on the press yesterday with their sticky printers' ink, I couldn't help lamenting the simplicity of the scribe and his desk, and his black ink and blue and red ink, and I almost felt ashamed of my press after all. I am writing a short narrative poem to top up my new book with. My wig! but it is garrulous: I can't help it, the short lines and my old recollections lead me on."

The volume of his own collected verses which, under the title of " Poems by the Way," was the second book issued from the Kelmscott Press, did not actually begin to be printed till July: but during May he was busy in collecting and passing judgment on those shorter unpublished poems of his own which were to form its main contents. He was habitually careless about his own manuscripts, and kept no record of what he had written or even of what he had published. Without the help of Mr. Fairfax Murray, into whose hands a number of the unpublished manuscripts had passed, and who had kept a record of all the poems which had ever been printed in magazines or elsewhere, the collection could hardly have been made. As it is, a number of his poems, which would have come within the general scope of the book, escaped his notice altogether. Apart from the longer narrative poems belonging to the period of " The Earthly Paradise," there are still sufficient of these yet unpublished pieces,—lyrics, sonnets, and ballads,—to make up a second volume of " Poems by the Way " as large as the first.

Among the pieces which had been rescued from total disappearance by Mr. Murray were a few belonging to the earliest years, the period of " The Defence of Guenevere." Of two of them he writes to Murray, " Catherine puzzles me: I have not the slightest recollection of any stanza of it. Did I write it? Is it a translation ? I think not the latter; but it is devilish like. It is much too long, and I fear it is too rude to be altered. The Long Land I like in a fashion. But O the callowness of it ! Item it is tainted with imitation of Browning, as Browning then was." None of these very early pieces were finally included in the volume published. The poem of " Goldilocks and Goldilocks," which concludes the volume, was the only one written for it now: the remainder of its contents, which are placed in a studied disarrangement, fall into two groups. One of these consists of poems written in the six or seven years between 1867 and 1874, the period which begins with " The Life and Death of Jason " and ends with " Love is Enough." The other is made up of poems of a period divided from the former by an interval of ten years. It begins with the first of the " Chants for Socialists " of 1884 ; and includes the political verses, as they might be called, of militant Socialism, the fragments which he thought most worthy of survival from his versified Socialist romance of the " Pilgrims of Hope," and the ballads and romantic pieces of the three or four years which had elapsed since the beginnings of his return to literature. Intermediate between the two main groups, and of very various dates, are the verses for his own tapestries, or for Burne-Jones's pictures, of which between thirty and forty are printed in the volume. Only one poem previously unpublished, " The Folkmote by the River," belongs to the more recent years.

Some of the poems of the earlier period have a special history or association. " The God of the Poor " (which had already been printed in the Fortnightly Review for August, 1868) was almost, if not quite, the first piece he wrote when he resumed the writing of poetry after he had left Red House. The two beautiful lyrics, " From the Upland to the Sea " and " Meeting in

Winter," are songs from " The Story of Orpheus," which had been written for " The Earthly Paradise," but never published.   "A Garden by the Sea " is a later version of the song of the water-nymph to Hylas in the fourth book of " The Life and Death of Jason."   The minute differences in language, in one of the most haunting and exquisitely finished of all his lyrics, are of no little interest. The lines " To the Muse of the North," it may be worth while to note, were written before his first visit to Iceland, and show more clearly than any comment how the land and all that had come from it filled his imagination.   The curious poem entitled " Pain and Time Strive Not," which is of a date somewhere between 1871 and 1873, is remarkable as the single instance in which Morris, after the first enthusiasm of his early years in London had cooled, has distinctly imitated the manner and versification of Rossetti.

"The title of my new book," Morris wrote to his publishers in June, " will be Poems by the Way; the *format* the same as the Glittering Plain.   It will be printed in red and black.   The poems will include some recently written and some written many years ago. Some have appeared in magazines, but with the two exceptions of a little piece out of the Jason and one out of the Ogier, they will none of them have been printed in any book of mine."

The " little piece out of the Jason " is the one just mentioned; that from " Ogier the Dane," which was in the end not included, was one of the versions of the song beginning *In the white-flowered hawthorn brake*, in that poem.   These two lyrics are, in the opinion of many judges, the most beautiful of all he ever wrote, and both are among the rare instances of lyrics which remained for years in his mind, and which he remodelled or retouched again and again.   Two earlier versions of this latter piece are extant: its original form, as a lyric in the "Scenes from the Fall of Troy," has been already quoted. An intermediate version occurs in the cancelled and rewritten Prologue to "The Earthly Paradise." Whether the lyric which he proposed to insert in the new volume was one of these two earlier versions, or (as in the case of the lyric from "Jason") a later version than that already published, and in that case a fourth version of the same piece, there are now no means of discovering.

In this pleasant work, and in the active joy of returning health, the spring and summer passed easily away. "The blossom is splendid," he writes on the 10th of May. "London in the older parts like the Inns of Court really looks well in this spring-time with the bright fresh green against the smoky old walls. Spring over, it becomes London again, and no more an enchanted city."

"I have the usual complaint at my pen's end of nothing to tell," he adds two days later. "The weather is beautifully bright and quite hot; the pear and cherry blossom is going off, and spring will soon have slid into summer, though the lilac is yet to come."

"It is a hottish close morning," says a letter of the 3rd of June, "rather dull with London smoke. I have just been down the garden to see how things were doing, and find that they are getting on. Not so many slugs and snails by a long way, and the new planted things are growing now; the sweet peas promising well, the peonies in bud, as well as the scarlet poppies. All well at the press: we are now really getting on, so that finishing the Golden Legend is looking something more than a dream."

At the end of July he writes from Folkestone to Mrs. Burne-Jones just before starting on a tour in Northern France with his daughter Jenny:

" I am ashamed to say that I am not as well as I should like, and am even such a fool as to be rather anxious—about myself this time.   But I suppose the anxiety is part of the ailment.   I hope you are better, as I have still some anxiety left for the service of my friends.

" On Sunday we had a strange show : a sea-fog came on in the afternoon after a bright morning, which gradually invaded the whole land under the downs ; but we clomb to the top of them and found them and all the uplands beyond lying under a serene calm sunny sky, the tops of the cliffs towards Dover coming bright and sharp above the fog, and throwing a blue shadow on it ; below a mere sea of cloud, not a trace of the sea (proper), wave on wave of it.   It looked like Long Jokull (in Iceland), only *that* was glittering white and this was goose-breast colour.   I thought it awful to look on, and it made me feel uneasy, as if there were wild goings on preparing for us underneath the veil."

The French tour of three weeks in August was the renewal of one of his earliest affections : and he writes that his delight in the country, "the river-bottoms with the endless poplar forest, and the green green meadows," and in the beautiful churches, was as keen and as unclouded as it had been thirty-three years before.   " I have given myself up to thinking of nothing but the passing day and keeping my eyes open."

The two letters which follow were written to Mr. Emery Walker on the journey.   In the first, the reference at the beginning is to the fount of Gothic type which he had just designed for the Kelmscott Press, and which was now in course of being cut by Mr. Prince. " By the Way " in the second was the familiar and disrespectful title of his new volume of poems.

"Beauvais,
"August 13th, 1891.

" My dear Walker,

" Many thanks for your letter and inclosures. I chuckled over the upside down A. I have written to Prince: he has now done e i h l n o p r t. The t does not look well: I think I shall have to re-design it. The e also looks a little wrong, but might be altered. The rest look very well indeed. I shall be pretty certainly at home on August 30. I leave for Soissons to-morrow, and I suppose shall get to Reims on Saturday. But I don't think we shall find any place better than this: the town is delightful quite apart from the Cathedral and St. Stephen's. Also our inn is comfortable, which is something. We went a long drive yesterday (morning drizzly, afternoon downright wet, but a jolly drive of near twenty miles and back) and saw the two churches of Gournay en Bray, and St. Germer en Fly: both early and interesting; the second exceedingly beautiful: a huge church, Norman, with vaulting and insertions of transitional, and a long lady-chapel with its vestibule, time of St. Louis (late thirteenth century). The chapel (not the vestibule) had been restored, pretty badly; but had three stained windows (of its own date) about as good as any I ever saw. The rest of the church quite unrestored : also there are grills of twelfth century round the choir. The west end, traditionally said to have been burned by the Burgundians (c. 1470), is very defective, but a plain (but good) abbey gateway remains. Altogether a wonderful church. Gournay, a much smaller church; the nave very early Norman (before the middle of century I should say), but with transition vaulting : transepts and choir mainly transition with each a big early decorated window in it : east end square and window coming low down. The carving on caps of nave very curious, no two alike; mostly rude (some very), but many beautiful.　I am sorry to say that this admirable nave has been badly restored, even to the re-cutting of some of the caps: perhaps the French Society might stop this game, as those that are left are extra-ordinarily valuable.　As to the west front it *was* thir-teenth century; but is now nineteenth, and bad at that; they have even done new sculptures for the tympanums. As for the town of Gournay it is uninteresting, but they make cream cheeses of the very best : *crede mihi experto.*

"Certainly the Cathedral here is one of the wonders of the world : seen by twilight its size gives one an im-pression almost of terror: one can scarcely believe in it. But when you see the detail, it is so beautiful that the beauty impresses you more than the size.

"We are just going to read the late stained glass at St. Stephen's, which is very amusing, lots of it.

"The arms of the chapter are gules a cross argent with four keys of the same cantoned if I blazon it right : the arms of the town, gules a pale argent.　The town has lost its walls, but they are in a way traceable, for the town ditch fed by two little rivers goes all round: there is a very big central *place* also, so that the plan of the town is very good.

"Yours affectionately,
"WILLIAM MORRIS."

"Reims, Marne,
"August 16th.

"My dear Walker,

"We have just come out of the Cathedral, which, though a wonderful place, is, if I am right, not so great a work as Amiens, Beauvais, or Soissons.　The latter was our last place on our way here.　I thought the church there most extraordinarily beautiful. Except for the end of the north transept (which is early decorated) it is all of the earliest Gothic, not very big (but wide), of great simplicity and of the utmost refinement. The south transept is much lower than the north and apsidal; the interior of it, of two vaulted stages, comparable in beauty to Hugh's work at Lincoln (though not like it), Gothic at its best. There have been some bad restorations there, but it is not destroyed. The worst is the black lining of the ashlar of the choir down to the triforium. Here the outside has already been restored (including the work they are doing to the south transept, which looks very bad), but excepting the west front with its amazing wealth of imagery: though they do not here seem to touch the figure sculptures. Perhaps it might be of use to memorialize the French Society upon this and some other points.

"Here the whole of the clerestory (except the windows of the choir blocked up by the restoration at present) has its stained glass, of the most splendid quality, though a good deal patched. If Grant Allen should see it he would find it justified his views of jewellery completely; for no collection of gems could come within a hundred miles of it. All the way from Beauvais to Compiègne, Soissons and here, the churches seem very fine and mostly early. The country round Soissons is very beautiful. It is built on the side of the Aisne, a river about as big there as the Thames at Reading: we saw vines there for the first time this journey. The arms of Soissons city are azure a fleur de lys argent. The chapter carries, I think, under a chief of France a tower. The tinctures I did not see, as I take my information from a lamp-post, of Napoleon's time, I suppose, as the fleur de lys were *bees*. There are some fine tapestries hung up in the aisles here in very good preservation, c. 1520 I think. They make splendid ornaments.   I intend studying them and the stained glass and the sculpture to-morrow properly.

"I heard from Bowden that he has sent on another sheet and some Golden Legend, but it has not yet come: will to-morrow, I suppose. Jacobi has sent me two sheets of the cheap By the Way: it looks well. I have not done one letter since I started, my work being mostly staring and walking and eating. We intend going on to Laon on Tuesday, which will probably mean getting to Folkestone on Saturday or Sunday next and home the day after. Get Hooper to do the colophon before he goes off if you can, as otherwise it might stick us.

"Yours affectionately,

"WILLIAM MORRIS."

"St. Remy a very fine church : some glass there even finer than that in Cathedral, twelfth century."

On the 23rd of September he writes to his daughter Jenny at Kelmscott: "I expect the book "—the "Poems by the Way "—"will be all printed to-morrow, and will go to the binders on Monday. They are printing the colophon sheet to-day, which is exciting. Item, Mr. Quaritch has sent me in a specimen copy of volume 2 of the Saga Library, so I suppose I shall bring it along with me. I shall probably bring along a copy of the cheap ' Glittering Plain,' and the cheap ' Poems by the Way ' will soon be out. So you see, my own, that if it doesn't rain ' blue elephants ' it may almost be said to rain new books of mine. Do you know, I do so like seeing a new book out that I have had a hand in. Mr. Prince is also getting on with the new fount of type, but when I shall begin to print with it I really don't know.

"Before I finish the news, I must tell you that about 6 o'clock yesterday a stout man called (like a Scotch farmer) and announced himself as the keeper of the dogs at the Doggeries; he said he had wanted to take the house again, but I had forestalled him, and now he wanted to rent the kennels of me : he was so polite that all I could say was that I did not *think* I would, also that I would ask my wife. Of course I won't let him have them.

"I am going to give a dinner party on Friday to Ellis, Phyllis and Cuthbert and Harry. And then on Saturday, ho for Kelmscott! I shall be *so* glad to see my dear again."

CHAPTER XX

THE life of Morris from that autumn until his last illness was one of placid continuity of production, with
little variety of external incident. From the illness of
the spring of 1891 he never fully recovered ; and though
he enjoyed several years more of fair health, his bodily
powers became gradually less able to respond to the
calls of his unflagging intellectual energy. The amount
of work he had already done, in literature, in art, in
politics, in handicraft, was enough to fill not one, but
many lives; and the machinery which had been working
at continuous high pressure for so long began to show
signs of permanent weakening. But in these latter years
his whole personality ripened and softened. The out-
bursts of temper so familiar to his earlier friends ceased.
The impatience born of intense craving for sympathy and
understanding died away. The training of the years of
co-operation with impracticable colleagues in the Socialist party had not been lost. Mr. Selwyn Image, speaking from intimate acquaintance as a colleague on the
executive committee of the Arts and Crafts Society and
in the Art Workers' Guild, records, as the deepest impression made on him, that of Morris's extraordinary
patience and conciliatoriness : and the same testimony is

borne by others who worked along with him. "O how I long to keep the world from narrowing me, and to look at things bigly and kindly!" Thus he had written, in a letter of more than usually intimate self-revelation, nearly twenty years before : and the prayer had been heard. Like the southern autumn of Virgil, the year remained fruitful in its mellow decline :

> *—dant arbuta silvæ,*
> *Et varios ponit fetus auctumnus, et alte*
> *Mitis in apricis coquitur vindemia saxis.*

The Kelmscott Press remained until towards the end of these years his engrossing preoccupation. Next to it in his interest were his own romances. He had practically ceased to write original poetry. As to one of these tales indeed, that entitled "Child Christopher and Goldilind the Fair," he wavered for some time whether he should write it in verse or prose, and actually began it in verse, but quickly gave it up. He announced this decision to Burne-Jones the next time they met, observing at the same time, in what is perhaps the most sweeping of all his generalizations, that poetry was tommy rot. But the prose romances all contain snatches of lyric verse, and besides his metrical rendering of "Beowulf," other verse, original and translated, was written by him now and again. Foremost perhaps in beauty among these lyrics of later summer, and deserving to be reclaimed here from the obscure pages of the Catalogue of the fourth Exhibition of the Arts and Crafts Society, are the verses which he wrote for an embroidered hanging, designed and worked by his daughter May for his own bed, a fine piece of carved oak of the seventeenth century, in the Manor House at Kelmscott.

> The wind's on the wold
> And the night is a-cold,

WILLIAM MORRIS'S BEDROOM AT THE MANOR HOUSE, KELMSCOTT,

And Thames runs chill
'Twixt mead and hill.
But kind and dear
Is the old house here
And my heart is warm
'Midst winter's harm.
Rest then and rest,
And think of the best
'Twixt summer and spring,
When all birds sing
In the town of the tree,
And ye lie in me
And scarce dare move,
Lest earth and its love
Should fade away
Ere the full of the day.
I am old and have seen
Many things that have been ;
Both grief and peace
And wane and increase.
No tale I tell
Of ill or well,
But this I say,
Night treadeth on day,
And for worst and best
Right good is rest.

Besides his own story-writing, he continued the pleasant labour of translating from the Icelandic and mediæval
French. He lectured, when time and strength permitted,
on the arts of life, more especially now on printing and
its kindred arts. He remained active in the service of
the Society for Protection of Ancient Buildings. Whether
in the defence of ancient buildings like Westminster
Abbey and Peterborough Cathedral against the injuries

of the restorer, or in the protection of the natural beauties of England, as in Epping Forest or on the upper Thames, against the inroads of planned ugliness or inconsiderate change, his voice and pen were always active when called upon. Nor did he decline from the unobtrusive work of education towards the growth of a future Socialism. It is to these last years that some of his noblest and most significant utterances on the ideals of human life belong —notably among them the preface to Ruskin's chapter " On the Nature of Gothic," and the letter of November, 1893, on the Miners' Question, his latest and most carefully-worded confession of faith.

In October, 1891, an exhibition of pictures of the Pre-Raphaelite School was held in the Municipal Art Gallery at Birmingham, and Morris was asked to open it with an address on the Pre-Raphaelite painters. The speech which he then made represents the most formal discourse he had yet given on the art of painting, as one distinct from, yet in the closest relation to, the arts which he himself practised. It perhaps expresses his views not the less exactly because it was spoken on the spur of the moment, and was the imperfect but immediate utterance of his habitual feelings. The curiously halting sentences and inconclusive termination are accounted for very simply. He had meant to think out what he would say on the journey down to Birmingham, but fell asleep in the train and arrived with nothing prepared.

Professing himself a humble member of the school, he stated as his deliberate conviction that its principal masters, Rossetti, Millais, Holman Hunt, and Burne-Jones, were names that ranked alongside of the very greatest in the great times of art : then, not labouring this point, he commended their example to all artists, not primarily for any technical quality, but for the virtues of patience, diligence, and courage. These were the qualities that went to make great men; and great men might be trusted to do great work.

As regards the technique of painting, Morris had, from his own early practice of the art as well as from the insight of his immense genius, a knowledge that was not less great because he seldom showed it. But the art of painting always took its place in his mind as one of the arts subordinate to architecture, though it might be the first of these. The inflexible naturalism and minute finish of the early Pre-Raphaelites, he held, were necessary at the time to startle men out of the lethargy of a long convention, but they hardly represented the permanent method in which the painter's art should employ itself. His own artistic intelligence had been as a matter of fact first awakened by that militant and, one might almost say, aggressive type of picture. "I remember distinctly myself," he said in this address when speaking of the Pre-Raphaelite revolt against an outworn academic tradition, " as a boy, that when I had pictures offered to my notice I could not understand what they were about at all. I said, ' Oh well, that is all right: it has got the sort of thing in it which there ought to be in a picture: there is nothing to be said against it, no doubt. I cannot say I would have had it other than that, because it is clearly the proper thing to do.' But really I took very little interest in it." For a short period he had been as profound an admirer of the earlier work of the Pre-Raphaelite Brotherhood as any of the school, and had himself worked hard at being a painter in the Pre-Raphaelite manner. When this temporary enthusiasm passed over, pictures took a place in his mind among the various methods of decorating surfaces. Except for his unbroken and almost daily intimacy with Burne-Jones, he did not see much of painters as such, nor was he a frequenter of studios or picture galleries. When he did see a picture he saw what there was in it at a single glance; his eye for both design and colour was here, as elsewhere, infallible, and his memory portentous. But easel-pictures seem, as a rule, to have given him the uneasy feeling of decoration disproportionate in labour and finish to its decorative object. With a painted book he had not this feeling; nor with the gem-like masterpieces of the Flemish and early Italian schools which approximate in method and finish to the pictures in a painted book. But for pictures on a larger scale and in a broader manner he would have preferred frescoes or even tapestries. Sir Edward Burne-Jones told me that Morris would have liked the faces in his pictures less highly finished, and less charged with the concentrated meaning or emotion of the painting. As with the artists of Greece and of the Middle Ages, the human face was to him merely a part, though no doubt a very important part, of the human body. In speaking of the qualifications required from tapestry-weavers, it was on their skill in rendering the feet and hands, not the faces, of the figures, that he laid special stress. He was quite satisfied with the simple and almost abstract types of expression that can be produced in tapestry; and he thought that the dramatic and emotional interest of a picture ought to be diffused throughout it as equally as possible. Such too was his own practice in the cognate art of poetry: and this is one reason why his poetry affords so few memorable single lines, and lends itself so little to quotation. Either quality would have been a merely incidental merit, and perhaps even a defect, in the view of his art which he himself held.

With the National Gallery indeed, or at least with those rooms in it which contained the works which were after his own heart, he was intimately familiar. Angelico, Van Eyck, and Holbein, his three greatest admirations

among the painters of past ages, he admired as profoundly as he did any artist whatever. In one of the
later numbers of the Commonweal, while discussing in
a fragmentary and parenthetic way what the art of the
future under realized Socialism might be like, he makes
some remarks on the pictures in the National Gallery
which incidentally open up his whole mind on the subject of pictorial art. "Perhaps," he says, "mankind
will regain their eyesight, which they have lost to a great
extent; people have largely ceased to take in mental impressions through the eyes, whereas in times past the
eyes were the great feeders of the fancy and imagination.
I am in the habit when I go to an exhibition or a picture
gallery of noticing their behaviour there; and as a rule I
note that they seem very much bored, and their eyes
wander vacantly over the various objects exhibited to
them. If ordinary people go to our National Gallery,
the thing which they want to see is the Blenheim
Raphael, which, though well done, is a very dull picture
to any one not an artist. While, when Holbein shows
them the Danish princess of the sixteenth century yet living on the canvas, the demure half-smile not yet faded
from her eyes; when Van Eyck opens a window for
them into Bruges of the fourteenth century; when Botti-
celli shows them Heaven as it lived in the hearts of men
before theology was dead, these things produce no impression on them, not so much even as to stimulate
their curiosity and make them ask what 'tis all about;
because these things were done to be looked at, and to
make the eyes tell the mind tales of the past, the present,
and the future." Yet deeply as Morris admired these
pictures, he scarcely loved them with his deepest love;
he would willingly at any time have exchanged the National Gallery and all its contents for the cases of painted
books in the British Museum. A man may be known

by his company, inanimate as well as human; and while Morris had a small but choice collection of painted books among his chief treasures, and gladly paid large sums to secure one, his house was, with a few exceptions for which there were special reasons, pictureless, and he never bought a picture after the early days when he had ceased trying to paint them.

From this brief excursion into art criticism he returned to the work of his printing-press. In November he was discussing the printing of all his own works, meaning then to begin with the "Sigurd." A second and larger press had been bought, and a new pressman and two new compositors engaged; and the printing of the Interminable, as "The Golden Legend" had come to be called, was making rapid progress. Before the end of the year he was discussing the form of the great Chaucer which it was his ambition to print. The Troy type, the first of his two Gothic founts, had been cut and was then being cast: but "it is so big that it is no use thinking of printing the Chaucer in double columns with it unless the book were to be as big as Eggestein's Gratian's Decretum,"—a leviathan among printed books, of which an uncut copy measures twenty inches by fifteen and weighs nearly thirty pounds. Before the end of the year he had determined on having another fount cut smaller from the same designs; and these two, with the original Roman or "Golden" fount, were the only three that he actually produced and printed from, though in the course of the year 1892 he partially designed another. "I am at work at my story and other trifles," he writes to Ellis just before Christmas. But he was so busy now with the Press that even story-telling had to be dropped. This was one of several romances which he began in these years, and discontinued either because he was not satisfied with them or from mere lack of time. "The Wood beyond the World," his next published romance, was not completed till quite two years later.

The small printing-press had been occupied during the earlier part of the winter of 1891-2 in turning out the third of the Kelmscott Press books, the volume of poems by Mr. Wilfrid Blunt. As soon as that volume was finished, it was set to work upon a reprint of Ruskin's celebrated chapter " On the Nature of Gothic" from " The Stones of Venice." It was the first thing that, when Morris met with it long ago at Oxford, had set fire to his enthusiasm, and kindled the beliefs of his whole life. In the preface to this reprint, dated 15th February, 1892, he states briefly and clearly the effect which Ruskin's teaching had had on himself, and the permanent value which he still conceived it to possess. " To my mind," he says, this chapter " is one of the most important things written by the author, and in future days will be considered as one of the very few necessary and inevitable utterances of the century. To some of us when we first read it"—in those dawn-golden days at Oxford—" now many years ago, it seemed to point out a new road on which the world should travel. The lesson which Ruskin here teaches us is that art is the expression of man's pleasure in labour; that it is possible for man to rejoice in his work, for, strange as it may seem to us to-day, there have been times when he did rejoice in it."

Even more : in this chapter, and in the subsequent teaching which did little more than expand and enforce it, Ruskin had laid, once for all, the basis for a true Socialism. For without art Socialism would remain as sterile as the other forms of social organization ; it would not meet the real and perpetual wants of mankind. The social doctrines of the thinkers and theorists who had preceded Ruskin, like those of the others who, coming after him, had ignored or denied this essential element in his doctrine, would in practice "certainly lighten the burden of labour, but would not procure for it the element of sensuous pleasure which is the essence of all true art." Of themselves they could go no further in their utmost success than create a world in which art would be possible : but that world would be a body still waiting, numb, joyless, and lifeless, for the entrance of the quickening spirit.

This preface was no sooner written, than Morris followed it by another utterance which has had little public circulation, but which gives his best literary qualities— his power of lucid statement, his immense and easily-wielded knowledge of architecture and history, his earnestness, his humour, and his mastery of biting phrase— with a perfection that is hardly equalled elsewhere. This was the paper on Westminster Abbey written by him for the Society for Protection of Ancient Buildings and finished on the 7th of March. Its immediate occasion was a proposal then being discussed for the "complete restoration" of the interior of the Abbey, and the addition to it, by public munificence or private enterprise, of some kind of annex which might give room for further monuments to distinguished men. That such a consummate monument of the noblest style and period of European architecture should be turned, as it long had been, into a "registration office for notorieties" was felt by him as wanton and inexcusable sacrilege : and this proposal not only to continue and extend that degrading usage, but to mutilate the Abbey still further under such a pretext by remodelling or enlargement, was one the mere mention of which roused him into fury. As regards the church itself, each fresh piece of restoration was in his deliberate judgment more scandalous and more ruinous than its predecessors. During the seventeenth and eighteenth

centuries it had indeed suffered heavily, but its worst
sufferings had been reserved for modern times.   " Being
situated in the centre of government," he bitterly writes,
" it has not enjoyed the advantages of boorish neglect,
which have left so much of interest in remoter parts of
the country."   On the work of Wren and his successors
down to Wyatt, the architects of " the ignorance," to use
that Arabian phrase which Morris was so fond of quoting, he touches with a light scorn, gibbeting their work
as "the Bible and Prayer-book style of the period,"
" the queer style of driven-into-a-corner Classic."   With
Wyatt and the first period of Gothic knowledge, whose
architects were far more destructive than those of the
Gothic ignorance, worse changes began.   Wyatt " managed to take all the romance out of the exterior of the
most romantic work of the late Middle Ages," Henry
VII.'s Chapel.   Blore, followed by Gilbert Scott, " completely destroyed all trace of the handwork of the mediæval masons " in the north aisle.   Scott, when he was
made architect of the Abbey and the second period of
Gothic knowledge had arrived, " carefully restored the
Chapter House, that is, he made it a modern building."
Finally Mr. Pearson, " driven by the necessity of making
some structural repairs," carried out the idea of making a
conjectural restoration of the north transept.   The façade
of the eighteenth century, a time when architects " had
not learned how to forge, and put some of their own
thought, poor as that was, into it," was accordingly destroyed.   It was replaced by "dead-alive office work,"
covered with " what is called ecclesiastical sculpture—
so utterly without life or interest that nobody who passes
under the portal of the church on which it is plastered
treats it as a work of art any more than he does the
clergyman's surplice," " a joyless, putty-like imitation,
that had better have been a plaster-cast."   As for the

"pieces of undertakers' upholstery" within the church, all that could be done with them was to let them alone. "The burden of their ugliness must be endured, at any rate until the folly of restoration has died out; for the greater part of them have been built into the fabric, and their removal would leave gaps, not so unsightly indeed as those stupid masses of marble, but tempting to the restorer, who would make them excuses for further introduction of modern work."

"It may seem strange," Morris adds, rising into the higher plane of his habitual thoughts, "that whereas we can give some distinguished name as the author of almost every injury it has received, the authors of this great epic itself have left no names behind them. For indeed it is the work of no one man, but of the people of south-eastern England. It was the work of the inseparable will of a body of men, who worked, as they lived, because they could do no otherwise, and unless you can bring these men back from the dead, you cannot 'restore' one verse of their epic. Rewrite the lost trilogies of Æschylus, put a beginning and an end to the Fight at Finsbury, finish the Squire's Tale for Chaucer, and if you can succeed in that, you may then 'restore' Westminster Abbey."

By this time the smaller Gothic fount was being cut for the Kelmscott Chaucer, after a momentary hesitation caused by his having seen for the first time the earlier or semi-Gothic type ("what asses they were to change it for the Roman type" is his characteristic comment) used by Sweynheym and Pannartz for the Subiaco Lactantius. Much of the immense vitality of earlier years still survived, though more and more fitfully: on the 9th of April, "happening to be awake at 6 a.m. I went and got my book and wrote several pages of story." In May he was beginning to see daylight at last with "The Golden

Legend." The two magnificent drawings by Burne-Jones of the Earthly and Heavenly Paradises had been completed, and the first was now being cut on the wood. Both were touched up for the wood-engraver by Mr. Fairfax Murray in a photographic copy. The last sheet of the text was read by Morris in proof on the 31st of May. The large printer's mark with a picture of the house at Kelmscott in it, which Morris then meant to design for his colophon, was not executed, and was replaced in the book as it appeared by the device which had already appeared in several of the smaller books, a small design with the words " Kelmscott " and " William Morris " in Gothic lettering on a floriated background and border.

Meanwhile Morris sought consolation for any occasional qualms that he may have had as to the artistic limitations of the finest printed books in a more and more impassioned devotion to thirteenth-century manuscripts. At the sale of the Lawrence collection this month he spent £250 on three of those, a little Psalter and little Book of Hours and the fragment of a folio Bible. Nearly all summer through he stayed in London by his Press, though with wistful thoughts now and again of haymaking going on fast in the big meadow, and of the hollyhocks in the garden at Kelmscott. Burne-Jones was beginning the series of drawings for Chaucer, and the form and detail of the great folio was taking definite shape in Morris's mind. By the middle of September the printing of the Interminable was done, the two great full-page woodcuts being the last part, as they were the most anxious, to print. On the 16th it went off, in two cartloads, in joyful procession to the binders. To celebrate the auspicious and long-awaited event Morris bought a vellum copy of Jenson's " Clementis Constitutiones " of 1476, and then took himself off to Kelmscott.

Once the Press was released from " The Golden Legend," the production of smaller books went on through
the winter of 1892-3 with accelerated and almost reckless
speed.   The reprint of Caxton's " Historyes of Troye,"
the first book issued in the large Gothic type which
Morris had designed in 1891, as the famous original
had been, more than four hundred years before, the first
book printed in English, is dated the 14th of October.
It was rapidly succeeded by the " Biblia Innocentium,"
dated 22nd October; " News from Nowhere," dated
22nd November; and the reprint of Caxton's " Reynard the Foxe" of 1481, dated 15th December.
This last Morris accounted far and away the best of
all Caxton's books in its literary quality: " he has the
true smell and smile."   Then followed the " Poems of
William Shakespeare," dated 17th January, 1893; and
after it, the reprint of Caxton's " Order of Chivalry" of
1484, dated 10th November, 1892, but held back in
order to be issued in a single volume together with
another little book.   This was the text and Morris's
own verse translation of " L'Ordene de Chevalerie," a
French poem of the thirteenth century which has been
thought to be the original of the fourteenth-century
prose treatise translated and printed by Caxton.   It is
dated 24th of February, 1893.   The translation had
first been made in prose by Ellis.   But Morris one day
suddenly remembered the fact that the Press, like the
firm of thirty years back, " kept a poet of its own," and
turned him on for the purpose.   Finally, to make up
the production of that remarkable winter, appeared
Cavendish's " Life of Wolsey," dated 30th March; and
the reprint of Caxton's " Godefrey of Boloyne" of
1481, dated 27th April.   In the " Order of Chivalry,"
and in parts of the " Historyes of Troye," the smaller
Gothic type which had been cut and cast for the Chaucer

made its first appearance. After this continuous torrent of production the Press for a time slackened off a little. Morris was advised that this rapid output of his books would depreciate the value of those already issued, and might end in the new books becoming unsaleable at their fair value. But for these warnings he did not greatly care: "the Kelmscott Press is humming" was his exultant comment, and he felt sure that his work was good enough to command a market. "I *shall* print that Froissart" was all his reply to an argument that it could only be printed as he designed it at a heavy loss. But the Froissart, which was to have taken the next place after the Chaucer among his most rich and elaborate productions, was little more than begun when the Press ceased after the death of its founder.

By the end of 1892 Morris had made up his mind to add the trade of a publisher to that of a printer. "There is really no risk in it," he said in summing up the situation: "I shall get more money; and the public will have to pay less." The reprint of Caxton's "Reynard the Foxe," then just finished, was in fact the last of his large books that he issued through a publisher, though with the smaller books the old practice was for some time continued. But the reprint of Caxton's "Godefrey of Boloyne," issued in the following May, bore on it for the first time the words "Published by William Morris at the Kelmscott Press": the "Utopia" of the following September was the last Kelmscott book issued through Messrs. Reeves & Turner; and thenceforth, except in a few cases of special arrangement (as when Tennyson's "Maud" was published by Messrs. Macmillan, and the two volumes of Rossetti's poems by Messrs. Ellis & Elvey), Morris published all Kelmscott Press books himself. Once more, as in so many previous ventures, he trusted to the existence of a market for excellence and was not disappointed. The Kelmscott Press was not carried on to make money: at first he would have been content if it had not cost him more than he could afford to spend, and even afterwards it was worked, and the prices fixed for its products, only with the view of making its receipts meet its expenditure. No expense was spared in getting everything connected with it as near his ideal as could be produced; yet in fact it brought in a profit which represented a fairly adequate salary for his own incessant work and oversight, and relieved him from the necessity of economizing on any expense which would really add to the excellence and beauty of his printed books.

In the immense detail of carrying on the work of the Press, which was beyond a single person's management unless he could give up the whole of his time to it, Morris was already being assisted by Mr. S. C. Cockerell, who was formally engaged as secretary to the Press in July, 1894. It is only due to Mr. Cockerell to say that these last years of Morris's life were greatly lightened by his diligence and devotion. For the first time in his life his papers were kept in order: the labour of correspondence, which had always been irksome to him, and was one of the few things that he felt as really hard work, was relieved : his library was catalogued; and the conduct, not only of the Press, but of his whole business, was made as easy to him as the nature of the case admitted. The relations between them grew to be of great intimacy and confidence, and added much to the happiness of both.

At the beginning of 1893 the beautiful little series of translations from thirteenth-century French prose romances which were printed by Morris in this and the following year began to be projected. "There is a little book," he wrote in January, "of the Librairie Elzévirienne hight Contes et Nouvelles de la XIIIme Siècle: two of these are amongst the most beautiful works of the Middle Ages, and I intend translating them, and printing in a nice little book in Chaucer type.   Probably I shall design some two-coloured letters for it."

The work of which he misquotes the title with his characteristic carelessness when he was writing a letter, "Nouvelles Françoises en prose du XIIIme Siècle," a little book published in 1856, had for thirty years been one of the treasures of literature to him.   Together with the " Violier des Histoires Romaines," which appeared in the same series two years later, it had been among the first sources of his knowledge of the French romance of the Middle Ages.   In thanking Morris for a copy of the last of the three little Kelmscott volumes, Mr. Swinburne recalls their delight in reading the French " in the days when we first foregathered at Oxford " nearly forty years before.   On two of the stories in the French volume, " Le Conte de l'Empereur Coustant " and " L'Amitié d'Amis et d'Amile," he had based two of the stories for " The Earthly Paradise "; the former appears in the work under the title of " The Man Born to be King "; the latter was the never published poem of " Amis and Amillion."   He now translated and printed these and two others.   The fifth, the famous pastoral romance of Aucassin and Nicolete, he left untouched, as it was already well known in two English versions.   The first of the stories which Morris published, a translation of the romance entitled " Le Conte du Roi Flore et de la Belle Jehanne," was issued under the title of " The Tale of King Florus and the Fair Jehane " at the end of this year.   It is dated 16th of December, 1893.   " Amis and Amile " succeeded it in April, 1894: " the Amis and Amile I translated in one day and a quarter, it was *very* easy: a most beautiful little book "; and " The Tale of the Emperor Coustans," with which was included a fourth story, " L'Histoire d'Outre-Mer," entitled in the English " The History of Over Sea," in the following September. The project of two-colour letters printed from double blocks was never carried out by him in these or any other of the Kelmscott Press books, though several designs in red and blue were made by him for that purpose.

" I am very busy all round, and ought to be busier, but can't be," he cheerfully writes in March. He had set to work on designing the ornament for the Kelmscott Chaucer. That for the first page was just finished to his complete satisfaction. " My eyes! how good it is!" was his own criticism on it. He had also begun his metrical version of " Beowulf." That great fragment of the earliest English epic he had hitherto only ad-mired from a distance. He was not an Anglo-Saxon scholar, and to help him in following the original he used the aid of a prose translation made for him by Mr. A. J. Wyatt, of Christ's College, Cambridge, with whom he also read through the original. The plan of their joint labours had been settled in the autumn of 1892. Mr. Wyatt began to supply Morris with his prose paraphrase in February, 1893, and he at once began to " rhyme up," as he said, " very eager to be at it, finding it the most delightful work." He was working at it all through the year, and used to read it to Burne-Jones regularly on Sunday mornings in summer. It was not fully finished till the end of 1894, and was published in February, 1895. It would seem on the whole, in spite of the love and labour Morris had bestowed on it, to be one of his few failures. Anglo-Saxon scholars do not regard it as a satisfactory rendering of the original ; and still less do ordinary readers find it a book that can be read with pleasure for its own sake. For the language of his ver-sion Morris for once felt it necessary to make an apology.

Except a few words, he said, the words he used in it were such as he would not hesitate to use in an original poem of his own. He did not add, however, that their effect, if slipped sparingly in amid his own pellucid construction and facile narrative method, would be very different from their habitual use in a translation which must in any case, if it were faithful to the original, be often both harsh and obscure. In his desire to reproduce the early English manner he allowed himself a harshness of construction and a strangeness of vocabulary that in many passages go near to making his version unintelligible. A poem which professes to be modern and yet requires a glossary fails of one of its primary objects. The obscurity of many parts of the original, made more obscure by gaps and corruptions in the text, cannot be got over in any translation which Morris would have regarded, or which it is possible fairly to regard, as faithful: but this means that the only translation practicable is a paraphrase, an " interpretation," as it was called in the old editions of the classics, which shall not profess to reproduce the original, but confine itself to the humbler use of being printed below the original to make it easier of comprehension. As the work advanced, he seems to have felt this himself, and his pleasure in the doing of it fell off. Between this, and the slow progress of the Chaucer, which was chiefly owing to the great difficulty of getting Burne-Jones's designs satisfactorily rendered upon wood—" we shall be twenty years at this rate in getting it out," he writes rather dolefully in May—he was not in the best of spirits that summer about his printing, and began to think that some caution in restricting his output might be not undesirable.

Another matter which seriously vexed him was the total defeat in Convocation, in June, 1893, of his attempt to save the mediæval statuary on the spire of St. Mary's,

Oxford, from the hands of the restorer.   Those images were much decayed and loosened by past neglect, and were as they stood admittedly unsafe : the question, therefore, became one in which Morris's principles as regards restoration came into the sharpest conflict with those of the ordinary architect. Stated briefly, the question was one of sacrificing truth and history on the one hand, or appearance on the other.   " Jackson took me up on the spire," Morris writes after his return from Oxford, " and I had a good look at the images and fought Jackson at every point. The fact is, he would now willingly keep the images, if he could do so without visibly banding and tying them, but this he funks. This was my chief point ; as I refused to be led into a discussion as to whether they could be tied up to look *neat*, but stuck to it that even if they had to be covered with a cage of bars it should be done rather than removing them "— and replacing them, it is to be understood, by copies professing to be originals.

The twelve statues grouped round the base of that magnificent spire, still in spite of all restorations and re-constructions the " eye of Oxford," the central crown of all her architecture, were among the noblest surviving examples of English sculpture of the early fourteenth century.   Time and neglect had seriously impaired several of them ; and in the first restoration of the spire, carried out by the architect Buckler according to the ideas of that " second period of Gothic knowledge " which Morris held in such profound contempt, just at the time when Morris himself went up to Exeter as an undergraduate, two had been wholly removed and replaced, and some of the others had been largely repaired. When the second restoration was decided upon and placed in the hands of Mr. T. G. Jackson, the ten ancient statues were the only important features of the spire which had not been already tampered with, and their importance was thus doubled. Mr. Jackson's first report was that they were all so much perished that it was not safe to allow even their ruins to remain. Owing to the decay of the hold-fasts, certain heads and hands were so loose that they could be lifted off. But the surface of the stone had weathered to such hardness that it resisted the point of a knife; and the bodies, which were solid set into the wall behind them, had actually to be sawn from their settings before they could be taken down. The noble figures of the Virgin, of St. Edward the Confessor, and of St. John the Baptist, as they now lie stored in the basement of the Convocation House, may be specially cited as examples, apart from any question of historic interest, of the purest feeling and most consummate artistic excellence. Of the copies by which they have been replaced on the base of the now doubly and triply reconstructed mass of pinnacles from which the central spire springs into the sunlight, it may be left to future generations to judge. But the judgment will be—so Morris insisted—upon works of the nineteenth century which profess to be, and are not, works of nearly six hundred years earlier.

The death of Tennyson in October, 1892, had left vacant the titular primacy of English poetry, which he had held for forty-two years. When the question of appointing a new Poet Laureate was opened, the name of Morris, as by amount and quality of actual work produced undoubtedly among the foremost of living English poets, was one of those which could not be ignored. His political creed would indeed have assorted but strangely with the holding of an office in the Royal Household; nor could any one who knew him, however slightly, think without a smile of his writing official odes, or posing as the eulogist of the existing order and the triumphs of the Victorian age. As regards his per-

sonal views on the matter, Mr. Gladstone, who had
then just become for the fourth time Prime Minister,
kept his own counsel : and it is matter of common
knowledge that no recommendation was ever made by
him to the Queen, and that the office remained unfilled
for three years during his Government and the administration which succeeded it. But after this lapse of
time it may not be indiscreet to say that Morris was
sounded by a member of the Cabinet, with Mr. Gladstone's knowledge and approval, to ascertain whether he
would accept the office in the event of its being offered
to him. His answer was unhesitating. He was frankly
pleased that he had been thought of, and did not under-
value the implied honour: but it was one which his
principles and his tastes alike made it impossible for him
to accept. The matter went no further. In private
conversation Morris always held that the proper function of a Poet Laureate was that of a ceremonial writer
of official verse, and that in this particular case the
Marquis of Lorne was the person pointed out for the
office—should the office be thought one worth keeping
up under modern conditions—by position and acquire-
ments.

While the Socialist organizations had been dwindling
as active forces, the permeation of public opinion by
Socialistic ideas had continued to make slow but noticeable progress. Taught by bitter experience, the more
thoughtful Socialists no longer held haughtily aloof from
the means at their hand by which they might take part
in the work of local government. The old idea of obstructing reform in order to precipitate revolution did
not now hold its place except among a few extremists.
Work directed towards common objects began to make
the differences on which the party had divided and sub-
divided itself fall back into something nearer their true

proportion: and in 1893 efforts began to be made towards re-uniting the party. In these efforts Morris cordially joined, though he no longer accepted the position of a leader, or allowed the work he contributed towards this object to encroach largely on his time and energy. He defined the work to be done as the promotion of common ideals based on the teaching of history. Towards that object, he this year carefully revised the series of articles which he had written for the Commonweal between 1886 and 1888, in collaboration with Mr. E. B. Bax, and issued them as a volume under the title of " Socialism, its Growth and Outcome." On the 1st of May—the anniversary which, under the name of Labour Day, it had been sought to constitute as an international festival of the working classes both in Europe and America—he joined with Mr. Hyndman and Mr. G. B. Shaw, as the representatives of the principal associations in England holding Socialist doctrines, in drawing up and issuing a new irenicon under the title of the " Manifesto of English Socialists." In this manifesto the common principles of the movement were once more stated, and a last appeal made towards the sinking of differences and the reinstatement of harmonious working on different methods towards common ends. It is signed by the fifteen members of a joint Committee which had been appointed for this purpose by the Social Democratic Federation, the Fabian Society, and the Hammersmith Socialist Society, and was issued with the authority of all three bodies.

The manifesto bears the traces of a joint authorship in which the hands of Mr. Sidney Webb and Mr. G. B. Shaw are more plainly visible than that of Morris. But it fairly represents the moderate and practical views which Morris held in the last years of his life. By a brief review of the facts it is shown that some constructive social theory is absolutely needed. Of these there are really only three. Two of the three must be rejected: the Feudal or Tory theory, which is incompatible with modern conditions and the fact of democracy; and the Manchester or Whig theory, which has completely broken down in practice. The third is Socialism. No amount of moralization of the conditions of a capitalist society based on private property can do away with the necessity for abolishing it, as a step towards the creation of the new social order. Legislative readjustments of industry and administration, while they may be desirable as temporary expedients, will not be permanently useful unless the whole state is merged into an organized commonwealth. For the realization of the new order, the whole community must possess complete ownership and control of the means for creating and distributing wealth; it must put an end to the wage-system; it must sweep away all distinctions of class, and finally establish national and international Communism. Anarchism, whether as a doctrine or a system of tactics, is formally repudiated in all its forms. The ameliorative measures which, under the heightened sensitiveness of the public conscience, are within the scope of practical politics, are not to be opposed, but supported and welcomed. The more that such measures give, either to individuals or to whole bodies of the working class, of leisure for thought and freedom from anxiety, the more will that working class be able to turn their attention and exert their powers towards the introduction of a new social order based on equality of condition. There is therefore no reason why Socialists should not constitute themselves into a distinct party with definite immediate aims. Among these are mentioned an Eight Hours Act, an adequate minimum or living wage for all working men or women employed either in the Government service or in monopolies under partial state-control, the suppression of sub-contracting and sweating, and universal suffrage. Ten years had elapsed since a theory and a programme not unlike this had induced Morris to join the newly-founded Democratic Federation. The wheel might seem to have come full circle. But the experience, the thought, the labour of ten years had given to all the terms employed, and to all the measures advocated, an enlarged and deepened meaning. There had been much disappointment, much disillusion, much wreckage of unverified beliefs and extravagant hopes. The work had been tried by fire and tempest; over and over again had the superstructure crumbled or been consumed away down to the foundations. But these foundations, such was Morris's permanent conviction, were in the rock, and imperishable.

Any later expressions of his mind with regard to the immediate duties which lay before Socialists are in complete consonance with the manifesto of 1893. One of the most significant of these occurs in an address on Art and Labour which he delivered to the Guild of Lithographic Artists in February, 1894. "The new birth of art," he said there, "will be brought about noiselessly, gradually, and without violent change. We already see springing up round us the germs of this new life, the outward signs of which are trades-unionism, socialism, and co-operation." Such at least were his reported words. Whether or not he actually employed the singular collocation of the last sentence, the fact remains that Socialism as a practical movement, though not as an ultimate ideal, had come in his mind to occupy a place alongside of other movements, all of which were incomplete manifestations of a single spirit. It no longer anathematized whatever lay outside of its own specific body of doctrine. From extreme intransigeance it had swung back to something approaching opportunism. *He that is not against us is on our part* was rapidly becoming its test of orthodoxy.

Thus the formal organization of a united Socialist party was a matter which, though he was willing to co-operate towards its realization, he did not think of the first importance.   On the 25th of October, 1894, he wrote on behalf of the Hammersmith Socialist Society to Mr. R. Blatchford, who had been urging this point in the Clarion newspaper.   In that letter he expressed his conviction that the union, if attainable, might and should be effected without any interference with the existing organizations.   But he was equally clear that all minor differences among these organizations should be sunk in view of a general assent in the aim of nationalizing the means of production.   A declaration of agreement in this aim would, he thought, be sufficient as a test of membership in a united Socialist party.

It may not be irrelevant to add here the last pronouncement on the subject which Morris made before his death. In answer to an American correspondent who had asked whether he had altered his views as to Socialism, he replied on the 9th of January, 1896:

"I have *not* changed my mind on Socialism.   My view on the point of relation between Art and Socialism is as follows: Society (so-called) at present is organized entirely for the benefit of a privileged class; the working class being only considered in the arrangement as so much machinery.   This involves perpetual and enormous *waste*, and the organization for the production of genuine utilities is only a secondary consideration.   This waste lands the whole civilized world in a position of *artificial poverty*, which again debars men of all classes from satisfying their rational desires.   Rich men are in slavery to Philistinism, poor men to penury.   We can none of us have what we want, except (partially only) by making

prodigious sacrifices, which very few men can ever do.
Before therefore we can so much as hope for any art,
we must be free from this artificial poverty. When we
are thus free, in my opinion, the natural instincts of
mankind toward beauty and incident will take their due
place: we shall *want* art, and since we shall be really
wealthy, we shall be able to have what we want."

But in truth, as Morris well knew, the work of the
Socialist party as a separate organization, whether acting
as a united body or in detached and conflicting fragments,
was for the time being already done. While Socialists
were busy over their friendly or embittered contests as
to methods, the course of events had already decided the
question, and the policy of permeation had slowly become
not so much an accepted theory as a realized fact. The
great lock-out in the English coal industry, which was the
most important social event of the autumn and winter
months of 1893, came at once as a result and a symbol
of a new spirit; and the ideas that underlay it, now
formally expressed in the celebrated phrase of the " living wage," were the first large outward manifestation of
the beginnings of a new order of things, a new theory
of human life. Almost for the first time, the cardinal
doctrine began to take shape and assume consistence that
the industrial and commercial system, no less than the
political system of the country, was a means and not an
end: and that the true end, for the sake of which alone
these systems had any claim to respect or any right to
existence, was the well-being of the nation, the humani-
zation of human life. Such a humanized life, in which
comfort and happiness should be alike within the reach
of all, and in which all alike, rich and poor, should share,
until the names rich and poor might finally become alike
obsolete in a common condition of civic and national
well-being, had been from the first what Morris had

striven after.   He had joined the Socialist movement as
a means, however indirect or uncertain, towards bringing
about that end : and neither in the State Socialism of his
earlier, nor in the Communal Socialism of his later theory,
did he see anything beyond stages towards the birth of a
final order.   That final order might be described, for
want of other terms, as the re-organization of the world
under Socialism : but its actual nature, or the actual steps
by which it was to be brought about, he perpetually insisted that it was impossible to lay out beforehand, or to
forecast except by instinctive conjecture, and the imaginings of a prophet or a poet.   As in Plato, the last words
of philosophy were only to be expressed in the terms of
a more or less conscious mythology.   As in the days of
the Hebrew prophets, the practical foundation of a king-
dom of God on earth was to be wrought out by aid of
that diffused imaginative ardour in which young men
should see visions, and old men dream dreams.   The
visions of his own boyhood, the dreams of his own more
advanced age, were but means towards expressing, and
influences towards stimulating, the human movement
itself, in which, through all doubts and discouragements,
he had a permanent and a growing faith.   No one insisted more strongly than he on the futility of any attempt
to organize the future, or to lay down what would actually
happen either in the progress towards the new age or in
the final epoch of its attainment.   In " The Dream of
John Ball " he had shadowed out, in an allegorical setting
of subtle and intricate beauty, the birth of a new world,
seen, for one hour of intense spiritual exaltation, when
the mediæval rebel and mystic and the modern Socialist
joined hands over the white poppy-flower in the doubtful
dusk between moonset and dawn.   In such a vision, the
prophetic soul of the world, dreaming on things to come,
ranges disembodied and unconfined.   The dreams which

the present may have of an elusive or dimly-conjectured future, no less than those which the past may once have had of a future that is not the present, must be no rational human forecast, but a tale told, like the Vision of Er in Plato's "Republic," by one neither alive nor dead. In "News from Nowhere" he had, with a reversion to a simpler and less august sphere of imagination, clothed his own dream of a new age in the innocent draperies of a romantic pastoral. But the dreamer of dreams, the poet and romance-writer who habitually moved in a strange world of his own, was also a man of keen-sighted practical intelligence. When called on for action, he could dismiss all that world of dreams, or only retain from it that deeper insight and that wider outlook which is forbidden to men not endowed with the more than human gift of imaginative insight. The letter to the Daily Chronicle on the Miners' Question, his last and most profound public utterance on the future of human society and the meaning of human life, is the voice of one who had lived both in Plato's cave and in the upper air, and who could adjust his eye to both. From that upper world of ideal art and creative imagination—of real things, as Plato would say—he could turn to the confused and perplexing movement of shadows in the cavern spoken and thought of by men as the actual world, and see breaking over the darkness no mere fluctuating glow from a fire behind the prisoners, but the glimmer of actual day.

This letter, headed "The Deeper Meaning of the Struggle," and written on the 9th of November, ran as follows:

"May I be allowed to say a word in supplement to your paragraph about my opinion on the future of the fine arts? You rather imply that I am a pessimist on this matter. This is not the case; but I am anxious that there should be no illusions as to the future of art.

I do not believe in the possibility of keeping art vigorously alive by the action, however energetic, of a few groups of specially gifted men and their small circle of admirers amidst a general public incapable of understanding and enjoying their work. I hold firmly to the opinion that all worthy schools of art must be in the future, as they have been in the past, the outcome of the aspirations of the people towards the beauty and true pleasure of life. And further, that now that democracy is building up a new order, which is slowly emerging from the confusion of the commercial period, these aspirations of the people towards beauty can only be born from a condition of practical equality of economical condition amongst the whole population. Lastly, I am so confident that this equality will be gained, that I am prepared to accept as a consequence of the process of that gain, the seeming disappearance of what art is now left us; because I am sure that that will be but a temporary loss, to be followed by a genuine new birth of art, which will be the spontaneous expression of the pleasure of life innate in the whole people.

" This, I say, is the art which I look forward to, not as a vague dream, but as a practical certainty, founded on the general well-being of the people. It is true that the blossom of it I shall not see; therefore I may be excused if, in common with other artists, I try to express myself through the art of to-day, which seems to us to be only a survival of the organic art of the past, in which the people shared, whatever the other drawbacks of their condition might have been. For the feeling for art in us artists is genuine, though we have to work in the midst of the ignorance of those whose whole life ought to be spent in the production of works of art (the makers of wares to wit) and of the fatuous pretence of those who, making no utilities, are driven to ' make-believe.'

" Yet if we shall not (those of us who are as old as I
am) see the New Art, the expression of the general
pleasure of life, we are even now seeing the seed of it
beginning to germinate. For if genuine art be impossible without the help of the useful classes, how can
these turn their attention to it if they are living amidst
sordid cares which press upon them day in, day out ?
The first step, therefore, towards the new birth of art
must be a definite rise in the condition of the workers ;
their livelihood must (to say the least of it) be less
niggardly and less precarious, and their hours of labour
shorter ; and this improvement must be a general one,
and confirmed against the chances of the market by legislation. But again this change for the better can only
be realized by the efforts of the workers themselves.
' By us, and not for us,' must be their motto. That
they are now finding this out for themselves and acting
on it makes this year a memorable one indeed, small as
is the actual gain which they are claiming. So I not
only ' admit,' but joyfully insist on the fact ' that the
miners are laying the foundation of something better.'
The struggle against the terrible power of the profit-
grinder is now practically proclaimed by them a matter
of principle, and no longer a mere chance-hap business
dispute, and though the importance of this is acknowledged here and there, I think it is even yet underrated.
For my part I look upon the swift progress towards
equality as now certain ; what these staunch miners have
been doing in the face of such tremendous odds, other
workmen can and will do ; and when life is easier and
fuller of pleasure, people will have time to look around
them and find out what they desire in the matter of art,
and will also have power to compass their desires. No
one can tell now what form that art will take ; but as it
is certain that it will not depend on the whim of a few

persons, but on the will of all, so it may be hoped that it will at last not lag behind that of past ages, but will outgo the art of the past in the degree that life will be more pleasurable from the absence of bygone violence and tyranny, *in spite* and not *because* of which our forefathers produced the wonders of popular art, some few of which time has left us."

CHAPTER XXI

FOR about a year from the date of this remarkable letter Morris's life was so quietly busy from day to day that it has left almost no noticeable records. At the end of 1893 he had written to his mother the last letter of the long series which begins when he was an undergraduate at Oxford.

"Kelmscott House,
"Dec. 23rd, 1893.

" My dearest Mother,

" If I do not write now I shall not be in time for Christmas Day, so please consider this as Christmas Eve. I asked Henny to get you some pocket-handkerchiefs when she was in town. I hope you found them nice. The weather here is very fine this morning; I hope the sun is shining in on your room as it is on mine, as I suppose it is, for I think they both look nearly south. Jenny (the younger) is sitting with me reading a paper, and we are both enjoying the fine day.

" I got a letter from Henny yesterday inclosing a nice neck-kerchief for me; that will be good for me to wear when the weather takes one of the sudden changes to cold, which come so often now. Thank you very much for it.

" Also, dearest mother, thank you very much for the handsome stands and dishes you were so kind as to send me; and the beautiful Dresden cups which I have always so much admired.   And they are so pleasant to drink out of.

"We are all very well at present, and have pretty much got over our colds.   I am looking forward to this Christmas as a quiet time, when there will be a lull in business matters: as I am hard at work, which I like very much.

"Dearest own mother, I send you my very best love and am

"Your most affectionate son,
"WILLIAM MORRIS."

Mrs. Morris died in the following winter in her ninetieth year. "Tuesday I went to bury my mother," he wrote a few days afterwards: "a pleasant winter day with gleams of sun.   She was laid in earth in the church-yard close by the house, a very pretty place among the great wych-elms, which, if it were of no use to her, was softening to us.   Altogether my old and callous heart was touched by the absence of what had been so kind to me and fond of me.   She was eighty-nine, and had been ill for nearly four years."

All that year Morris had been working hard at his press.   But at Whitsuntide he took a holiday, and spent it in his favourite haunts of Northern France.   He renewed there his delight in the indestructibly beautiful country, and the still lovely towns which seem as if they had grown out of the country like the fruit on a tree. The spring, too, was one of exceptional beauty; the countryside was one flame of flowers, and "the nightin-gales," as Morris put it to Burne-Jones after he came back, "O my wig, they *were* peppering into it."   The effect of the visit may be clearly traced in an address which he gave, soon after his return to England, to the

Ancoats Brotherhood at Manchester.   The subject he chose to speak upon was " Town and Country."   The greater part of the address was delivered without notes, and of that portion no trustworthy record has been preserved.   But for the earlier portion a few pages of manuscript had been carefully written out : and the fragment is notable for the clearness of its historical view, and for the temperate practical ideal, which, not without reasonable hope, it sets up for a near future.   It has also a direct autobiographic value from its personal touches, not only in the allusion to the Oxford of his own youth, but where he speaks of the havoc wrought in country villages by the wasteful neglect, or still worse by the destructive attention, of the modern landowner.   In both cases he had in his mind actual instances in his own neighbourhood on the upper Thames.   But beyond all, it sums up, with the ripeness of long experience, the instincts and beliefs which guided him in his view of what kind of human life was desirable, and possible, and a duty, in a naturally beautiful world.

" Town and country are generally put in a kind of contrast, but we will see what kind of a contrast there has been, is, and may be between them ; how far that contrast is desirable or necessary, or whether it may not be possible in the long run to make the town a part of the country and the country a part of the towns.   I think I may assume that, on the one hand, there is nobody here so abnormally made as not to take a pleasure in green fields, and trees, and rivers, and mountains, the beings, human and otherwise, that inhabit those scenes, and in a word, the general beauty and incident of nature : and that, on the other, we all of us find human intercourse necessary to us, and even the excitement of those forms of it which can only be had where large bodies of men live together.

" In the Roman times of the Empire, when the lands were cultivated almost wholly by well-organized slave labour with its necessary concomitant of brigandage and piracy in out-of-the-way places, I can't think that the countrysides were very pleasant places to live in; whereas' the Roman city with its handsome buildings and gardens, its public baths, and other institutions of almost complete ' municipal socialism,' must have been very pleasant to well-to-do people, and perhaps, under the Empire at least, not quite intolerable to the proletarian, whose form of pauper relief did not include the prison system of the modern workhouse. In those days the town decidedly ' scores'; all the more as manufacture was, as its name implies, wholly a matter of handicraft. But the Roman city-system was pretty much swept away by the barbarism which took the place of the Empire. In this country, and wherever the people were not completely Romanized, the town was almost always merely the development of the agricultural district ; it was the aggregation of the cultivators of the soil, and its freemen were always landowners, though mostly collective ones. In fact, for a long time after the Teutonic invasion which made this country England, there were no towns at all : the English clans lived in scattered homesteads along the side of the sea, or some river, or in clearings of the wild wood, as their Anglish, Jutish, or Saxon forefathers had done, and when they took a Romano-British town they had nothing better to do with it than to burn it and let it be : though, when they got more civilized, the long extinct glories of Rome took some revenge for this destruction, by the impression which they made on the descendants of the destroyers : e.g., an Anglo-Saxon poet of about the time of Athelstane wrote a poem on the ruins of an old Roman city which is as pathetic and beautiful as any lyric extant in any language, and you may, if you please, look on it as a forecast of the glories of the cities that were yet to come.

"Gradually, as civilization grew, the population thickened in certain places where the protection of the feudal lord—Baron, Bishop, or Abbot—made a market possible ; and in short the growth of such places made our mediæval towns ; though, as was like to be, where an old Roman town like York or London was still in existence, it was used as such a centre. But doubtless our mediæval towns were very small, smaller than our imagination of them pictures them to us; while on the other hand, the country villages were in many cases much larger than they are now. In fact in those days it was not so much the houses that made the town, as the constitution, the freemen and the guilds, which gradually grew into the Corporation. My familiarity with Oxford makes it easy to me to see a mediæval town of the more important kind: a place of some extent within its ancient walls, but the houses much broken by gardens and open spaces within the walls, and without them, a small estate it may be called, the communal property of the freemen. On the whole, then, the towns of the Middle Ages, in this country at least, were a part of the countrysides where they stood.

"In the Middle Ages even London was no more of a centre than Bristol or York, or indeed other places now become almost extinct. But in the eighteenth century London was become very decidedly the centre of England, and now the distinction was not between the towns and the countrysides, but between London and the rest of the country, towns and all. And here properly begins the opposition of town to country. The only further development of this was the work of the Great Industries which created the big manufacturing town, a thing so entirely modern that even London, with all its enormity, has more relation to the cities of the past than these manufacturing towns have.

" On considering further the contrast between town and country we must be careful not to forget this special quality in London. For now we see that we have three things to deal with : London, the external beastliness and sordidness of which is in some degree compensated by its intellectual life; the commercial centres, which have no such compensation, and even in externals are far more horrible than London; and the country, which, instead of being the due fellow and helpmate of the towns and the Town, is a troublesome appendage, an awkward incident of town life, which, commercial or in-tellectual, is the real life of our epoch.

" The result of all this is the usual make-shift jumble which oppresses all our life in this epoch of strange and rapid change, when we have fallen into such grievous want of reasonable organization. Even London, though far better than the commercial towns, is sordidly vulgar in its rich quarters, noisome and squalid beyond word in its poor quarters. And the country—at this end of May I am not going to say that it is not beautiful—beautiful everywhere more or less where there are not many modern houses in sight. But I know the country well: and even for a rich man, a well-to-do one at least, it shares in the make-shift stupidity of the epoch. Amongst all the superabundant beauty of leaf and flower, all the wealth of meadow, and acre, and hillside, it is *stingy*, O so stingy ! In an ordinary way not an hour's work will be spent in taking away an ugly dead tree, in mending a shattered wall, setting a tottering vane straight (even if it be pulling down the roof-beam it is fastened to), in short in mending any defacement caused by wind and weather. Not a moment's consideration will be given as to whether the sightly material shall be used, if the unsightly one be a fraction cheaper for the time being. You can scarce have milk unless you keep a cow: you can't have vegetables unless you grow them yourself. I say this is the ordinary rule : it is true that when there is a rich squire, he does sometimes take some pains in beautifying his cottages, restoring his church, and so forth—with the result in *all* cases, that the village he has so dealt with has become as vulgar as Bayswater. Nor can I leave this subject of the outward aspect of the country without reminding you that through forty years of my life I have diligently and affectionately *noticed* the countryside in its smallest detail, and that the change for the worse in its aspect has been steady, and, especially within the last twenty years, startlingly rapid. Indeed, sometimes I feel selfishly glad to think that I shall not live to see the worst of it. Now you may well say that all this suffering to men who are in the habit of taking in impressions through the eyes is a due reward for our living on other people's earnings ; for our suffering the human live-stock of the country to live such a wretched scanty existence as they do. True, and over true ; but then why should *we* of the nineteenth century be so extra punished, when our fore-fathers were involved in the same sin ?

"I take it that after all this is the case, that we feel it because it is at last tending to change—that we at last can do something to alter it. For this is what I want done in this matter of town and country: I want neither the towns to be appendages of the country, nor the country of the town ; I want the town to be impregnated with the beauty of the country, and the country with the intelligence and vivid life of the town. I want every homestead to be clean, orderly, and tidy; a lovely house surrounded by acres and acres of garden. On the other hand, I want the town to be clean, orderly, and tidy; in short, a garden with beautiful houses in it. Clearly, if I don't wish this, I must be a fool or a dullard; but I do more—I claim it as the due heritage of the latter ages of the world which have subdued nature, and can have for the asking."

The great work of the Kelmscott Chaucer, which had been so long in preparation, was now fairly begun. "Chaucer getting on well; such lovely designs," is a note made by him in early spring. At the end of June he writes that he hopes to begin the actual printing within a month, and that, in about three months more, all the pictures, and nearly all the borders, will be ready for the whole of the Canterbury Tales. His delight in the growing row of volumes from his own press was un-abated; and almost as great was his delight in giving copies to his more intimate friends. To Mr. Philip Webb, who had made some remonstrance against the extent of his generosity, he replied in the following letter:

"Kelmscott House,
"August 27th, '94.

"My dear Fellow,

"A traveller once entered a western hotel in America and went up to the clerk in his box (as the custom is in that country) and ordered chicken for his dinner: the clerk, without any trouble in his face, put his hand into his desk, and drew out a derringer, where-with he covered the newcomer and said in a calm historic voice: Stranger, you will not have chicken, you will have hash.

"This story you seem to have forgotten. So I will apply it, and say that you will have the Kelmscott books as they come out. In short you will have hash because

it would upset me very much if you did not have a
share in my 'larx.'

"As to the Olaf Saga, I had forgotten what you had
had; chiefly I think because I did not prize the big-paper
copies much.   They were done in the days of ignorance,
before the Kelmscott Press was, though hard on the
time when it began.

"You see as to all these matters I do the books
mainly for you and one or two others; the public does
not really care about them a damn—which is stale.   But
I tell you I *want* you to have them, and finally you *shall*.

"Yours affectionately,

"WILLIAM MORRIS."

The autumn at Kelmscott was unusually quiet and
happy.   A certain degree of physical feebleness had now
become his normal condition; he was seldom able to take
long walks, or to spend whole days fishing; but he
delighted in driving among the beautiful and familiar
villages, and in shorter walks near home.   It was on
one of these walks, at the end of September, that when
his companions perched on a gate to rest he sat down on
the roadside with his legs straight out in front of him,
saying, "I shall sit on the world."   It would be difficult
to convey to any one who did not know him well the
sense of mingled oddness and pathos that the words gave.
Two days later, on a Sunday morning in Buscot Wood,
he talked for some two hours on end on the principles
of conducting business, with all his old keen insight and
fertility of illustration.   It was noticeable how he seemed
to speak of the whole matter as, for himself, a past experience.   One of the visitors at Kelmscott that week
was Sir Edward Burne-Jones's little grandson, in whose
favour Morris discarded any prejudices which he might
have against children other than his own; for outside of

his own family he was not a lover of children, and seldom took any notice of them. "As to Denis, he is the dearest little chap," he writes on the 3rd of October, "and as merry as the day is long—all that a gentleman of his age should be: everybody paid him the attention which he deserves." The Kelmscott holiday—during which, however, he was steadily at work designing borders and initials for the Chaucer—was prolonged till the beginning of November.

Soon after he returned to London the first elections were being held under the Local Government Act of 1894, which had been the latest and the most important achievement of Mr. Gladstone's administration. Morris was at once too preoccupied with his own work, and too disillusioned by his own experience, to feel any very deep interest in the matter. He did not go to Kelmscott to attend the inaugural parish meeting: in London he voted, but did no more. It was claimed for the Act by some enthusiasts that it reconstituted a framework of administration which was essentially that of the Middle Ages, and indeed went back in some points even beyond them. But to him it seemed too artificial, and too much encumbered with those checks and balances which he hated, to be a source of any great hope. To Lady Burne-Jones, who was standing for election to the Parish Council at Rottingdean, he wrote on the 14th of December:

"Well now, I hope you will come in at the head of the poll; and I hope we shall beat our Bumbles. No one here can even guess how it will go. I daresay you think me rather lukewarm about the affair; but I am so depressed with the pettiness and timidity of the bill and the checks and counterchecks with which such an obvious measure has been hedged about, that all I can hope is that people will be able to keep up the excitement about it till they have got it altered somewhat. However, I shall go and vote for my twelve to-morrow morning, but I am lethargic and faint-hearted."

A week later he wrote again : " Many thanks for your book "—a brief, but admirably lucid printed address to the electors, explaining the scope of the Act and the nature of their rights and duties under it—" which is as good as the subject admits of, and for the first time makes me know something about the parish councils. Could you let me have two or three more ? Now I congratulate you on the election, and I am really quite pleased that you beat the Bumbles. Here they beat us properly ; though I didn't think, all things considered, that it was so bad, as we polled about half of what they did. You see all through London the middle class voted solid against us ; which I think extremely stupid of them, as they might as well have got credit for supporting an improved administration. But you see they have an instinct, which they can't resist, against any progress in any direction. Item, they are very fearful lest the rates should be raised on them ; as they certainly will be, whoever is in. We did better with the Guardians' election, getting eight out of twelve."

At the beginning of 1895 Morris was carrying on all his multifarious occupations with unimpaired activity. Two presses were at work upon the Chaucer, and a third on smaller books. He was designing new paper-hangings; he was going on daily with the writing of new romances; he was completing, in collaboration with Mr. Magnússon, the translation of the Heimskringla which they had begun some three and twenty years before, and seeing it through the press for the Saga Library; and he was busily increasing the collection of illuminated manuscripts, chiefly of the thirteenth and fourteenth centuries, which towards the end of his life became his chief treasures and gave him extraordinary delight.

With the two presses at work it now seemed possible to finish the Chaucer in a year, and the panics into which he sometimes fell over its slow progress were greatly allayed.   Among the smaller books which the third printing-press was turning out was the volume of selected poems of Coleridge.   As to that book the following interesting passage occurs in a letter to Ellis when the contents were under discussion :

"As to the Coleridge-Keats question, you don't quite understand the position I think.   Keats was a great poet who sometimes nodded : we don't want to make a *selection* of his works.   Coleridge was a muddle-brained metaphysician, who by some strange freak of fortune turned out a few real poems amongst the dreary flood of inanity which was his wont.   It is these real poems only that must be selected, or we burden the world with another useless book.   Christabel only just comes in because the detail is fine ; but nothing a hair's breadth worse must be admitted.   There is absolutely no difficulty in choosing, because the difference between his poetry and his drivel is so striking.

" I have been through the poems, and find that the only ones that have any interest for me are—1. Ancient Mariner, 2. Christabel, 3. Kubla Khan, and 4. the poem called Love.   This would make a very little book, about 60 pages.   There is one other which at least has some character, though rather tainted with Wordsworthianism ; it is called The Three Graves, and is about as cheerful as the influenza.   But then it is copyright ; and at the best it would rather water down the good ones."

This volume, which finally included thirteen of Coleridge's poems, was the last of the series of reprints of modern poetry issued from the Kelmscott Press.   It was not printed till a year later, having been postponed to another volume of selected poems of Herrick, for whom Morris had only a modified liking. "I like him better than I thought I should : I daresay we shall make a pretty book of it," was all he would say after looking through the "Hesperides" and "Noble Numbers" when the Kelmscott edition was in preparation.

In March he was buying manuscripts of Messrs. Quaritch and Leighton, and also at sales at Sotheby's and Christie's, and hungering after more, though indignant at the prices which were asked for them. "I bought," he writes to Ellis on the 19th, " for £15 10s. (much too dear) a Guldin Bibel (Augsburg, Hohenwang, *circa* 1470), a very interesting book which I much wanted. Also I bought for £25 (much too dear) a handsome 13th century French MS., but with little ornament, because it looked so handsome I hadn't the heart to send it back. The Mentelin Bible Quaritch bought for himself : 'tis a *very* fine book, and I lust after it, but can't afford it. The prices were preposterous. There is a sale at Sotheby's this week, and I am just going up there, though I don't expect much in my way. I expect to meet Mr. James there with the two leaves from the Fitzwilliam."

On the 23rd he continues : " As the history of sales seems to interest you, hear a tale of the Phillips sale, of which to-day is the third day. Two books I bid for. A 13th century Aristotelian book with three very pretty initials, but imperfect top and tail; I put £15 on this with many misgivings as to my folly—hi! it fetched £50!! A really pretty little book, Gregory's Decretals, with four or five very tiny illuminations ; I took a fancy to it and put £40 on it, expecting to get it for £25— ho!! it fetched £96 !!! ·Rejoice with me that I have got 82 MSS., as clearly I shall never get another. I have duly got my two leaves, and beauties they are."

The two leaves mentioned in these letters have an interesting history attached to them. In the previous July Morris had bought for upwards of £400—the highest price he had ever then paid for a book—an English Book of Hours written about 1300 in East Anglia, and containing the arms of Grey and Clifford. It was subsequently found that two missing leaves from this manuscript were in the Fitzwilliam Museum at Cambridge. After long negotiations, it was agreed that Morris should sell his book to the museum for £200, and in return have the possession of it and of the two leaves belonging to it for his own lifetime. He had the leaves inserted in their places, and the manuscript remained one of his chief treasures. After his death it went to Cambridge, where it is now.

Notwithstanding the great rise in prices, a fine painted book was always worth more to Morris than it cost: and within the next two months he had added two of the first rank to his collection. One of these was the so-called Huntingfield Psalter, a superb book of the end of the twelfth century. The other was the Tiptoft Missal, a work of about thirty years later, with illuminated borders throughout, of which the best are of unsurpassed beauty.

At the beginning of April he went down to Kelmscott. The Manor House, of which his tenure had hitherto been precarious, had, by an arrangement made the month before, passed practically, though not formally, into his ownership.

"It is just a month," he wrote to his daughter on his arrival, "since I was here, and there is a great change in the grass, which shows green everywhere and looks beautiful. As to the flowers, there are not many of them actually out. The snowdrops nearly but not quite gone; a few purple crocuses, but of course not open this sunless day.   The daphne very full of blossom.   Many daffodils nearly out, but only two or three quite.   The beautiful hepatica, which I used to love so when I was a quite little boy, in full bloom, both pink and blue: the hyacinths not out yet, but more advanced than our London (outdoor) ones.   Several of the crown imperials show for bloom; but are not due yet, nor are the yellow tulips.   There are a few primroses, but not many; but the garden with all its springing green looks lovely.

"As to birds, I have heard very little singing except the rooks, who are all agog: I suppose the cold weather has belated the breeding season.

"Giles has patched up the punt, and is sanguine about its holding water: so am I; but think the water may be rather inside than out—however we shall see.   There has been a little flood since I was here; which will do good.   The house is as clean as a new pin."

By the end of the month he had cleared off long arrears of translation and romance-writing by finishing his Heimskringla and the romance of "The Water of the Wondrous Isles," and was working harder than ever for the Society for Protection of Ancient Buildings. The main object of their defence at the moment was Peterborough Cathedral.

It was one of the churches which had been his earliest admirations; he had known it in his boyhood, and felt towards it as though he had been one of its own builders. One of the most brilliant pieces of imaginative description in "The Earthly Paradise" is put in the mouth of a wanderer who had seen that magnificent western front rising. It occurs in the introductory verses to the tale of "The Proud King."

—I, who have seen

So many lands, and midst such marvels been,
Clearer than these abodes of outland men

Can see above the green and unburnt fen
The little houses of an English town,
Cross-timbered, thatched with fen-reeds coarse and
    brown,
And high o'er these, three gables, great and fair,
That slender rods of columns do upbear
Over the minster doors, and imagery
Of kings, and flowers no summer field doth see,
Wrought on those gables.   Yea, I heard withal
In the fresh morning air, the trowels fall
Upon the stone, a thin noise far away ;
For high up wrought the masons on that day,
Since to the monks that house seemed scarcely well
Till they had set a spire or pinnacle
Each side the great porch. . . . I am now grown
    old,
Yet is it still the tale I then heard told
Within the guest-house of that minster-close
Whose walls, like cliffs new-made, before us rose.

A long and bitter controversy was carried on between
the Dean and Chapter on one side and the Society for
Protection of Ancient Buildings on the other.   It ended
inconclusively ; and the work proposed by Mr. Pearson
has in the main been carried out.   But here as elsewhere
the real result of the Society's action is to be sought, not
so much in what they failed to prevent, as in the effect
which their vigilant and jealous criticism had on the
manner in which the work was carried out.

Equally strong was Morris's feeling in another matter
on which that same spring he helped to excite public
interest, that of the injuries done to Epping Forest, the
playground of his own childhood, by the Conservators.
Alarm had been aroused by the amount of "restoration"
that had been carried out in it for some years by lopping

and felling, as well as by changes which smoothed down the characteristic wildness of the Forest. The strangely romantic aspect of the dense hornbeam thickets, the plashy dells, and the rough cattle-tracks winding among the hollies and beeches of the upper ground, had been already impaired and was in further danger: and Morris was roused to alarm and indignation by the prospect of seeing one of the last fragments of ancient England turned into a modern park. On the 7th of May he spent a long day in walking through the Forest with a party of four or five friends. He was relieved to find that the evil had been exaggerated. Here and there damage had undoubtedly been done ; but whole tracts of the Forest remained as wild and beautiful as ever; and he drew little but pleasure from the visit to the glades and coppices, every yard of which had been familiar to him as a boy.

His anxieties about the Kelmscott Chaucer were not yet over. At the end of May the discovery was made that a number of the printed sheets had become discoloured, owing to some failure in the exact preparation of the ink. Fortunately it proved that the yellow stain was fugitive, and could be removed by careful bleaching in sunlight without affecting the colour of the ink. But it was not till late in the autumn that he could fully satisfy himself that the stain had been permanently removed, and might not reappear.

" The check of the Chaucer flattens life for me somewhat," he writes on the 19th of July, " but I am going hard into the matter, and have found out the real expert in the matter of inks and oils, and in about a fortnight hope to know the worst of it.

" On Wednesday I went a journey into Suffolk for the S. P. A. B., a pretty journey all through my native Essex. The upland pastures were all burnt up, and were cocoa-nut matting ; but the corn did not look bad : they were cutting oats in many places, which should not be ready till the end of August. Blythborough was what we went to see; once a good town in the Middle Ages, now a poor remnant of a village with the ruins of a small religious house and a huge 15th century church built of flint after that country manner : a very beautiful church, full of interest, with fine wood-work galore, a lovely painted roof, and some stained glass; the restorations not much noticeable from the inside : floor of various bricks, a few seats in the nave, all ancient, similar ones in the chancel, and the rest open space. We were cumbered of course with the parson, since we came to advise him, but I much enjoyed myself and sat about while Turner did his measurings, etc. The place is close to Southwold on the little tidal river Bly at the end of the marshland valley, where they were busy with their second hay crop. Little spits of the sandy low upland covered with heather and bracken run down to the marsh, and make a strange landscape of it; a mournful place, but full of character. I was there some twenty-five years ago ; and found I remembered it perfectly.

" By the way, there was a review of the Wood "—his romance of " The Wood beyond the World," which had been issued from the Kelmscott Press the year before, and of which an ordinary edition had recently been published—" in last week's Spectator, which was kind and polite, but amused me very much by assuming that it was a Socialist allegory of Capital and Labour! It was written with such an air of cock-certainty that I thought people might think that I had told the reviewer myself; so I wrote a note to explain that he was wrong."

During this summer the gradual failure of Morris's strength became clearly noticeable. Languor insensibly stole over him. " It is sad," Sir Edward Burne-Jones wrote in autumn, "to see his enormous vitality diminishing." He was less ready for any active expeditions, and began to suffer from sleeplessness. In summer mornings it had long been a luxury with him to be awakened at dawn by the first birds and then fall asleep again; but now that first waking was not always succeeded by a second sleep, and he often, even when summer passed into winter, got up at three or four o'clock and sat down to write at one of his prose tales in order to pass the time. He found that the clipping of a yew dragon which had been for some years in progress under the gable of the tapestry-room at Kelmscott was too fatiguing a task for him. His country walks became shorter in their range, and fishing was almost given up. "Ellis was with us for three days," he writes at the beginning of August, "and took me fishing every day: I did not much want to go, but I daresay it did me good." Even writing began to be a fatiguing task. "I am worn out," he says on the 13th of August, "with writing a long letter to the Athenæum about the tapestry at South Kensington Museum, and so cannot attempt to fill up this sheet." A week later, however, he was well enough to make his annual expedition to the White Horse. Lady Burne-Jones, who was staying at Kelmscott, was of the party. "Topsy looks very happy, and is so sweet down here," she wrote home. "The garden is enchanting with flowers, one mass of them, and all kept in beautiful order. The trees and bushes are of course grown in the last nine years, and the whole place is leafier; otherwise I feel as if I had been here last week, the place is so little changed—but I feel the added years in Janey and Topsy and me, so that it seems like visiting something that is not quite real."

"The garden looks rich and pleasant," Morris himself had written at the beginning of the month, "though the autumn flowers (for we are practically in autumn now) are so much less delightful than those of spring and early summer.   One pleasant walk is cut off from us at present, the one up to Buscot Wood. It is guarded by a dragon; *i.e.*, a savage Bull; we (Jenny and I) on Friday last were just going into the first Berkshire field when the lock-keeper stopped us and told us awesome stories about the said beast; so we abstained. We, safe on the other side of the river, saw the gentleman after-wards, as he walked away from his harem, sometimes throwing up his head and bellowing, sometimes faring along with that expressive half inward growl, which is so interesting to hear when you *are* on the other side of the Thames. We were both of us compelled to admit that he was a gallant-looking neat—red-roan of colour."

The lock-keeper's cottage, a pretty but tumble-down building of grey stone, walls and roof, was about to be rebuilt by the Thames Conservancy; and one of the last instances in which Morris was able to ward off encroach-ments on the beauty of the riverside was when he now prevented, by a temperate and dignified expostulation, the replacement of the old silver-grey roof which lay in sight of his own house by one of blue Welsh slate. At his urgent instances, too, the Conservators consented to give instructions that the men who cut the weeds on the river should spare the flowering plants on the banks as much as possible. But beyond his own immediate reach he had to confess with despondency that it seemed use-less to struggle against the pervading flood of evil change in that lovely region. "I was thinking just now," he writes from Kelmscott at the end of August, "how I have wasted the many times when I have been 'hurt' and (especially of late years) have made no sign, but swallowed down my sorrow and anger, and nothing done! Whereas if I had but gone to bed and stayed there for a month or two and declined taking any part in life, as indeed on such occasions I have felt very much disinclined to do, I can't help thinking that it might have been very effective. Perhaps you remember that this game was tried by some of my Icelandic heroes, and seemingly with great success. But I admit that it wants to be done well.

" It was a most lovely afternoon when I came down here, and I was prepared to enjoy the journey from Oxford to Lechlade very much : and so I did ; but woe's me ! when we passed by the once lovely little garth near Black Bourton, I saw all my worst fears realized ; for there was the little barn we saw being mended, the wall cut down and finished with a zinked iron roof. It quite sickened me when I saw it. That's the way all things are going now. In twenty years everything will be gone in this countryside, which twenty years ago was so rich in beautiful building : and we can do nothing to help it or mend it. The world had better say, 'Let us be through with it and see what will come after it !' In the meantime I can do nothing but a little bit of Anti-Scrape—*sweet to eye while seen*. Now that I am grown old and see that nothing is to be done, I half wish that I had not been born with a sense of romance and beauty in this accursed age."

But a week afterwards he had so far rallied from this fit of depression as to be in great excitement over the new scheme for the folio edition of his own " Sigurd the Volsung," for which Burne-Jones had just agreed to design at least five and twenty pictures. "I am afire to see the new designs," he wrote to Burne-Jones, "which I have no doubt *will* do—and as to the age, that be blowed ! "

During the winter he still went on lecturing from time to time as his strength allowed. On the 30th of October, at the request of Mr. Hines, a Radical and

Socialist chimney-sweep in Oxford, with whom he had a long-standing acquaintance, dating from the early days of the Socialist movement, he gave an address to inaugurate the newly-founded Oxford Socialist Union. A month later he spoke—"to the point and impressively," a hearer says—at the funeral of Sergius Stepniak, in the foggy drizzle outside Waterloo Station. During December he lectured twice in London, on English architecture and on Gothic illustrations to printed books. The latter lecture, delivered at the Bolt Court Technical School, was the last he gave with his old vigour. On the 3rd of January he attended the New Year's meeting of the Social Democratic Federation at the Holborn Town Hall, and made there a short, but noble and touching speech on behalf of unity. Two days afterwards, he gave the last of his Sunday evening lectures at Kelmscott House. The subject of the lecture was "One Socialist Party." "Could not sleep at night," he writes in his diary the next day; "got up and worked from 1 to 4 at Sundering Flood." On the 31st of January he attended a meeting, at the Society of Arts, of the Society for Checking the Abuses of Public Advertising, and made a brief speech in support of the first resolution moved. He never spoke in public again after this. On the day before, he had been for the last time at the weekly meeting of the Society for Protection of Ancient Buildings. As he walked up Buckingham Street after the meeting, a friend ventured to observe, noting his obvious weakness, that it was the worst time of the year. "No, it ain't," he returned, " it's a very fine time of the year indeed : I'm getting old, that's what it is."

On the 27th of November he had written from Rottingdean, where he had gone for a few days by himself, to Lady Burne-Jones:

" To-day has been quite mild, and I started out at ten

and went to a mountain with some barns on the top, and
a chalk pit near (where you took me one hot evening in
September, you remember), and I walked on thence a good
way, and should have gone further, but prudence rather
than weariness turned me back. They were ploughing
a field in the bottom with no less than ten teams of great
big horses: they were knocking off for their bever just
as I came on them, and seemed very jolly, and my heart
went out to them, both men and horses.

"I brought my University book"—this was Mr.
Rashdall's "Universities of Europe in the Middle
Ages," a work for which he expressed the highest respect and admiration—"down with me, but deserted it
yesterday afternoon for Jane Austen's 'Pride and Prejudice,' which I have just finished. I am getting better
here, but was better on Sunday for the matter of that.
The doctor called on Monday, and told me it was good for
me not to be victimized by bores, and that I had better
not be: this seems to me such very good advice, that I
pass it on to you; but am just struck with fear that you
may begin the practice of it on me. Anyhow I will be
cautious enough of it not to make this letter longer."

In December the Chaucer was making such good progress that he began to design a binding for it. Even
here he was confronted by the difficulty of obtaining
sound material. "Leather is not good now," he said
in talking about this matter; "what used to take nine
months to cure is done in three. They used to say,
what's longest in the tanyard stays least time in the
market: but that no longer holds good. *People don't
know how to buy now; they'll take anything.*" The truth
in this last sentence goes very deep. The manufacturer
—so Morris perpetually urged—is but the servant of
the public, and the buyer is equally responsible with the
seller (each, he would add, doing their best to cheat the

other) for a state of things which floods all markets with cheap dishonest work.

As the Chaucer approached completion, Morris became nervous about anything which threatened, however remotely, to delay it. "I'd like it finished to-morrow," he answered, when asked how early a date would satisfy him for its appearance: "every day beyond to-morrow that it isn't done is one too many." In his own library one day before Christmas, a visitor looking over the sheets that were lying on the table remarked on the added beauty of those sheets following the Canterbury Tales where picture-pages face one another in pairs. Morris took alarm. "Now don't you go saying that to Burne-Jones," he said, "or he'll be wanting to do the first part over again; and the worst of that would be, that he'd want to do all the rest over again, because the other would be so much better, and then we should never get done, but always be going round and round in a circle." The last of the eighty-seven pictures was finished two days after Christmas. In the same week Morris had begun to write the story of "The Sundering Flood," the last of his prose romances. During that December he had enriched his collection of manuscripts by two splendid examples of the thirteenth century, for which he paid upwards of a thousand pounds; one a folio Bible, in three volumes, of French work of the end of the century, and the other a Psalter of slightly earlier date, variously ascribed to Rouen or Beauvais, and richly adorned with miniatures in the finest manner of that fine period.

With the turn of the year the weakness that had been gaining on him for some months became much more pronounced. He now suffered from an exhausting cough; he was losing flesh noticeably, and sleeplessness became a regular feature of his nights. He wrote a

WILLIAM MORRIS'S STUDY. KELMSCOTT HOUSE. HAMMERSMITH.

little of " The Sundering Flood" every day, and did work
nearly every day for initials and borders for the Kelmscott Press editions of " The Well at the World's End "
and " The Earthly Paradise." But his working hours
became shorter and shorter. In February another visit
to Rottingdean was tried, but he was languid and made
no improvement. On his return he was induced to
consult Sir William Broadbent. The existence of diabetes
and other complications was confirmed, but not to a
degree which implied immediate danger. There were
fluctuations and slight improvements followed by relapses,
but on the whole he was now steadily losing ground, and
as his weakness increased, losing heart. " I don't feel
any better : so weak," is a pathetic note in his diary of
work at the end of February : and a journey round his
garden at Hammersmith was now sufficient to tire him.
The daily progress of the Chaucer was the one thing that
kept up his interest. It was now within sight of completion. The last three of the wood-blocks had been
brought him on the 21st of March. The Easter holidays in April, " four mouldy Sundays in a mouldy row,
the press shut and Chaucer at a standstill," were almost
more than he could bear. But his eagerness over the
acquisition of fresh manuscripts was unabated. In
March he had bought from Mr. W. A. S. Benson a
fine folio Testament of the twelfth century, which he discovered, to his great delight, had belonged to the same
religious house near Dijon as a Josephus which he had
acquired a few months before. Towards the end of April
he was roused to great excitement by news of a splendid
twelfth-century English Bestiary, containing one hundred
and six miniatures, which was offered for sale by Mr.
Rosenthal of Munich. He at once began to negotiate
for it : as Mr. Rosenthal would not take the risk of
sending it on approval, Mr. Cockerell went to Stuttgart,

where the book was, with full powers. It turned out to
be even finer than had been expected; even the British
Museum possessed nothing in Bestiaries equal to it. A
contemporary note in the book itself recorded that it had
been given in the year 1187 to Worksop Priory, together
with other books, by one Philip, Canon of Lincoln. Both
writing and miniatures, with which it is profusely illustrated, were of the best and most characteristic English
style of the period. Mr. Cockerell bought it for £900,
and brought it back with him to Kelmscott, where
Morris had gone for what turned out to be his last visit.
He was delighted with it beyond measure.

From Kelmscott he wrote, during this visit, to Lady
Burne-Jones;

"I cannot say that I think I am better since I saw you
a week ago; and I hope I am no worse; only you see
down in this deep quiet, away from the excitements of
business, and callers, and doctors, one is rather apt to
brood, and I fear that I have made myself very disagreeable at times.

"However, I am going on with my work, both drawing and writing, though but little of the latter, as Walker
was with me Saturday and Sunday, to my great comfort.
Ellis comes on Saturday, and will stay till I go back.
Here everything is as beautiful as it can be: up to now
the season is a fine one, the grass well grown and well
coloured; the apple-blossom plentifuller than we have
ever had it here. The weather with lots of sun, though I
should have preferred that alternated with a few warm
showers instead of the veil of cold cloud which has no
promise of rain in it (like Hud's dry cloud that hung
over the city of Sheddad, the son of Ad the Greater) and
withering wind with it.

"However I have enjoyed the garden very much, and
should never be bored by walking about and about in it.

And though you think I don't like music, I assure you that the rooks and the blackbirds have been a great consolation to me.   We are still between the flowers, for nothing stirs this beastly weather.   The thing that was the pleasingest surprise was the raspberry-canes, which Giles has trellised up neatly, so that they look like a mediæval garden: they are thriving splendidly.

"Moreover Hobbs has been re-thatching a lot of his sheds and barns, which sorely needed it, and used to keep me in a fever of terror of galvanized iron: so that this time at least there is some improvement in the village."

At Kelmscott he had written the last of his contributions to the literature of Socialism, a brief article for the May-Day number of " Justice." When he returned to London on the 6th of May he found that all the picture sheets of the Chaucer had been printed off, and the block of the title-page was ready for approval.   The printing was completed two days later.   At the end of May he went for a few days to Mr. Wilfrid Blunt at Newbuildings Place; he was then too weak to work, but could enjoy the beautiful West Sussex country.   He returned to London on the 30th: and on the 2nd of June the first two copies of the Chaucer came from the binder, one for himself and the other for Burne-Jones.   Morris's own copy is now in the library of Exeter College.   The other was given on the 3rd of June by Sir Edward Burne-Jones to his daughter for her birthday.   " I want particularly to draw your attention," Burne-Jones wrote of the volume when complete, and the feeling is one which Morris himself fully and cordially shared, " to the fact that there is no preface to Chaucer, and no introduction, and no essay on his position as a poet, and no notes, and no glossary; so that all is prepared for you to enjoy him thoroughly."

Thus the work which had been for just five years in project, and for three years and four months in actual preparation and execution, was brought to a conclusion. The printing had occupied a year and nine months. Besides Burne-Jones's eighty-seven pictures, it contains a full-page woodcut title, fourteen large borders, eighteen borders or frames for the pictures, and twenty-six large initial words. All of these, besides the ornamented initial letters large and small, were designed by Morris himself, as was the white pigskin binding with silver clasps, executed at Mr. Cobden-Sanderson's bindery by Mr. Douglas Cockerell, in which the Kelmscott Chaucer receives its complete form.

CHAPTER XXII

IT was his last finished work. His weakness was already so great that the ambiguous reports of professional advisers could no longer conceal the fact that the end was not far off. He still, on days when the depression of his illness was less severe, cherished the hope of going on with the great Froissart, which was to be a sister volume to the Chaucer, and with the sumptuous folio edition of his own "Sigurd the Volsung." The series of woodcuts for the "Sigurd" from drawings by Sir Edward Burne-Jones had been already planned, and a number of designs for them made. In May Burne-Jones, though with but little hope that the work could ever be carried out, had offered to increase the number of these pictures to forty. The proposal had been joyfully accepted by Morris, and roused him for a little into fresh life. His daily work was now mainly designing borders for the "Sigurd," and he still was able to do a little at it every day. Before either of these large works, however, another small book was to have been printed, which would have been one of the most beautiful products of the Kelmscott Press. This was the tale of "The Hill of Venus," to be written in prose by himself and adorned by the twelve exquisite designs made by Burne-Jones for the story nearly thirty years before.

At the beginning of July he completed his collection of painted books by a Psalter which for style, colour, and

execution was the finest of them all. He gave it the name
of the Windmill Psalter from a windmill which was prominent in the design upon the page next following the
"Beatus." This book, a folio of about the year 1270, had
been acquired, with several leaves missing, about five and
twenty years previously, by Mr. Henry Hucks-Gibbs,
now Lord Aldenham. Four of the missing leaves were,
however, extant, and had been sold many years before by
Ellis to Mr. Fairfax Murray, who after much solicitation
had consented to exchange them with Morris for five
sheets of drawings on vellum by an Italian master of the
fifteenth century. Lord Aldenham's book was exhibited
among the English manuscripts collected and shown in
the summer of 1896 by the Society of Antiquaries in
their rooms at Burlington House. To that exhibition
Morris also lent the four leaves in question, together
with six of the best of his own English painted books.
They were placed next the book to which they had
originally belonged. When Morris went with Burne-
Jones on the 5th of June to see the collection, the re-
lationship of the two portions of the book was obvious.
" We looked," Morris writes exultantly the next day to
Ellis, " and lo ! there was no doubt—there was the book
with the due hiatuses. And now, whatten a book was
that, my man ? Why, as soon as I saw its second leaf,
I recognized it as the book which I saw in your shop in
Bond Street, and which I have talked so much to you
about, and which you told me you sold, or some one
else sold, to Hucks-Gibbs. Are you thunderstruck ?
But now the question is, How am I to get hold of the
Hucks-Gibbs ' fragment' ? Perhaps you can suggest
some course of procedure. Come up and talk about it."

Finally, after much debate, Morris wrote to Lord
Aldenham explaining the case, and offering him £1,000
for the Psalter. He was out of town; and the three

days that passed before his answer came were spent by Morris in much agitation. At last the answer came. "Letter in morning," Morris notes in his diary, "from Lord A., kind and friendly, *will* let me have the book. Sent Cockerell after it with cheque in afternoon, and it came back at 4: a great wonder."

There were two other books in the exhibition at Burlington House which he coveted as much or even more. One was the famous Apocalypse from the Archbishop's Library at Lambeth, "a book with the most amazing design and beauty in it." This was, of course, unattainable. But the other was in private ownership; it was a Psalter, even finer than Lord Aldenham's, belonging to the Duke of Rutland : " *such* a book ! *my* eyes ! and I am beating my brains to see if I can find any thread of an intrigue to begin upon, so as to creep and crawl toward the possession of it." He entered on negotiations, and offered a much higher sum than he had paid for the Windmill Psalter, but in vain; and this last pleasure was denied him.

For the greater part of June he had been, by medical advice, staying at Folkestone to try the effects of change of air, but without any beneficial result. His nervous prostration had by this time become very great. The news which he learned on the way down to Folkestone of the death of his old friend, John Henry Middleton, completely broke him down. "I did like him very much," he wrote mournfully to Lady Burne-Jones a few days afterwards : " we had a deal to talk about, and much in common as to our views of things and the world, and his friendliness to his friends was beyond measure." But he enjoyed strolling about the harbour and walking on the Leas, and on one very fine bright day he managed to go to Boulogne and back with Mr. Cockerell. Relays of friends came down to keep him company: Sir

Edward and Lady Burne-Jones, Mr. Ellis, Mr. Cockerell, Mr. Wilfrid Blunt, Mr. E. Walker, Mr. Catterson-Smith.   On the 24th of June the first fully bound copy of his Chaucer was brought down to him by Mr. Douglas Cockerell, and was approved by him as in every way satisfactory.   On his return to London early in July, he went to report himself to Sir William Broadbent. " He thought me a little better (I'm not), and ordered me a sea voyage."

The voyage fixed on was one to Norway, on an Orient liner which was making a special trip as far as Spitzbergen for the solar eclipse of that year.   It was hoped that the keen northern sea air might prove beneficial, and that the historic associations of Norway might serve to alleviate the monotony of the voyage.   Much to his satisfaction, his old friend, Mr. John Carruthers, the companion of other journeys in previous years, found himself at the last moment able to go with him.   They started on the 22nd of July.   The last entry in his diary had been made on the 20th.

But the voyage, whether wisely counselled or not, was not happy either in its progress or in its results.   His beloved books and manuscripts had to be left behind : he suffered from almost constant weariness and restlessness : he was not able to make any excursions inland, and the melancholy of the firths struck a chill on his spirits in spite of fine weather and warm suns.   Off Bergen a last gleam of the Viking spirit came over him as he gazed on " the old hills which the eyes of the old men looked on when they did their best against the Weirds."   But his own fighting days were over.

He stayed at Vadsö near the North Cape for the week in which the steamer went on to Spitzbergen and returned.   On the morning of the 18th of August he arrived again at Tilbury, with only one anxious wish, to

get away to Kelmscott as soon as possible.   But his illness took a serious turn a day or two afterwards, and the
doctors had to forbid his removal.   He never left
Hammersmith again.   He was so weak now that he had
to dictate the few letters he wrote, though on some days
he did a little designing of letters and ornaments for
the Press.   To his old friend, Mr. Thomas Wardle of
Leek, who had written pressing him to try the effect of
rest and the pure Derbyshire air at Swainslow, he wrote
as follows, the body of the letter being dictated and the
signature added feebly in his own hand :

" Kelmscott House,
" August 26th, 1896.

" My dear Wardle,
        " It is very kind of you to invite me to share in
your paradise, and I am absolutely delighted to find
another beautiful place which is still in its untouched
loveliness.   I should certainly have accepted your invitation, but I am quite unable to do so, for at present I
cannot walk over the threshold, being so intensely weak.
The Manifold is the same river, is it not, which you
carried me across on your back, which situation tickled
us so much that, owing to inextinguishable laughter, you
very nearly dropped me in.   What pleasant old times
those were.

"With all good wishes and renewed thanks,
" I am yours very truly,
" WILLIAM MORRIS."

On the 8th of September, with some difficulty, he dictated the last dozen lines of "The Sundering Flood" to
Mr. Cockerell, and seemed to find relief in having been
able to bring it to a conclusion.   The last letter he had
been able to write himself was one of a few lines to
Lady Burne-Jones, who was at Rottingdean, on the 1st

of September. "Come soon," it ends, "I want a sight of your dear face."

During his absence two more books had been issued from the Kelmscott Press. One of them, "Laudes Beatæ Mariæ Virginis," consisted of a series of Latin poems to the Virgin, from an English Psalter of the early thirteenth century which was one of the manuscripts in his own possession, and one of extreme beauty as regards both writing and ornament. For the first time he had, in this beautiful little volume, tried the experiment of printing in three colours. The result was entirely successful, and the effect of the red was much enhanced by the fine blue which he used as the third colour. The other book was the first volume of a sumptuous eight-volume edition of "The Earthly Paradise." A second volume was issued in September. The remaining six, all of which include borders and half borders specially designed by him and not used in any other book, were completed and issued after his death. In these posthumous volumes, however, there are three borders which had been designed in Morris's manner by Mr. Catterson-Smith; these being the only instances of any letter, border, or ornament (with the exception of a little Greek type which occurs in two books) printed at the Kelmscott Press and not actually designed by Morris himself and drawn with his own hand.

Among the projects that had dated from the earliest days of the Press were two which various circumstances had from time to time put off, and which were now once more much in his mind. One of these was the printing of a selection of mediæval English lyrical poetry. He had discussed the plan of such a book with Mr. Wyatt when they were working together at " Beowulf," and just before he started on the voyage to Norway Mr. Wyatt had sent him a list of early English poems for consideration. But he was too weak then to do anything with it. The other proposed volume was one which lay even nearer his heart; it was a volume of the Border Ballads, which had been his delight since boyhood, and which he often maintained to be the highest achievement in poetry which the language had to show. This also had been planned years before; and early in 1894 he had been discussing the thorny question of a text with Ellis. He had persuaded himself that it was possible to form such a text by selection from the different versions. "You see," he said, "no one version has more authority than another; it is a matter of literary merit;"—and no doubt were the formation of such a text at all possible, it would have had its best chances of success in his hands. During this autumn, when he was too ill to do anything else, he amused himself by having the ballads read aloud to him and beginning to form his own version. Mr. Ellis, who was daily with him, and who did most of this work for him, was well aware that the selection could never be completed, and no longer argued the question with him.

Among the larger unexecuted projects which had at one time or another been formed for the Kelmscott Press, the Shakespeare in three folio volumes, which had been announced in 1893, had been definitely abandoned, and the reprint of the English Bible of 1611, though not formally given up, had receded into a problematical future. The "Sigurd" and the Froissart would have been the work of at least two years; and after them the next work planned was to have been a volume of even greater magnificence than the Chaucer, a folio edition of Malory's "Morte d'Arthur," for which Sir Edward Burne-Jones was to design at least a hundred pictures. With the added experience and increased technical skill now available, it should have eclipsed even the Chaucer in splendour of design and beauty of execution. Of other items in the mass of work which lay before the Press, an account is given in the last book issued from it before it was finally wound up in March, 1898. In that little volume Mr. Cockerell has added to Morris's own account of his aims in founding and conducting the Press, a description of its inception and progress, and an annotated list of the books printed at it, with a fullness, lucidity, and accuracy which leave nothing to be desired.

Morris himself was now known by his friends to be a dying man. On his return from Norway congestion of the left lung had set in, which remained persistent, and the general organic degeneration made steady progress. His old fear of death had long left him, but his desire to live remained almost as strong as ever till he became too weak to desire anything. As the power of self-control slackened, the emotional tenderness which had always been so large an element in his nature became more habitually visible. On one of her latest visits, Lady Burne-Jones tells me, he broke into tears when something was said about the hard life of the poor. He had a longing to hear for the last time some of that older music for which he had so great an admiration. Mr. Arnold Dolmetsch brought down a pair of virginals to Kelmscott House, and played to him several pieces by English composers of the sixteenth century. A pavan and galliard by William Byrd were what Morris liked most. He broke into a cry of joy at the opening phrase, and after the two pieces had been repeated at his request, was so deeply stirred that he could not bear to hear any more.

The weariness of that September was also alleviated by the thoughtful kindness of Mr. R. H. Benson, who took to him, one after another, several of the priceless thirteenth-century manuscripts from the Dorchester

House library : among them a Psalter written at Amiens, and a book even more fascinating to him, a " Bible His- toriée et Vies des Saints " containing, besides initial and marginal ornament of unsurpassed wealth and beauty of invention, no less than one thousand and thirty-four pic- tures, beginning with the Creation and concluding with the coming of Antichrist and the end of the world, *toutes ymaginées et ētitulées et p escripture exposées.* This last book he had by him for a week, and though he was too weak to look at it for more than a few minutes together, he always went back to it with fresh delight.

During the last weeks he was attended, beyond his own family, by the untiring devotion of his friends. Miss Mary De Morgan brought to this last service all the skill born of long experience, and the intelligent sympathy of an affection which Morris had for many years cordially returned. Sir Edward and Lady Burne- Jones, Mr. Webb, and Mr. Ellis were with him almost daily. Mr. Cockerell was ceaseless in his zeal and care ; and Mr. Emery Walker nursed him with the patience and tenderness of a woman. On the morning of Satur- day the 3rd of October, between eleven and twelve o'clock, he died quietly and without visible suffering.

No man on earth dies before his day: and least of all can the departure be called premature of a man whose life had been so crowded in activity and so rich in achieve- ment. To one judging by the work done in it, his working day was longer and ampler than often falls to the lot of our brief and pitiable human race. But the specific reasons why that life was not protracted beyond its sixty-third year are not difficult to assign. On the paternal side of his family there was a marked neurotic and gouty tendency. Himself of powerful physique, deep-chested, sound-lunged, big-hearted, he yet carried in him that family weakness, which was developed under the pressure of an immensely busy life. On a constitution made sensitive by gout, the exposure of the years of the Socialist crusade, when he had perpetually spoken in the open air in all weathers, and in the worse than open air of indoor meetings, and had often neglected or forgone proper food and rest, told with fatal effect. " I have no hesitation," his family doctor writes to me, " in saying that he died a victim to his enthusiasm for spreading the principles of Socialism." Yet this was only the special form that, in those years, his unceasing and prodigious activity had taken : and these words may be enlarged or supplemented by those of an eminent member of the same profession : " I consider the case is this : the disease is simply being William Morris, and having done more work than most ten men."

" Remembering those early years," says Sir Edward Burne-Jones, " and comparing them with the last in which I knew him, the life is one continuous course. His earliest enthusiasms were his latest. The thirteenth century was his ideal period then, and it was still the same in our last talks together ; nor would he ever wander from his allegiance. The changes that have come over later impressions about art passed beside him or under him with scarcely any notice."

With all the patience and conciliatoriness of his later years, he remained absolutely unshaken in his loyalty to his old opinions and to his old associates. " He was most tolerable with the opinions of others," are the quaint but touching words of one of his colleagues of the Socialist League. But his own opinions were never withdrawn or concealed ; and to the last he could be roused to anger by any slighting words about things for which his own admiration was a fixed article of faith. Among the younger men who came about him in these

years were some who, full of the latest ideas and methods
in painting, were ready to disparage the work of Burne-
Jones.   One of them ventured, one day at Kelmscott
House, to give some expression of this disparagement,
fancying perhaps that Morris might not find it wholly
ungrateful.   Morris, as his wont was when things were
not going to his mind, began to walk about the room
and fidget with the things lying on his study table. His
visitor continued, undeterred by these warnings.   Then
Morris broke out.   " Look here, ——," he said, " you
mustn't say that sort of thing in mixed company, you
know, or you'll run a great chance of being taken for a
fool."

For Burne-Jones his own admiration was undulled
by their complete and lifelong fraternity, and untouched
by any later divergence in social habit or doctrine. Even
in matters of art they did not see alike.   Just as the
restless energy of the one was in strong contrast to the
other's patient scholarship and continuous absorption, so
they received or re-incarnated the Middle Ages through
the eyes and brain in the one case of a Norman, in the
other of a Florentine.   But these very differences only
made them the more fully complementary to one another.
Morris's deep feeling for Burne-Jones's work is expressed, though in studiously restrained language, in the
Birmingham address of 1891 on the Pre-Raphaelite
School. But it may be even better judged from a more
casual utterance.   Once at the Grange he was—perhaps
for the hundredth time—pressing for more and yet more
designs for woodcuts for the Kelmscott Press.   " You
would think," Sir Edward said, turning to me with his
wonderful smile, " to listen to Top, that I was the only
artist in the world."   " Well," said Morris quietly,
" perhaps you wouldn't be so far wrong."

With well-meaning persons who came to him for

advice or information he had grown wonderfully tolerant. In reply to an earnest correspondent who had asked his views on the subject of temperance, he replied in a letter which deserves record for its exquisite interplay of demure humour and solid sense.

" Dear Sir," he wrote, " I think the question of the advantage of alcoholic liquors is a matter which each man must find out for himself, having admitted that one may easily drink too much even without getting drunk. My own experience is that I find my victuals dull without something to drink, and that tea and coffee are not fit liquors to be taken with food: in fact the latter always disagrees with me palpably, and probably tea isn't good for me. It is a remarkable fact that in Iceland toothache was almost unknown till the introduction of tea and coffee : the latter drink the Icelanders are now much addicted to.

" If I were to say what I really think I should say that tobacco seems to me a more dangerous intoxicant than liquors, because people can and do smoke to excess without becoming beastly and a nuisance. I am sure that Oriental countries have suffered much from the introduction of tobacco. N.B.—I am a smoker myself. A great point would be to try to get the liquors free from adulteration. But that I fear is impossible under a capitalistic *régime*."

His patience even extended to others less worthy of it : to those who came to him with the more or less concealed intention of getting something to their own advantage out of him, or in order to instruct him on matters in which he had taught their teachers. When his activity in the Socialist movement brought round him a mass of more or less disreputable professing adherents, whose application of the principles of Socialism did not go much beyond the idea that Morris should share his money with them, he carried his indulgence to an extreme pitch.   He told a friend of his once that a young man and woman, quite unknown, had called on him and asked him to give them a start, as they were going to be married. "Were they Socialists?" his friend asked. "I don't know," Morris answered; "I suppose so.   I gave them five pounds to get rid of them, as I was busy."

The life of insults through which he had passed both before and after he became a Socialist had at last left him almost secure of his own temper.   His friend, Mr. Newman Howard, has told me that once when they had been doing business together, he took Morris to his own club, which was a Conservative one.   An acquaintance of Mr. Howard's, who did not know Morris, sat down at the same table with them, and opened conversation with Morris by asking, " Well, what do you think of these strikes? I can tell you: it isn't so much the workmen: it 's those damned Socialist leaders.   They are infernal thieves and rascals, the whole lot of them."   Bland and impenetrable, Morris only answered " Indeed," in such a quiet flat voice as made it impossible to continue the subject.

One result of that growing patience was to make him more indifferent to criticism.   As much from a certain "childlike shamelessness" which has been noted by one of his most intimate friends as his deepest quality, as from his no less unique self-absorption in his own thoughts and feelings, external criticism had never much affected him.   No doubt there must have been a certain loss in this carelessness to the effect which his work, and he himself, made on others.   Criticism has its value in letting an artist, or a human being, see, more clearly than he could do of his own self, to what he and his work really amount for his fellow-artists and fellow-creatures: and

the absence of sensitiveness in an artist to the effect produced by his work may imply even for the work itself
a certain loss of sensitiveness and flexibility. With
Morris one often felt that it would make little or no
difference to him if no one else ever saw his designs or
read his books. Certainly it made no difference to him
whether they met with approval from the world, or even
from other artists in other methods. He might have
taken for his own an ancient Celtic saying : "God has
made out of his abundance a separate wisdom for everything that lives, and to do these things is my wisdom."

To criticism of his writings, whether in prose or verse,
he was particularly indifferent. In his poems and his
prose romances alike, he had set before himself an object
or an effect with perfect clearness : how far he had
executed his own design, how far fallen short of it, he
felt he knew better than any one could teach him ; and
that his design was not what this or that other person
would have chosen, was not what the public liked or
understood, was not, in a word, something else instead
of being itself, were matters to him of infinite unconcern.
The adverse criticisms encountered by his prose romances
on the ground of their mannerisms of vocabulary and
construction never induced him to modify the diction
which he had chosen, and which was in truth natural to
him in a much deeper way than modern newspaper
English is natural to the ordinary educated writer. The
common literary English of the present day Morris denounced as "a wretched mongrel jargon," corresponding
in its own vices to the so-called modern architecture.
His own prose style, so difficult to the average careless
reader, he maintained to be far simpler and more natural.
So indeed it essentially is, as may be seen by the sudden
contrast, like a patch of bad colour in a tapestry, when
from carelessness or weariness or the mere overwhelming

force of surroundings, he has here and there allowed his style for a few lines together to slip into modernism. But he confessed mournfully that for working men (and he thought that working men had a natural intelligence at least equal to that of the middle classes) his writing was "too simple to be understood." The debased modern journalistic style, like the debased modern typography, had grown so familiar from universal use, that a reversion to older and purer types threw people out, and made them complain of a difficulty which they quite honestly felt.

"Verse has a privilege to be more old-fashioned than prose," observes one of the most scholarly and accomplished of his critics in discussing "The Roots of the Mountains"; "but Mr. Morris's prose is more old-fashioned than his verse." This is true; it seems, however, to miss or ignore the fact which is essential to a sympathetic understanding of the whole of Morris's work, that in literature as well as in the manual arts he was throughout his life striving to take up and continue the dropped threads of the mediæval tradition; and that his work in both fields, while it was in one sense completely modern and even in advance of his age, was based on the return to and development of methods which had long since gone out of fashion, if they had not become completely obsolete. To go back to the fourteenth century, not with the view of staying there, but of advancing from it on what he conceived to be the true high road out of which the arts had long wandered, was his perpetual principle. But it so happens (whether from anything essential to the art or from particular causes to be sought in history) that the fashion of poetry has changed much less since Chaucer's time than the fashion of prose. The English version of the "Gesta Romanorum" (a work which Morris considered to be the perfection of English prose) is, though more recent in date, more old-fashioned

than either Piers Plowman or the Canterbury Tales: or
in Chaucer himself, the Tale of Melibœus, or the Treatise
on the Astrolabe, is more old-fashioned than the Knight's
Tale, or than the Book of Troilus and Cressida.   It
was some feeling of this sort, in combination with his
inveterate love of paradox, that made Morris repeatedly
startle his friends by casually alluding to Chaucer as
" the great corrupter of the English language."   For in
matters of style and diction, Chaucer, as is proved by
the fact that English poetry made no sensible advance for
a hundred and fifty years after him, was far in advance
of his own day.   Whether Morris's attempt to launch
English prose style on this fresh pathway was successful
is a different question, and one which perhaps few scholars
would hesitate to answer in the negative.   But his prose
was as sincere, and as little a forced copy of mediæval
work, as were his illuminated manuscripts, or his painted
windows.   This may be a reason, if reason has to be
assigned, why none of the various parodies of his style
bear much resemblance to the original.

For the refined products of modern ingenuity which
did not root themselves back on that old tradition, he
had as little taste in literature as in painting.   The
modern books which in later life he read with the greatest enjoyment were those which, without artifice or distinction of style, dealt with a life, whether actual or
imaginary, which approached his ideal in its simplicity
and its close relation to nature, especially among a race
of people who remained face to face with the elementary
facts of life, and had never become fully sophisticated
by civilization.   In this spirit, he admired and praised
works like Mr. Doughty's " Arabia Deserta," or " Uncle
Remus," from which he was always willing and eager to
read aloud, or " Huck Finn," which he half-jestingly
pronounced to be the greatest thing, whether in art or

nature, that America had produced.   For refinement of style, for subtle psychology in creation, he had but little taste.   He could not admire either Meredith or Stevenson.   When he was introduced to Ibsen's plays, and called on to join in admiring their union of accomplished dramatic craftsmanship with the most modern movement of ideas, they were dismissed by him in the terse and comprehensive criticism, " Very clever, I must say."   But neither did elaboration of style nor advanced modernism of treatment stand in the way of his appreciation when the substance of a book was to his liking ; and among the books which in recent years he praised most highly were the masterpieces of Pierre Loti and Maurice Maeterlinck.

" Master of himself and therefore of all near him," Morris at the same time retained the most childlike simplicity in the expression of his actual thoughts or feelings on any subject, and was as little hampered by false shame as he was guided by convention.   In some points he remained an absolute child to the end of his life.   If you introduced him to a friend, and he had the faintest suspicion that he was there to be shown off, his manners instantly became intolerable.   As childlike was another of his characteristics, the constant desire to be in actual touch with the things he loved.   He became a member of the Society of Antiquaries for no other reason than that he might be part-owner of one of their mediæval painted books.   The mere handling of a beautiful thing seemed to give him intense physical pleasure.   " If you have got one of his books in your hands for a minute," Burne-Jones said of him, " he'll take it away from you as if you were hurting it, and show it you himself."   He never in any case could conceal his hand in a matter of business : but when he was bargaining with Quaritch for an old book of which the possession meant more to him than the price, he would make the fact plain by carrying

on the negotiation with the book tucked tightly under
his arm, as if it might run away. The resemblance
already glanced at between him and Samuel Johnson
had grown stronger in these latter years: and it was as
visible in his eager width of interest as in the contradic-
tiousness and love of paradox in which he was perhaps
excelled by Johnson alone. Both men had this spirit of
contradiction constantly acting in curious combination
with what was, if not fair-mindedness, at all events an
unshaken and fundamental integrity of intellect. Like
Johnson, Morris had a way of applying hard logic to
matters in which most men are content to be guided by
compromise or fashion. Both were acute and severe
critics of what is called women's work, and were fas-
tidious in their appreciation of women's dress and looks,
yet were little affected by what women thought of them,
and preferred men's to women's society. Morris allowed
himself to be drawn freely by inquisitive acquaintances,
and was ready to lay down the law on any conceivable
topic ; but any amateur Boswell was liable to be suddenly
turned upon and tossed. His large tolerance for bores
was united with a keen insight into their character: he
would allow one of that class to make heavy drafts on
his time, and purse, and patience, and only incidentally
note him in a quiet, but scathing phrase, as "hen-headed,"
or "a sponge," or "a cripple whose smoking flax I have
not conscientious boldness enough to quench." Like
Johnson ("I am well-bred to a degree of needless scru-
pulosity" are the immortal words recorded by Mrs.
Thrale), he "looked upon himself as a very polite man,"
prided himself on his manners, and was capable of the
most amazing and almost supernatural rudeness towards
both men and women. Many of Johnson's sayings sound
most natural in Morris's familiar intonation, and accompanied by his tricks of gesture ; and his own familiar

talk was full of sentences which, were they inserted in Boswell, could hardly be distinguished from the true Johnsonian context.

But this likeness was crossed and shot by the vein of high romance which coloured all he ever thought or did. In him this turn of mind had all the seriousness, though not the lack of balance, that is associated with the name of Quixotry. Seriousness was what lay deepest of all in him; and the comparison which clings most intimately, of all the many made, in sport or in earnest, by his friends, is one incidentally and lightly dropped, only a few months before his death, by one for whom familiarity had not dulled the edge of observation. The figure seen by him one evening, in the cloak and satchel, the soft hat pulled down over his eyes and the stick firmly grasped and held point forward as he walked straight on, seeming to see nothing of all that was round him—yet in fact seeing it and taking it all in with incomparable swiftness—through the glare and bustle of the Strand, was like one other person and one only, Christian passing through Vanity Fair.

That seriousness and simplicity of mind, even more than the less approachable and intelligible qualities of his lonely genius, was what held his friends to him with a strength of attachment that neither his own inner aloofness nor his swift turns from one interest to another could loosen. They often had a sense of being dragged at his heels, perplexed and out of breath; but they felt through it all that to his own eyes the way lay perfectly straight forward. " He led us all a dance," one of his closest friends said to me in speaking of one of those times when, without troubling himself to give much explanation, or to break his new departure gently to his panting followers, he swung rapidly round on a new front—" not for the first or last time: would he could lead us some more!" For as long as he lived those who knew him felt confident that he would be in the fullest sense, and at every moment, alive: this or that interest might pass, one or another occupation be taken up or discarded, but the interest of living, the occupation of creating and working, would never lessen or falter.

To the same central quality, the seriousness and simplicity which walked, without noticing them, through all the hedges and over all the ditches of worldly convention, it was due that he was so conspicuously at his ease in the society of a class different from his own. Civility to inferiors was certainly not one of his strong points; and the aristocratic temper of his youth would show itself even in his latest years. But it was a temper rather than a principle; in a very real sense he treated his servants or workmen as he treated his social equals; and though he often, in the terse phrase of common usage, wiped his boots on a man, he never either showed or felt towards him the more stinging insolence of condescension. To working men he was like one of themselves, one who worked as they did and lived a quite intelligible life, but who was full of queer, and for the most part fantastic or unintelligible, ideas. Yet many letters received after his death show that working men held him in real honour, and felt a personal grief for the loss of one who had been on their side, who had meant well by them, who had brought to some degree a new meaning into their own life. Such tributes are apt to be paid in an artificial currency; but in these letters a sincere emotion struggles to express itself through the worn and ill-fitting phrases, the stock of cheap ready-made clothing for ideas which the industry and keen intelligence of commercial journalism, copying with a fatal instinct all that is worst in its models, produces wholesale for an ever widening market.

In an ill-spelled and touching letter, the Walthamstow Branch of the Navvies' and General Labourers' Union expressed their admiration for his " noble works and genuine counsel," " the seed that so noble a man sowed in his great and useful life."   On behalf of a Lancashire Branch of the Social Democratic Federation their secretary wrote, " Comrade Morris is not dead there is not a Socialist living whould belive him dead for he Lives in the heart of all true men and women still and will do so to the end of time."   In even simpler words one of the textile workers at Merton Abbey wrote to Mrs. Morris, " Dear Madam, I loved and honoured my Master, therefore I mourn with you, excuse this intrusion, I cannot help it.   May God support and comfort you is the prayer of your faithful servant."

In the Northern Sagas, as in the heroic cycle of ancient Greece, a man's life is not fully ended till he has been laid under ground, and the accident of death has been followed by the sacred offices of burial.   That reluctance to end the story, to part with its hero until the funeral pyre was out and the last valediction over, was an attitude of mind which Morris himself specially loved; and if we may believe that any sense of the last rites performed over them may touch the dead, he might find a last satisfaction in the simple and impressive ceremony of his funeral.   He was buried in the little churchyard of Kelmscott on the 6th of October.   The night had been wet, and morning lightened dully over soaking meadows, fading away in a blur of mist.   As the day went on, the wind and rain both increased, and rose in the afternoon to a tempest.   The storm, which raged with great violence over the whole country, with furious southwesterly gales, reached its greatest force in the upper Thames valley.   The low-lying lands were flooded, and

all the little streams that are fed from the Cotswolds ran
full and deep brown.   The noise of waters was everywhere.   Clumps of Michaelmas daisies were in flower in
the drenched cottage gardens, and the thinning willows
had turned, not to the brilliance of their common October
colouring, but to a dull tarnished gold.   The rooks were
silent in the elms about the Manor House.   Apples lay
strewn on the grass in the orchard.   In the garden, the
yew dragon, untrimmed since his own hand had last
clipped it, had sprouted out into bristles.   A few pink
roses and sweet peas still lingered among the chrysanthemums and dahlias of the autumnal plots.

One of the farm wagons, with a yellow body and
bright red wheels, was prepared in the morning to
carry the coffin from Lechlade station; it was drawn
by a sleek roan mare and led by one of the Kelmscott
carters.   The wagon was wreathed with vine, and strewn
with willow boughs over a carpeting of moss.   In it
the coffin, simple and even beautiful in its severe design, of unpolished oak with wrought iron handles, was
placed on its arrival, and over it was laid a piece of
Broussa brocade which had been long in Morris's possession, and a wreath of bay.   The group of mourners
followed it along the dripping lanes, between russet
hedgerows and silver-grey slabbed stone fences, to the
churchyard gate, and up the short lime-avenue to the
tiny church.   There the Rev. W. F. Adams, Vicar of
Little Faringdon, Morris's schoolfellow at Marlborough,
and the friend and neighbour of later years at Kelmscott, read the funeral service.   With the family and
friends were mingled workmen from Merton Abbey and
Oxford Street, comrades of the Socialist League, pupils
of the Art Workers' Guild, and Kelmscott villagers in
their daily working dress.   There was no pomp of organized mourning, and the ceremony was of the shortest and

simplest.   Among associates and followers of later years were the few survivors of that remarkable fellowship which had founded the Oxford Brotherhood and the Firm of Red Lion Square; and at the head of the grave Sir Edward Burne-Jones, the closest and the first friend of all, stood and saw a great part of his own life lowered into earth.   " What I should do, or how I should get on without him," he had once said when Morris's increasing weakness became alarming, " I don't in the least know.   I should be like a man who has lost his back."   *Si unus ceciderit, ab altero fulcietur : væ soli! quia cum ceciderit, non habet sublevantem se.*

As dusk fell, the storm swept more fiercely over Oxford. The driving rain found its way through the roof of the Union Library, and carried away patches of the faded painting with which, in the ardour of his first devotion to art, amid an unbroken band of kindred spirits, confident in youth, united in faith and friendship, he had adorned it thirty-nine years before.   A new age had since then risen over a new England, and those early days were already receding into the dimness of an almost fabulous past.

Principes mortales, rem publicam æternam esse : proin repeterent sollennia : the cold and august words of the Roman Emperor may best express the feeling with which that funeral company dispersed to their homes.   A great personality had ceased : yet the strongest feeling in the minds of the survivors was rather that it had returned to, than, in the customary phrase of common usage, passed away from earth.   Among the men and women through whom he had so often moved as in a dream, isolated, self-centred, almost empty of love or hatred, he moved no more.   It seemed natural that he should go out from among them, not being really of them.   " He doesn't want anybody," so his most intimate friend once said of him : "I suppose he would miss me for a bit, but it wouldn't change one day of his life, nor alter a plan in it.   He lives absolutely without the need of man or woman.   He is really a sort of Viking, set down here, and making art because there is nothing else to do." Far less easy to realize was his absence henceforward from the surroundings in which and through which he lived almost as in a bodily vesture : from his books and manuscripts, from his vats and looms, from the grey gabled house and the familiar fields, from the living earth which he loved with so continuous and absorbing a passion.

"It came to pass," says the ancient forgotten author of the Volsunga Saga, when he has to tell of the death of the father of King Volsung, "that he fell sick and got his death, being minded to go home to Odin, a thing much desired of many folk in those days."   With no such desire had this last inheritor of the Viking spirit approached his end. To be, " though men call you dead, a part and parcel of the living wisdom of all things," still to live somewhere in the larger life of this and no other world, such had been his desire, such his faith and hope throughout the loneliness and fixedness in which he had passed his mortal days. He might seem, now the entanglement of life was snapped, to have resumed his place among the lucid ranks that, still sojourning yet still moving onward, enter their appointed rest and their native country unannounced, as lords that are certainly expected, and yet there is a silent joy at their arrival.

THE MANOR HOUSE, KELMSCOTT, FROM THE HOME-MEAD.

INDEX